SPARTANS
at the
GATES

Also by Noble Smith

Sparks in the Park
Stolen from Gypsies
The Wisdom of the Shire

The Warrior Trilogy
Sons of Zeus

SPARTANS

— *at the* —

GATES

Book II of the Warrior Trilogy

NOBLE SMITH

THOMAS DUNNE BOOKS · ST. MARTIN'S PRESS · NEW YORK

This is a work of fiction. All of the characters, organizations, and events portrayed in this novel are either products of the author's imagination or are used fictitiously.

THOMAS DUNNE BOOKS.
An imprint of St. Martin's Press.

SPARTANS AT THE GATES. Copyright © 2014 by Noble Smith. All rights reserved. Printed in the United States of America. For information, address St. Martin's Press, 175 Fifth Avenue, New York, N.Y. 10010.

www.thomasdunnebooks.com
www.stmartins.com

Designed by Steven Seighman

Library of Congress Cataloging-in-Publication Data

Smith, Noble Mason, 1968–
    Spartans at the gates : novel / Noble Smith.—First edition.
        p. cm.
    "Thomas Dunne Books."
    ISBN 978-1-250-02558-6 (hardcover)
    ISBN 978-1-250-02643-9 (e-book)
    1. Soldiers—Fiction. 2. Greece—History—Peloponnesian War, 431–404 B.C.—Fiction. 3. Plataiai (Greece)—Fiction. 4. Athens (Greece)—Fiction. I. Title.
    PS3569.M537837S66 2014
    813'.54—dc23

                                                            2014008412

St. Martin's Press books may be purchased for educational, business, or promotional use. For information on bulk purchases, please contact Macmillan Corporate and Premium Sales Department at 1-800-221-7945, extension 5442, or write specialmarkets@macmillan.com.

First Edition: June 2014

10 9 8 7 6 5 4 3 2 1

For Kendra

The god of battle is our liege lord.
—Spartan saying

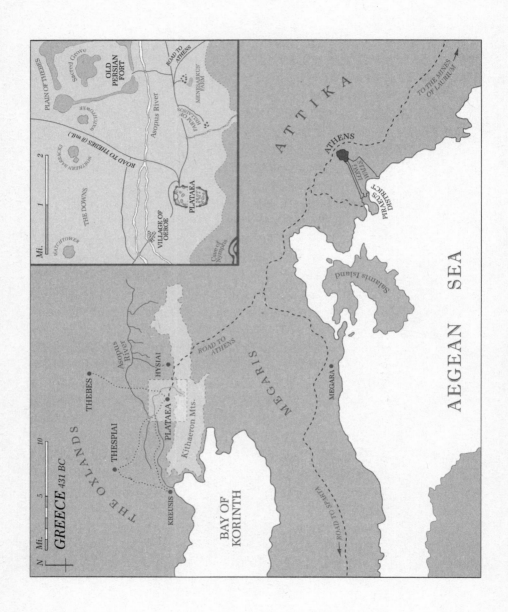

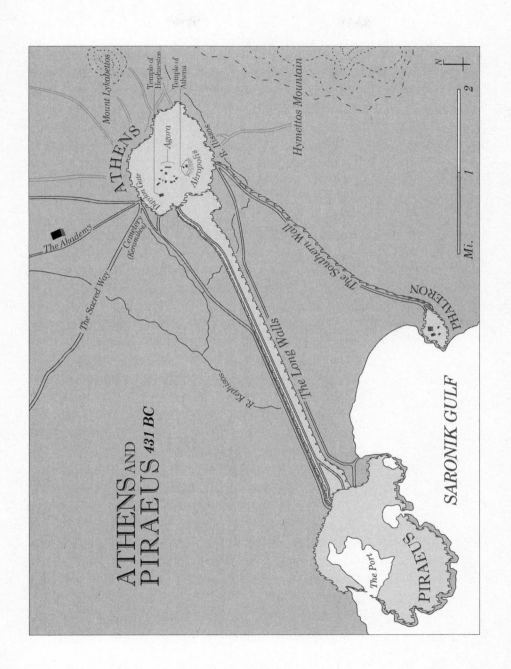

ATHENS AND PIRAEUS 431 BC

The Akademy

Mount Lykabettos

Temple of Hephaestus

Temple of Athena

ATHENS

Agora

Acropolis

R. Ilissos

Hymettos Mountain

Dipylon Gate

Cemetery (Kerameikos)

The Sacred Way

The Southern Wall

R. Kephisos

The Long Walls

HALERON

PIRAEUS

The Port

SARONIK GULF

N

Mi.   1   2

Part I

Many famous adventures begin with a foolhardy young man defying his patriarch and charging headlong into grave peril. This tale is no different.

—Papyrus fragment from the "Lost History" of the Peloponnesian War by the "Exiled Scribe"

ONE

———◆———

She was a creature foaled from the West Wind—a muscular white mare racing down a fog-covered road at dawn. A young horseman leaned over her neck, his strong legs hugging her rib cage, moving with the rhythm of the animal's strides, floating above her lather-slick back. He uttered the name of the Great Protector, begging him for help with every exhalation from his heaving chest:

"Zeus . . . Zeus . . . Zeus . . ."

The rider's name was Nikias of Plataea, and the god of death was hunting him down yet again.

He could hear the enemy's hooves pounding the road behind him. They had chased him for over two miles, and showed no signs of giving up. They were Megarian Dog Raiders—the vicious marauders who inhabited this rugged region. They wore helms covered in the hides of wild dogs and they peeled off the faces of their living victims as a warning to all who would challenge them.

Nikias squinted against the rushing wind, his scarred but handsome face wet with mist, long blond hair whipping out behind him. He wore the tall leather boots, plain tunic, and short wool cape of an Oxlander—the hardy farmers who inhabited the region north of the Kithaeron Mountains. A Sargatian whip, coiled like a long and deadly snake, was tied to his belt. And strapped securely to his broad back, in a battle-scarred travel sheath, was a sword with a pommel bearing the image of a boxing Minotaur.

The thick fog gave Nikias the unsettling sensation that he was riding in a murky gray sea. He imagined that the road might end at any moment, sending him and his mare plummeting off the edge of the world. For they were in rough country—the rocky and barren foothills of the southern slopes of the Kithaeron Mountains. But there was no turning back on this dangerous road.

And the enemy was getting closer.

One of the Dog Raiders let forth a wordless hunting call—a sound full of bloodlust and hate. The other riders took up the noise. It wouldn't be long before he'd be within range of their javelins: short spears they could throw with deadly accuracy even at full gallop. Soon the fog would be gone, burned off by the rising sun, and no longer offer protection. He could almost feel a spear tip in his spine.

"Keep going, girl!" Nikias urged. He could see his horse's eyes bulging from the sides of her head in terror and she was starting to lag. Photine was the fastest creature he had ever known, but she was only good for short bursts of speed, and became unnerved when chased.

Nikias wished that Kolax was still riding by his side. The child had been raised in the wild grasslands of Skythia, far from Greece and could shoot three arrows in as many heartbeats, hitting his mark every time. Damn that boy for riding off! If they had stuck together they might have stood a chance.

The two had made the journey down the mountainside the night before. They had just found the road marker at dawn—the stone that pointed the way to Athens—when the Dog Raiders had appeared out of nowhere. Kolax had bolted in the opposite direction, leading half of the two dozen enemy riders back toward the mountain. The boy, no doubt, was dead by now.

Nikias felt Photine slow as she came to a bend in the road. He glanced quickly over his shoulder and caught a glimpse of the riders—dark shapes in the fog wearing plate armor and black cloaks . . . spear tips glinting in the gray morning light. He dug his heels into his horse's sides and she jolted forward.

Another mile or so. That's all Photine had in her.

His heart sank. Athens, the city he was urgently trying to reach, was twenty-five miles away at the end of this treacherous white limestone road—a road scored on either side with deep tracks that had been carved by cart and chariot wheels. And it was getting harder to keep Photine in the center of the road. She kept veering to one side. If she stepped in one of those tracks her leg would snap like a stick and he would be thrown over her neck, landing in a helpless broken heap upon the road.

"Better to die facing your enemy than with a spear in your backside," he mused grimly. "Better to go out swinging." That's what his grandfather always said.

He kicked Photine with his heels and she went faster, putting some distance between them and the Dog Raiders. Nikias hoped he might come to a bridge or someplace where the road narrowed. There at least he could make a stand, using his bow and arrow to kill the enemy horses from a distance, blocking the way with their corpses. He would much rather fight on his feet than on horseback, for he had been educated since childhood in the art of the pankration—the battle training that turned every part of a man's body into a weapon, from the heel to the crown of the head. Despite his youth he was one of the best pankrators in the Oxlands, quite possibly in all of Greece. He was the grandson of a renowned Olympic pankration champion—a man who'd taught him to be fierce by punching fierceness into his flesh, like a blacksmith hammering a sword.

His training had worked.

Even though Nikias had just turned eighteen, he was already famous in his independent city-state of Plataea. He'd fought men to death with his bare fists and wielded sword and spear in the wild and bloody chaos of battle. He'd faced down the enemy Theban invaders with the courage of the Nemean Lion—the legendary beast whose name his family of warriors had taken as its own.

But now, chased on horseback down the road to Athens with a pack of Dog Raiders gaining on him with every second, Nikias felt more like a terrified fawn than a deadly predator. He touched his elbow to the Sargatian whip coiled on his belt. His grandfather's Persian slave had braided it from the entire hide of an ox, and it was an excellent weapon, especially when wielded with skill. By the time he was eight years old Nikias could snap a fly off a wall from twenty feet away. But the whip was impossible to use when riding at full gallop.

He heard something made of wood clatter on the road behind. One of the Dog Raiders had thrown a javelin at him, but it had fallen short. Nikias was still just out of range. He touched his stomach—the place where he wore a heavy leather pouch strapped to his midriff. The pouch was filled with Persian gold coins: enough wealth to buy several prosperous farms in the Oxlands. The coins had been found hidden in the traitor Nauklydes's house. It was blood money paid to the traitor for his part in opening the city gates of Plataea and letting in a Theban attack force. A little more than a week had passed since that terrible night—the night when Nikias's mother and most of his friends had been killed by the invaders. But the Thebans had failed to conquer Plataea.

Nikias planned to use this tainted fortune in Persian gold to lure a small army of mercenaries back to Plataea to help defend the walled citadel from Plataea's newest threat: an army of Spartans that had appeared in the Oxlands hard on the heels of the defeated Thebans. The Spartans had demanded that Plataea break its alliance with Athens, or else they would lay siege to Plataea. Nikias knew that his city needed good fighters—especially archers—to help man the two and a half miles of walls that surrounded the citadel. Too many good Plataean warriors had been killed during the Theban sneak attack. But to get to Athens and its abundance of sellswords, Nikias had to first pass through Megarian territory: a land crawling with Dog Raiders.

"Watch for it!" cried one of the horsemen behind him. "Up ahead! We're close."

Nikias wondered what the rider was shouting about. He glanced around but could see nothing through the fog except the lead-colored shapes of rocks and trees. He couldn't see any place to get off the road and make a break for it overland. He was stuck on this road, running out of time. . . .

"Faster!" he said, slapping Photine on the neck. She responded by bearing down and surging forward.

Nikias had defied the new Arkon—the leader of Plataea and a renowned general—by making this journey to Athens. The Arkon had ordered him to help round up food and animals from the countryside and bring them into the citadel while the tenuous truce with the Spartan invaders lasted. The Arkon had sent envoys to the Athenian leader begging his help, but Nikias knew that this assistance would not come. The Athenians were spread too thin in their own wars to send an army to aid in Plataea's defense—at least, that is what an Athenian spy working in Plataea had told Nikias. But there was no use arguing with the Arkon . . . the fact that he was Nikias's grandfather didn't help matters. The great Menesarkus, the Bull of the Oxlands, demanded obedience from his heir above all other traits—even above courage.

Nikias was far more brave than obedient, and so he had decided to take matters into his own hands. Hadn't he been the one to escape from the citadel during the Theban sneak attack? He'd warned the border garrisons and led them to the gates of Plataea, heading off the army of Theban reinforcements and saving the city in the fields in front of its gates. And then, with the help of the Athenian spy, Nikias had exposed Nauklydes as the traitor and brought him to justice.

Rounding up animals in the hills was work for a sheep-stuffing shepherd, not a warrior!

"Now! Here it is!" barked a voice from behind. "We'll stay behind!"

The shout jolted Nikias from his thoughts like the crack of a whip in his ear. He glanced to the right. The fog had thinned considerably now and he could clearly see the shapes of horses leaping off the road and onto a path that wended its way through a wooded area of pines and oak. He counted nine of the Dog Raiders going that way.

He peered ahead into the gloom to where the road curved sharply and became narrower, dropping off into a gully. He would have to slow down soon. The riders who'd just gone off the road must be taking a shortcut. A way of bypassing this stretch of the road so they could loop back around and cut him off at the narrowest spot.

He glanced back. There were only three riders on the road behind him now. He reacted instinctively, reining in Photine hard. She came to a dead stop so fast that her hindquarters nearly touched the ground and her hooves skidded on the gravel. Then she raised her front legs in the air and he tumbled off her back, slamming onto the road on his right side. A split second later a blinding pain erupted in his shoulder.

"Gods!" he screamed.

The three startled-looking Dog Raiders charged past him in single file, but pulled up when they realized that their prey now lay helplessly in the road. As they turned around to face him one of the horses stepped into a deep wheel rut with both its hind legs. The animal's bones fractured and it let forth a piercing neigh. It flipped onto its side, crushing its rider underneath, breaking the man's neck.

Nikias ignored the searing pain in his right shoulder. He reached behind his back with his left hand and started to draw the sword that was strapped there, but then he stopped, shoving the blade back in its sheath.

He grabbed the handle of his Sargatian whip with his left hand, yanked it free from the breakaway knot on his belt, then got up and sprinted at the two remaining Dog Raiders, snapping the rawhide tip at the nearest rider, who was just about to throw his javelin.

Crack! The Dog Raider slumped over his horse in shock, holding a hand to his eye, howling with agony. The other horseman charged Nikias with his javelin raised. But Nikias moved his arm in a fluid motion—the leather braid made a figure-eight pattern in the air—and the whip looped itself around the surprised warrior's neck. Nikias yanked, pulling the man from his mount. He landed on his tailbone and dropped his javelin, then clawed wildly at the leather noose around his neck, gasping for air.

Nikias tried to reach for his sword with his right hand, but his arm hung useless at his side. It was dead. He heard his grandfather's voice shouting in his brain—

Your body is the weapon!

Nikias jumped toward the whip-choked Dog Raider and pulled fiercely on the whip, causing the man to lunge toward him. The man's face met the heel of Nikias's fully extended foot. It was a savage blow that sent the enemy's front teeth down his throat. Before the stunned man could topple over, Nikias kicked again, pushing his nasal bones straight into his brain.

Instant death.

Nikias uncoiled the lasso from around the dead man's neck with a quick flick of his wrist and turned to face the final mounted Dog Raider. The man held one hand to his ruined eye. He swiped the blood from his cheek and bared his teeth viciously as he drew his sword.

"You took my eye!" he howled with indignation. "I'll make you eat both of yours, you—"

Before he could finish his sentence Nikias snapped the whip again, catching him in the other eye and blinding him. The astonished warrior clutched his face and sucked in his breath. Nikias glanced down. A javelin lay at his feet. He dropped the whip, then slipped the tip of his riding boot under the spear and flicked it into the air, catching it with his left hand. The spear flew from his grip like a lightning bolt, passing through the mouth of the blinded Dog Raider with a crunch of teeth and bone. He slid off his horse backward and lay there, bleeding his life onto the road.

Nikias took a deep breath and peered down the road. He could just make out the shapes of the other Dog Raiders—the ones who'd ridden through the woods to cut him off—about a quarter of a mile away.

He glanced over at Photine, who trotted in a big circle around the scene of carnage, blowing through her nostrils, wild-eyed, with her tail up in the air. If they'd been back home in the Oxlands, Nikias reckoned, she would have already bolted for home—something she had done in the midst of the Battle of the Gates with the Theban invaders. But here she didn't know where to go.

"Come here, girl," he said softly, holding out his left hand and forcing himself to make his voice sound calm. He looked behind him and saw the peaks of the Kithaerons, covered in snow, shining white in the morning sun. If he could get his skittish horse to come back to him he could ride that way. The Plataean fortress of the Three Heads was only a few miles away. Inside that stronghold was an entire garrison of his kinsmen guarding the narrow pass into the Oxlands. Nikias and Kolax had skirted around the fortress on their clandestine ride over the mountains. If only he could get to the safety of the fort! He'd go back home with his tail between his legs and beg his grandfather to forgive him. He would gladly round up every stray sheep left in the Oxlands.

His hand was almost within reach of Photine's reins when she trembled and snorted, dropping her head and shying away from him with the agility of a cat.

"Zeus's balls!" roared Nikias, lunging toward her with a face twisted with wrath. "Come here, you stupid goat!"

Photine turned and ran for a few strides, then faced him again with her head low, glaring at him, ears laid flat.

He took a deep breath and tried to smile. "I'm sorry," he said. "Just—"

He stopped as he heard shouts coming from down the road. The other Dog Raiders were now coming back. They were calling out to their brethren: the three men turned to shades by Nikias's hand.

"Where is he? Where's the Oxlander?"

"Answer us!"

"Go back! He's tricked us."

Nikias took another step toward Photine. She let forth a neighing scream, then bolted past him, galloping up the road in the direction of the mountains and home.

"I'll never see her again," he thought. He wondered what his grandfather would say when he saw her running riderless in the fields in front of the citadel.

He reached behind and grasped the bow and quiver that were slung on his back. But his heart lurched as he realized the bow was broken—it had snapped when he had fallen off Photine. He tossed it aside angrily. He had to think of a way to hide! And then he thought of a plan. A crazy idea, but it might just give him a chance.

Working fast, he bent over one of the Dog Raider's corpses and traded his own short gray cape for the warrior's black cloak. He pulled off the man's helm and squeezed it over his head, then hunched over the man's body, kneeling with his back to the approaching riders. He stared at his dead father's signet ring on his middle finger—a boxing Minotaur carved from jasper.

"Steady," he said to himself. "Stay calm."

But his brain screamed at him to run. And his hand trembled.

He heard the sound of approaching riders. Keeping his back to them, he stole a glance over his shoulder and saw eight riders enter the killing grounds. They reined in, stopping fifty paces away from him. The raiders eyed the scene warily, but none dismounted.

"Where is he?" asked one of the Dog Raiders.

"Come," said Nikias, gesturing at the corpse and imitating the enemy's harsh accent. "I killed him."

Nikias waited without turning around, hunched under the black cloak. His heart beat wildly. He listened hopefully for the sounds of feet hitting the road. But the only noises he heard were horses puffing air through their cheeks.

The Dog Raider who'd spoken before gave a malicious laugh and spat, "Clever. But none of us has pretty blond hair like you, beardless one."

Nikias felt as though his stomach had been pitched down a well. He'd forgotten to tuck his long hair under the helm!

He thought of his beloved, Kallisto. She would never know what happened to him now. The thought filled him with despair. There was no chance of escape. But he wouldn't let the Dog Raiders torture him. He glanced down at his belt and saw his long dagger in its tooled leather sheath.

"There's an artery in your neck," his grandfather had told him when he was a boy, instructing him never to let himself be taken alive by Dog Raiders or Thebans. "Slice your neck there and you'll soon be dead."

He would take a few of them down first, though. "I am Nikias, son of Aristo of the Nemean tribe," he said under his breath, readying himself for death, forcing back the urge to piss himself with fear.

He got up slowly, letting the whip uncoil as he stood, and turned to face the Dog Raiders. He saw the black-robed horsemen lined up in a semicircle, far out of range of his whip, with their javelins and bows raised, and their dark eyes regarding him with hate from under their helms.

His gaze flashed to a warrior seated on a dun-colored horse in the center of the pack. He had a long, black, forked beard, like a satyr. And he stared down the shaft of a tautly strung bow, a glinting bronze arrowhead pointing directly at Nikias's head.

"Stand still," ordered the Dog Raider commander.

Nikias didn't have time to make a move. An arrow, unloosed by one of the other riders, slammed into his gut and his knees buckled. He hit the road in a heap and lay there, blinking, trying to breathe, but his lungs wouldn't work. He felt as though he'd been punched by a Titan's fist. He lay very still, with the sound of his heart throbbing in his ears, his mind dazed.

"Who shot that arrow?" shouted the Dog Raider commander. "Damn you! The Spartans wanted him alive!"

A roaring sound filled Nikias's ears. He squinted in pain, gazing up at the sky, and realized that the fog had burned away to reveal a few patches of bright blue sky. And then he heard a harsh voice snarl, "Let's peel his face before he dies!"

TWO

———————— ◆ ————————

Chusor the smith rubbed his callused hands over the dome of his recently shaved scalp, as if he might massage a clever idea from his brain. But he couldn't think of anything to convince Diokles the Helot to come out of the storage room where he hid, and so Chusor could only grit his teeth in frustration.

He pounded on the door with the flat of his hand. "Come out, you great goat-stuffing ape!" he snarled. He tried to force the door open but Diokles had barricaded it from within. The Helot race—the thralls of the Spartans—were a spectacularly stubborn people. And, thought Chusor with annoyance, Diokles was the exemplar of his kind.

Chusor coughed and rubbed his watering eyes. "Gods, that damnable smoke!" he muttered.

It was just after dawn and the citadel of Plataea was starting to come to life. Thousands of farmers and shepherds—terrified of the Spartan army camped two miles away from Plataea—had sought protection inside the city walls. Now they were cooking their breakfasts on campfires, and the overpowering reek of wood-smoke wafted in through the open windows of the smithy, giving Chusor a queasy feeling and stinging his eyes.

"Not coming out," came Diokles's muffled voice.

"He's not coming out," said Leo confidently. The short teenager stood next to the towering smith, holding an oil lamp that lit the dark hallway. "His wits have left his body for another place."

"Leave the Oxlands and join the school of Athens, lad," replied Chusor sarcastically in his clipped Athenian accent. "You've got the makings of a philosopher." He glared at the young Plataean who served as his apprentice.

Leo ignored Chusor's sarcasm and spoke in a serious whisper. "Maybe if we offered him breakfast?"

"He's got enough desiccated goat in there to feed a trireme's crew."

Ever since the morning of the battle with the Theban army one week ago, when Diokles had seen the thin line of Spartan Red Cloaks snaking their way down a path on the Kithaeron Mountains toward the citadel of Plataea, the escaped Spartan slave had fallen into a morbid stupor. But when the hideous noseless Spartan emissary, Drako, and his contingent had actually been allowed inside the city walls to discuss terms with the Arkon—the leader of the Plataeans—well, Diokles had nearly lost his mind with fear and had hidden in the storeroom like a dog.

Chusor knew that Diokles had suffered the torments of Hades at the hands of his former masters, and the Helot had been terrified for years that one day the savage Spartans would track him down. But Chusor was shocked that Diokles had reverted to this state—he was like a child hiding from monsters. Years ago they had been shipmates on a privateer's crew and had become fast friends. During those years on the sea they had been through many perils together. But Chusor had never seen the Helot this frightened before. And it galled him.

"He's got it in his head, the daft bull," Chusor explained to Leo, pitching his voice so Diokles was sure to hear, "that the Spartans have come for him *alone*."

"The Red Cloaks aren't here looking for you, Diokles," Leo said soothingly, as if he were a cheery grandmother speaking to a frightened little boy. "They've come to kill us *all*."

A whimper emanated from the locked chamber and Chusor rolled his eyes. He pushed Leo away from the door and said, "You're not helping a bit, Leo."

"Sorry," Leo said, and leaned against the wall, moping.

Chusor put his mouth to the crack in the doorframe and tried to mask the frustration in his voice. "Listen, Diokles, my friend. The Spartans are merely trying to threaten the Plataeans into breaking their alliance with Athens. The Spartans do not know how to besiege a high-walled citadel like Plataea. They never have and never will. Because they're as dumb as doorknockers outside of forming up a phalanx. They don't even know how to till the soil, the poor buggers, and that's why they had to enslave your happy race of Helots to do their labors! So why don't you come on out and get back to work in the smithy. I need your help."

There was a long pause before Diokles said in his halting voice, "The masters are smarter than you think. They smart enough to find other people. To help them lay siege this city. They find smart men like *you*. They find a way in. They will capture me and cut off hands, lips, eyes, ears, and cock and make me eat them."

Leo cringed. "Gods! That *is* horrible."

Chusor took in a deep breath, puffed out his cheeks, and exhaled slowly. He tugged on his long braided goatee for a few seconds, then turned and strode up the stairs to the sunlit workshop above. Leo raced up behind him, immediately shielding the lamp flame and blowing out the wick lest it start a fire—this part of the workshop contained highly flammable items. They stood next to each other, staring off into space, grimly contemplating what Diokles had said.

The two were an odd pair. Leo was a short, pale, and notoriously homely eighteen-year-old prone to acne, with a head of thick black hair and overlong arms. Chusor—the tallest man in Plataea—was over forty years of age yet still in the prime of his manhood, with skin the color of roasted sesame, the musculature of an Olympian, and the proud face of a Phoenician god.

The men and women of Plataea called Chusor "the Egyptian" because of his dark brown skin and exotic features. To them he was a *barbaroi*—one who babbled "bar bar bar" like a savage. Except this so-called barbarian spoke their language fluently and with the accent of an educated man born and bred in Athens.

Chusor and Leo had been thrown together a week ago during the Theban sneak attack, and had come to admire each other's unique skills. Leo worshipped Chusor for the way he'd taken control of the panic-stricken Plataeans and led the citizens to victory against the Theban barricades with his invention: a deadly liquid fire that stuck to the enemy's skin. And Chusor respected Leo's tenacity—his wrestler's will to never let go of an opponent.

"Who *would* the Spartans get to help them lay siege to Plataea?" Leo asked.

"Persians," said Chusor. "Something I've been worried about. There's many a Persian siege-master who'd gladly give his balls for the honor of bringing down Plataea."

Fifty years ago, not a mile from the citadel, the Persian king Xerxes had watched nearly half a million of his men die in the Battle of Plataea—the greatest loss in the history of their ancient empire. Xerxes's own siege-master had been captured and put to work for the rest of his life improving the walls and towers of Plataea—the city he had come to destroy.

"Well, I've got work to do grinding the sulfur stones," said Leo as he went into the other room. Chusor had taught Leo how to make the fire pots they'd used against the Theban invaders. The sticking fire was composed mainly of a highly combustible distilled pine resin called naptha, and the explosive gray-colored mineral gypsum. Chusor added to this a secret ingredient that he'd learned from the great Naxos of Syrakuse: the volatile *niter* crystals extracted from bat guano. These three ingredients—when contained in a pot, set alight with a fuse, and hurled at an enemy—would turn an armor-clad warrior into a human torch. Leo had shown a knack for working with the dangerous chemicals when he had helped Chusor prepare his "pandoras," as he called them, for the battle with the Thebans.

Chusor walked through the workshop and sighed as he took stock of all of the armor and weapons piled up. The place was a mess. He wasn't the only black-smith in the city, but he was—by his own admission—the very best, and so the

Plataeans with money to spare wanted him to do the work on their valuable tools of war. A single well-made set of armor could cost a man three years' wages. And Chusor stood to earn a small fortune in the coming months.

If he were mad enough to stay in Plataea, that is.

He sat down and chewed pensively on a piece of bread. His mind wandered back to the day he'd first seen the citadel of Plataea. It had been a hot spring morning and the air had been scented with flowering olives. He and Diokles had just crested the heights of the Kithaeron Mountains and caught sight of the green plains of the Oxlands below, stretching far north into the distance. Below they saw a walled city—the famous Plataea. The citadel was a rambling circular shape, over two miles in circumference with many guard towers, enclosing a collection of dwellings, public buildings, and temples. From the distance it had resembled a child's creation made from stones and clay.

Chusor had come here because of a legend telling of a vast treasure hidden in a network of underground tunnels beneath the city.

As they got closer to town they saw that a celebration was taking place. The entire population of Plataea and the surrounding countryside—twenty thousand or so—had turned out to celebrate the Festival of Hermes. In his travels, Chusor had noticed, men prayed to the gods who were most important to their livelihoods. The Plataeans relied on sheep and wool for their economy. Hermes was said to be the protector of sheep and shepherds. And so they feted and feasted this particular god in hopes he would turn his attentions their way.

The Plataeans encouraged Chusor and Diokles to enter the festival's games. Strangers always brought luck to the city, they told them. Diokles politely refused and sat contentedly in the shade eating a leg of mutton bought from a vendor. Chusor always loved contests, however, and so he took part with enthusiasm. He won the long footrace, narrowly beating a sixteen-year-old blond farm boy. He outthrew this same competitor at the discus by no more than a foot. This infuriated the young Plataean and he challenged Chusor to enter the pankration tournament. But Chusor had no desire to humiliate the youth further. He had trained with the best pankrators in the city of Kroton and knew how to punch, grapple, and choke the strongest man into submission, let alone a beardless teen. He'd also been a member of a privateer's crew for nearly five years where he'd fought for his life many times over.

Chusor watched the pankration event from the sidelines. He was impressed by the young fighter's skill. The Plataean lad destroyed all of his competitors except the last—a leonine old man with a black beard who was remarkably well preserved for his age. This pankrator fought dirty and knocked out the teenager with a sucker's punch to take the olive wreath.

Menesarkus was the old man's name. *General* Menesarkus. Chusor had heard stories about this Plataean his entire life. He was famous in Athens and even far-off Syrakuse: a hero of the Persian Wars, a fighter who'd never been beaten in the arena, and the pankrator who'd killed Damos the Theban at the Olympics years before, nearly starting a riot. And the young fighter he'd just pummeled into the dirt was Menesarkus's own grandson—Nikias. No wonder these Plataeans had stopped the Persians on their doorsill! They even fought their own kin.

The Plataeans were unsophisticated, just as the Athenians always said, but Chusor felt welcomed in their city. He used the little money that remained in his purse to set up a small shop. He and Diokles built a forge and Chusor painted an old shield with an image of the patron god of smiths—the crippled Hephaestos—hanging it over the entrance. His first jobs were simple: fixing door hinges, mending cartwheels, and making plows.

Over the next couple of months he got his hands on some good bronze and fashioned a breastplate with inlaid designs: bulging pectorals and rippled stomach muscles. He put this on display out in front of his shop and instantly drew crowds. One of the admirers was Menesarkus's heir.

"My name is Nikias," announced the lad with a broad smile. He'd just come from the gymnasium and his face was covered in bruises and sweat. He touched the gleaming breastplate with awe, with reverence, with lust. "And you and I are going to be friends."

"Indeed?" asked Chusor, raising a bushy eyebrow. He forced himself not to smile at the young man's ingenuous enthusiasm.

"Of course," said Nikias as he ogled the armor. "For I'm a warrior and you are the god of the forge. Our lives will be intertwined forever."

Chusor laughed. A great, rolling, mellifluous belly laugh.

"I'm serious," said Nikias with a roguish grin.

Chusor squinted at the lad. The young athlete held out his hand—his ugly, scabbed, gnarled pankrator's hand. Chusor took it in his own hoary palm and clasped it tight.

"I can see you're serious," said Chusor.

"Intertwined," repeated Nikias, pumping his hand. "Whether you like it or not."

That meeting with Nikias had been two years ago. Chusor had watched him grow into the bravest man he'd ever known. He wondered where the young hero was now. He should be at least halfway to Athens if he hadn't run into trouble. The road to Athens was dangerous enough, of course. But the capital of the Athenian Empire was worse. It was like entering the Minotaur's labyrinth. It was a foolhardy journey to make alone, but the young Plataean seemed to have Tyke—the goddess of luck—wrapped around his finger.

So why did Chusor have such a sinking feeling in his gut? As if something terrible had happened to Nikias?

He rubbed his bald scalp pensively. He had cut off his long black hair on an impulse the day before and then shaved his head. Afterward he had burned his locks on the coal fire of his forge. He didn't know why he had made this burnt offering. The Plataeans incinerated their cut hair in honor of Zeus when they came of age: they believed they were the sons of the father of the gods. The strange Thebans set their shorn tresses alight in honor of Ares—the hateful god of war. Chusor had muttered the name of Hephaestos, the fire god, when he had set his own curls ablaze. But he didn't really believe in any of the gods, and so his prayers were pointless. After he had done it Leo had told him that he looked fiercer without his hair. The truth was that Chusor *felt* fiercer after the events of the Theban invasion and the terrible things that had happened in Plataea . . . the barbaric punishments he had witnessed the enraged Plataeans inflict on the captured Theban prisoners. Something in him had withered. Perhaps it was his love for the Oxlanders.

" 'Those whom the gods intend to destroy, they first turn mad,' " said Chusor to himself, quoting a play he had seen in Athens.

He tossed the hunk of bread he held aside. He had no appetite this morning. He got up and went to check on the forge fire. He'd hired a pair of scrawny brothers to tend the charcoal flames, a tedious task that demanded constant vigilance. The boys had lost their father—a fellow smith and member of the Artisans' Guild—in the sneak attack, and their mother had begged Chusor to take them on as apprentices.

They were hopeless little fools. Skinny and stupid and full of mischief. The kind of boys who poked each other with hot irons, and got drunk on wine and pissed on one another for sport. Chusor had wanted Diokles to watch over them and keep them in line. But the Helot had been useless for weeks and Chusor had let the boys run wild.

"Ajax! Teleos!" Chusor barked. Neither one of the boys was by the forge. The fire—which should have been a red-hot blaze by now—was nearly out.

"They're in the courtyard," called Leo. "I saw them trying to kill something."

Chusor stepped into the courtyard and caught sight of the two boys chasing a terrified bird, trying to smash it with the bellows.

"Don't let them kill the poor thing," called a female voice from the window above the inner courtyard.

Chusor glanced up to see a woman's pale face staring down at him from one of the upstairs windows. It was Kallisto . . . Nikias's lover. The teenaged girl had been recovering in his house from a head wound she'd suffered in the battle with the Thebans. Chusor admired her. She was brave and beautiful. But she was the daughter of a man who'd been in league with the traitor Nauklydes, and so it wasn't safe for her to leave his home. She'd been tainted by the crime of her father. He'd seen up close what sort of savagery the Plataeans were capable of committing. He'd watched men of his own guild take apart a Theban prisoner, piece by piece, to extract information. It was a gruesome memory he would take to his tomb.

Chusor had promised Nikias to keep Kallisto safe. As long as she was under his roof, nobody would touch her. For the smith had helped save the city from the Theban invaders, and for a time, at least, his protection meant something. But someone had painted the words TRAITOR'S DAUGHTER on the outside wall of the smithy one night. And many men and women gave Chusor's house dark looks as they walked past.

"Get back into bed, girl," said Chusor, not unkindly. "You should not be up."

"The pretty pigeon," said Kallisto. "It flew through the window and sat on my bed, looking at me. I thought it was a sign from Nikias."

"Pigeon?" said Chusor. He glanced across the courtyard and saw Ajax about to impale the bird with an iron rod. Moving with the speed of a striking snake, he picked up an empty wooden bucket and flung it at the boys. It hit Ajax in the knee, bounced off, and smashed Teleos's foot. The pair howled with pain and shot angry looks at their master.

"By the shriveled leg of Hephaestos!" yelled Chusor as he charged them, filled with the wrath of a vengeful deity. "Leave the bird alone!"

Ajax pointed at his brother and said, "Teleos made me!"

Chusor snatched the bellows from Ajax. Teleos, a year older, took the opportunity to punch his brother in the face. Ajax screamed and struck back at Teleos. Chusor shoved them off to the side and let them fight.

"Do me a favor and go out in the street and kill each other," said Chusor, his eyes riveted on the bird.

He set the bellows down and walked slowly to the pigeon, making a low clucking sound in the back of his throat. The pigeon took one look at Chusor and strutted toward him, swaying its head from side to side and blinking its red eyes. Chusor knelt down and gently cupped his hands around the bird, then brought its head to his mouth and gave it a gentle kiss.

"Hello, old friend," he said, inspecting the animal's wings to make sure the boys hadn't harmed her.

Chusor realized that Teleos and Ajax—and even Leo, who'd popped his head out the window to take in the fun—were staring at him with surprise. He glanced up at the window and saw Kallisto regarding him with an odd expression.

"If either of you ever so much as ruffle a feather on this creature," said Chusor to the boys, "I will cut off your balls and cook them on the forge."

The boys nodded vigorously and went back inside.

Kallisto said, "I had a terrible dream about Nikias just now. I'm—I must tell you about it." She looked stricken and held a long hand to her throat.

Chusor replied, "I will come later. You must rest now."

She nodded silently, and then moved away from the window, disappearing into the shadows of her bedchamber.

Chusor walked quickly into the kitchen and grabbed a jar from off a shelf, and then carried the pigeon to his private chamber and set the bird on his desk. The pigeon inspected everything with an officious air—some scrolls, quills, a wine bowl holding only dregs—while Chusor regarded the creature with an apprehensive gaze. Finally, he took the bird in one hand and found the bit of parchment that he knew would be tied to her leg. He opened the jar he'd gotten from the kitchen, took out some millet seeds, and scattered them on the desk. The pigeon cooed and got to work snatching up the tiny grains.

Chusor unrolled the tiny scroll. He shook his head in amazement as he scanned the coded words written on the parchment. It had been nearly a decade since he'd used the ciphers, but ever so slowly they came rising back into his brain from the depths of his memory, like corpses from a shipwreck floating slowly to the surface of the sea.

After he finished reading he reached for his wine cup and realized his hand shook. He refilled the empty cup, took a long drink, then wiped his mouth on his arm, staring at the pigeon. After all this time . . . they had come! They had finally tracked him and Diokles down.

He tore the parchment into tiny pieces, placed them in a bowl with some white powder, and scraped a flint with a knife, causing a spark. The powder ignited and burned the pieces of parchment to ash. He tossed them out the window and the ashes vanished on the breeze.

He reached for a hidden drawer under the desk and took out a scroll, unrolling it on the table and holding the corners down with different rock samples he'd collected from the mountains. He stared at the map of Plataea he'd drawn—a bird's-eye view of the citadel, with all of the buildings' walls and bastions clearly marked. It was a secret map he'd been working on for years, ever since coming to Plataea. The only person who'd seen it other than Diokles was Nikias. He hadn't intended on showing the young fighter the map. Nikias had come into his workshop unbidden and seen it lying on the table—a careless mistake Chusor would never have made in his younger days. It was a map that would earn him a "tunic of stones" if anyone found out about it. For who could make such a map other than a spy? An enemy of Plataea?

The pigeon walked to the edge of the table and jumped onto Chusor's lap with a little flutter of wings. It sat there contentedly, cooing. Chusor gently stroked the bird's head with one of his giant thumbs.

"I'm heading to the market," called out Leo from the other room. "Need anything?"

"Bread and cheese," said Chusor immediately. "And some fresh vegetables for the girl if there are any."

"Of course," said Leo. "I'll be back soon."

After the front door slammed shut Chusor put the pigeon on his shoulder, where it sat nestled against his ear. He went to work quickly, cutting a slip of parchment, writing a reply in the secret language with quill and ink, then rolling the message up and tying it to the pigeon's ankle. He cupped the bird in his big hands and took it to the window.

"Fly to your mistress, now," he said in the pigeon's ear, then tossed it into the air. When he was satisfied the pigeon was headed back in the direction of the Kithaeron Mountains he gathered up his gear: a long walking staff, a wooden basket that fit onto his back—which he used to collect sulfurous stones from fissures on the mountain—and his leather mountain boots.

He put on the boots and laced them, then unscrewed a cap on the bottom of the walking stick to reveal a hollow core. He rolled the map into a tube and held it to the opening of the secret compartment, hesitating for a moment. Then he sighed and pushed the map into the tube and replaced the cap. He hoisted the pack onto his back and pulled the leather straps tight.

Snatching his wide-brimmed reed hat from its hook, he placed it on his head and exited the house, striding up Artisans' Lane.

THREE

———◆———

Nikias lay stunned on his back in the middle of the road, breathing in ragged breaths. He lifted his head with a great effort, squinting down the length of his body at the mounted Dog Raiders. He counted twelve of them. Twelve ruthless killers who were going to skin him alive.

The satyr-bearded commander had turned his mount around to face the other eleven riders and shouted angrily at his men:

"The Spartans said they'd give us silver for any captured Plataean!" he roared, glancing over his shoulder at Nikias. "He's no good to us dead. They'll want to extract information first."

Nikias probed his stomach fearfully, expecting to find an arrow sticking from his guts and his bowels leaking out. But all he felt there was a hard and lumpy mass.

"Oh, thank you, Zeus," he whispered, for the bag of gold that he wore under his tunic had turned the point of the arrow! He touched some of the Persian darics that had slipped out from a tear in the leather pouch. The traitor's blood money had saved his life. At least for the moment.

"I'm not kissing the arses of the Long Hairs for a few shitty silver coins!" barked a one-eyed Dog Raider. "That Oxlander cunt over there killed my nephew." He pointed at one of the corpses on the road. "I want him peeled while he's still got breath. He's dying from a gut wound. He'll be meat before we can get him back to camp."

Nikias shuddered and clenched his teeth, banishing the blinding fear from his brain. He had to think. He was running out of time!

"I've seen men live for days with stomach wounds," said the Dog Raider commander.

"You can stick his bleeding stomach in my puckered old arse!" spat One Eye, pulling his knife from its sheath. The other raiders laughed.

The hunters can quickly become the prey.

It was his grandfather's voice in Nikias's head. When Nikias was a boy his grandfather used to tell him the story of a wolf caught in a trap. When the hunter came close enough to skin his prey, the wolf leapt up and tore out the hunter's throat: the clever wolf had merely been pretending to be caught. "Deceit," his grandfather had explained, "can be as sharp as a sword."

Guile was the only way he could beat these Dog Raiders now.

A memory flashed in his mind: a wandering bard singing the "Song of Troy"—the scene with the wretched Trojan Adrestus, defeated on the field of battle, pleading piteously for his life.

He tried to flex his right arm, but it was still numb and useless. No matter. He'd fought with his right arm tied behind his back before, pummeling a much bigger warrior named Axe in a pankration bout. Nikias's grandfather had trained him to be ready for any shift in fortune. A hoplite might lose a hand or an arm in the midst of battle.

He snatched his dagger from his belt with his left hand, then cut a large gash in the bag of gold. He carefully tucked his blade under the pit of his wounded arm, hiding it from sight.

"It's on your heads, then," the commander said, nervously smoothing his satyr's beard. "You can be the one to tell King Kyros you lost him a valuable prize that he could trade to the Spartans." He pointed at a trio of riders including One Eye. "Make it fast."

"Gods!" Nikias cried out in a grief-stricken voice. "My stomach." He let forth an agonized cry, tucking his legs into the fetal position and clutching his abdomen. He'd seen men with gut wounds after a battle. He knew how to feign this terrible injury. He watched as the men chosen to be his torturers sauntered toward him.

"Bring me that pretty hair, will you?" called out one of the Dog Raiders. "I'll put it on my helm."

The three riders sauntered over and surrounded him, peering down and gloating.

"Please," Nikias said in a high-pitched, pathetic voice. "I beg you." He pretended to weep. "Take me alive to Kyros. My father is rich. Ransom me."

"You gave us quite the chase," said One Eye, standing on Nikias's right. The raider held a coil of rope with which to bind Nikias's arms and truss him up like a dead animal. The old man started looping one end to make a slipknot.

"Those Oxlanders are good riders," commented the Dog Raider standing at Nikias's feet. This one spoke with a lisp—he had two missing incisors. He knelt and grabbed Nikias around the ankles to pinion him in place.

"They make good screamers too," added the raider to Nikias's left. Nikias stole a glance at him. He was the youngest. Brown of beard. Cold, dead eyes. He scraped a hunting knife over a sharpening stone.

"Take me alive!" screamed Nikias. "There are treasures in my father's house!" He prepared his body to strike. A tingling heat coursed through his spine and left arm. He felt a sudden mad urge to laugh.

Brown Beard squatted and squinted at Nikias's face with the casual air of a butcher deciding where to cut first, running his hunting knife back and forth over the stone. "Scared?" he asked without pity.

Nikias squirmed, crying out in mock agony. Writhing wildly, he scattered the Persian coins onto the road. "There!" he shouted. "Look!" The coins clinked with the unmistakable sound of gold and glimmered yellow in the sun.

"Hey," said Gray Beard with a start. "This one bleeds darics!"

All three warriors, dazzled by the gold, lunged greedily at the coins, turning their eyes away from the young man, who they thought was dying on the road.

And then Nikias attacked.

His dagger flashed quickly to the right and to the left—as fast as a snake striking a hare.

Brown Beard clutched the side of his neck with an expression of mystified surprise as his lifeblood spouted from the mortal wound gushing beneath his fingertips. One Eye toppled backward, killed instantly by the blade, which had passed through the soft underside of his chin, the roof of his mouth, and into his brain.

The raider with the missing incisors—both hands still clenched on the coins—glared stupidly at Nikias, utterly bewildered. He blinked once before the bloodied dagger plunged deep into his eye, all the way up to the hilt.

Nikias was on his feet before the third Dog Raider's head hit the road. He flipped the bloody dagger, caught it by the flat of the blade, and sent it flying at the archer's horse.

Thwack!

The blade sank into the animal's chest. The horse reared and the archer somersaulted off. He reached out desperately to break his fall and landed awkwardly, his face hitting the road. His horse, meanwhile, turned and ran straight into another mount, knocking its rider to the road. That man hit the ground headfirst and lay unmoving.

The commander scrambled to his knees, screaming through a mouthful of blood, "Kill him!" His left forearm was broken and dangled at a weird angle.

Nikias grabbed his Sargatian lasso and ran headlong at the pack of Dog Raiders, cracking his whip in a frenzy of unleashed rage, striking their horses on the legs, rumps, and heads. The animals went wild, bucking and turning, throwing their riders. The road became a churning mass of terrified horses and trampled raiders with Nikias darting nimbly this way and that, his whip working ceaselessly, scarring flesh and hide, throwing up a red mist.

"Thanatos!" Nikias shouted, calling on the god of death.

One of the dismounted riders broke from the chaos, limping over to Nikias with his javelin held high, screaming openmouthed as he came. But Nikias whipped him full in the gaping maw with the Sargatian lasso—a knifelike blow that split the man's tongue in two.

The Dog Raider dropped his spear and reached for his mouth with both hands, his voice catching in his throat as the blinding pain hit his brain. Before the enemy could take another step Nikias cut his forehead to the bone. The Dog Raider covered his face with his arms, like an injured child. The next blow from Nikias's whip sliced clean through the artery in his neck. Blood spurted. His knees buckled and he fell to the road.

"Come on!" Nikias yelled, raging. "Fight me now!"

Another Dog Raider jumped off his horse, holding his armored forearm to his face to ward off any whip blow, and charged at Nikias with his sword raised. Nikias let the man approach a few steps before lowering his arm and snapping the whip at the raider's ankle. The braided leather cord wound itself around the warrior's leg. Nikias leapt back, pulling up on the whip, jerking the man's leg up high, and flipping him onto his back. And then Nikias was on him, driving his heel into the Dog Raider's throat, breaking his larynx. Nikias backed away as the man writhed, gasping for air. He wouldn't live more than a minute or two.

Nikias quickly surveyed the scene. Brown Beard and One Eye were dead. The raider with the missing incisors—dead. The raider with the whip-lashed neck—dead. The one with the crushed larynx—dying. And two who'd been thrown from their mounts lay motionless on the road.

Seven Dog Raiders were either dead or dying. He'd whittled them down to five. Those were good numbers. He snapped his whip over and over again, terrifying the horses.

The commander had remounted but was having trouble controlling his bucking horse because of his broken arm. The other four horsemen were having the same difficulties with their spooked mounts.

Nikias lowered his whip and glanced down. The Dog Raider whose throat he'd smashed with his heel had turned purple about the face, his eyes bulging from his head. He glared at Nikias with a look of profound hatred as he tried to suck in air through his destroyed windpipe.

The dying man's horse—a giant black gelding—came over and sniffed its master's head. The animal trembled, blood trickling down its haunch from where Nikias had struck it with the Sargatian whip. The horse stared goggle-eyed at Nikias out of one side of its big head, its reins dangling tantalizingly just out of reach. If only he could grab the reins. He could mount the animal and ride it back to the Three Heads!

He glanced at the five Dog Raiders up the road. They were an arrow shot away, spinning in circles, cursing at their frightened horses.

Nikias took a slow step toward the gelding. But the instant he moved his foot the horse flinched and whinnied angrily at him, snorting. It wheeled and kicked out with its hind legs, and then ran away, tossing its head as it went. It disappeared into the fog, heading north in the direction of the mountains. Nikias swore under his breath and turned to face the mounted Dog Raiders. The five men had finally gotten their horses under control and were lined up in a row, ready to charge with their javelins pointed at him.

Nikias clenched his teeth and breathed through his nose. He realized that all fear had left him.

"Come on!" The shout was ripped from his throat. "Die like your brothers!" He felt his skin tingle with excitement. His heart swelled. He suddenly felt powerful. Unbeatable. It was a sensation that he had experienced recently in battle. His grandfather called it "the ikor of the gods"—the sensation that the blood of the Olympians coursed through a warrior when his life was balanced on the edge of a knifepoint, making him potent . . . making him fierce and strong. He cracked the whip and the enemy horses reacted again with terror, bucking and rearing. Nikias could plainly see fear in the eyes of the raiders. They were hesitating. They didn't want to attack him. Nikias laughed and sprinted toward them—

And then a black blur rushed past from behind and slammed him to the road on his back. It took him a few seconds to realize that the black gelding had come back, running past him, kicking out with one of its back hooves as it passed—an act of revenge for the whip blows. If the hoof had hit him in the head it would have broken every bone in his face. But the horse had caught him on the thick pectoral muscle on his right breast.

Yet the animal's blow had done damage.

He rolled onto his stomach and fought for air, staring up the road in a daze. He saw the black gelding galloping crazily toward the four Dog Raiders. The other horses danced aside to let the enraged gelding pass, and then the beast was gone, bolting up the road in the direction of Athens.

Nikias felt the trembling in the ground before he heard the hooves. Many horses. Coming up the road from the direction of the mountains. He realized why the gelding had returned.

It was being chased.

He heard the distant war cry of a Dog Raider from that direction and his stomach sank. The horsemen who'd gone after Kolax . . . they must have killed the barbarian boy and were now returning to rejoin their brethren. Nikias was trapped like a wild boar—hemmed in between two packs of hunters.

Nikias shot a glance at the Dog Raider commander, who glared back at him malevolently. The raider cupped his hands to his mouth and answered the approaching riders with a full-throated scream.

"Hera's jugs!" spat Nikias. He got to his feet with a great effort and stood there swaying. He would die standing up. That's what his grandfather would have done. He might even take one or two more of them to Hades with him. He pulled back his arm and readied his whip. But his arm was shaking uncontrollably now. From behind he could hear the fast-approaching horses—their hooves pounding the hard road like thunder. They would be on him in seconds. Driving their spears into his body.

The Dog Raider commander ordered his men to attack, while he stayed back from the fray. The four remaining horsemen charged toward Nikias, their black capes flying, javelins raised.

Nikias's heart throbbed in his chest. His ears roared. Soon he would be caught in the maelstrom. Crushed and speared. Trampled. Pounded to blood and shit and dust.

And then something curious happened. A thing his mind could not fathom at first. He heard a sound like a hummingbird flying past his ear from behind. The face of the enemy rider closest to him was struck by an arrow and he fell from his mount.

Three more arrows buzzed over Nikias's head, one after the other, and three other charging Dog Raiders fell from their mounts, the last toppling into the dirt almost at Nikias's feet.

Four riders felled in a few heartbeats!

He caught a glimpse of the Dog Raider commander, a dumbstruck expression on his face, kicking his mount. The horse jumped off the road into the gully, where he vanished.

Then the world became a rush of noise and a swirl of dust as the pack of horses that were coming from behind rushed by Nikias on either side, passing so close that their coats brushed his shoulders. Only one of these horses bore a rider—a boy wearing the embroidered coat and leggings of a Skythian. He reined in, breaking from the pack, and turned, trotting back to Nikias. His long red hair was tied in an elaborate topknot that bobbed like a horse's tail as he trotted around the scene of carnage, guiding his horse with his knees alone, holding his bow in one hand and an arrow in the other, seeking out more men to slay.

"Did you see that?" shouted Kolax gleefully in broken Greek. "One, two, three, four! I did that at full gallop. Four in a row!" His horse, a small Theban mare of Persian blood that Kolax had captured on the battlefield two weeks before, lifted its hooves daintily, stepping over dead men and pushing air through its nostrils with a prim expression on its long face.

"One of them got away," said Kolax, pointing in the direction that the Dog Raider commander had gone. "Should I chase him?" He let forth his perfect imitation of a Dog Raider war cry—the same cry he had just used to trick the enemy as he'd charged up behind Nikias, driving the pack of horses.

Nikias shook his head. "No." He slumped to his haunches, trembling violently. "Let him go. We have to keep moving toward Athens."

Kolax leapt off his horse, wrapped his bow around his neck, and stowed the arrow he clutched in his hand in the lidded quiver at his back. Then he was on his knees, a knife gleaming in one hand, moving from one black-clad Dog Raider to the next, slitting their throats to make sure he'd done his job, then yanking out the arrows, clutching the gory things in his fist. The cart tracks carved into the white road were soon running red—gutters filled with blood.

"Counting those eight I killed earlier who chased after me," said Kolax proudly, "that makes twelve for the day. Twelve of these Fur-heads! Wasn't that funny how I herded their stupid horses?" He stood over the warrior whose throat Nikias had crushed. The man was still wheezing ever so slightly, in the final stages of death from asphyxiation.

"This one isn't quite dead," said Kolax, glancing at Nikias with a hopeful look.

There came a sudden gust from the north, and Nikias could smell the faint scent of pine borne on the wind. He closed his eyes and breathed in through his nostrils, savoring the fact that he had slipped from the hands of the god of death yet again.

Out of the corner of his eye he saw Kolax gesturing impatiently at the dying Dog Raider at his feet.

"This Fur-head needs help to the Other World," said Kolax.

"He's yours," he said, giving an exhausted wave of his hand.

Kolax smiled and bowed slightly at the waist, as if Nikias had offered him a modest but respectable gift. With a rapid movement he bent over and sliced off the Dog Raider's head with a few strokes of his long dagger. He held it up and looked into the face of the dead man.

"Not so fierce now," he said in a chiding tone. He tossed the head high into the air, counting quickly from one to eleven as the head spun against the sky, spurting blood.

"Thirteen," said Kolax under his breath as the Dog Raider's head slammed onto the road.

FOUR

———◆———

"The Gates of Pausanius are shut by the Arkon's orders! No foraging this morning!"

"You heard him, now back off!"

Chusor stood amongst a throng of irate people milling about near the city's gates. Most mornings men and women were allowed to venture outside of the walls to seek firewood and hunt for game. But today guards were shoving people back from the two massive oak-and-iron portals that were shut and barred.

"I need to retrieve something from my farm!" yelled a man.

"And I have to check on my flock on the mountain!" fumed another.

"Arkon's orders!" said one of the guards. "Now clear off!"

The crowd dispersed with dark looks, but they obeyed.

Chusor said an oath under his breath and glanced up at the mountain looming above the city. He could almost feel someone watching him from up there. How was he going to make his assignation now? There was no other way out of the citadel except through these gates. A secret tunnel did exist—Nikias had found it on the night of the Theban attack—but it had caved in, nearly burying the lad alive.

The sound of heated voices made him turn. He saw a crowd gathering near the statue of the hero Androkles in the center of the agora: the square in front of the gates. The statue was the figure of a young man raising a leaf-bladed sword toward the sky—the symbol of Plataea's democracy. Two debaters stood face-to-face in the shadow of the monument. Chusor wandered across the agora in that direction.

Thousands of inhabitants from the countryside, fleeing their homes after the Spartans had invaded the valley, had set up makeshift dwellings in the agora. Many people had removed the valuable doors and shutters of their farmhouses and brought them here, using them to fashion crude lean-tos. Some had even toted their beds and furniture, anything made of wood—a scarce resource in the

Oxlands—for fear that the Spartans would rip them from their unprotected homes and use them for firewood. It was a sight that depressed Chusor. What would happen if the Spartans did indeed besiege this place? How long would all of these people remain civilized in the face of overcrowding and starvation? How long until they were at each other's throats?

He had seen the aftermath of a year-long siege in Sicily. It was a terrible sight to behold.

"—but as I have argued so many times before, brother," one of the debaters was saying derisively as Chusor got nearer to the statue, "breaking our allegiance with Athens and offering earth to the Spartans makes us nothing more than their dogs. We might as well change our name from Plataeans to Helots!"

"And as I have reiterated countless times, my dear brother," responded the other, eyes wide with frustration, "Sparta does not want us to be their slaves. They merely require our neutrality. I don't understand why this fact seems to elude your brain. . . ."

Chusor had always been fascinated by public debates, even as a child growing up in Athens. There was nothing more civilized, in his opinion, than two citizens having a contest of words and ideas rather than a battle of brawn. One of the highest honors of being a citizen was the right to debate in this way, both in public and in the Assembly Hall. An honor he, Chusor, would never get to have, because he'd been born a slave—a citizen of nowhere.

"And I suppose you would rather Perikles of Athens make all of our decisions for us in this time of great crisis? Eh? Perikles the king?"

"Perikles is no tyrant. Athens is the general. And we are the hoplite. It is as simple as that."

"There is nothing simple about this situation, brother. I would remind you of the words of the noble orator . . ."

Chusor glanced around at the faces in the crowd. He saw resignation. Boredom. They were quickly losing interest. They'd all heard the arguments countless times over the last two weeks. The issue was an ox beaten long after it had died. Tensions would not be diminished until the Plataean emissary returned from Athens with Perikles's answer: whether or not they would be given permission to sign a peace accord with the Spartans.

Chusor hoped Perikles would agree to the Arkon's request, if merely to give the Plataeans time to stall the Spartans and build up the city's defenses. That would give Perikles enough time to raise an army to send to Plataea's aid as well. But he reckoned the Athenian leader would deny the request. If Plataea were to be allowed to sever its alliance with Athens, then other city-states, already rebellious, would secede also, and the Athenian Empire would start to crumble.

Out of the corner of his eye he spotted three city guardsmen, wearing light armor, striding toward him from the direction of the jail.

"Chusor!" one of them called out. "Just the man we're looking for."

Chusor knew all of the guardsmen—they were Arkon Menesarkus's hand-picked warriors: grizzled veterans of many campaigns.

His heart started pounding. Had someone caught the messenger pigeon and found his note? It was unlikely, and even if they had they would not be able to read his coded message. But still, he had to suppress a sudden urge to run away, back to his smithy, and lock himself in the storeroom with Diokles. He glanced toward the gates. They'd just been opened for a troop of cavalry to enter. The horses and men were dusty from the road. The gates were quickly shut with a loud clash, and heavy beams inserted into iron slots to lock them into place.

"What's wrong, Telemus?" Chusor asked the senior of the guardsmen. "What do you want?"

"The Arkon wants to see you, Chusor," Telemus replied.

"I was on my way to the—"

"You're on your way to see the Arkon," cut in Telemus, pointing in the direction he wanted him to walk—toward the city jail and the Arkon's headquarters next door. "Let's go."

Chusor tightly gripped his walking stick and obeyed. The other guards each took up a position on either side of him with the third leading the way toward the black marble steps of the city jail.

Inside the building a clerk relieved Chusor of his pack, and then held out his hand for the walking stick. Chusor reluctantly gave it up to the man, who took stick and pack to another room. A servant then led Chusor down a long hallway, opened a heavy oak door, and bade him enter. Chusor stepped into a long rectangular room and the servant shut the door behind him with a thud.

At the end of the chamber, behind a desk, sat a burly man writing with a stylus. He didn't glance up when Chusor entered, but remained hunched over the parchment upon which he worked. He had a black beard streaked with gray, and was balding. His sleeveless tunic exposed his massive arms, and he wore no sandals on his large feet. Even though he was well into his sixth decade, his powerful frame made him resemble Herakles come to life; for he was Menesarkus, hero of the Persian Wars, five-time Olympic pankration champion, general of Plataea, and Arkon of the city-state.

Chusor glanced around the chamber. There were several buckets filled with scrolls sitting on the floor, and a plate of uneaten breakfast on the desk. In the corner, behind the desk, was displayed Menesarkus's armor and helm, supported on a wooden stand. The armor seemed to float there, hovering behind the general like a spectral guardian. Chusor knew every square inch of that armor, for he'd made it with his own hands over a year ago. Menesarkus's battered shield, protected by a leather cover, leaned against the wall. The flap was open, revealing the image painted on the shield—a boxing Minotaur.

"Arkon?" Chusor asked hesitantly and resisted the urge to wipe away the beads of sweat forming on his brow. He wondered if the men in the other room had already found the secret compartment in his walking stick and his heart beat faster.

Menesarkus put down his stylus, rubbed his eyes and the dented bridge of his slightly crooked nose, then he spoke without looking up: "You've stepped in bilge water, Chusor."

"He knows," thought Chusor, feeling his guts turn.

Menesarkus put down the stylus, lifted his big head, and pierced Chusor with his stern gaze. "Where's that idiot boy, my grandson?"

Nikias!

The Arkon hadn't dragged him in here to interrogate him as a suspected spy. He wanted to know where Nikias was!

"He's gone to Athens," said Chusor with a sigh. "I tried to dissuade him, but it was no good."

Menesarkus cocked his head to the side and squinted at him, dumbfounded. "Eh?" he asked, as if he hadn't heard Chusor's reply. "Gone where?"

"He's gone to Athens. To recruit mercenaries to come back to Plataea."

"Gone to Athens?" repeated Menesarkus with a laugh. "To recruit mercenaries?"

"Yes, Arkon."

"*Mercenaries?*" Menesarkus asked again with an astonished expression, as if Chusor had just told him that his grandson had gone to fetch water from the moon.

"Archers and peltasts, Arkon," explained Chusor.

Menesarkus's smile faded and he scratched his beard with the end of his stylus. "Archers and peltasts," he repeated under his breath.

"To defend the walls, Arkon," offered Chusor. "During a siege."

Menesarkus shot Chusor a look that said, "I know what purpose archers and peltasts serve." And then he asked, "How did my grandson expect to entice these mercenaries? With his good looks alone?" he added with biting sarcasm.

"A bag of Persian gold darics," said Chusor, a hangdog expression on his face.

The ironic smile on Menesarkus's face disappeared to be replaced by a thin-lipped scowl. He crossed his big arms on his chest, leaned back in his chair, and bore into Chusor's eyes. He raised his eyebrows slightly, a sign for Chusor to continue.

"There's a story to tell," offered Chusor lamely.

"Indeed," said Menesarkus. "The plot of this play grows ever more intriguing." Menesarkus gestured for Chusor to sit in the chair opposite the desk.

Chusor sat down, considering how much of the tale to actually tell.

"The gold came from the traitor Nauklydes's storeroom," he said at last.

Menesarkus chewed on the end of the stylus for a few seconds, his eyebrows raised in wonder. "And you found this gold?" he asked.

"Not I, young Leo."

"That scab-faced lad? Nikias's friend? How did he find it?"

"He was searching in Nauklydes's office," said Chusor. "On the morning before the traitor's trial when he and Nikias were searching for evidence to help convict Nauklydes of treachery. The lad found it and gave it to me for safekeeping."

Nauklydes had been one of the most prominent and respected members of Plataean society: a factory owner and magistrate who, in his youth, had served as Menesarkus's battlefield protégé and Olympic herald. But Nauklydes had been terrified at the prospect of a Spartan invasion of the Oxlands, and so he had forged a secret alliance with the Thebans—allies of the Spartans. Over the years Nauklydes had been bought off with a fortune in Persian gold, paid to him by the Theban spy Eurymakus, and he had used this wealth to expand his business to as far away as Syrakuse, falling deeper and deeper into collusion with Plataea's enemies. Nauklydes had bribed the men guarding Plataea's gates on the night of the sneak attack, allowing Eurymakus and his invasion force to enter the citadel. After the Thebans had been defeated, Nikias had exposed Nauklydes as the traitor, and Menesarkus had prosecuted the man in court. Nauklydes had been found unanimously guilty and sentenced to the "tunic of stones" as a punishment: buried up to his waist in the marketplace and stoned to death by citizens of Plataea.

"How much gold are we talking about?" asked Menesarkus.

"Fifty darics or more."

Menesarkus let forth a scoff that could have been taken as a sign of either amazement or exasperation.

"And you gave it all to my grandson?" he asked. "This fortune in gold? Enough gold, I might add," he said, slapping down the stylus and peering at Chusor, "to build a very fine little temple to the goddess of fucking Mirth!" He raised his hand and slammed a fist onto the table with such force that the ink pot jumped and spilled ink across the parchment like a spray of dark blood. "Because this adventure of his is a pathetic joke. He'll be lucky if he makes it to Athens alive, and even luckier if he comes home with his balls intact, let alone with a band of cutthroats from the port of Athens!"

"I wanted to assist him," said Chusor, abashed. "He was going to Athens no matter what I said to him. I reckoned the gold could be put to good use. When your grandson sets his mind to something, he cannot be diverted from it."

Menesarkus ground his teeth together, staring back at Chusor under heavy lids.

The door opened and the servant peeked in his head, saying, "Arkon, you're needed for a moment."

Menesarkus got up, scowling, and limped toward the door on his bad right knee. "Stay here," he said to Chusor, and shut the door behind him.

Chusor swiped at his forehead, wiping away the stinging sweat that dripped into his eyes. He could hear the sound of activity in the offices on the other side of the door: the chattering voices and scribes hard at work. His gaze wandered to a big vase sitting on a table behind Menesarkus's desk. It was painted in the old style, from perhaps a hundred years before, when artists colored the bodies of men with black paint. The vase bore the image of a preposterously muscular man, the hero Herakles, lifting a much larger opponent—the Libyan giant Antaios, son of Mother Earth—and squeezing him in a bear hug. The artist had captured the action of this moment vividly. Antaios had thrown back his head and howled in pain and surprise, his toes straining to reach the earth. Chusor could almost hear Antaios gasp as Herakles crushed his ribs, driving the bones into his organs.

Chusor had seen Menesarkus beat a man in a pankration bout in just such a manner. By squeezing the air from his lungs until he'd passed out.

The door opened again and the Arkon came back in holding a jug of wine in one hand and two drinking cups in the other. "Leave me," he said to the servant, who was trying, ever so gently, to pry the jug from his hands. "I can do it myself! Now leave us."

The servant bowed, scurried out, and shut the door behind him. Menesarkus hobbled back to his desk, placed the jug and cups down with a sigh, then poured the wine. He handed Chusor a cup, then took a long draft from his own, wiping his mouth on his forearm, then nodding his head as though responding to an unspoken question.

"No, I can't blame him for having my blood," he said at last, though more as if speaking to himself than for Chusor's benefit. "I would have done the same at his age." He stared at Chusor and gestured at him with his cup. "You are an interesting man, Chusor," he said. "I didn't trust you when you first came to Plataea. Not because you're half Aethiope. But because you seemed to be too clever a fellow to merely be a vagabond. I reckoned you must be either a spy or a criminal on the run. I encouraged the old Arkon to have you watched closely and he agreed. Every aspect of your life was scrutinized that first year you were here. But after you became friends with my grandson, and I saw what a good influence you had on him, my feelings about you started to change. Nikias talks about you constantly, you know? You're one of his heroes. And when I saw what you have made with your hands, well, I was convinced you were some kind of genius. The beautiful armor and helms"—here he gestured toward the armor on the rack behind him—"and your inventions! Nobody has ever seen the like, I'll wager, not even in Athens. You have a gift that few men ever hope to have."

Chusor didn't know what to think. His head was spinning. The revelation that he'd been spied upon didn't surprise him. He'd known he was being watched back then. But to have Menesarkus, the great general of Plataea, offer him praise in such a manner—it disconcerted him.

"Many thanks," said Chusor softly.

Menesarkus stroked his beard and said, "When the Athenian whisperer Timarkos told me you'd killed one of Kleon's men in Athens . . . well . . . everything finally made sense. You came to my city to hide."

At the mention of Timarkos's name Chusor's heart sank. He knew Timarkos well from his days in Athens. He was one of the most dangerous spies who inhabited the viper pit of that vast citadel. And the skinny, goat-bearded whisperer had been partially responsible for Chusor losing the woman he loved.

"I do not deny that I killed a man," said Chusor at last. "But I did it in self-defense. I had to flee Athens because I would not have been given a fair trial. And Timarkos, who helped orchestrate my downfall, is a liar and not to be trusted."

"He said the same of you," replied Menesarkus. "On several occasions. He even suggested I have your throat slit."

The casual way in which Menesarkus had said this last sentence was chilling.

"But Timarkos does not concern me now," continued Menesarkus, peering directly in Chusor's eyes. "He has proved to be most unreliable. Now *you*, on the other hand, have proved your worth countless times over the last two weeks. Without your help this city might have fallen to its most hated and ancient enemy. This invention of yours, this sticking fire that you used against the Thebans . . . I think it is the key to defending Plataea from a Spartan siege."

Chusor thought back to the night of the sneak attack. The small army of Theban invaders, an advance force that had been let into the citadel by Nauklydes, had trapped the stunned Plataeans in their own city. The Thebans had built a wooden barricade in front of the gates using carts and timbers while mounted archers had patrolled the high walls. Anyone who had tried to get to the gates—the only entrance out of the citadel—was shot down by the archers on the walls. Nikias had been chosen to attempt a daring escape through an ancient and crumbling tunnel that led under the citadel. He was sent to round up all the warriors in the countryside as well as warn the border cavalry garrisons what had happened and bring them all back to Plataea.

But the men in the citadel had not known if Nikias would succeed. They knew they had to attack the barricade. If the Theban reinforcements arrived at dawn, they were all dead men, and every woman and child in Plataea would be turned into a Theban slave. Fortunately for the Plataeans, Chusor had been taught the secret of the sticking fire. Using clay vases as containers for this powerful weapon, they attacked the barricade, hurling the "pandoras," as he called them, using two-man slings. The makeshift fortification turned into an inferno. Many of the Theban invaders were burned alive. . . .

"You have been doing an excellent job as Master of the Walls," said Menesarkus abruptly, pulling Chusor from his thoughts. "You did a remarkable job repairing the gates after the Thebans destroyed them. There is no doubt in my mind that we need you. And so I have asked you here today to make you a proposition."

This time it was Chusor's turn to be flummoxed. "A proposition?" he asked with a catch in his throat. He tugged on his braided beard and stared into Menesarkus's eyes.

"You were born a slave," said Menesarkus.

"Yes," said Chusor, blood rushing to his cheeks. "But my master gave me my freedom."

"Freedom, yes, but not *citizenship*. The most you can ever hope to be in any city in Greece is a *metic*. A foreign worker isn't much better than a slave. You're like a confused shade that finds itself lost in that netherworld between life and death."

Chusor had never heard his own situation put so bluntly before. Menesarkus was right, of course. And it made him sick at heart. "Such is my fate," he said, staring gloomily at the vase behind Menesarkus.

Menesarkus followed his gaze to the jar. "Herakles could not beat Antaios by throwing him to the ground," he explained, gesturing at the painted image, "because it was the *earth* that gave Antaios his strength. So Herakles had to change tactics and trust in the gods. The solution was simple, really."

"All he had to do was lift Antaios off the ground," said Chusor.

"And then Herakles could squeeze the life out of him," put in Menesarkus with a wicked gleam in his eye. "These Spartans . . . all *we* have to do is get *them* off their feet, and then we can crush them."

"Why am I here, Arkon?" asked Chusor. "What is your proposition?"

"Haven't you figured it out?" asked Menesarkus with a sly smile. "I am offering you citizenship as a Plataean."

Chusor stood up as though he'd been stung by a wasp. Wine sloshed from his cup, splattering the stones. This was an offer of a treasure more valuable to him than a mountain of gold. Citizenship! To no longer live as a paltry freed slave, or a lowly *metic,* but rather a full-fledged citizen of a city-state that was in league with the great Athenian Empire. A gift once given that could never be taken away and would serve as a passport anywhere in the empire, even were Plataea to fall.

"Do you toy with me?" he asked.

"I would never toy with such a man as you," said Menesarkus. "But this gift I offer you comes at a *very* high price."

FIVE

Nikias and Kolax had been riding hard for many miles with a strong wind at their backs. It felt like the hand of a friendly god pushing them toward Athens.

The fog had burned away completely to reveal the rocky and barren terrain of this region: Attika. Hardscrabble hills and parched fields waiting to be plowed and sown; many hues of brown under a bright blue and cloudless sky. The landscape reminded Nikias of a desiccated old man. It was as though the fog, like a white death shroud, had been pulled away to reveal a dried-up old corpse.

Nikias glanced at the barbarian boy riding a few strides ahead—always a few strides ahead in an impatient manner that irked the Plataean. The Skythian kept looking back at him and frowning as if to say, "Can't you go any faster?"

The truth was that Nikias could not. But he didn't want to admit this to Kolax. His recent injuries were preventing him from keeping up with the boy. His right shoulder, injured in the fall from Photine, felt as though it had been branded with an iron. And the place where he'd been kicked in the chest by the black gelding hurt more now than it had an hour ago. It throbbed with every hoofbeat, radiating a dull ache through his torso and into his spine. He longed to come to a stop and lie down under the shade of a tree.

He could sense his horse was at the end of her limits too. He was on one of the Dog Raiders' mounts—a lithe gray mare that had been the only animal to escape injury from his Sargatian lasso in the chaos of the fight. She was fast, but a little too small for Nikias's heavy build. And she was getting tired. He would have to stop soon to let her drink and nose around for some food.

"How much farther to Athens?" asked Kolax.

The barbarian boy had asked this question so many times that Nikias had lost count. Kolax was anxious to be reunited with his father—an archer in the employ of the Athenian police force. But the truth was that Nikias didn't know the answer. He was in a daze.

"Have to stop soon," he said. "Need to rest."

"Rest?" scoffed Kolax. "I've got a bag of gold and I'm on my way to see my papa! No rest for me!"

After Kolax had saved him from the Dog Raiders, Nikias had given the boy half of the gold to carry, thinking it better to split the treasure between them in case they were attacked again. He was beginning to regret the decision, however. The boy might just leave him in the dust and head off to Athens on his own. Or cut his throat.

No. That was a foolish notion. Kolax was as loyal as a dog. "I'm being mistrustful," he thought. He touched his head with the back of his hand. His forehead burned and he sweated profusely. He realized that he had a fever.

After another mile the road wended its way through a flatter area—there were fields on either side of the road that had been cross-furrowed to kill the weeds. In the distance, to the right, he could see a single farmer plowing with a bony ox, preparing the field for spring planting. Probably millet, Nikias considered with the eye of a farmer. That's what he would grow in this cracked rocky ground that was so unlike the verdant Oxlands, where you could practically scatter seed in the red earth without plowing and know it would come up strong.

The cart ruts were deeper on this part of the road than they had been closer to the mountain range. If he were to step into one of these tracks his leg would go in all the way up to his calf muscle. He wondered how many years men had moved along this road. A thousand? More? He could see a little cluster of farmhouses on top of a low hill surrounded by trees and vineyards. It looked like a happy place to live. And easily defensible from enemy attack.

"But I thought that our home was safe from attack," he thought. "And I was wrong."

His mind wandered, lulled into a sort of waking sleep by his fatigue and the rhythm of the galloping horse. A vision of his mother, standing at her loom and singing, flashed before his eyes, and he felt a stabbing sensation in his gut. She was dead now, murdered by Thebans on the night of the sneak attack. After Nikias had escaped from the citadel through the secret tunnel, he had gone straight to his family's farmhouse and had found it in smoldering ruins. The Theban called Eurymakus, who had a blood feud with Menesarkus, had tried to wipe out Nikias's entire family.

The next morning Nikias had come face-to-face with Eurymakus in the battle in front of the gates of Plataea, when the Theban reinforcements had clashed with the Plataean cavalry that Nikias had led from the border garrisons. But the Theban spy had fled in the confusion of the battle. . . .

"Where is my mother's shade now?" Nikias thought morosely. He should have been at the farm on the night of the invasion. He would have saved her.

She had not received a proper cremation and interment. For her body had been consumed in the inferno that had obliterated their home. Nor had she been given a funeral feast. Would her shade be angry? Confused?

Nikias's father, Aristo, had died on a battlefield when Nikias was six, and his grandfather had brought the corpse back home in a cart. It didn't take much effort to recall that memory. He could see his father's body in his mind as clearly as the day it had happened. Aristo's long, lean body laid out like a plank, almost blue and drained of blood from a terrible spear wound to his abdomen—a wound from which no man could recover. His grandfather had found his only son on the battlefield with his face buried in the dirt, hands frozen in the act of pushing dirt to either side of his face. He had smothered himself to stop the terrible agony.

"He looked as though he were shouting to the Underworld that he was on his way," Menesarkus had said.

Nikias had been allowed to help wash his father's corpse. He'd even been given the honor of placing a silver coin in his father's hand to pay the Ferryman who would transport him across the river Styx. After that his father had been wrapped in his best robe, and then burned on a bier. The ashes and bits of bones were collected and stored in a funeral jar painted with Aristo's image: a beautiful man with long limbs holding a tortoiseshell harp and staring into space with sad eyes. He had been a poet and a runner, one of the fastest in the Oxlands. "Not meant for the battlefield," his grandfather had said several times over the years. Not with disgust or anger. Just regret. But Nikias had always bristled at this description of his father. Who *was* meant for the battlefield? It seemed, in Nikias's opinion, that whether or not you survived was based almost solely on pure luck.

His grandfather had an answer for that too. "Some men are born lucky, others seize luck by the balls and take it. Others can't buy luck even if they have a cartload of gold."

Nikias had kept his father's funeral jar and tortoiseshell harp in his bedroom. Both had been destroyed in the fire. His mother's remains were mingled in the cinders of the abandoned farmhouse as well. There was nothing left of her body. No hand in which to place a silver Plataean coin for the journey to the Underworld.

"The Athenians put the Ferryman's coin in the mouths of the dead," he mumbled aloud. Nikias also knew that the poor kept money in their mouths when they went to market.

His mother had told him this when he was a child. She'd come from Athens. She'd been poor, but so very beguiling. His parents' marriage had been arranged, but Aristo had fallen in love with her the moment he'd seen his bride. At least that's what his mother had told him.

He hoped his mother had found her way to the Underworld. Perhaps the

Ferryman would give her passage for free, enraptured by her beauty. And then she would search the Land of the Dead, drawn by the sound of her husband's playing and singing. Would his parents still love one another if they were reunited? Could the dead hold each other? Make love as shades? How terrible to be nothing more solid than a fog. A mere vapor craving life. . . .

The sound of laughter startled him from his grim reverie. He glanced to the left of the road and saw a small olive grove. Some boys were beating the trees with long sticks to shake out the last of the harvest. A pair of toddlers, barely able to walk, were picking up the fallen olives and gleefully tossing them into a basket.

"Stop," said Nikias, pulling back on the reins and coming to a halt. Kolax stopped, too, trotting back to him.

"What is it?" asked Kolax.

"There's a road marker," Nikias said, sliding off his horse's back. When his feet hit the ground his brain exploded in a blinding flash of pain. Bending over, he took several ragged breaths to compose himself, and then clutched the horse's reins, walking the animal over to a statue by the road: a stone head with long curling beard and hair stuck onto a rectangular column. A phallus protruded from the center of the block of marble, pointing the way to Athens like a fat finger.

Kolax walked his horse over and looked the strange statue up and down. His lips curled in an expression of haughty disdain. "What's he so happy about?" he asked, pointing at the stone erection with his bow.

"It's a herm statue," said Nikias.

Hearing a high-pitched screech, he looked up: an eagle soared high in the sky overhead. The messenger of Zeus! This was a good sign.

"What does the stone say?" asked Kolax, pointing at the words etched on the marker.

"Ten miles to Athens," said Nikias. He couldn't hide the weariness in his voice. He could barely speak.

"Then let's go! Let's go! To Athens!" cried Kolax enthusiastically.

"I have to rest," said Nikias softly. "And my horse is going lame." He looped his mount's reins around the statue's erection, adjusted the straps on his small pack, then stared across the field, past the olive grove, to a cluster of farm buildings in the distance. Suddenly the world swam before his eyes. He slumped to the ground with his back against the cool north side of the marble statue. He shut his eyes.

"Are you taking a nap?" asked Kolax. "Great Sky-God! Are you joking?"

Nikias ignored him, his thoughts drifting. He thought back to several days before he'd departed Plataea. His grandfather had ordered him to meet him at his offices. Thinking that he was being summoned for a tongue-lashing, Nikias had been surprised when his grandfather led him down a dark hallway to a portal guarded by armed men.

"There's a man in this room," Menesarkus had said. "And he's worth his weight in gold. . . ."

"Nikias!" said Kolax urgently.

Nikias shook himself from his reverie and opened his eyes. "What?"

"You were about to swallow a fly," said Kolax.

Nikias scowled at him, then got slowly to his feet, taking the horse's reins from the herm statue. He started walking in the direction of the farmhouses, leading his mount.

"Where are you going?" asked Kolax.

Nikias tripped in one of the cart ruts, falling onto his knees. The reins slipped from his fingers, and the Dog Raider's horse bolted instantly and galloped across the road, heading north, away from the direction of Athens. Even Kolax was caught off guard by its sudden act of escape.

"Stupid horse!" cried the Skythian as he kicked his mount and took off in pursuit.

"Wait!" yelled Nikias, struggling to his feet. "Leave the horse! Come back, you idiot barbarian!"

But Kolax ignored him, whooping madly as he chased the fleeing animal across a field, churning up a cloud of dust. Nikias watched with helpless fury as first his horse and then Kolax and his mount disappeared over the crest of a hill and vanished from sight. Nikias staggered up the hill, but by the time he got to the top Kolax was far away—a tiny dot riding hard in the distance, chasing another dot heading north. Nikias turned toward Athens. From this high vantage point above the road he could clearly see the Athenian citadel ten miles to the southeast. The Temple of Athena, where it sat atop the Akropolis, was plainly visible even from this distance. The brightly painted building shone in the sun like a beacon. He was so close now.

He waited on the hill for the longest time, sitting on his haunches, focused on the temple, shivering with chills. At first anger boiled within him. But then it changed to concern. And then finally a wave of despondency overcame his soul. The Skythian boy was gone. Something must have happened to him. He would not be gone so long otherwise.

He realized that his teeth were chattering noisily in his head. But his head was burning. How would he ever make it to Athens?

He got to his feet and clambered down the hill and over the dusty field toward the farm. He could see the figures of women in the distance, balancing tall amphoras on their heads, moving to and fro from a well to the farm buildings.

His feet felt as though they were cast of iron. He plodded on, mouth parched, while waves of nausea passed over him. By the time he got to the well only two women remained standing there—two old women in their sixties, veils thrown to the wind with their backs to him.

The sound of Nikias clearing his throat caused the women to turn around with startled expressions. They gasped at the sight of him: pale, covered with dried blood, and his teeth chattering like knucklebone dice in a clay cup.

One of the women pulled a long kitchen knife from a sheath she kept on her hip—a knife for cutting the heads off chickens, though it looked as sharp as any warrior's sword. Nikias saw the blade shining in the sun, and the looks of fear on their faces. He held up his left hand in a sign of peace and slowly sank to his knees, dropping his chin to his chest.

"Mothers," he said in a croaking voice. "I need water. Please. I can pay." He tried to grasp the leather pouch at his belt, then swayed. He heard one of the women scream as everything turned to blackness before his eyes.

SIX

"As wily as Odysseus," grumbled Chusor as he climbed the steep goat path that wended its way up the Kithaeron Mountains.

He still reeled from his meeting with the Arkon. He'd known Menesarkus for only two years, but he'd seen enough of the man in action to realize that he was a strategist without compare. Their conversation of an hour ago reinforced this notion beyond a doubt.

"How could he have known my greatest desire?" Chusor asked the stones, the trees, and the birds of the hillside. "How did the Arkon know the one thing that would keep me here in this doomed city? Risking my neck against a Spartan siege?"

If Chusor helped defend Plataea, then he would be granted Plataean citizenship. But only after the Spartans had departed the Oxlands. That was the preposterous stipulation that Menesarkus had presented to him.

It was a ludicrous arrangement . . . so why had Chusor said yes without hesitation?

He paused and wiped the sweat from his brow, staring down at the citadel five hundred feet below the trail. His gaze wandered from the jumble of hovels in the agora to the overcrowded marketplace, and then to the gates on the eastern wall. One of the great portals had been opened to allow people to exit the citadel, and men and women were heading into the countryside, looking around fearfully for Spartans as they went. Nobody knew how much longer the Spartans would let Plataeans move about unmolested.

Chusor peered to the northeast—two miles from the citadel of Plataea—to where the massive earthen-walled structure of the Persian Fort loomed. This fortification was big enough to hold four citadels of Plataea within its twenty-foot-high bastions. It had been constructed almost fifty years ago by King Xerxes's army of half a million warriors and slaves. It was a marvel of engineering and industriousness, for it had been erected in less than a week. But the place had become a killing ground when the Greek allies had broken through the Persian and Theban shield walls, trapping the invaders inside their own fortress: a battle in which Menesarkus, only sixteen years old at the time, had won renown by slaying the Persian general Mardonius.

The Persian Fort became a tourist destination after that, visited for decades by warriors from all over Greece. Nikias told him that he and his friends used to play inside the fort when they were children, searching in the tall grass for treasures: bronze arrowheads and spear points, pieces of armor, and even Persian gold and rings. For the Persian nobles had gone to battle vainly arrayed in all their wealth—riches that had been divided up between the Greek allies after the Persians were wiped out. The Plataeans had used their share of the gold to make Plataea's walls higher and stronger, and to construct public buildings and temples, turning their city into one of the strongest and most beautiful in Greece.

Two weeks ago, after the Theban reinforcements had been defeated in front of the gates of the citadel, the Spartans had arrived in the Oxlands—too late to help their Theban allies. The Spartans had taken over the Persian Fort as their base of operations, swarming into the place like a flock of predatory birds into abandoned nesting grounds. And now they were waiting silently . . . waiting for the Plataeans to join them in their war against the Athenians, or suffer the torments of a siege.

From the center of the Persian Fort a gray haze rose toward the blue sky—smoke from hundreds of campfires. And on the parapets of the walls, moving about like ants, Chusor could see hundreds of Spartan sentries. The noise of hammers and axes pounding and chopping wood carried faintly on the wind. Thousands of Helot slaves were hard at work, building the equipment to besiege Plataea: scaling ladders, mobile towers, and battering rams. The northern road leading from the Persian Fort to the city of Thebes six miles away was alive with activity: oxcarts and riders moving back and forth between the two strongholds. The Thebans were Spartan allies, and had been responsible for the unsuccessful sneak attack on Plataea two weeks ago. If the Theban plan had worked, Plataea already would be occupied by the Spartan invasion force. But Plataea's ancient enemy had failed, and the Spartans had arrived too late to defeat the citizens of Plataea.

Citizenship!

The word echoed in Chusor's brain. Citizenship would change his life forever. He could go back to Athens without fear of reprisal. As a citizen of Plataea, independent democratic city-state and an ally of Athens, he would be on equal footing with even a man as lofty as Perikles himself—the leader of the Athenian Empire!

Twenty years ago Chusor had been the apprentice of the great architect

Phidias—a kindly genius who had recognized Chusor's talent for mathematics and had purchased him from his first master and taken him into his own household. For the next ten years Chusor had helped Phidias construct the new Temple of Athena atop the Akropolis. The architect had treated Chusor like a son and the young apprentice had been allowed to attend gatherings hosted by wealthy Athenians. At one of these salons Chusor had fallen in love with a regal courtesan named Sophia. She and Chusor had started an affair, incurring the murderous wrath of her lover, a politician named Kleon. Chusor had been forced to run. For the next seven years he'd traveled the Mediterranean Sea, from Byblos to Carthage and beyond. In Sicily he became the student of the great inventor Naxos, and learned the secrets of the sticking fire and siegecraft. But after running afoul of a wealthy Syrakusan he'd fled that island's chief citadel. He fell in with a band of pirates, journeying with them beyond the Pillars of Herakles to the western shore of Africa.

On this extraordinary and eventful odyssey he'd discovered that half of what Herodotus had written in his book was true, and the other half was pure horseshit.

But something had always drawn Chusor back to Greece. He could never return to Athens—he would be imprisoned and tortured—and so he'd headed north to the Kithaeron Mountains: the place where the god Dionysus had been born.

And now here he was. Standing on a cliff, peering down at a doomed citadel. Everything looked so peaceful. But Plataea was like a town built upon the edge of a volcano . . . a volcano that was about to erupt.

He picked up a stone and threw it in frustration against the trunk of a weather-beaten olive tree nearby. It made a satisfying crack as the missile found its target. A flock of crows that had roosted in the branches took flight, squawking angrily.

He saw something move in one of the tree's upper limbs. At first he thought he was looking at a great bird. Then he realized it was a human head. The shape of a body materialized before his eyes—a body that had been hidden amongst the leaves. He picked up another rock and tested the weight, cocking his arm to hurl it at the man who was spying on him.

"I know you're up there, Ji," said Chusor. "You can come down now. Or shall I knock you down with this rock?"

The man in the tree made a ludicrous imitation of a crow. Chusor smiled and watched as the diminutive figure climbed quickly down to the ground and walked over to Chusor. A lithe, brown-skinned man of indeterminate age, he wore a smile across his round face, his almond-shaped eyes squinting with delight. He bowed and said in the Phoenician tongue, "Greetings, Big Man."

Chusor bowed back, speaking the same language. "You look well, Ji, my old friend."

"And you look nearly the same," said Ji, "even after these four years."

"*Nearly* the same?" asked Chusor with a laugh.

"Your body has not aged," said Ji, staring at Chusor's bald scalp, "but it seems your hair has died."

Chusor rubbed a hand over his shaved skull. "An experiment," he said.

"She won't like it," said Ji, showing his teeth and squinting as he laughed amiably. "She'll say you look like an Egyptian scribe." He mimed the actions of a scribe, holding one hand out like a piece of papyrus, and pretending to write on it with the other.

Men who didn't know Ji would have been lulled into thinking he was a gentle buffoon. But Chusor wasn't fooled by the man's good humor. He'd been raised as an assassin in a Chinese governor's house and had been trained to kill his lord's enemies around the same time he'd learned to wipe his own arse. Not even young Nikias would stand a chance against Ji. He was the fastest man Chusor had ever seen.

"I care not if your mistress likes my looks," said Chusor. "Take me to her."

Ji grinned, nodding, and then turned on his heels, walking quickly up the slope. They continued on the goat path for a hundred paces, and then turned left through a stand of pines. Chusor knew where they were headed. The Cave of Nymphs. It was a grotto the Plataeans believed to be inhabited by *daimons*—evil spirits who were neither gods nor men. He glanced back over his shoulder, down the slope, toward the citadel of Plataea shining in the sun. A voice in his head told him to turn back. That he was in danger.

Ji glanced over his shoulder and asked, "Does the Helot live?"

"In a manner of speaking," said Chusor.

Ji didn't press Chusor to explain this cryptic reply. Instead he said, "The Sponge is dead."

"Pity," said Chusor in a monotone.

"She killed him," said Ji. "They got in a fight. It was a mess."

"I'm sure the Sponge got what was coming to him."

"Oh, and Barka has returned to our crew."

Chusor stopped dead in his tracks, his heart sinking to his knees. The world seemed to shift as his mind reeled from the shock of this news. Barka the eunuch. Barka the Soothsayer. Barka the murderer. He thought he would never again see the wretched man again. But the evil little creature had returned.

Something on the trail up ahead caught his eye. It was a sun-whitened goat's skull moving slightly, as though it were alive. Shreds of its hide and tufts of wool were scattered about the path—the goat must have been killed and eaten by some animal. But what was making the skull move? Then he saw a large tortoise on the other side of the path. It had become entangled in a long tuft of the dead goat's wool. This strand of brown fleece was wrapped around its neck and hooked onto the jagged bottom of the goat skull. The tortoise struggled in vain to free itself from this trap. Chusor went over and untangled it and the tortoise moved quickly away—at least, Chusor thought, quickly for one of its kind.

He realized Ji was scrutinizing him with a half-mocking expression, scratching his head contemplatively.

"A strange sign," said Chusor.

"Barka could tell you what it means."

"I no longer wish to ask Barka to interpret anything for me."

Chusor wanted more than anything to turn and flee. To run down the mountainside to the citadel. But he knew he couldn't outrun the little man who stood before him, gesturing with his dagger in the direction he wanted Chusor to go—toward the mouth of the cave above. "Where is the ship?" asked Chusor, stalling for time. "The Bay of Korinth?"

"I'll let Zana tell you, Big Man," Ji said flatly. The twinkle in his eye had vanished. "Let's go. We've kept her waiting long enough."

Chusor clenched his teeth and nodded, then forced his feet to move up the flinty slope toward the Cave of Nymphs, looming in the hillside above like the gaping mouth of a beast.

SEVEN

"A handsome face once the blood is off him," said a woman's kindly voice.

"And the dirt," replied another.

"Look at all the scars on his body."

"He's seen battle before."

Nikias had been listening to the old farm women chattering for a while with his eyes closed. He felt so exhausted he could barely move a muscle. He didn't know how long he'd been unconscious. The chills had subsided. But his body felt strangely heavy, as though it were carved from marble. He forced himself to open his eyes and saw the faces of the two old women staring down at him with concern.

"I'm not going to hurt you," he muttered.

The old women smiled and laughed gently. "Of course you're not," said one of them and patted him on the cheek.

"You couldn't fight a kitten in the state you're in," added the other.

"What happened to you, lad?"

"Fell off my horse," said Nikias. "Then I was attacked by Dog Raiders."

"Achh! These days are sad days!"

"Sister, you said the very words that I was thinking!"

"How did you survive?"

"Where are you from, sweet love?"

"Plataea," said Nikias, and the women dropped their jaws in unison.

"But my husband heard news just yesterday in the market—" one of the women began.

"—of Thebans and a battle!" finished the other.

"True," said Nikias. "I was there."

"And you walked all the way here straight from the fight?"

"No wonder you're such a mess."

Nikias laughed softly. "No, the battle was two weeks ago. I looked fine until this morning. I'm on my way to Athens."

"I am the wife of Solon," said the elder of the two women. "My name is Anastasia. And I live nearby. You must come to my home and eat something and rest."

"Maybe I could just stay *here* awhile, by the well, wife of Solon," said Nikias, closing his eyes again and drifting off.

"My grandson is coming with the cart," said Anastasia. "He'll take you to the house."

Nikias shook his head. "I can walk," he insisted. He tried to stand but his legs were wobbly and he sank back down. Soon a young man arrived pulling a wooden cart. His left arm was missing at the elbow, so he had yoked the cart to himself with an ox harness. He stared curiously at Nikias as he approached.

"Is he dead, Grandmother?" asked the young man.

"Not yet," croaked Nikias.

"This is my grandson, Konon," said Anastasia.

Konon, a strong farmer with stout legs, wrapped his arm around Nikias and heaved him into the cart, setting his pack and sword by his side. Then he yoked himself to the cart again and started walking, pulling Nikias through an olive grove toward the main farmhouse.

Nikias reached for the pack and thrust his hand inside, feeling for the pouch in which he'd placed the gold. It was still there. He sat up and swiped his long hair out of his eyes. "My name is Nikias," he said. "Son of Aristo."

"Konon," replied the lad. "Son of Periander."

They approached the first of the farm buildings—a shed filled with barrels for the fermenting of wine. An old man with a humped back stood outside the shed tasting some mash from a cup. As the cart approached he ordered it to stop and shuffled over to it, thrusting the cup into Nikias's hand saying, "Taste this."

Nikias took a swallow and coughed. "A little on the pickle side, as my grand-father says."

The man gave a colossal sigh—as though the world were coming to an end. He took the cup from Nikias's outstretched hand.

"My thoughts exactly, boy," he said and tossed the rest of the wine to the side. An instant later his face lit up. "Now try the juice from this other vat and—"

"Husband," interrupted Anastasia, who had come up behind them, "this poor boy has come all the way from the Oxlands and a battle with Thebans. He's been thrown from his horse and beaten by Dog Raiders. And now you are making him taste your wine? Stop!"

"I thought he was the young fellow who lives down the road," said Solon. "The one who shits himself and has to be carted around."

"He's a traveler from Plataea, Grandfather," explained Konon.

"And he's very ill," said Anastasia with a chiding tone.

"Take me to court, why don't you?" Solon muttered to himself and went back into his shed.

"He's nearly blind," Anastasia said to Nikias.

"But not yet *deaf*," countered the cranky Solon from inside the building.

Konon pulled the cart up to the front of a farmhouse and helped Nikias to his feet, supporting him as they entered the front door.

"Take him to the kitchen," Anastasia told Konon.

She made Nikias a delicious meal: flatbread, olives in brine, goat cheese, chickpeas in oil and vinegar with herbs, little fish drowning in oil, and a delicious wine mixed to the perfect proportion with good, clean water. Nikias hadn't realized how hungry he was. He kept the slave girl busy working at the bread oven. Anastasia was pleased that he ate so much.

"Poor dear," she said after he'd finished off his second plate of fish and beans. "Poor starving creature. You must have been dying."

Nikias wiped his mouth on his arm and smiled at Anastasia. "Bless you, wife of Solon," he said. "I think you have saved my life."

"My other grandson, Konon's elder brother, is an oarsman on a trireme," said Anastasia proudly. "I hope some other mother would do the same for him if he was ever in trouble in the colonies." She took a painted plate off the shelf and set it before Nikias. It bore the image of a fierce-looking young Athenian man throwing the javelin and written beneath was the name TIMON.

"He looks like a brave fellow," said Nikias. "I have a cousin who's on the *Sea Nymph*."

"My Timon is on the *Freedom Bringer*," she said. "We haven't seen him for a year." She took the plate, gently dusting it off with her sleeve, then carefully placed it back on a high shelf. "We don't know where the fleet was sent. Somewhere in the north. A blockade," she added and her face fell. She smoothed her dress over her ample chest and brightened. "Come," she said. "You can't go about wearing that bloody torn tunic. You look like a barbarian."

She led Nikias to an upstairs bedchamber where she opened a large cedar chest and took out an Athenian-style tunic—it was shorter than the kind worn in the Oxlands and made of finer wool. She crossed her arms and watched unabashed while Nikias undressed until he wore nothing more than his Oxlander boots. She inspected his naked body, commenting on his dozens of bruises and cuts.

"You're a fine specimen," she said. "You're almost the same size as my Timon, and he's one of the strongest men in the fleet."

Nikias tried to slip on Timon's tunic but he couldn't lift his right arm and winced with pain.

"Poor lad! What is wrong?"

"My arm," said Nikias. "Tore the shoulder muscle."

Anastasia helped him put on the rectangular cut of cloth, fastening the square at the shoulder with a copper pin. Nikias put on his own heavy leather belt and adjusted his Sargatian whip. He turned around and Anastasia regarded him with an appraising eye.

"Timon is a little bigger than you," she said. "He *is* an oarsman, after all. But the folds at the waist look elegant. You appear to be a proper Athenian."

"Thank you, good woman," said Nikias.

"Except for those ugly boots," said Anastasia. "No Athenian would be caught dead in those. It's either barefoot or sandals in the city."

Nikias shrugged. "They're my favorite boots. They're not coming off unless I *am* dead." He reached for his pack and took out a cone-shaped traveling hat. It was made of gray felt and had a geometric design. He put it on. "What do you think?" he asked.

Anastasia smiled. "Only an Oxlander would wear a pilos as ugly as that one."

"My mother made it for me last year," said Nikias. "She said it would bring me luck."

"Then don't lose it," said Anastasia.

Just then a deep male voice boomed from the courtyard below. "Where is he?"

"In the house," came Konon's reply.

"Call him down here, then!" ordered the man.

"Wife!" shouted Solon. "Bring the Plataean!"

"Come, Nikias," said Anastasia with a sigh, as if she knew what this was all about. "Let's get this over with."

Nikias followed her down the stairs and into the courtyard. He saw Solon and Konon, and next to them was a giant in farmer's clothes—a man in his late fifties with a long beard and close-cropped hair and the pugnacious bearing of a pankrator.

"Nikias," said Anastasia, gesturing toward the giant, "this is my son, Periander, Konon's father."

"Where are you from, lad?" demanded Periander with a belligerent tone.

"Plataea," replied Nikias proudly.

"So are the stories true?" asked Periander, his eyes ablaze. "Did the Thebans take Plataea?"

Nikias scoffed. "Take Plataea? Thebans? Never! A traitor let them through the gates and they held the city for a time. But our citizens rallied together and drove them out. And our cavalry smashed their relief forces outside the walls. We slaughtered them."

All of the faces in the courtyard showed various degrees of amazement.

"And you were in this fight?" asked Periander.

"I fought in the streets," said Nikias. "Then I escaped from the city and helped raise the countryside."

"But you've still got your long hair," said Konon, indignant.

Nikias didn't want to tell them that he was eighteen and of age . . . that he should have gone through the ceremony of manhood three weeks ago and burned his long hair on the altar of Zeus . . . but he'd been in jail at the time, falsely accused of murdering Kallisto's brother. He said, "Everyone fought that night. Even our women and children and slaves."

"Gods, what a story!" said Periander, his big mouth breaking into a smile. He clapped Nikias a great opened-handed blow to his right shoulder. Nikias cried out in pain and his knees buckled.

"Father, he's injured!" cried Konon. "A fall from a horse."

Periander, Solon, and Konon all came to Nikias's aid at once. They led him to a chair and bade him sit. He cradled his shoulder with one hand, clenching his teeth.

"I'm sorry," said Periander. "Please forgive me."

"How could you have known?" asked Nikias, forcing a smile.

"And what are you doing here? Are you with the Plataean contingent that arrived in the city the other day to see General Perikles?"

"No," said Nikias. He hesitated. He didn't want to divulge that he had come to Athens to look for mercenaries. "I'm here on an errand . . . to my Athenian relatives," he lied.

"What is your name, lad?" asked Periander.

"Son of Aristo—Nikias by name. Nemean tribe."

"Nemean tribe?" asked Periander, his face contorted in astonishment. "Are you related to the Bull of Plataea?"

Nikias realized there was no getting out of this one. He had to tell the truth.

"He's my grandfather," he replied with trepidation.

Periander smiled again, showing four missing lower incisors. He pointed to the gap and said proudly, "See this? Your grandfather took my teeth in the Panathenaic Games! One punch and I was out like a smashed lamp!"

EIGHT

After walking east for half a mile below the ridgeline, Chusor and Ji arrived at the Cave of Nymphs. Chusor looked for signs of other men, but he couldn't see anyone. As they approached the mouth of the grotto, the pigeon that had delivered Chusor the message flew out and alighted on his shoulder, cooing in his ear.

"She's waiting for you," said Ji, and came to a stop. He bowed slightly and made a sweeping gesture for Chusor to enter.

Chusor squinted into the blackness, but he couldn't see anyone. Only a fire burning far back in the cave. He wondered if Ji had betrayed him. If this was an elaborate trap set up by Barka. But Ji could have easily murdered him on the walk here if he had desired to do so.

"Come to the fire," said a woman's commanding voice from the blackness behind the fire. She, too, spoke in Phoenician, but without an accent, for the language was her native tongue.

Chusor obeyed and set his staff on the ground along with his pack.

"Now strip."

He took the pigeon off his shoulder and set it on a rock. Then he pulled off his climbing boots, slipped off his belt and tunic, and stood facing the flames. In the firelight his muscular torso seemed to be carved from bronze-colored marble. The dozens of puckered scars on his body reflected the light like the edges of silver coins.

A naked woman appeared from the shadows on the other side of the fire. Her physique was a perfect female counterpart to Chusor's. She was freakishly tall for her sex, with an ample chest, powerful legs, and broad shoulders. She would dwarf nearly any other man besides Chusor. Her black hair—shining like obsidian—grew all the way down to her waist in two thick plaits.

Chusor noticed she wore no ornaments except for earrings of beaten gold that hung nearly to her shoulders. They were in the shape of miniature triremes dangling from hoops. Chusor had fashioned them with his own hands—hammered them out in the hold of a ship using a spare anchor as an anvil—and he was pleased to see she still owned them.

She was not considered a ravishing beauty by the standards of the day, in any port. But she wasn't manly or unlovely. Her face was just too strong—as if a sculptor had roughed out her features and had not yet made the delicate refinements. There was something about her, however, that aroused Chusor's animal nature like few other women had. She was confident and happy in her own skin. She loved pleasure as well as pleasing him. And those qualities made her very appealing.

Her big sleepy eyes looked him up and down with a languorous gaze. She crossed her arms under her breasts, pushing them together in a beguiling way. Zana—the daughter of a deposed Phoenician king who'd become a pirate queen and captain of a band of cheerful cutthroats.

"What did you do to your exquisite hair?" she asked wistfully.

"I grew tired of it," explained Chusor. "Where is your ship, by the way? Your crew?"

"The ship is lost," she said with a tiny shrug, as if she had misplaced a trinket and not the fastest pirate ship on the seas. She stared at his smooth pate and chewed the inside of her cheek petulantly. "I don't like your bald head."

"I'm happy to leave you in peace," he said. But the way he gazed hungrily at her body said otherwise.

She looked at his loins, grinned, and said, "Spears ho!" imitating the battle cry of Phoenician mariners.

"Is there someplace soft for us to lay ourselves down, Zana?" asked Chusor with a world-weary voice.

Ever so slowly Zana stepped back into the shadows, but her hand remained in the firelight. Beckoning . . . beckoning. . . .

After an hour of reacquainting themselves with each other's bodies, Zana fell asleep sprawled on Chusor's chest, snoring softly. He recalled his first glimpse of her seven years ago. She had been dressed as a man, brandishing an axe over his neck. "Why *shouldn't* I kill you, stowaway? You stinking bilge rat!" she had demanded.

"Zana," Chusor said now, gently stirring her awake. "How did you find me?"

"It was Barka," she said in a drowsy voice. "He was sure you were here. Then I remembered that story you used to tell about the legend of the gold hidden under Plataea, and I knew Barka was right. That you'd come here. We arrived only yesterday. The bird found you."

"Her name is Jezebel," said Chusor. He glanced over and saw the pigeon nestled in his clothes, sleeping contentedly with one eye half opened. He realized the animal must be ten years old by now. He wondered how long a pigeon could possibly live. "Who else is left of your crew?" he asked.

"All gone except for Ji," said Zana. "We were at port in Tyre when a fleet of Persians came into the harbor unexpectedly. The ship was seized. Ji and I weren't on board at the time. We fled to Italia. That was where we eventually ran into Barka. Or rather where *he* found us." She put one elbow into his chest and rested her head on her palm, looking him in the eyes. "When you left me I swore that I would find you and kill you one day."

"Because you loved me?" asked Chusor sarcastically.

"Because you took two of my best men," came Zana's reply.

"And gold as well," added Chusor.

"The gold was your fair share," she replied. "But *not* the men. They were loyal to me—would have killed themselves for me—before they met you."

Chusor sighed. "I didn't ask them to come with me."

"That makes it worse," said Zana.

"I grew tired of marauding and murder," said Chusor.

She traced a finger across his lips and looked at him coldly. "I should murder *you* now."

Chusor felt the hairs on his forearms rise. He knew she wasn't making idle threats. "You already killed me today," he said and closed his eyes. "Put me in a funeral jar. I'm dead."

She smiled, showing her pearly teeth, and moved her hand down to stroke him between his legs. "And that's why I always liked you the best, Chusor. Because you were never afraid of me *or* death. When my men found you hiding on my ship—a miserable stowaway, reeking of filth, fleeing the wrath of the Tyrant of Syrakuse—I asked you why I should spare your life, and you made some stupid joke." She grabbed his balls quickly and squeezed.

Chusor clenched his teeth and said, "*Life* is a stupid joke."

She smiled and relaxed her grip, stroking him sensuously again.

Chusor thought back to his days in Syrakuse where he'd studied with the inventor Naxos and learned the secrets of the sticking fire. The city-state of Syrakuse was a flimsy democracy—one firmly under the reins of an oligarchy. And Chusor had made a mistake of monumental proportions: he had seduced the wife of a wealthy man named General Pantares. The leader was so powerful in Syrakuse that he was known far and wide as "the Tyrant." Chusor had escaped the general's henchmen by jumping into a pipe that carried waste into the bay. Fortunately Zana's ship was nearby.

"Have you found the treasure?" asked Zana, moving on top of him and grinding her hips. "Ummmm," she groaned softly.

"No," he replied.

"Are you telling me . . . uhhhh . . . the truth?"

"I wouldn't still be here if I'd found it, Zana."

"Is it . . . uhhhh . . . there?"

"I think so," he said. As they made love again he told her about the night of the Theban invasion and how they'd found the secret tunnel entrance under the Temple of Zeus. "It fits with the legend. We haven't had time to explore the place. But I've created a map of the entire citadel. I've brought it with me. I'll show you—"

"Stop talking." Zana grunted. She obviously hadn't been listening to him for some time. She was touching herself now as she moved faster and faster. She put one hand on the back of his head and guided his mouth to her left breast. Chusor cupped her dark areola with his generous lips, biting her nipple gently with his incisors. She sucked in through her teeth and he pushed himself deep inside her, again and again.

At last she breathed, "I'm almost there." He lashed her breast with his tongue and she let forth a cry of pleasure as her body jerked uncontrollably. She brought both hands to the sides of his face and leaned down, meeting his lips with her own.

"Stop thrusting," she said between kisses.

He did as he was told. She gave a sultry smile and adjusted her body. Then her muscles clenched and unclenched rapidly on the crown of his manhood as though she were stroking and squeezing it with a hidden hand.

"Gods!" he bellowed, his legs going rigid. It felt as though Zeus's bolt had just shot from his loins . . . as though he had melted inside her.

He fell back, staring at the ceiling of the cave. She laughed softly, toying with him awhile longer, taking her own pleasure while he was still firm. When she was satisfied she pulled away from him and draped herself across his broad chest, stretching like a cat, and purring like one, too, with her hair completely covering her face.

"Where did you learn to do *that*?" he asked hoarsely.

"Perhaps I always had that skill," said Zana coyly. "I was just saving it for a special occasion."

"You should have done that sooner," he replied. "I might never have left you."

"I have you again," she said softly. "At least one of my treasures is found."

"So good to see old friends reunited," cooed a honeyed voice from the darkness.

The sound of that voice, like a chill wind on bare flesh, made Chusor shiver.

"What are you doing, lurking there?" asked Zana, sitting up and glaring. "How long have you been watching us, you little owl?"

Barka crawled into the light and sat at their feet. The eunuch's black, limpid eyes regarded Chusor with a placidity that unsettled him to the core.

"Hello, Barka," Chusor said to the creature he'd hoped he would never lay eyes on again. Barka the Sooth—a walking oracle who could look into a man's eyes and tell him his past as well as predict his death.

"Chusor," said Barka, "I had a funny dream about you. I think you'll laugh. You were in a ship laden with treasure . . . but the hold was slowly filling with water. And you were far from shore."

"I don't find that dream amusing," said Chusor, moving away from Zana and covering himself with his tunic.

Barka pulled a map from his sleeve and dangled it by two fingers. "This is quite interesting."

Chusor's skin crawled. Barka had managed to find the map in the secret compartment in his staff. He forced himself to smile back at the feminine, feline face—the pretty face of a Phoenician girl on a boy's body. "I'll look forward to hearing about your dream," he said at length, trying not to betray his unease. "And maybe you can use your skills to see if the treasure exists."

"Oh, it is there," said Barka, nodding his head confidently. "I've already seen it. Enough gold to buy a fleet of ships."

Zana sat up straight and her eyes shone in the firelight. Chusor could tell she was already standing on the deck of a new ship, sailing into the unknown.

"Now!" said Barka, setting aside the map and clapping his hands together. "Since Chusor-the-Cunning has already revealed that my darling Diokles is still with him, may we know what happened to our other friend who ran away with you?" The eunuch snickered. "I don't need the sooth-sight to see what Ezekiel is *doing* right now: drinking himself into a stupor. But I dreamt that he'd set up the sign of his skull in . . ." He closed his eyes, shifted his head back and forth, then popped open his lids. "Athens? Am I right? Ezekiel the Babylonian is living in Athens now?"

Chusor did not need to answer, for Barka was smiling confidently. The eunuch *knew* that his guess was right.

"Ezekiel will meet your young friend," said Barka in an offhand manner. "Whether good or ill will come of the meeting, I cannot say."

NINE

———◆———

Konon drove Nikias to Athens in a mule cart. The young farmer had jumped at the chance to help the Plataean, telling Nikias that he was happy to get away from the farm for a few hours.

Konon was nearly eight years older than Nikias but had yet to serve in a military expedition, and he never would. He'd lost his left arm in a childhood accident—it had gotten caught in the mechanism of an olive press. Without the ability to hold shield and sword at the same time, or to pull an oar, he was useless as either a hoplite or sailor. He devoured Nikias's stories of battle with a combination of wonder and unconcealed jealousy.

Nikias felt sorry for Konon. He would rather be dead than share a similar fate. Even this injury to his shoulder—an injury he knew would eventually heal—gave Nikias a feeling of impotence. He couldn't even put a tunic on without an old woman's help! He couldn't imagine what it would be like to lose his shield arm.

He told Konon about the Battle of the Gates and his fight with Eurymakus, the Theban assassin who'd led the sneak attack on the city and who'd burned down Nikias's farmhouse. Eurymakus had tried to kill Nikias with a poisoned blade, but the Plataean had used the invader's own weapon against him, slicing his hand with the knife. Eurymakus had instantly drawn his sword and chopped off his own arm at the elbow to keep the poison from coursing upward through his veins.

Nikias would never forget the sight of that evil man fleeing the battlefield, blood spurting from his severed limb. He had tried to chase down the Theban, but he'd been thrown from a horse and been knocked out.

"Well, it makes me feel a little better," said Konon, "to think a Theban now shares my fate."

"Do you know how to use a leather sling?" asked Nikias.

"Of course," replied Konon, indignant. "I can kill a hare at a hundred paces." He paused and smiled. "Well, maybe fifty paces. But I've got a good eye."

"Then you could be a peltast," said Nikias. "Kill Spartans from the walls of Athens." He gestured at the mighty western walls of Athens looming a mile down the road.

"I tried to enlist with the Guards," said Konon and sighed morosely. "But they wouldn't take me. And you can't be a knight unless you're stinking rich and can afford your own mounts."

"Come to Plataea," said Nikias, half joking. "We'd welcome a man with one arm. Just so long as he was willing to kill Spartans."

Konon laughed at this prospect. "My father's heart would freeze up if I did that. And my poor mother would throw herself down a well. I am their youngest son and still a child in their eyes."

They were a half mile from the walls of Athens when they passed a long ar-caded building that Nikias recognized as the Akademy. He saw fifty or so bearded athletes training in the gymnasium—they were running footraces, throwing the javelin, and practicing the long jump with weights. In an arena next door some prepubescent boys fought in the pankration with padded gloves on their hands. Nikias's grandfather had never let him train with gloves and would scoff at the "Athenian" style of training their young.

The cart continued on a well-rutted road lined with tombs on either side. In the distance, through the gaps in the plane trees that lined the road on either side, Nikias could see glimpses of the redbrick walls of Athens meandering across the uneven ground.

"Do you think you'll enter the pankration in the next Olympics?" Konon asked Nikias.

"I will," said Nikias, staring to his left at the hundreds of tombs and monu-ments that lined the other road. "I mean . . . my grandfather and I were plan-ning on it."

Nikias wondered now if he *would* be able to journey to the Sacred Games this year. He hadn't even thought about the fact that the impending Spartan siege might completely disrupt movement to and from Olympia. The Olympic committee had demanded truces in the past. Maybe they would this time? Hope-fully, the Spartans would decide that besieging mighty Plataea was a foolhardy option and just decamp from the Oxlands. At least that's what Chusor thought would happen.

He thought of his best friend Demetrios, whose father had sent him away to Syrakuse two years ago to live with a famous general. Demetrios and Nikias had trained together in the gymnasium since childhood, pushing each other to the edge of endurance, the dream of Olympic glory burning in both of their hearts. Nikias missed Demetrios and wondered if his friend would ever return to the Oxlands. He hoped that, for Demetrios's sake, he would not. For he would learn how his father, Nauklydes, had been tried and convicted as a traitor and given the dreaded "tunic of stones" as punishment. And Demetrios's heart would be broken when he found out that his beloved sister, Penelope, had been raped, tortured, and murdered by the Thebans, all because of his own father's treachery.

"Please stop here for a moment," Nikias asked, touching Konon's armless shoulder and pointing to a little glade where carts could pull off the grooved road.

Konon looked questioningly at Nikias, but pulled on the reins and clicked his tongue. The disconcerted mule, not used to stopping here, looked around with a daft expression and let out a bray.

Konon said, "Come on, you silly beast," and gave the mule a gentle tap on the rump. As soon as the cart came to a stop Nikias got out and started walking across a patch of grass to the Cemetery Road. Konon followed without speaking.

Nikias had only been here once—when he was ten years old—but he remembered the way. He walked past the marble and limestone miniature replicas of temples and homes that displayed the funeral jars with pictures of loved ones. There were dozens of unveiled and painted women loitering about in this area. They eyed Nikias as he walked past. This was the most popular place in Athens, Nikias knew, for men seeking a quick copulation. These prostitutes were also the cheapest. "Paying my respects to the dead" had a double meaning in Athens.

"Only two drachma for you, love," an older woman said with a ghastly smile. "I've a nice place for us to lie down in the shade."

"No, thank you, mother," replied Nikias politely.

"I'm nobody's mother, you Oxland bumpkin!" sneered the prostitute. "And I'm not old enough to be yours either."

Nikias crossed the Cemetery Road to the other side and saw a marble signpost that read, I AM THE BOUNDARY OF THE TOMBS OF HEROES. This was where the war monuments stood—bronze statues of men fallen in battle for Athens with the names of the dead carved in the plinths.

Nikias knelt in front of a base of black marble—Plataean marble—upon which stood a statue of a warrior holding a notched shield of the Oxlands. Nikias found the name carved on the base and ran his finger over the letters. ARISTO, SON OF MENESARKUS, NEMEAN TRIBE. Lichen had grown in some of the letters, obscuring them.

"Your father?" asked Konon with a tone of reverence.

Nikias nodded. "Killed by Thebans at a battle near Koronea."

Thebes had been the only Greek city that offered earth to the Persian king Xerxes when he invaded fifty years before. After the Persians had been defeated at Plataea, Thebes was punished severely by the Greek allies and put under the control of the Athenians. Fourteen years ago, the Thebans had revolted and thrown out the Athenians, defeating them and their Plataean allies at the

Battle of Koronea. And that is where Nikias's father had breathed out his life into the dust, speared in the guts after the Plataean shield wall had broken and the hoplites had run for their lives.

Nikias picked the lichen out his father's name with his fingernail. When he finished cleaning all the letters, he started working on the other Plataean names that had become obscured. Konon squatted down beside him and started rubbing the marble with his wet tunic. The dirt and lichen came off quickly, soiling Konon's shirt black and green.

"There's a fountain just over there," said Konon. "Bring me some more water in your cupped hands and we'll have this clean."

Nikias could not hold back his tears as he walked to the fountain. He knew there was no shame in crying for the dead. But he felt so raw, and Konon's small act of kindness had put him over the edge. He dipped a hand into the fountain and wiped the tears from his face. Then he made a cup with his hands, filled it, and walked back to the monument, splashing the water onto the memorial stone. He got down beside Konon and rubbed the names with his tunic until his clothes were stained.

"Looks like the day it was carved," said Konon, smiling broadly.

"Thank you," said Nikias.

"I'm embarrassed for my fellow citizens," said Konon with disgust. "Letting moss grow on the names of heroes who died for Athens."

They went back to the cart and found the mule was asleep and hadn't budged an inch. Konon had to scratch the animal's ears to wake it up. Soon they were back on the cart path and within minutes they'd arrived at the mighty Dipylon Gate—one of the fifteen entrances to the walled city, and the biggest.

It was an awe-inspiring sight, Nikias thought. A vision to make any invaders turn on their heels and go away. Two square towers stood on either side of two open portals. Patrolling the flat tops of these massive towers and the walls directly beside them were Skythian bowmen and Athenian spearmen who kept a watchful eye on the road below. The foundations of the walls were made of huge rectangular blocks of limestone with bricks on top. The battlements were over four times the height of a tall man.

The wall followed a curve to the north and Nikias could see more towers in that direction. To the south the wall went as far as the eye could see, curving and then connecting with the Long Walls—a protected corridor that linked Athens with the walled port city of Piraeus. All along the top of the wall he could see warriors.

Konon left the mule and cart in a roped-off area outside the wall. An attendant pinned a metal disk to the mule's ear—a disk inscribed with numbers. Then he handed an identical disk to Konon.

"You have to give up your sword," Konon said, pointing to a brick building with barred windows. "None are allowed inside the gates."

Reluctantly Nikias handed over his sword at the weapons depository and received a numbered disk just like Konon's. He put it into his belt pouch.

They walked over to the nearest gate and got into line behind three woodsmen with blackened hands and forearms who toted enormous bags of charcoal on their shoulders. Nikias became nervous, wondering if the gatekeepers would turn him away. They were sure to ask him why he'd come to the city. Would they know that he had run away from home? Would they send him back to Plataea? But when he and Konon finally got to the entrance, one of the guards merely said, "Stay out of trouble, lads," and waved them both through with a casual gesture, and Nikias smiled, feeling foolish for having been so worried.

They passed under the narrow arch and entered the citadel, making their way down the road of the inner graveyard—a pathway lined with more tombs and markers for the dead. To the right, standing atop a little hill, Nikias saw the handsome shape of the Temple of Hephaestos. The columns, pediments, and friezes had been completed but the roof had yet to be added on to the temple, and it made Nikias think of a bald man without a hat, standing in the hot sun.

Up ahead and to the left he caught sight of the Painted Stoa—an open colonnade that was filled with paintings of famous battles and gods. Thirty years ago his grandfather had proudly posed for an artist who had depicted him as Herakles slaying the Nemean Lion. When they got to the gallery Nikias stopped and peeked in at the painting and saw the lifelike image of his grandfather scowling back. He shuddered slightly and peered across the busy agora to the courts of law and the jail and other public places. Wooden cranes and scaffolding showed where new buildings and temples were under construction all around the perimeter of the agora. Directly in front of them lay the paved street that led up to the Akropolis. The high limestone plateau, capped by its sturdy walls, seemed to rise from the ground like a majestic ship that had been crafted by Gaia, the goddess of the earth.

Nearly fifty years ago, after the defeat of the Persians at the Battle of Plataea, all of the Greek allies had sworn to let lie in ruins any temples—like the old Temple of Athena that once stood atop the Akropolis—that had been destroyed by the invaders. These ruins were to be eternal reminders of the war and its cost. But after the Athenians had started to grow rich from taxes, they had begun this rapid program of rebuilding, ignoring their vow.

Nikias's grandfather had always told him, "A man should love and protect Plataea as though the city is his child. The Athenian men, however, love their city as if it's their sweetheart." Nikias, who hadn't been to Athens in four years, finally understood what his grandfather was talking about. Almost every single building in the city, including the walls themselves, had been built up in the last fifty years—after Athens had been razed by the Persian invaders. The agora, like the rest of the city, was a festival of alluring colors, sounds, and smells that made Nikias's heart swell.

They started walking again, moving into the marketplace. Thousands of men were shopping at the open-air stalls and eating in wineshops and food booths. There were magicians and flute players, acrobats and seers. It seemed as if everything in the world was for sale in the place, from fancy scabbards to spindles to lobsters. The noise of voices and music was so loud it made Nikias's already sore head ache even more. The woodsmoke made him a little queasy.

He turned his gaze again toward the Akropolis—and the almost impossibly beautiful building that stood on top: the Temple of Athena. The brightly painted temple was one of the most remarkable things he'd ever seen in his life. The beauty of it all made him proud to be Greek. Old vows about leaving temples in ruins be damned! He hoped that the Athenians would keep on building their shining city until the world's ending.

"Come on, Oxlander," said Konon with a smile. "You're going to wear out your eyes."

Nikias followed Konon as he weaved in and out of the crowds of men and stalls and barbershops filled with customers getting their curly hair and beards trimmed short. Nikias was struck by the lack of women in the market—so unlike Plataea, where women worked and shopped alongside the men. The few women that he saw were heavily veiled and covered with long shawls.

"Hey!" Nikias shouted as a hand snatched his felt traveling hat from off his head. He whirled and saw an urchin dashing through the crowds. Nikias started to take off after the boy, but Konon grabbed his arm.

"You'll never find him," said Konon. "Leave him."

"But that was my lucky hat," growled Nikias, brushing the hair from his eyes.

"You stood out too much with it on," said Konon.

Nikias frowned and followed Konon, cursing under his breath. They went past a theatre with wooden bleachers and Nikias paused to look at a sign advertising the show for later that day.

"*Alkestis* by Euripides," Nikias read aloud. He scanned the bottom of the poster and asked, "What's a 'tragicomedy'?"

"It's a new kind of play that starts out full of woe and ends with a laugh," said a young man standing by the sign. He was a few years younger than Nikias and had a sharp hawk face and intelligent eyes.

A Euripides play had been performed in Plataea a couple of years ago. Nikias hadn't been too impressed. But Kallisto—who'd seen it at a special performance for women only—had loved it. At the finale a magical creature came and rescued two lovers trapped in a high castle. If only life were so easy, he mused.

"Euripides needs to write something more realistic," said Nikias. "He needs to write about war."

"Euripides is more interested in the war in our heads," replied the young man smugly, going on his way.

Nikias chewed on this curious notion silently, following Konon as he headed into a dark alleyway.

"This is the place where the doctor that you're looking for lives," said Konon. "The Street of Thieves."

Konon stuck a few silver obols into his mouth, making a "slave's purse" as it was called in Athens. This was the seedier part of the agora, where stolen goods could be bought and sold, and it was full of criminals. Here there were "brothels of last resort" as his friend Stasius used to call them, and food stalls that sold less-than-fresh fish. Stasius's father had owned a fancy brothel in Plataea. But both father and son were dead, killed in the invasion. Nikias wished his irreverent friend were with him now to make him laugh.

"Anybody know where Dr. Ezekiel Pittakos's place is at?" asked Konon in a carrying voice.

"By the stall that sells speckled eggs," called out a young drachmae-boy with rouged cheeks and dyed hair. He pointed at a dark and dingy alley across the way. "Go toward the Akarnian Gate and look for the sign with the skull. Though I can play doctor for you if you like."

Konon politely declined and said in an aside to Nikias, "What quality of physician is this man?" They walked into the alley cautiously.

"I don't know," said Nikias, echoing the farmer's growing suspicions as to the doctor's standing in Athenian society. "My friend Chusor told me he's an expert."

Konon stepped over a pile of garbage and said, "An expert on filth? And what kind of name is Ezekiel?" he added with a touch of disapproval. "Ah, look! There's his sign."

"My friend Chusor said he's Babylonian," said Nikias, and knocked on the door. When nobody answered he tried to open the portal, but it was locked. He peered through a small window into a messy room littered with scrolls, bowls, and medical equipment. No lamp was burning.

"You'll have to come back," said Konon.

Nikias rubbed his aching shoulder and sighed. "Let's go," he said.

They returned to the marketplace and Nikias was glad to be back in the sunlight after the musty alleyways of the Street of Thieves.

"Let's get something to eat," said Konon. "I've still got the silver my mother gave me"—he took the coins from his mouth and held them up—"and we could . . . hey, where are you going?"

Nikias marched away in the opposite direction. He'd seen something bobbing above the crowd: a felt hat in the style of the Oxlands. He pushed his way through a group of laughing teenagers and strode up to a well-muscled young man who wore the hat and spoke in a stupid version of an Oxland accent. Nikias snatched the hat from his head and the Athenian spun around, shouting, "Hey, that's my hat!"

"No, it's not," said Nikias, barely containing his fury. "It's my hat. My mother made it for me and you stole it."

The big Athenian put his hands on his hips and laughed in Nikias's face. "Only a sheep-stuffer like you would admit to owning that piece-of-crap hat," he said in a throaty, highborn Athenian accent.

The young man's friends crowded around Nikias, eyeing him menacingly. There were five of them. All big and muscular. Pankrators by the looks of them.

"Then you admit you stole it?" asked Nikias.

The Athenian teenager said, "I found it on the ground. You can take it back and stuff it up your mother's dirty twat. How dare you call me a thief, you Oxland cunt."

Nikias's eyes narrowed and everything in the world went out of focus except for the Athenian's face. He was deciding which to break first. The long nose with the big, flaring nostrils? His yellowish, widely spaced teeth? His pointy jaw with the deep cleft?

The Athenian tough—who was several inches taller and at least fifty pounds heavier than Nikias—poked a finger into his chest and said softly and without fear, "Why don't you just turn around and go before you get hurt."

Nikias felt Konon's hand touch his shoulder but he didn't take his eyes off the Athenian.

"Come on, Nikias," Konon hissed in his ear. "You're about to go diving into a ditch."

"Leave me alone, Konon," said Nikias.

"Hey Konon-half-arms," said the Athenian with a sneer. "Get your boyfriend out of my face before I send him back home on a cart."

Nikias looked at the crowd that had formed around them. Scores of shoppers and stall-workers were eyeing them intently. He even saw the unveiled and brightly painted faces of a trio of gorgeous hetaeras—the famous courtesans of Athens—wearing elaborate headdresses and regal gowns. They were staring at the scene with curiosity and smiling.

"I can't walk away," said Nikias to Konon. He smiled wryly and raised his voice so all could hear. "I'm an Oxlander. We never walk away from a fight."

Nikias's words made the young Athenian throw back his head and laugh. "There's a theatre just over there," he said and pointed to the nearby structure. "We can fight on the floor of the orchestra."

"I accept," said Nikias.

"The Oxlander has eggs!" shouted one of the vendors. "He just agreed to fight young Apollo!"

"A fight!" yelled another. "A fight!"

Apollo turned and strutted toward the theatre, followed by his friends. He mocked Nikias's accent in a loud voice as he went, causing the crowd to snicker. Nikias followed, moving along with a crowd of fifty or so people who were already heading into the theatre to enjoy the spectacle. Konon wrapped his arm around Nikias's shoulder and put his mouth to his ear.

"Apollo is the best young pankrator in Athens," said Konon, speaking fast. "One of the city's hopefuls for the Olympics. And I think I'd better remind you in case you've forgotten—which I'm pretty sure you have—that your right arm doesn't work." He gave Nikias a look that said, "Wish you'd listened to me now, don't you?"

Nikias felt a pang in his guts. He'd completely forgotten about his arm. He tried to lift it and could barely raise it more than an inch—it was worse than an hour ago. He didn't slow his pace, though. As he strode into the theatre he squeezed the felt hat onto his head. Squeezed it hard. Then he started to laugh.

"Why are you laughing?" asked Konon. "Are you crazy?"

Nikias said, "I just realized this isn't my hat."

TEN

———— ✦ ————

In the last two changes of the moon Kolax had been kidnapped from his tribe and sold as a slave, escaped from bondage, fought warriors in the dark streets of Plataea, defeated an assassin with nothing more than his teeth, and ridden straight into a phalanx of two thousand hoplites on a suicidal charge—a battle in which he'd killed eight grown men in hand-to-hand combat. But nothing scared him more than what he faced right now, for he was on one side of a deep, wide, and swiftly flowing river while Nikias's runaway Dog Raider horse stood on the opposite bank, calmly grazing in a field of lush grass, drying its wet black coat in the sun.

For Kolax was terrified of water.

The barbarian boy cursed the name of every god he knew, pulled out his hair, and stomped his feet with indignation. But he could not summon enough courage to cross the river to retrieve Nikias's horse.

"Why am I so frightened, Fire Feet?" he asked his own mount, a Theban mare he'd captured two weeks ago after the Battle at the Gates. "I will tell you. Because on the day of my birth the village seer prophesied that I would die in a river. There is no way I am going to put a toe into *this* one."

Fire Feet stared across the river at the black horse and pawed the rocky ground. Then it let forth a long neigh. The black horse tossed its head and answered back with a piercing whinny.

"Get over here, you stupid spawn of a pus-ridden donkey!" Kolax screamed in Skythian. "I'll make you into a tent-rug if you don't come back!"

He threw himself on the ground and screamed into the earth. He thought that maybe if his voice was loud enough his mama would hear him in the Underworld and help him in some way. Maybe she could fly up and scare the Dog Raider horse into coming back to this side of the river?

Kolax heard a splash and when he looked up he saw that Fire Feet had plunged into the river.

"Fire Feet!" yelled Kolax in astonishment. He jumped up and ran to the water's edge. "Fire Feet, come back! What madness is this?"

The black horse looked up lazily, chewing on a mouthful of grass. Then it pranced away in the opposite direction. Kolax picked up a rock and threw it into the river.

Skamander, the god of rivers, must have done this! He'd made both the horses go insane!

Kolax looked to the right. Fire Feet was far downriver now, struggling against the strong current. She had tried to cross at the deepest part where the current was swiftest. Her nostrils and eyes were the only things above the water. A moment later her head disappeared and it was gone, swallowed by the torrent.

Kolax stopped crying. He swallowed the lump in his throat and wiped the tears from his cheeks. Fire Feet was dead! And it had happened so fast. He craned his neck to catch sight of the black steed, but she was long gone, heading north—back to the lands of the Dog Raiders.

Watching Fire Feet die made Kolax feel like less of a coward. If a strong horse couldn't make it across this river, then surely he, Kolax, son of Osyrus of the Bindi tribe, would have perished, thus fulfilling the prophecy. Perhaps this was the awful day the Skythian seer had foreseen in his vision? Maybe he, Kolax, had cheated Death.

"Skamander-River-God!" proclaimed Kolax. "I give you Fire Feet as a sacrifice!"

Now what to do? He needed to get back to Nikias but he'd ridden for over an hour chasing that crazy Dog Raider horse.

He laid out all of his weapons and supplies on the grass. He had his short wooden bow captured from the black-clad people called Thebans. It was nothing like the recurved-horn-and-sinew bows made in Skythia . . . but it was well made and strung with quality gut. He reckoned that he'd killed at least twenty men with it. He kissed it and thanked it for its good work. He also had a lidded quiver with thirty-three arrows. This was a very lucky number and made him happy. There was a knife he'd found on the field of battle with a leather handle and sharp edge. He wore it strapped to his ankle just above his short buckskin boots. It was a weapon good for skinning animals . . . or Theban prisoners, of course.

And there was a short sword given to him by the dark-skinned smith Chusor. This was of the finest quality and his prized possession, forged by the smith's own hands. He could see his reflection in the iron blade, and used it now to admire his tattoos. Kolax could not wait to show this man-killer to his father once he got to Athens. All in all his weapons were good and this fact raised his spirits a little more.

He took off his pack and looked inside. It contained some dried fruits and meats as well as a skin filled with water and another with decent Plataean wine.

He touched the leather pouch that he wore around his neck. It held the Persian gold—the coins that he had collected from the road. He was not going to lose those precious coins. They were going to be a gift to his beloved papa.

He decided to drink half of the wine to lighten his load. In a few minutes he felt a warm glow in his belly. He took a hunk of dried meat and gnawed on it as he headed back in the direction he'd come, following the hoofprints that his and Nikias's horses had made. He figured it would take him about three hours to get back to the road marker where Nikias—the silly sheep-milker!—had tripped and let go of his horse's reins.

Kolax could not wait to see his papa and show him the gold coins. His father would no doubt be surprised to see his boy in Athens. And all grown-up, too, with a fine topknot and several comely tattoos.

Kolax wished his mother could see him now as well. But she had been sleeping under the grass for six summers. She'd died giving birth to Kolax's sister, but the girl hadn't even lived through her first winter without her mama. Before his mother had been buried in her tomb, Kolax's father had placed his torque on her lovely neck. The torque was made of solid gold and depicted a horse attacked by two gryphons—beasts with the head and wings of an eagle and the body of a rampant lion. Kolax often pictured his mama awaking in the afterlife, surprised and pleased to find the fair thing around her white throat. When the first grass had sprouted on her mound Kolax's father had departed for the Land of the Hellenes to serve as an Athenian archer, for he was one of the best bowmen in Skythia, and had beaten all others in the annual contest sponsored by the great warrior General Perikles of Athens.

Before his father had left Skythia he had tattooed Kolax's back with the family symbol—a snarling gryphon—so that he would always know his son, even if many years went by before they saw each other again, or if they died apart and had to find each other in the Underworld. Kolax could remember the agony of those thousands of needle pricks hammered into his skin.

Kolax knew his father would be outraged when he told him the story of what had happened to him. How old King Astyanax—leader of the Bindi tribe—had died. And how his bad son had killed his good son with poison and took his seat on the Horse Throne in the High Tent. Kolax's father, Osyrus, had been an enemy of the bad son—Krouspako, the Snow Dog—and so Kolax had been kidnapped by Krouspako's men and sold into slavery.

And that was how he had ended up in Plataea.

As soon as he found his father he was certain his papa would ride straight back to Skythia, enter the High Tent, cut off the head of the Snow Dog, and craft a drinking goblet from his skullcap. And then he would fill it with sweet uncut wine and he and Kolax would drink the wine until they were properly drunk. Then they would burn hemp seeds and inhale the smoke and sing songs like "Death to Cowards."

He stumbled a little and realized the wine he had drunk was very strong. He noticed the sun was at its highest point in the sky for this time of year and the sky was blue. He thought, "The sun warms you from the outside, but the wine warms you from the inside." And this notion made him laugh out loud. He didn't like being forced to walk, but things could be worse. There were interesting things to look at, like the olive trees and little ruined god-places made from crumbling stone.

The question that nagged at him was how he would tell Nikias he'd failed to bring back his horse. Back in Skythia horses were sometimes struck by lightning. One of his father's horses had died that way. He glanced at the sunny sky and frowned.

No lightning today.

He reckoned the best thing to say was the truth—that Nikias's horse had gone in search of a better rider. Sometimes the truth was like a dagger in the guts, but Nikias was a warrior and could take it. Coming to this conclusion made Kolax feel much better. He was almost looking forward to teaching Nikias-the-farmer this valuable lesson. Plataeans were good at growing things, but they were shit when it came to riding horses.

Kolax reckoned that being a farmer was one of the most horrible fates. He did not understand how these Hellenes could spend so much time digging their dry soil. And their grass was pitiful. He wondered why they didn't beg Zeus to give them more rain. Silly sheep-milkers, all of them!

His path took him across a barren field, then down a culvert and up the side of a steep hill. As he approached the top he heard the sound of a girl weeping. It scared him at first because it sounded just like his mama when she cried in his dreams. He crept through a little grove of oak trees and saw a girl—a pretty girl a few years older than himself—sitting high up in the bough of a tree. Her face was streaked with tears and she kept clenching and unclenching her fingers.

Kolax was fascinated by the vision of the tree girl. These Hellene girls looked so different from Skythian girls with their brown hair and dark eyes. He stayed there for a long time, crouched low, as still as a hare. Finally, she nodded her head vigorously and stood up on the branch. She bent down and picked up a length of rope and tossed it up and over another branch above her head. At the end of the rope was a slipknot. Kolax noticed the other end of the rope tied around the trunk of the tree.

The girl stepped out onto the limb so she was under the dangling rope, then put her head through the noose and pulled the slipknot so it was snug around her throat.

Kolax's face tingled. His heart tripled its pace. His hands moved instinctively for his bow and arrow. As she took a step and walked into air, Kolax was already sighting along the length of the shaft. And as she fell he unloosed the arrow.

The girl dropped the ten feet to the ground and landed hard. The severed rope fell down on top of her like a dead snake.

Kolax ran to her. The girl's face was white with pain. Blood seeped from her mouth where her face had struck a rock. A tooth was chipped. Kolax could not take his eyes off her lips. They were perfectly shaped . . . like a Skythian bow.

ELEVEN

Nikias stood alone at the center of the stage waiting for the large crowd to file in and take their seats on the wooden benches. Word had quickly spread that Apollo the pankrator was going to teach a young Oxlander a harsh lesson in Athenian civility. Several hundred people were already in their seats and many more were pouring through the entrance. Apollo stood off to the side laughing with his friends as if he didn't have a care in the world.

Nikias had no desire to be either humiliated or pounded senseless by Apollo. But his body just wasn't up for the fight. He knew he couldn't beat the Athenian with his muscles. So he'd have to use his mind. His grandfather had told him over and over again that a fight could be won before the first punch had even been thrown. The trick was to get inside the head of the adversary. And then blindside him.

Once, after making a stupid boast, Nikias's grandfather had forced him to fight a much bigger man—a brutal warrior named Axe—with one arm tied behind his back. His grandfather had intended on teaching a Nikias a lesson at the hands of the other man's fists. But Nikias had humiliated Axe in public, beating him down before the man had even thrown a punch. He had used Axe's own hubris to trick him into making the wrong attack, and then Nikias had knocked him senseless.

He took off his pack and tossed it to the side along with the felt cap. Then he walked to the center of the stage and addressed the crowd. "Good citizens of Athens," he said in a steady voice. The people quieted down a little and looked at him with interest. "Apparently my opponent is well known to you, but I am a stranger to the city, having just arrived from the Oxlands, where we are at war with Thebes."

Now a hush fell over the audience and even Apollo stopped jawing with his friends and watched Nikias with a predatory curiosity.

"I am the son of Aristo of Plataea, Nemean tribe, Nikias by name."

There was a slight pause, and then the crowd erupted into whispers. Nikias glanced at Apollo. One of the Athenian's companions said something in his ear that made his face grow dark. Finally, a man in the bleachers said in a stentorian voice, "Gods! He's the Bull of Plataea's heir!"

"Menesarkus's heir?" shouted another.

"My money's on him, who'll wager?"

"Fifty silver owls on the Oxlander!"

The noise in the theatre was suddenly deafening as men made frantic bets. This would be a real fight!

So far so good, thought Nikias. He'd planted a seed of doubt in the haughty Apollo's brain. Now he had to twist the knife a little more.

"Now I must apologize to my opponent," said Nikias over the din, "for I do believe I falsely accused him of stealing my favorite traveling hat, which started all of this nonsense. And I am sorry for it."

Apollo turned to his friends and threw up his hands saying, "I knew he had a hare's heart. He won't fight me."

Nikias caught Konon's gaze and saw that the young farmer looked relieved. He gestured for Nikias to hurry up and leave the stage. There were many disappointed groans in the crowd. The men in the audience had wanted to see a bloody pankration bout.

"But," continued Nikias, "I cannot forgive him for the disparaging remarks he made against the Oxlands. And especially the evil words he said against my late mother. And if he makes an apology to me immediately, I will call us even."

Apollo walked onto the circular floor of the stage and stood close to Nikias, eyeing him up and down. Then he turned to the audience and crossed his arms on his chest. "I'd rather stuff a sheep, you Oxland piece of crap."

Nikias smiled. "Excellent. That is what I hoped to hear. Because now you and I may settle an old score from when we were boys and you bit me like a dirty little rat."

Apollo's lip curled back in rage but he was speechless.

"You see," continued Nikias to the spectators, "Apollo and I have met before, and I'm certain he now remembers our bout. When we were children my grandfather and I visited your illustrious Akademy. I fought several of the very best pankrators of my age. I beat them all. My final opponent was Apollo here, and I was pounding him to a pulp when—during a moment of grappling—he clamped his teeth upon my neck in desperation. I still have the scar to this day and you can see it clearly here."

He turned his face to expose his neck, pulling back his long hair to reveal a livid scar in the shape of an open mouth. The crowd voiced their disapproval at this story of a young cheating Apollo. The Athenian pankrator looked mortified.

"His silence," said Nikias, "proves that Apollo remembers that day and still feels shame for stooping to Spartan tactics to beat me." He paused. Out of the corner of his eye he'd caught sight of the three exotic-looking hetaeras he'd seen in the street outside. They were the only women in the packed audience and the men around them neither bothered them nor paid them any undo attention. Chusor had told Nikias that hetaeras were like a race unto themselves in Athens— creatures from another world and treated as such. Only the richest men in the city could afford to hire these courtesans to entertain and comfort them. They were like sacred beings.

Nikias locked eyes with the tallest of the three hetaeras. She was the most beautiful amongst the trio, with high cheekbones and dark intelligent eyes. She looked like a statue of a goddess come to life. Cocking her head slightly, she smiled and winked at him. That little gesture made his heart flutter and Nikias grinned from ear to ear. Standing at her side was a little dark-skinned slave girl who stared back at Nikias with an unflinching and sullen gaze.

"Let's fight," said Apollo with murder in his voice.

"Not yet," said Nikias, tearing his eyes away from the hetaera. "I propose a new rule for our fight."

"A new rule?" asked Apollo. "What do you mean?"

"Just what I said," replied Nikias, looking directly at Apollo. Here was the crucial moment. This was the moment where he knew he would either win the fight or lose it. He had to push Apollo so far over the edge that he would become unhinged and fight foolishly. Push him so that he would lash out and attack without thinking straight.

"Since you were unable to beat me as a child," said Nikias, "even after biting my neck and drawing blood, and since I have been training nonstop since that day with the greatest living fighter in the world, thus putting the advantage considerably in my favor, I propose to even the odds."

"And how do you suppose to do that?" asked Apollo, outraged.

"I propose to fight you one-armed," said Nikias. "In honor of my friend Konon."

The theatre was utterly silent except for a woman's melodious and mirthful laugh. Nikias glanced at the hetaera who had winked at him and saw she had put a hand to her mouth to contain her laughter, but the sound of her sweet voice still rang out clearly.

Apollo took a step back from Nikias and stared at him in amazement. "You will fight me with one arm?" he asked, his mouth slowly shaping a smile.

"Yes." Nikias glanced at Konon, who had slid down in his seat and was covering his face with his hand and shaking his head. The young farmer stared at Nikias with an expression of pity.

Nikias made a great show of lifting his left arm—his unwounded arm—and putting it behind his back, leaving his useless right arm dangling at his side.

"You promise only to use one arm?" asked Apollo.

"My word of honor as an Oxlander," replied Nikias. "I will only use *one* arm."

"I accept your offer," said Apollo.

Those who had bet on Nikias sighed morosely, or cursed Tyke, the goddess of luck, or did both and started counting out their coins. This idiotic Oxlander had gone beyond arrogance. He was apparently mad.

The fighters faced each other and the crowd burst into the eerie war chant that all Greeks sang before battle or a pankration match: "Eleu eleu eleu eleu." The sound vibrated in the theatre, filled Nikias's body, and made his skin crawl. He felt as though the chant were singing itself into his bones.

"I'm going to crush you!" bellowed Apollo. "You conceited bastard!"

Nikias looked him in the eyes and let all the hate and rage he'd felt over the past two weeks course through his veins like a molten fire in the blood. It was the final trick his grandfather had taught him—a way to channel pain into his fists. He could almost feel his hand swelling with power.

Apollo lunged toward Nikias, reaching out with both hands to grab Nikias's exposed right arm, intending to yank it from the socket. Nikias let him take it like an animal seizing bait in a trap. Then he swung his left arm—the arm he'd been holding behind his back—in a furious haymaker.

Sheep-stuffer!

Nikias's huge craggy fist caught Apollo on the jaw, snapping his neck to one side with the force of a horse's kick. Apollo didn't even see it coming. Wasn't expecting it. Nikias knew that his opponent would assume that he would be keeping his left arm behind his back for the entire fight.

The Athenian was unconscious before he hit the floor.

The crowd had never seen anything like it. The men got to their feet and yelled with delight, shock, and fury.

"Apollo bested!"

"With one punch!"

The noise was deafening. Before Nikias knew what was happening he was in the street, dragged out one of the side exits by Konon. They ran together all the way across the agora, and finally stopped in an alley near the Street of Thieves.

"I had to get you out of there," said Konon. "Apollo's friends were going to kill you."

Nikias wiped the sweat from his brow and laughed softly. "Probably."

"Zeus's eggs! I can't believe you pulled that off!" said Konon, smiling with admiration.

"Neither can I," said Nikias. "I hope you didn't swallow that coin you put in your mouth because I need a drink." They started walking quickly toward the Street of Thieves, but then Nikias stopped dead in his tracks, his heart skipping a beat. He turned and sprinted back toward the theatre.

"What is it?" shouted Konon.

"My pack!" yelled Nikias over his shoulder.

But when he got back into the theatre his pack was gone and the theatre was nearly empty of people. He and Konon searched everywhere in vain.

"Someone stole it," said Nikias with despair.

"What was in it?" asked Konon.

"I've lost everything," uttered Nikias, sitting on one of the benches and covering his face with his hand.

"I found your pilos," said Konon, holding up the ugly felt cap, smiling ruefully.

TWELVE

———◆———

Nikias and Konon ate a dinner of bread, boiled eggs, fish, and goat cheese at a crowded wineshop in the Street of Thieves, right around the corner from Dr. Pittakos's home.

Night had fallen and the narrow lane was now lit by pitch torches and little oil lamps hanging from chains. This part of the agora was just coming to life now and was packed with men looking for cheap entertainment.

Every so often a passerby would recognize Nikias from the fight at the theatre and come over to pat him on the back and offer their congratulations. The young Plataean was already something of a hero to the denizens of this part of Athens for besting the haughty and aristocratic Apollo—the nephew of the wealthy magistrate Kleon.

But Nikias could take joy in neither the food nor the adulation, for he had lost the gold with which to hire mercenaries. His first day in Athens and he had already failed in his quest.

"I can't wait to tell my father about the fight," said Konon, his face shining with delight and too much wine.

"You'd better go home soon," said Nikias morosely. "They're going to be worried about you."

Konon frowned. "You're coming back to the farm with me, aren't you?"

"No," said Nikias. "I'm staying here. I'm going to find a way to talk to Perikles."

"You might as well try to get an audience with Zeus himself," said Konon with a laugh, stuffing a boiled egg into his mouth.

"I have to do something," said Nikias, "if I'm going to get my grandfather to let me marry Kallisto."

"Ah!" said Konon. "She's a girl you love?"

Nikias scowled and glanced at a nearby table where a woman was loudly berating her husband. She had a fussy, red-faced toddler on her lap whose nose was running, as well as a baby in a ceramic high chair who was sitting close to Nikias. The husband was hunched over his wine krater, doing his best to ignore his wife.

"You're as drunk as a Skythian already," she hissed. "And not a scrap of food in the house except the few drops of milk left in my ragged bosom."

The infant was bouncing up and down excitedly and pushed herself away from the table with her feet. Suddenly she tipped the high chair over backward. Nikias instantly reached out with his good hand and caught the back of the baby's head, preventing her from smashing onto the hard stone floor, but the clay high chair broke apart with a noise that startled the baby and made her scream.

"Gods!" said Konon with a laugh. "You even save babies."

The mother leapt out of her seat and scooped the girl in her arms, clutching her to her chest. She thanked Nikias profusely, and then rounded on her husband and cursed him to Hades and back for being a neglectful, drunken bastard of a father, then she stormed out of the wineshop carrying both of her children on her skinny hips.

The husband sighed, rubbed his eyes, and poured himself another cup of uncut wine. He was on his way to getting thoroughly drunk.

"Are you sure you want to get married?" asked Konon, eyeing the drinker with disdain. "You're so young. Athenian men usually don't get married until they're in their late twenties. Look at what marriage has done to this poor bastard," he added, gesturing at the drunk.

"I've wanted to marry Kallisto since I was a little boy," said Nikias. He briefly told Konon the history of their love—how they'd grown up as neighbors, separated by nothing more than ancient boundary stones and the enmity that her father Helladios and Nikias's grandfather had shared for one another.

When Nikias and Kallisto were children they would sneak off and build houses together out of branches and stones, hiding their friendship from everyone except Aphrodite, whom they called on as their protector. As they grew older they plotted their escape. They decided that if they were not allowed to marry, then they would run away together. Nikias reckoned he could make a living off prize money from fighting at the festivals, and eventually they could save enough silver to buy some land far from their feuding families.

But all of that had changed with the Theban invasion. Kallisto's father Helladios had been revealed as one of the conspirators in league with the traitor Nauklydes. And even though Helladios was now dead, Nikias's grandfather had told him that he would not let him marry a traitor's daughter.

"In my grandfather's mind Kallisto is tainted by her father's crime," Nikias said.

"Well, I certainly wouldn't defy *my* father," said Konon. "You should see him when he's angry. Once I broke an oil jar—the big kind—and he chased me all over the farm with a willow branch. I can't imagine what he'd do if I tried to marry a woman without his consent."

Nikias stifled a laugh. "My grandfather once chased me with a *spear*," he said.

"What did you do?" asked Konon, nearly choking on a mouthful of wine.

"I hid in the mountains for a couple of days," said Nikias. "Until his iron cooled off."

The drunk turned his chair and faced the two young men, giving them a lopsided smile. "I couldn't help overhear your story of love, young man," he said with an unknown accent. "And I am compelled to offer my advice."

Nikias looked closely at the foreigner—a dark-skinned man with bushy eyebrows, a proud beaky nose, and wine-stained teeth. He was around forty years of age, and handsome in his way, but possessed one of the scrawniest physiques Nikias had ever seen. If the man had been a Plataean citizen he would have been fined annually by the state for being unable to meet the battle fitness of a hoplite: to wear the fifty pounds of armor, and bear a twenty-five-pound shield—a prerequisite that lasted into a man's eighth decade.

"What's your advice, friend?" Nikias asked.

"Don't ever," said the foreigner, "under any circumstances, no matter how lonely or drunk or depraved"—a pause to take a long drink from his cup—"be so foolish as to marry a woman and thus forever seal your miserable fate. And furthermore, do not procreate." The foreigner put his cup to his lips and drained the wine, then chewed on some lees between his incisors. Then he stood and tried to bow, but pitched forward.

"Now I must be off, young fellows," he said politely, after they'd put him back on his feet. "I must attend to some business. I hope that you will heed my advice."

He staggered out of the wineshop and disappeared into the street.

"Crazy drunken foreigner," said Konon, fingering the metal disk he would use to redeem his mule and cart. "I pity the man's sad wife."

"What's this, then?" asked Nikias.

A tall, willowy, and dark-skinned slave girl, of perhaps twelve years of age, approached their table and looked Nikias straight in the eye. She was unveiled and had a self-assured expression on her intelligent face.

"Nikias of Plataea?" she asked, raising her chin regally.

"Yes," replied Nikias. "Who wants to know?"

"My mistress sent me with a message." She handed Nikias a tiny scroll bound with ribbon.

He took the proffered message and pulled on one end of a rose-scented ribbon, then held the papyrus up and read it silently.

"Well," asked Konon impatiently. "What does it say?"

Nikias read aloud. "'To the great pankrator, Nikias of Plataea. Please come to my symposium tonight and make me laugh again. Blessings, Helena.'" He handed the note to Konon, who read it for himself, openmouthed.

"She must be the hetaera I saw in the theatre," said Nikias. He looked at the slave girl. "You were there, too, weren't you? Standing beside your mistress?"

The slave girl nodded.

"I've heard of this hetaera," said the amazed Konon. "She is very popular! You've only been in Athens for an hour and you've been invited to one of her symposiums. Unbelievable!"

Nikias thought for a while. He didn't have anything better to do until he found the doctor. And this Helena might be able to direct him to Chusor's old lover—the hetaera named Sophia. Maybe he would be able to find someplace to sleep at the symposium—on a cushioned couch. And he had to admit that the woman he'd seen at the theatre was gorgeous. The thing about her that had intrigued him most, however, was the cheerful sound of her laughter.

Nikias stood up and pulled on Konon's tunic, forcing him to rise to his feet. "Come on, then."

"I—I can't go with you!" spluttered Konon. "I won't know what to say! It's a symposium! There will be philosophers and playwrights and Zeus knows what other students from the brain-factories!"

"Stuff that!" said Nikias. "I'm not going without you. And you don't have to say anything. Eat and drink and if you have to fart, well, just find yourself a lonely corner and stuff a pillow over your arse."

Nikias followed the slave girl, who was already walking fast up the Street of Thieves with a determined stride.

THIRTEEN

———————•———————

The hetaera lived in a new two-story house in a neighborhood at the northeast base of the Akropolis. The house was lit up on the outside with hundreds of oil lamps, and Nikias heard odd, frenetic music playing from within.

Two well-built men who stood guard at the front door to the courtyard stepped aside as the slave girl approached. She led Nikias and Konon inside and told them to sit on a stone bench that encircled a splashing fountain. She called for slaves to attend to their feet.

"She has her own fountain," whispered Konon with awe as one of the slaves took off his sandals and washed his feet in a bucket.

Nikias said, "Let's hope she has good food, because I'm still hungry."

"Me too," said Konon. "One silver owl doesn't go very far in the Street of Thieves."

"Hey!" said Nikias, appalled. "What are you putting on my feet?" The young foot-cleaner was dousing his toes with scent from a phallus-shaped bottle.

"Everyone in the *city* does this, master," replied the slave with barely contained contempt.

"Smells good," said Konon, lifting one of his feet to smell it.

Nikias gently slapped the slave's hand away before he could spray the scent into his hair. "Not in my hair," he said. "I like the way it smells just fine." The slave curled his upper lip slightly, but did as he was told. Konon was grinning as his attendant sprayed copious amounts of perfume into his hair.

After the attendants were done with their work they bowed and departed. Konon leaned over and sniffed Nikias's head. "You do smell of horse," he said with a newfound superiority.

"I like the way horses smell," said Nikias. "If they'd sprayed me with horse sweat I would have been perfectly happy."

"I think the perfume is brilliant!" said Konon, rubbing his hair and sniffing his palm.

The slave girl returned and handed each an empty wine cup, then asked them to follow her. Nikias looked into the bottom of his cup and saw an erotic painting of a young woman pulling back her dress to mount an aroused young man.

"Did your mistress pick this one out herself?" Nikias quipped.

"Yes," said the slave girl, very serious. "Specifically for you."

That put Nikias back on his heels a little.

Konon frowned as he peered at the painting on the bottom of his cup. "Mine's got a dirty old satyr raping a goat's arse," he said, disappointed.

The girl led them across the courtyard and down a long corridor. The walls were hung with erotic scenes—images more graphic than anything either Nikias or Konon had ever seen.

"Gods," whispered Konon reverently, pausing to gawk at an orgy scene set in a glade. "I didn't even know centaurs could do *that*."

"And in a pond, no less," said Nikias.

The girl stopped them at the threshold to the drinking room and asked them their full titles and told them she would announce them once the music had ended. An older slave woman emerged from an alcove and put a garland of flowers around their necks.

Nikias peered into the small room. It had couches along all four walls and a raised dais in the center upon which sat the musician. The kithara player was strumming rapidly on his harp in a mysterious style that Nikias had never heard before. About a dozen men were lounging on the couches, holding wine cups and nibbling on food.

"Where is your mistress?" he asked the slave girl, looking everywhere in the room for the hetaera but not seeing her.

"She is still dressing," she replied. "She will come down soon."

The musician ended with a flourish—scraping the catgut so forcefully with his plectrum that Nikias thought he would snap the strings right off the tortoise-shell body. When he was done the men in the room cheered loudly. Several put down their drinking cups and clapped to show their appreciation. The musician smiled and bowed his head.

"That was awful," Konon whispered to Nikias.

"Waste of a good cat," said Nikias, slapping his hands together unenthusiastically.

When the noise had quieted down, the slave girl took a step into the room and announced their names in a high, clear voice.

Nikias and Konon walked hesitantly into the silent room. Nikias scanned the faces and saw mostly bearded men and only one or two beardless boys, all wearing garlands. Some of the guests stared back with bemused expressions, others with curiosity, a few with out-and-out hostility.

"Somebody usher them in," called out a stout man who was past military age. He carried an elaborate ceremonial staff showing that he was the symposiarch—the appointed master of the symposium. "You! Aristophanes. You're the youngest."

Nikias recognized the smiling face coming toward him. It was the young man with the hawkish features he'd spoken to outside of the theatre in the agora.

"Remember me?" he asked, giving Nikias an ironic smile. "My name is Aristophanes."

Nikias smiled and bowed his head politely. "Of course. You told me what a tragicomedy was all about."

"And you demonstrated one for us soon thereafter," said Aristophanes. "When you beat young Apollo with one punch." He glanced at Konon and acknowledged his presence with a curt bob of his head.

"Aristophanes is famous for playing women upon the stage," said the aged symposiarch.

Aristophanes smiled and bowed slightly. "And Aeskylos, here," he said, gesturing at the symposiarch, "is simply famous." He put a hand on Nikias's shoulder. "Come, both of you, I'll show you to the wine."

He led Nikias and Konon to a gigantic clay vessel—big enough for Nikias to crawl into—sitting on a marble table at the back of the room. It looked several hundred years old and was decorated with little black painted figures. A slave boy stood inside it up to his waist in wine and dipped a ladle into the liquid, filling their cups to the top.

Nikias and Konon sipped their wine and smiled.

"Quality stuff," whispered Konon.

A voice broke the silence, asking, "What's the news from the Oxlands?"

"Yes," demanded another partygoer. "Tell us about the battle with Thebes."

Aeskylos put his hands on his hips. "What is this?" he asked peevishly. "News corner at the agora? We are in a symposium, the subject of which was chosen by our hostess, the hetaera Helena. I will not insult her wishes by allowing the talk in this room to degenerate into gossip."

"What is the subject of this symposium?" asked Nikias politely.

Aeskylos grinned at Nikias, showing a mouth missing several teeth. "Dear lad," he said, "the subject of this gathering is 'The Delights of Lovemaking.'"

"Gods," said Konon, choking on his wine. "I guess I'll be keeping my mouth shut tonight."

A dashing fifty-year-old with brooding eyes and a thick black beard said, "What does some sheep-stuffer from the Oxlands know about lovemaking?" The man was sprawling on a cushioned chair, glaring at Nikias.

Several of the men in the room laughed at this insult. But Nikias raised his cup in a mock salute, then asked the man, "What do you call an Oxlander with a sheep under each arm?" After a suitable pause he delivered the punch line: "A pimp."

The room exploded with guffaws.

"What do you call his best customer?" asked Nikias. "A Theban!"

The laughter was much louder this time and the drinkers raised their cups, praising his wit. But the dashing man was not amused. He gave Nikias a slight smile and returned to his wine.

Nikias was pleased with himself. Now all he had to do was get through the night without putting his foot in his mouth. He hoped the hetaera would come soon. He didn't have to wait long.

"Gods, look at her!"

A chorus of exclamations—Nikias turned to look at the doorway. The figure standing there took his breath away. At first he thought it was a human-sized version of the giant golden statue of Athena in the temple on the Akropolis. But when the statue's eyes turned to him, he realized it was Helena—naked to the waist. She was painted gold and dressed like the statue. She even wore a Korinthian helm perched on the back of her head, though it appeared to be made of papyrus. And with her platform shoes she stood as tall as Nikias.

She smiled at everyone in the room, until her eyes finally locked onto Nikias. He bowed low. Helena nodded and walked over to her chair—a gilded, high-backed seat like a tyrant's throne—followed by four scantily clad young slave women whose job it was to hold the train of her skirt. She sat down and rested her hands on her lap, staring about the room with a regal expression.

"This is what it's like in the home of the gods," said Konon in a voice of reverence.

A swarm of attendants bearing platters hustled into the room and handed out plates of steaming food to all of the men. Nikias took his plate and breathed in the aroma, smiling happily.

"Bless Helena," he said and started gorging himself on the sheep's stomach packed with innards. He finished off his meal in no time and called for another. When he was done eating three more he licked his fingers, leaned back on a couch, and sighed contentedly.

He glanced over at Helena and saw the black-bearded man who'd insulted him earlier was kneeling by her and speaking in a hushed yet vehement tone. She was listening to him with an expressionless face. She flicked her gaze over to Nikias and they held each other's stares.

She stood abruptly and said, "I have been in this room now some time and yet I have not heard any talk about lovemaking." She wore an expression of mock outrage. "All I have seen is a lot of hungry men gorging themselves on my food and wine. I am rather put out." She sat down again and cast an imperious look about the room—a look that made the men smile and laugh. She whispered something to Black Beard and he skulked back to his seat.

Aeskylos got to his feet and shuffled to the center of the room. "My gracious host," he said and bowed to Helena. "We are honored to be in your home and partake of your wine—the blessing of Dionysus. Nearly every man in this room is either an actor or a playwright, and as you know how difficult it is to make a living in this business, you have taken pity on us once again. Now that our physical appetites have been satiated, we are ready to nourish our minds and, hopefully, entertain you in the process. I propose to begin with a debate between two members of our present company on the subject of this symposium. I defer to you now to pick the men who will expand on the subject of the delights of lovemaking." He went back to his cushioned seat and took a drinking cup proffered by a slave.

"Thank you, dear Aeskylos," said Helena. "I would be pleased to listen to the debate you have proposed. Since Euripides here"—she waved a hand at Black Beard—"seems so anxious to express his views on the subject to me in private, I would ask him now to express them in public for all to hear."

Euripides scowled, but he stood and bowed to Helena.

"I've heard," Konon said to Nikias, his voice already slurred from too much wine, "that this Euripides spends much of his time in a cave on the island of Salamis writing his plays. Isn't that strange? I wonder who she'll choose to take him on?"

Nikias said under his breath, "I think I can guess."

Helena smiled. "Now for your opponent I pick someone whom I think can stand up to your threatening manner. I saw him defeat a pankrator today before the first punch was thrown, using only his words." She turned her face to Nikias and made a sweeping gesture. "Nikias of Plataea."

The crowd voiced their approval for this choice and Nikias stood up and faced Euripides. The two threw their wine lees at a spot on the floor to see who'd go first and Euripides won the honor, for his lees stuck together in the bigger clump.

The playwright bowed his head for some time before raising his dark eyes to look at Helena. "When love first struck me," he said bitterly, "I tried to figure out how best to bear it. At first I thought silence was the thing, because my tongue is a fool. It criticizes others for the same faults that it possesses, yet brings down a heap of troubles upon my own head. You see, I believed I could defeat love, subdue it with caution and good judgment. And when that also let me down I resolved to die. Aphrodite, in her anger, has cast me into a vast sea of love! And my pathetic swimming will not bring me to shore."

Helena shook her head slowly, digesting his words, a bemused smile on her gold-painted lips.

"But my dear Euripides," said Helena in a goading voice, "you were supposed to elucidate on the delights of lovemaking. What you have described would be better suited to a symposium concerning the torments of unrequited love."

"How peculiar," said Euripides, "that doctors have found remedies for snake venom, but against a bad woman—far deadlier than snakes and crueler than fire—no one has concocted a cure."

"Perhaps you should not step on them," shot back Helena. "Perhaps then they will not bite you."

"I take no delight in any of this," replied Euripides with a growl. "Let the Oxlander excite you with his rustic notions of pleasure." And with that he stormed out of the room.

The room was uncomfortably silent. Helena sat back down in her chair, trembling with fury. She looked as though she, too, might get up and leave the chamber. Nikias knew that Euripides had insulted her in some deep and painful way that went beyond his scathing words. Obviously there was a history between the two.

"Euripides was right," said Nikias. Helena shot him a wounded look, but he winked at her and continued. "He was right earlier when he said that farmers from the Oxlands like me have scant knowledge of the arts of lovemaking. I know men who believe that plowing a field should be considered a kind of foreplay." Cordial laughter followed this little joke and Nikias took a deep breath to steady his nerves. "Our women, on the other hand," he continued, "do know something about the delights of lovemaking. And it's their task to tame us men and break us like wild horses—"

"And then ride you across the plains of the Oxlands!" called out Aristophanes jovially, imitating a woman's voice.

Nikias smiled and nodded. "I tell you this: a man who is unwilling to bow before the altar of Aphrodite is nothing more than a stubborn and stupid beast. Euripides spoke of drowning in a sea of love. Well, I say, 'Swim in that sea!' You, Aristophanes, may wear gowns and pretend to be a woman when you're on the stage, but until you've lived in the same house with three strong women like I have, you will never be able to understand their desires. They love and hate and dream just like us men." He glanced at Helena out of the corner of his eye and saw she was smiling slightly. "Euripides talked about the cruelty and counterfeit nature of womankind. In my experience it is *men* who exhibit this kind of behavior, not women. And everything that I have learned about love has come from women, not men."

The guests clapped politely and Aeskylos called out, "Excellently said! Most excellent!"

Helena stood up slowly and walked over to Nikias, stopping a few feet from him, regarding him with an inquisitive glint in her eye. "Would you agree, young bull," she asked flirtatiously, "that lovemaking is like the pankration?"

"Like the pankration?" asked Nikias with surprise.

"Yes," said Helena. "The lovers are the two fighters—"

"The bed—the arena," added Nikias playfully.

Helena gave him a mischievous look and said, "The opponents face one another. Flexing their muscles. Eyeing each other haughtily. And then the fight begins with the first blow."

She stepped forward and kissed him briefly but sensually on the lips.

"I wish this sort of fight were an Olympic event," commented Aristophanes drily.

"It's an event that I would gladly enter," said Nikias, "if my opponents were as beautiful as Helena."

"Hear him!" shouted Aeskylos merrily, and the other men in the room started talking all at once, calling for more wine and making jokes.

Nikias's eyes locked with Helena's and her smile slowly faded. A queer look darkened her features and she turned away. She went back to her seat and sat staring into space, sipping her wine, brooding in silence.

Nikias picked up a tortoiseshell harp that lay nearby and started plucking out a tune. His song was nothing like the frantic music that had been playing when he and Konon had entered Helena's home. This was a melancholy ode, full of yearning, full of anguish. It was an ancient song that Nikias's father had played. Nikias had spent many hours alone in his room, practicing upon his late father's harp, as though to conjure the dead man back to this world. And he had written the words to accompany the music.

"Hush!" said Aeskylos to the room. "It appears the Oxlander is going to play for us."

The crowd quieted down and Nikias started singing in his deep and mellow voice:

> *"A shimmering star that hangs in the sky*
> *An apple on a limb too high*
> *A fragrant wind that rushes by*
> *Love's sweet yearning*
> *A gentle hand that touches skin*
> *Kisses that never wear thin*
> *Eyes that drown me therein*
> *Love's sweet yearning . . ."*

Nikias stared at Helena as he sang, and saw that her eyes were welling up with tears. And when the tears finally trickled from the corners of her eyes they looked like drops of quicksilver racing down her golden cheeks. When he was done he set down the harp and looked shyly about the room. He had not planned on singing. In fact he'd never sung anything other than drinking songs in front of a crowd. The chamber burst into hearty cheers and thunderous applause.

"You can play *and* sing," said Konon, coming up and slapping Nikias on the back. His face was flushed with wine.

As the evening progressed the men became drunker and more ribald. A merchant who imported a fabric called silk—a dark-eyed Lydian with a handsome face who smiled too much for Nikias's liking—arrived late. He wore an outlandish garment made of the material he sold, and he kept trying to corner Nikias, begging him to tell him news of the Theban sneak attack.

The somber mood cast by Euripides had evaporated almost completely, and Helena became a charming and friendly host. Later, as the guests started to depart, she called Nikias to her and asked him to drink from her cup. He flushed with pride and drained the proffered wine.

A few minutes after sipping from her cup Nikias started to feel dizzy. Thinking he had imbibed too much, he sat down on one of the cushioned chairs and picked up the harp, strumming the strings absentmindedly. They made a weird sound, reverberating in his brain and rising and falling in volume. The harp slipped from his fingers and landed on the floor with an echoing crash. He stared at his hands with fascination, for they seemed to be stretching and bending as though they were made of dough. He regarded them for the longest time, unable to tear his eyes away. Finally he managed to squeeze his eyes shut, but when he did he saw bright colors and lights exploding behind his closed lids. Suddenly he felt as though he were flying—like Ikarus toward the sun. It was an unnerving sensation.

When he finally opened his eyes the room was dark and empty. The only other person still there was Konon, but he was passed out on the floor with a smile on his face.

Nikias heard footsteps. When he looked up he saw that the two burly men who had been guarding the entrance to the house were now standing over him. Their faces were not friendly.

"Where's Helena?" asked Nikias with a slurred voice.

The men ignored his question and pulled him from his seat.

"He's heavy," observed one of them.

"Like carrying a side of beef," said the other.

Nikias tried to move his feet, but they were dead. The men gripped him under the armpits and dragged him down a dark hallway, then up a flight of stairs. They took him into a darkened chamber and threw him on a bed, then stripped off his belt and tunic.

"What are you doing?" asked Nikias, frightened all of a sudden. Were these two going to rape him?

The men exited the room, shutting the portal behind them. Nikias lay on the bed, unmoving, listening to his own heartbeat pounding in his ears. He heard something move.

"Who's there?" he asked fearfully.

After a while a man whose face Nikias did not recognize appeared from the shadows, leering down at him. Nikias tried with all his might to sit up but he couldn't move a muscle.

He was utterly paralyzed . . . frozen like a corpse.

The stranger ran a hand over Nikias's chest, then up his throat to his lips. He put a finger in Nikias's mouth and pulled down his jaw so that his mouth was agape. Then he took a small vial from the folds of his robe and unplugged a stopper. He put the spout to Nikias's lips and poured a burning draft down his throat.

"Now we begin," said the stranger.

FOURTEEN

———— ◆ ————

Nikias choked on the thick and bitter liquid. A few seconds later he felt a wave of euphoria rushing through his body. Every nerve was on fire with pleasure. Not once had he ever experienced such intense joy. Such peace and clarity of mind.

"How are we feeling?" asked the stranger in an aristocratic Athenian accent.

Nikias smiled and nodded.

"Excellent," said the man.

Nikias saw the figure of a naked woman standing at the foot of the bed, holding an oil lamp. Her face was obscured in darkness, but her perfectly shaped breasts were illuminated by the flickering light, the areolas staring at him like eyes in a face, the navel a tiny mouth shaping an O.

"What's wrong with him?" Helena asked with a worried tone.

"It's the drug I just gave him," replied the man, stepping back into the shadows. "A very powerful drug. Touch him now."

"Can he hear us?" asked Helena.

"Yes," said the man. "He can hear us. He's in a dreamlike state."

Helena set the lamp by the bed and crawled on top of Nikias. She had washed off all of the gold paint. Her flesh was warm and smelled of roses. With all of her makeup removed she looked much younger. Nikias realized she was only a few years older than him. She pressed herself onto him, pushing her hard nipples against his chest.

"Who's that man?" asked Nikias, and wondered why his own voice sounded like it came from so far away. She started kissing him. Her mouth tasted delicious . . . like wild mint. And within a few seconds he'd forgotten what he had just asked her.

"I've found this technique works far better than torture," said the man. "And so much cleaner. Ask him why he came to Athens. And touch him below."

"Why are you here?" asked Helena, stroking Nikias's quickly growing erection with her soft fingertips.

"I came to hire mercenaries," Nikias replied without hesitation. "To help defend Plataea. Gods! Keep doing that."

"And where did you get the Persian gold?" asked Helena, moving her lips down to play on his chest.

Nikias laughed softly. "So you're the one who stole my pack. . . ."

"Not her," said the man's unctuous voice. "It was one of my whisperers. You were a fool to pick a fight with Kleon's nephew on your first day in Athens. Draws a crowd, you know? Now tell me: Where did you get such a treasure in Persian gold?"

"The gold coins," said Nikias, chuckling. "They spilled from my guts onto the road. The Dog Raiders . . ." He drifted off, adrift in a sea of delight.

"Tell him," said Helena anxiously. "Please tell him, Nikias."

"It was the traitor Nauklydes's pay for opening the gates to the Thebans," said Nikias dreamily. "We found the darics at his pottery factory."

"Interesting," said the man. "And who wrote the letter that was in your pack? The letter of introduction to the woman named Sophia."

"That was my letter," said Nikias jovially. "You shouldn't have taken it. You're lucky I'm in such a good mood."

Helena moved her mouth lower and Nikias felt a rush of pleasure crash through his body like a wave breaking against a shore. Then she stopped, and he thought he might lose his mind if she didn't continue.

"Please!" he begged. "Keep going!"

"Answer his question, Nikias," said Helena urgently. "Please." There was fear in her voice. He wondered why she was afraid of the man in the shadows. He seemed nice enough.

"My friend Chusor," said Nikias, even though a voice in the back of his mind was screaming at him to stay quiet. That he was revealing too much. "He wrote the letter. Sophia was his lover. He thought she might help me."

"What does this Chusor look like?" asked the man, his voice tense.

"Tallest man in Plataea. Speaks with an Athenian accent. He's half Aethiope."

"He's alive!" said the man in a tone that was no longer serene.

"Who are you?" asked Nikias.

"I am a friend of Plataea," said the man. "I hate the Spartans, just like you. If I were the leader of the League I would send an army to help defend your citadel. But Perikles refuses to listen to reason. He looks to the sea for victory. The countryside means nothing to him. He will let Plataea burn."

"We have a Spartan prisoner," said Nikias proudly. He knew he shouldn't be telling this secret, but he couldn't help himself. The words were spilling from him like liquid from a water clock.

"Really?" asked the man with a tone of wonder. "Please, tell me more."

"A Spartan royal," continued Nikias. "Worth his weight in gold. He was thrown from a horse and paralyzed. Our men found him near the city walls. My grandfather keeps him in a secret room. He's going to use him to trade to the Spartans. To gain passage for our women and children to Athens if the city comes under siege."

"This is fascinating information, my young friend," murmured the man. "Tell me. Why did you come here? To Athens?"

"I came to see Perikles," Nikias said. "I don't know where to find him, though. I must find him. I'll convince him to send an army."

"Never put your faith in a leader who sees himself as a god," said the man bitterly. He moved close to the bed so that Nikias could see his face in the dim light. He studied the stranger's features. He was in his fifties. Sleek beard and curled hair. Strong face—scar above the eye. A warrior. A leader. Nikias liked the look of him.

"You're my friend," said Nikias. "Aren't you?"

"Yes," cooed the man. "A friend. But to Perikles you are nothing more than a tool to further his purpose. I'm a warrior, just like you and your grandfather. Timarkos is not your friend either. Do not trust him. He plays more than one game at a time. And Chusor is trash. An arrogant freed slave who will get his comeuppance soon enough. Now. You must leave Athens. There are Persian spies here. They will try to capture you and take you to Thebes. One of them was at the party tonight."

"Euripides is a Persian spy?" said Nikias, bursting into laughter.

"The Lydian silk merchant," said the man. "He's in league with the Spartans and Persians. One of the pitfalls of a city like Athens that is open to the world. But this freedom allows us to keep an eye on our enemies too."

"That merchant was very slippery," said Nikias, laughing softly. "I think it was his silk outfit."

"Shh," said Helena with a worried expression. "Nikias, stop laughing. I don't want them to hurt you."

The man put a hand on the back of Helena's neck and held it firmly. "Why would I hurt this lad?" he asked, forcing her face toward Nikias. "Kiss him. Take your pleasure now. I can see how wet you are for him. You've earned this little treat. He's given me everything I need." With his other hand the man brushed the hair away from Nikias's forehead. "Such a handsome lad. He's my gift to you, my little bird," he said, pushing her face into Nikias's. "Kiss now. Oh, yes. Move your hips, girl. Yes. Like that. Squeeze him inside you. Yes. Yes."

Nikias tried to ignore the face of the man ogling them as they made love. He wanted him to go away. He didn't like him anymore. He wanted to kill him. But he still couldn't move a muscle. He forced himself to look into Helena's eyes. She was weeping. He wanted her to stop but he was helpless.

"Gods!" groaned Nikias. It felt as if every atom of his body was exploding with ecstasy.

Helena ceased her movement and held her trembling hands to her eyes, wiping away the tears. The man leaned over and kissed her roughly on the mouth, saying, "You did well, girl." Then he left the room.

Helena sat for a while on the edge of the bed, breathing slowly. Then she picked up the oil lamp and held it between them so that it illuminated her face.

"You're far more beautiful like this," Nikias said softly, "than when you were in your hetaera costume. I love you."

"You love a puppet, then," she said. "A thing without a soul."

She got up and quickly put on her gown, slipping from the room without another word.

"Helena?" Nikias called out.

The men who had dragged Nikias to the bedchamber reappeared and gagged him, putting a cloth sack over his head. They carried him down a flight of stairs, then threw him on the ground. They took turns kicking him in the stomach. When they were tired of this sport they picked him up and threw him into a cart. Nikias was conscious of a searing pain in his shoulder and stomach—or rather the *notion* of pain—but he was beyond caring, lost in a netherworld.

"This is what a shade feels like," he thought.

Eos, the goddess of morning, woke him.

He was lying on the ground, face pressed against the brown grass wet with dew, shivering from the cold. His stomach muscles ached and his head throbbed as though it might burst out through his eyes and ears. The back of his throat was parched and his tongue swollen, as though he'd swallowed a hot coal.

"I was drugged," he remembered, and the events of the previous night came rushing back—the humiliation of Helena's bedchamber. How he'd been helpless to move and unable to keep himself from answering the man with the dulcet voice.

He sat up and looked around. He was outside the city walls, near the graveyard. He could see the Akropolis and the Temple of Athena atop the hill. The sun was rising with a fiery glow.

The truth of what had happened hit him like an uppercut—an Athenian whisperer had gotten ahold of him. Chusor had warned him about Athens. That the citadel was crawling with spies, keeping an eye on everything, watching anyone suspicious who came to their city.

"Careless idiot!" he cursed himself. The symposium had merely been a trap. And Nikias, like some stupid rabbit, had walked right into the snare. Not only had he lost the gold, but he had endangered Chusor, and given up secret information about the Spartan prisoner.

And Helena had been forced to make love to him in front of that twisted man.

He looked down and saw a piece of papyrus pinned to his tunic, like a sign stuck to a slave at an auction. He ripped it from his clothes and read the message with blurry eyes.

RETURN TO ATHENS AND DIE.

They'd tossed him from their city like garbage and sent him on his way with a warning, as though he were nothing more than a vagabond.

"I've been the worst sort of fool," he said out loud. The face of Timarkos— the Athenian spy he'd dealt with in Plataea—flashed before his eyes. How the spy would mock him if he were to find out what had happened.

He reached for his belt. His Sargatian whip was gone. He opened the small pouch sewn onto the belt and put his hand inside. He found the disk for his sword that he'd left at the Dipylon Gate yesterday. And in the corner of the pouch, tucked under a fold of leather, was the object he was looking for. He pulled out the gold-and-carnelian signet ring that he'd taken from Eurymakus the Theban's severed hand. He didn't know why he'd kept the wretched enemy's ring in the first place. But he was glad that the Athenian whisperer had not found it and taken it last night. He put the ring back into the pouch and stood up. Then he started walking back toward Athens.

Out of the corner of his eye he saw a man standing under a tree about five hundred paces away, watching him intently. This man—dressed in the clothes of a vagabond and wearing an old tattered woven hat—started following him, keeping his distance warily, like a fox following a wounded prey.

Nikias heard the sound of a mule cart's wooden wheels behind him, rattling on the stone pavers.

"Timarkos told me you were clever," said an old man's voice, "but I beg to differ."

Nikias glanced in surprise but the old man holding the reins dropped his head and hissed, "Don't look at me. Just keep walking. They're watching us."

Nikias did as he was told. He made to wipe his face on his sleeve, masked his mouth in the crook of his arm, and asked, "Who are you?"

"An enemy of Thebes and Sparta," said the old man. He wore a farmer's tunic and a wide-brimmed leather hat that hid his eyes. "Now, you must do exactly what I tell you to do. There is an orchard across from the gymnasium. There is a horse tethered to one of the trees. Take the horse and ride to the Piraeus District.

Leave the horse at the gates and go to the shipyards—the harbormaster's offices. A one-eyed slave boy will find you."

The old man turned the cart onto a little side road and was gone.

"Do I trust him?" thought Nikias.

He could see the gymnasium up ahead. He glanced to his left and saw that the man dressed like a vagabond was getting closer. The stranger raised his fingers to his lips and let forth a piercing whistle. Another man emerged from a field on the opposite side of the road. A third dropped from a tree and started walking quickly toward Nikias. Soon the three would converge and be on him.

Nikias dashed off the road and into the orchard. He saw a horse there, undid the tether, and leapt onto the animal's back. The three spies shouted for him to stop but he was already galloping away, headed toward the bay as fast as the horse would run.

FIFTEEN

———— ◆ ————

"By Ashtarte's swollen tits," uttered Zana in a nervous whisper as she walked tentatively toward the citadel of Plataea with Chusor at her side. The walls and area in front of the gates were swarming with armored men.

"I told you not to worry," said Chusor. "Just don't say anything. Let me do all the talking. I know every one of those warriors by name." He held Jezebel in one of his huge hands, and the bird made itself smaller, as though sensing his tension.

Barka—dressed as a woman—followed close behind. Ji came last, nearly doubled over from the belongings that he carried on his back in a great sailcloth sack.

"I like Greek men," Barka observed with a girlish titter. "They're so much gentler than Persians or Egyptians. And their pricks are smaller, which is nice."

"And you," said Chusor, snapping his head around and shooting the eunuch a withering glare. "None of your games. Behave yourself. I don't want another Byblos incident on our hands."

"I can't help being pretty," said Barka. "I'm popular wherever I go."

As they got closer to the open gates they could see a group of traveling merchants who'd been stripped of their robes and tunics. The naked men had their backs to the wall and watched angrily while guards pulled their wares out of a cart and tossed them haphazardly into the dirt, searching for weapons.

"I won't let them strip me," said Zana through clenched teeth.

"I said not to worry," repeated Chusor.

"They can strip me if they like," said Barka.

When they got within twenty paces of the entrance a young guard approached and held up his hand for them to stop. Zana gripped Chusor's arm, digging her fingernails into his flesh. The smith made a growl deep in his throat and yanked his arm away from her.

"Hello, Chusor," said the guard. "You can enter but these others must be checked."

Chusor was about to protest when the captain of the Guard—one of Chusor's neighbors—strode over and pushed the young warrior aside.

"I'll handle this," said the captain, his eyes riveted on Barka.

"Hello, Damon," said Chusor, and gestured toward Zana. "This is my cousin, come from Athens with her two slaves."

Damon flicked his eyes over Ji and Zana, then returned to staring at Barka. The eunuch batted his eyes and turned away shyly.

"They'll be staying at the smithy?" asked Damon hopefully.

Chusor said, "Of course."

Damon ordered Ji to set down his burden and untie it. Then the guard made a cursory inspection of the contents, picking through the clothes, cooking pots, and dried food. When he was done he gave Chusor a friendly smile and a nod. "Go on in." A moment later he called out, "I'll be coming soon for that sword of mine—the one with the horse head pommel." He flicked a lascivious glance at Barka.

"I'll have it in two days," Chusor replied over his shoulder.

After they'd walked through the gateway tunnel and emerged into the agora Barka said, "That man Damon felt my arse as I walked past."

"Damon has the sort of wife," warned Chusor, "with very sharp fingernails."

Barka sniffed.

"This city is not what I expected," said Zana, looking around at the stately temples and public buildings—many of them made of the local black marble. "It's beauteous."

"It would look better without all this rabble," said Barka, turning up his nose at the makeshift homes of the refugees scattered across the open space. "Can we please get off this filthy street? I want to see Diokles."

Chusor pushed open the front door to the smithy and stepped inside. "Leo? Are you here?"

"Coming!" shouted Leo. He appeared from the back of the shop moments later cleaning his hands on a rag. His face lit up with surprise when he saw Zana, Barka, and Ji standing in the front room. "Who's this?" he asked with a pleasant smile.

"My cousin Zana," said Chusor. "From Athens."

"I didn't know you had a cousin," said Leo. "Pleased to meet you, Zana. My name is Leo."

Zana nodded slightly and cast her haughty gaze around the messy workshop.

"Chusor didn't tell me you were coming," said Leo apologetically, reading the expression on her face. "I would have cleaned up if I'd known ladies would be coming."

Chusor pointed at Ji, who was wiping the sweat from his face with a dirty sleeve. "This is her servant Ji. And this other one here is Barka."

"Where's Diokles hiding?" asked Barka.

"He hasn't come out of the storage room," said Leo. "He's been in there for days now. I'm worried he's going to die in there. Do you know him?"

"Lead me to him," commanded Barka.

Leo gave Chusor a questioning look but the smith nodded and said, "Take Barka to him."

Leo led Barka down the hall. Ji asked Chusor where Zana would be sleeping and the smith told him to take her things upstairs—to the master bedchamber. Ji lumbered up the stairs with his heavy burden.

"Must that ugly Greek boy live here?" Zana asked when they were alone.

"He's my assistant," said Chusor. "The lad is indispensable. I could give a fig if he had the face of a baboon's arse." He set Jezebel on the table and the pigeon immediately strutted about, inspecting every item with her sidelong glance.

Zana took off her cloak, folded it neatly, and put it on the table. Then she tied her hair into a knot at the back of her head and set to work cleaning up.

"You don't have to do that," said Chusor.

"Who else will do it?" asked Zana. "I am not so proud as you think."

"I could bring a woman in to clean."

"No."

He could tell by the sullen look on Zana's face not to argue with her. She had always run a neat ship and would not abide filth or clutter of any kind, even on a galley full of criminals and miscreants. He realized that he had never seen Zana doing anything domestic before. He wondered what her life had been like as a youngster—in the palace of her youth, before her father, a local ruler, had offended the Persian king and was strangled with a silken cord. Could she cook? Did she know how to weave? It was obvious she was ill-suited to life in a city, or a poky little home and workshop like this one. A woman of her grandeur needed the vast sea as a backdrop, and a trireme's open top deck to prowl.

"Stop watching me and do something," she snapped and took a pile of dirty plates into the kitchen.

Chusor went into the smithy and started going through the various items he needed to work on. He hefted a wooden torso used to display breastplates into a corner, then rummaged through the pile of swords until he found Damon's weapon with the horse head pommel. He reckoned the man—a notorious lover of eunuchs—would come sniffing around sooner rather than later. But it was good to have a man like Damon in Barka's pocket. A captain of the Guard could be a useful ally.

He stubbed his toe on a heap of scrap iron lying on the floor and cursed every god's name he could think of. He sat in a chair staring at the nail of his big toe, which had been bent backward. Blood oozed out.

His eyes glazed over. There was just too much to do. How would he ever get it done? Especially with Diokles cowering in the storeroom like a scared cat. He ran a hand over his bald pate and sighed.

And then he heard a familiar voice calling out joyfully, "You brought my little Lylit!" Diokles came running into the smithy with a laughing Barka clinging to his back.

"Diokles!" shouted Chusor, amazed at the sight.

Diokles spun around in a circle, beaming like a child. "You brought the sweet girl," he said, "my little goddess—my Lylit."

Leo appeared in the room and he was laughing, too, pleased that his friend had emerged into the sunlight.

"How did you do it, Barka?" asked Chusor.

Barka merely shrugged his slender shoulders and gave Chusor a complacent grin.

"Lylit told me how I would die!" said Diokles, exuberant.

"Who is 'Lylit'?" asked Leo.

"It's a Phoenician word for goddess," said Chusor. "Diokles's nickname for Barka."

"Lylit, use the inner eye and tell me I will die in the great Eyam," continued Diokles, using the Helot word for the sea. "That means the Spartan masters will never catch me. I will drown instead! I am invincible in this place!" Diokles set Barka down and took the eunuch's hand. "Come, Lylit," he said. "I will show you the citadel." And he led Barka out of the house.

"You could knock me over with an acorn," said Leo. "Well, I'm glad he's out of there. But do you think Diokles really believes that nonsense?"

"Oh, he believes," said Chusor. "He saw too many of Barka's predictions come true for him *not* to believe."

"Then this Barka—she's really an oracle?" asked Leo.

"*He,*" said Chusor. "Barka is a eunuch."

Leo looked stunned for a moment, then scratched his chin and said, "Oh, of course. I knew all along."

"But he likes to be called *she,*" said Chusor. "So if you want to be in his good graces, do as such."

"Does Diokles know he's a . . . she's a . . . he *was* a . . . ?" Leo gave up and picked his ear with his littlest finger.

"A physiological conundrum?" offered Chusor.

Leo nodded his head.

"I think I explained it to him once," said Chusor. "But he is convinced Barka is female. Regardless of the fact that he's got a cock between his legs."

Leo scratched his head pensively, then went back to his work.

Chusor became aware of a noise in the courtyard. A loud scraping of metal on rock. "What have those two little rat-brained fools gotten into now?" he raged, and launched himself from his chair.

The boys—Ajax and Teleos—were each digging furiously in the dirt floor of the courtyard. They had already made waist-deep holes and showed no signs of flagging. Chusor saw Ji standing off to the side, arms crossed on his chest, watching them with a stern countenance.

"What is going on?" Chusor asked Ji.

"These boys," said Ji. "Their chi—their spirit—is not in balance. Probably because of their father's death. They mourn him in the curious way of children. With violence and chaos. I gave them a task that pits one against the other. Their energy is now directed toward something useful."

"Useful?" asked Chusor. "You call that useful? They're digging two use*less* holes in my courtyard."

"Look again," said Ji. "You see two holes. I see two *diggers*."

Ji stared into Chusor's eyes and raised his eyebrows as if to say, "Do you understand now?"

Chusor turned and looked at the boys, who were frantically shoveling, focused for the first time since they had been living under his roof. If Chusor and the others were going to find the treasure buried under Plataea, they would need to mine the collapsed system of secret tunnels.

"Keep them at it until they're tapped out," said Chusor, then headed back into the smithy to light the forge fire.

SIXTEEN

———◆———

Menesarkus waited at the front entrance to his private house in the citadel of Plataea, leaning on his staff and chewing his lip anxiously, when a small troop of guards arrived bearing the Spartan prisoner, Arkilokus, on a palanquin.

Arkilokus—a tall, broad-shouldered man in his early thirties with blue eyes and sandy-colored hair—lay still, eyeing Menesarkus as the guards carried him into the entrance hall. Menesarkus's wife and granddaughter, who were standing off to the side, let out shocked gasps the moment they saw the prisoner. At first glance they'd both thought that Nikias had been brought home, such was the strong resemblance between him and the Spartan.

"Upstairs," Menesarkus said to the guards. "Lay him on the bed in the first room and then take up position outside the entrance to this house. No one is to come in without my leave." The guards nodded, then headed up the stairs with their burden.

"Who is that man?" asked Eudoxia in a whisper. Menesarkus's silver-haired wife held a hand to her mouth, as though she'd seen a shade.

Menesarkus took her hand, covering it with his scarred fingers. "Eudoxia," he said with a sigh, "I must tell you something that will shock you. But there is nothing for it but the blunt truth. That is a Spartan prisoner. He was thrown from a horse outside the city walls. He has lain in the city jail, in secret, until now. And he is my . . . my grandson."

"Grandfather!" said Phile with a startled laugh. "What a strange thing to say. My brother Nikias is your only grandson." But she gripped her grandmother's arm and her eyes traveled up the stairs to the second floor where the guards had just disappeared, the sound of their feet treading on the wooden floor above.

Eudoxia looked up into Menesarkus's eyes with a horrified expression.

"After the Persian Wars," continued Menesarkus, staring back into Eudoxia's eyes, "when I was invited to Sparta to participate in the funeral games for Leonidas, one of the dual kings sent his daughter to my bed. This was after I had defeated

Drako in their pankration championship. You've heard of the Spartan 'wise-breeding.' Well, I was chosen to strengthen their bloodline. That young man is the heir to one of the Spartan dual thrones."

Eudoxia had lived through the Persian invasions, the deaths of two of her children, and the many vicissitudes of life. She stared into space for a moment, blinked, then nodded her head, standing up a little straighter, her face hardening.

"Weren't you and Grandmother already married when you visited Sparta?" asked Phile, seeing the stony look on her grandmother's face.

Menesarkus rolled his eyes—a vexed expression that very few people had ever seen on the old pankrator's face other than his granddaughter. "Don't you have something to do, girl?" he asked impatiently. "Leave your grandmother and me to ourselves."

Phile scowled and looked to her grandmother for support, but Eudoxia said softly, "Go to the kitchen and see to the afternoon meal."

Without another word Phile nodded and moved swiftly from the room.

"That child will be the death of me," said Menesarkus under his breath.

"If Phile had been born a boy," said Eudoxia archly, "she would be Nikias's twin, and you would love her much more than you do." She pulled her hand from Menesarkus's grasp. "How do you know this Spartan is your grandson?" she asked in a forced voice.

"He's the one who found me in the wreckage of the farmhouse," said Menesarkus. He thought back to that terrible night a week ago when the Theban raiders had attacked their home in the country and burned it to the ground. The women had escaped to the ground from the rooftop. But Menesarkus had been trapped up there, and had only survived by climbing into the chimney, where he'd become stuck like a stopper in a bottle but protected from the flames.

"Arkilokus came to the farm with a Spartan scouting party," he explained. "He brought me to the Spartan camp. That night Arkilokus came to the tent where I was being held prisoner and told me that I was his grandfather. He's always known that he was my grandson."

"Plataeans are better at keeping secrets than Spartans, it seems," said Eudoxia in a scathing tone. "Well, what *do* you want us to do with him, husband? And *have* you heard any news of Nikias?"

Menesarkus shifted his weight, moving his staff to his other hand. The fierceness burning in Eudoxia's eyes prevented him from evading her questions.

"Nikias is in Athens," said Menesarkus. "Chusor the smith told me. He's run away on some foolhardy quest."

Eudoxia looked at Menesarkus and pursed her lips for a moment before saying, "Why did you bring this Spartan to our house? A house where your brother and his family were butchered by the Thebans in their beds. Thebans who do the bidding of the Spartans."

"Arkilokus is valuable to us," said Menesarkus. "The Spartans will pay a warrior's weight in silver to get back one of their captured hoplites. Who knows what a prospective heir to a Spartan throne is worth? He may be a bargaining piece. But if he is crippled he is worthless. The Spartans throw their deformed babies off of cliffs. And a warrior paralyzed in battle is awarded a knife to the heart. I need you to nurse this man back to health. Between me and Nikias you've healed more injuries than any doctor in the citadel."

"What makes you think his spine isn't severed?" asked Eudoxia.

"He feels tingling," said Menesarkus. "He can move his toes and fingers. But the prison is no place to recover. I found Arkilokus stewing in his own shit today. He needs careful looking after and you are the only one to whom I can entrust this important task."

"I will care for him on one condition," said Eudoxia.

"Name your terms," replied Menesarkus, full of relief.

"You allow us to care for Kallisto here as well. Let us bring her here from Chusor's smithy and give her the protection she deserves. There are men in the city who would kill her for being the daughter of Helladios."

Menesarkus felt a surge of anger. "The daughter of a betrayer," he said. "The daughter of a man who allied himself with Nauklydes the traitor—a man who tried to sell Plataea to the enemy and opened the gates to this citadel."

"Kallisto had nothing to do with that," said Eudoxia. "And you know this is true. Her father nearly beat her to death when he found out that she and Nikias had made love. Kallisto's father was going to sell her as a sex slave to the Makedonian, but she escaped and came to our farm and helped to defend it from the enemy—"

"You don't have to tell me the tale," growled Menesarkus. "I was there."

"And then she was nearly killed at the Battle of Oeroe," continued Eudoxia, as if Menesarkus had never spoken. "But most of all you should protect her and let us care for her under our roof because your grandson and heir loves her and would marry her if only you would let him."

"Which I cannot," said Menesarkus. "The blood of Helladios runs in her veins. I will not let Nikias breed scions of a traitor."

"Would you rather have him bed a Spartan wench?" asked Eudoxia hotly, and her eyes flashed to the top of the stairs where the guards, having delivered their prisoner, now stood staring down into the entrance hall with embarrassed looks.

Menesarkus gestured impatiently for the men to descend the stairs. He waited until they exited the house. "Now, what is your decision about Kallisto?" Eudoxia asked.

Menesarkus took in a deep breath and puffed out his cheeks, letting out a long slow exhalation. He thought, "What harm could be done bringing the girl here?" She had fought valiantly. But she was tainted by Helladios's crime, and that stain would never be washed clean. "Yes, yes," he said at last. "Bring her here. But she is not to be under the false impression that she is Nikias's betrothed. They will never marry."

Eudoxia sniffed and pulled on her plait of long hair. Menesarkus knew from long experience that she did not agree with what he had just said, but that she had given up for the time being. She turned and started walking up the stairs.

"Where are you going?" asked Menesarkus.

"To meet your Spartan grandson," she responded.

When they entered the upstairs chamber they found Arkilokus staring at the ceiling and gritting his teeth.

"Arkilokus," said Menesarkus. "This is my wife, Eudoxia."

"I've got to piss," said Arkilokus. "I can feel it coming. But I can't stop it."

Eudoxia shouted downstairs, "Phile! Bring a chamber bowl!" Then she went to the bed, saying to Menesarkus, "Help me get him up."

Together they lifted the Spartan to a sitting position. He had a torso like Menesarkus—broad and husky. It was difficult for the two of them to maneuver his bulky, corpse-like form. Phile entered the chamber, breathless and holding a large clay bowl.

"Hold the pot under his penis," ordered Eudoxia.

Phile knelt and held the bowl, wrinkling her nose in disgust as Eudoxia gripped the Spartan's penis and aimed it into the bowl. A jet of urine shot into the container and Arkilokus let forth a great sigh of relief.

"He pisses just like Nikias," said Phile.

"It's a good sign," said Eudoxia. "The fact that he can feel the urine coming." Menesarkus nodded.

"Good thing it's such a big pot," said Phile.

"I'm paralyzed, but not deaf, girl," said Arkilokus wryly.

Phile was so surprised she dropped the bowl and it shattered on the floor.

"And this is my granddaughter, Phile," Menesarkus said to Arkilokus with a sardonic tone.

"Go get sponges, Phile," Eudoxia said.

"Do you not have slaves to clean up such a mess?" said Arkilokus, his face red with shame. "Must your own women be forced into this humiliation?"

"All of our slaves were murdered in the raid on our farmyard," Eudoxia replied curtly. "Slaughtered in the dormitory."

Arkilokus looked at Menesarkus, who raised his eyebrows and nodded.

"The Theban Eurymakus did it," said Menesarkus. "The one whose brother I killed at the Games."

Arkilokus dropped his eyes. "I know the man far too well. He's a viper upon whom I have tried to step many times in the past. But the Spartan Elders see him as a useful tool. And my father esteems Eurymakus's connection to the Persian court."

Menesarkus smiled inwardly. The Spartan had just revealed something about Eurymakus that Menesarkus had not known: he was in league with the Persians! What else would Arkilokus let slip in his vulnerable state?

"One doesn't step on snakes," said Eudoxia, interrupting his thoughts. "You chop them in half with a sword." And looking at Menesarkus she said, "Now, husband. Help me lower him."

Gently they lay Arkilokus back down upon the bed and then Eudoxia set to work examining his body, smelling his breath, and probing different parts of his body with a pin that she wore clasped to her dress, softly poking him from the flat of his feet to the crown of his head. Phile came back during this assessment and cleaned up the mess. Then Eudoxia led Menesarkus and Phile from the room and shut the door behind them.

"Well?" asked Menesarkus.

"He flinches when prodded," said Eudoxia.

"I saw."

"My own father had this happen to him at the Battle of Plataea," said Eudoxia.

"I remember," said Menesarkus. "I helped drag his body from under a Persian horse."

Eudoxia frowned. "My father's paralysis only lasted a week, but he could never really feel his feet again."

"He could walk, though," said Menesarkus.

"You've been starving him," said Eudoxia. "I can smell it on his breath. He's living off his muscles."

"He refuses to take food," said Menesarkus. "It's one of the reasons I brought him here. The doctor has tried to spoon soup into his mouth but—"

"He needs ox blood," said Eudoxia. "Phile can feed it to him with a spoon."

"Disgusting," said Phile, who was crouched over, staring at Arkilokus through the crack in the door.

"Spartans live on congealed blood," said Eudoxia.

"Spartan *warriors* live on black pudding," corrected Menesarkus. "This man was raised in a royal house."

"Well, we have no pomegranates and goose liver in the larder," said Eudoxia snidely, "so it's ox blood for him. Phile, go and find Saeed and send him to the smithy. He is to tell Chusor and Leo to bring Kallisto here immediately. Now I'm off to the butcher for the blood."

Menesarkus watched his women go downstairs, then went back into the bedchamber, pulled up a chair, and sat by Arkilokus's bed. The Spartan was staring at the ceiling, his eyes pools of water. Menesarkus had never before seen a Spartan cry.

"Why are you crying?" asked Menesarkus bluntly. "Humiliation?"

"On the contrary," replied Arkilokus. "Your wife reminds me of my grandmother."

Menesarkus saw the woman in his mind's eye—the fetching and brazen Spartan princess who had climbed into his bed, taken her pleasure of him, and stolen his seed. He felt a familiar rush of shame that he'd never shaken, even after nearly fifty years.

"Eudoxia and your grandmother look nothing alike," said Menesarkus.

"I wasn't talking about her looks," said Arkilokus. "Her spirit."

Menesarkus crossed his arms on his chest and grunted. "You see why we cannot bend to the Spartan yoke?" he asked. "Our women would cut off our balls."

Arkilokus burst into laughter—a surprising sound that echoed throughout the mirthless house.

SEVENTEEN

———◆———

Kolax heard frantic barking in the distance and knew instantly what breed of dog was on their scent—Mollossian hunting hounds. Dogs trained to track and kill men. His father used to tell him that three of these animals could take down a lion.

"There's at least ten dogs coming after us," Kolax thought, ear cocked toward the carrying wind. He didn't have much time to get the girl someplace safe. The dogs would rip her apart.

They'd spent the last day and a half hiding in the woods near the place where she had tried to hang herself. Kolax had snuck into a nearby farmyard that evening and stolen food.

The Skythian boy was not fluent in Greek, but he'd been able to piece together the girl's story—she was good with gestures and could draw wonderful pictures in the dirt to show words like "warrior" and "city."

Her name was Iphigenia, and she was from an island that the Athenians had conquered. She had been brought back to this place by her new master—a Greek warrior named General Lukos—as his war prize. The general had defiled her body every night and beaten her. Iphigenia would rather die than live in constant shame. Her parents had been killed by the Athenians and she longed to join them in Hades.

But Kolax wasn't going to let that happen.

"Up, Iphigenia," he said, pointing to the gargantuan olive tree under which they sat huddled together.

"I'm ready to die, right here, right now," she said.

Kolax had never been in love with a girl before. But he was now. He'd held her in his arms all through the night. The scent of her hair made him giddy. Whenever she spoke he was transfixed by her bow-shaped mouth. He loved the sound of her voice.

The decision to keep her for his own—steal her from this sheep-milker of an

Athenian—had come to him in a flash. It was exactly how his father had won his own mother! Snatched her from a rival and brought her home in triumph to share his round-tent.

The sound of the dogs approaching shook him from his thoughts. The Mollossians were calling to each other. Forming up ranks. Closing in on their prey—the runaway slave.

Kolax got on his knees, bent down, and patted his shoulders. "I lift you up," he said. Iphigenia reluctantly obeyed and Kolax stood to his full height, allowing her to climb onto a low branch. He kept saying, "Up, up," and she ascended as far as she could before the limbs became too weak to support her weight.

"I will come back," he said in Skythian. "No matter what happens." Then in Greek he said, "Stay."

She nodded and hugged a limb, nestling in the bough of the tree.

Kolax took out his knife and cut a leafy branch, then slashed a gash on the top of his thigh. He tore a leaf from the branch, smeared some blood onto it, and dropped this on the ground. Then he took off running, grabbing leaves, smearing them with blood, and leaving a trail for the dogs.

He ran as fast as he could for about half a mile before pausing to listen. His heart pounded in his ears but he could still hear the Mollossians—they were on his trail and gaining.

He looked around and recognized the surroundings. He'd come this way the other day when he'd chased Nikias's horse. He remembered there was an old, crumbling temple nearby. He kept running until he came to the place. It was the size of a little hut, with three walls, an altar, and a ceiling of rotting timbers. The ancient holy place stood at one end of a glade.

Kolax dashed inside the temple, pulling down the roof timbers that were hanging down, and made a barricade with them. Now he was fully enclosed except for the open ceiling. He took off his quiver, dumped the arrows on the dirt floor, and stabbed each of the bronze points into the dirt, all of them lined up in a row. Grabbing his bow, he nocked the first arrow but kept the string loose to prevent his arm from getting tired, aiming through a narrow gap in the makeshift barricade.

And then he waited. The sound of barking got louder and louder. He sang his father's favorite drinking song under his breath to keep the fear from creeping into his brain.

"Cut off his head and now it's mine, gild it with gold and fill it with wine."

He saw the lead Mollossian burst through the undergrowth and into the glade, two hundred paces away. It was a big dog. At least a hundred pounds, with mottled brown fur. The cur sniffed the final bloody leaf Kolax had dropped, and raised its big intelligent head to look right at his hiding place. Then it let out a bloodcurdling howl.

"Pretty drinking cup, my favorite drinking cup."

The Mollossian's shoulder blades went up and its head dropped as the animal hunkered down into its stalking trot, dewlap flopping from side to side. It growled, showing its teeth as it approached the temple at a quickening pace. Three other Mollossians burst into the glade, saw their leader running toward the temple, and barked excitedly, trying to catch up.

"Don't put down the skull cup, raise it up, up, up!"

Kolax let the first arrow fly directly at the lead dog's head. But the Mollossian ducked at the last second, and the shaft struck the animal behind it, dropping the dog to the brown grass. The lead animal dodged and Kolax's next arrow went wide. The Skythian cursed and reached for another arrow, darting his eyes to the temple floor for a split second to grab the shaft. When he looked back the leader was no longer in sight.

Kolax felled two other hounds with perfectly aimed shots. But a few heartbeats later six more Mollossians ran into the glade. When they saw their dead companions they stopped short, looking for their quarry. Kolax held his arrows, waiting for them to get closer. He didn't want them to scatter and come at him from different sides. He knew these dogs could climb twenty feet up a tree using their sharp claws. It would be no effort for them to scale the crumbling walls of the temple and attack him, dropping down through the open roof.

His eyes darted around as he looked for the mottled brown leader. He could sense the hunting hound was out there somewhere, trying to figure out the best way to get to him. Some sort of bestial signal had passed between the pack, and the dogs were starting to spread out as if obeying orders.

Kolax was a natural mimic. He'd been taught to make hundreds of animal sounds before he could speak words. He made one now—a perfect imitation of a terrified fox. All of the Mollossians turned their heads toward the temple and ran at it. They couldn't resist the idea of tearing apart a fox.

When they were fifty paces away Kolax let fly a flurry of arrows. He stuck each dog with a bronze-headed shaft. Four of them dropped, but two stayed on their feet, running straight at him, growling with hatred. One was hiding behind the other, using the dog in front as a shield. At twenty paces Kolax took down the one in the lead. The dog following it immediately dropped and hid behind the corpse, waiting there, snarling with fury.

There was nothing more dangerous, Kolax knew, than a wounded hunting dog. This one had an arrow sticking through its hind end—straight up like a stiff tail.

Kolax pulled back on the bowstring as hard as he could, hoping to drive an arrow straight through the dead Mollossian's exposed belly and into the one hiding behind it. But the bow was not strong enough and the arrow merely went into the dead dog halfway up the flights.

"Stupid Greek bow," he spat.

A scrabbling sound on the outside of the temple wall made Kolax jump. He turned just in time to see the head and front paws of the mottled brown Mollossian appear at the roofline. Kolax shot an arrow through the dog's muzzle, but that didn't stop it. The hound flung itself over the wall and landed on top of him, snapping its teeth, reaching for his throat, and clawing at his chest with its sharp nails.

Screaming, Kolax kicked out with both feet, gaining a split second. He grabbed an arrow from where it was stuck in the earth, and plunged it into the dog's eye—into its brain. The body jerked and slumped.

Kolax grabbed his bow, nocked an arrow, and looked out through the barricade. The wounded dog with the arrow in its rump was gone.

Stuffing his remaining arrows into the quiver as fast as he could, Kolax kicked aside the barricade and started walking cautiously. Which way should he go? He was surrounded on all sides by trees. He knew the Mollossian would be at an advantage in the woods. It could be hiding anywhere. The best thing to do was taunt it—bring the creature into the open where he could get a clean shot.

He stopped and stood in the center of the glade. He could hear something coming through the brush behind him—footsteps. He put an arrow to his string and turned.

"Zeus's eggs!" said a stunned man, staring in shock at the dead dogs everywhere. He looked at Kolax with wonder. "Who are you?"

Kolax noticed the man had a net in one hand and a cudgel in the other. Slave-hunter. He glanced behind him and saw the man's mount standing at the edge of the glade.

The slave-hunter's eyes flashed at something behind Kolax. Without hesitating the Skythian put arrow to bow, turned, and pulled the gut-string.

And the bowstring snapped.

The wounded Mollossian with the arrow in its hind end was ten paces away, running at him at full speed, blood and saliva dripping from its mouth.

Kolax drew his long dagger and fell flat on his back, holding the blade with both hands at his loins. The Mollossian leapt on him and Kolax thrust upward, gutting the dog and spraying his chest with gore.

The moment Kolax got to his feet something wrapped around his neck like a snake. He clawed at his throat and felt leather—a whip! It was cutting off his air and crushing his larynx.

"Bastard!" yelled the slave catcher, pulling tighter with his powerful arms and shouting, "There's a wild Skythian boy over here! Help! He's killed all the dogs!"

Kolax's vision started to go black at the edges. He knew he didn't have much time. Only a couple of seconds. He lifted his leg and grasped the handle of the small Theban dagger he kept strapped to his ankle, pulled it from the sheath, and jabbed backward with all the strength left in his body. The whipcord went slack and the slave-hunter fell backward.

The Skythian boy rolled over and yanked the dagger from the dead man's heart. He wiped the tears from his eyes and tried to swallow, but there was a lump in his throat that made him gag.

He heard horses galloping toward the glade and the shouts of men. He turned at a sound coming from the opposite direction and saw a lone rider burst through the thickets not twenty paces away. The horseman was a blond-bearded Athenian with a jagged scar running the length of his face. Kolax knew the man the instant he saw him—General Lukos. Iphigenia had described her tormentor's scar.

Kolax watched as the Athenian's gaze danced from the dead dogs, to the corpse of his servant, to the bloody dagger in Kolax's hand. Then Lukos's expression shifted from astonishment to outrage.

The barbarian boy stared down the Athenian and started walking slowly backward toward the dead slave-hunter's horse tethered at the edge of the glade. General Lukos raised his short spear and flung it at Kolax, but the Skythian was too quick and jumped aside. The spear stuck in the ground, vibrating like a plucked bow.

Yanking the spear from the earth, Kolax turned and flung it at the general's chest with a lightning-fast motion. But the wily Athenian pulled back on his reins, making his horse rear, and the spear struck the animal in the breast. The beast screamed and Lukos was thrown.

Kolax sprinted to the other horse, undid the tether, jumped on its back, kicked it hard, and took off. He looked back over his shoulder and saw Lukos climbing onto another mount, shouting furiously at his men to give chase.

"Follow me if you can!" Kolax cried out in Skythian. "Follow me to your deaths, you rapers-of-sheep!" He let forth a croaking war whoop and laughed with wild joy, turning his horse toward Athens, leading the slave-hunters in the opposite direction of the girl in the tree.

EIGHTEEN

———— ◆ ————

The bay was swimming with dozens of double- and triple-decker galleys with huge eyes painted on their prows and bronze rams jutting from their cutwaters like the teeth of peculiar and deadly ocean creatures. Nikias had never seen so many of the powerful warships in one place at one time, and the sight was awe inspiring.

He'd followed the old mule driver's instructions and ridden cross-country to the port city of Piraeus, situated six miles southeast of Athens. As far as he could tell he'd left the spies who'd been chasing him in the dust. He'd abandoned the mount outside the city walls and entered on foot, making his way along the dock road to the first of the two harbors—a place swarming with shipbuilding activity. The noise of adzes and hammers, furiously shaping and fitting timbers, filled the air with a cacophonous music. The smell of brine, fir, and pine pitch filled his nostrils.

He paused to look at the hulks of at least fifty vessels, all in various phases of construction, sitting inside the open boat sheds. Some were just the beginnings of ships—the keels laid from aft to bow. And there were completed hulls that had yet to be planked, their wooden rib cages exposed to the sun. Near the water's edge, perched on log rollers, was a nearly finished triple-decker, already rigged with ropes and sails. He saw men painting the entire hull with dark pitch, staining the ship black like all the others out in the bay.

"It'll be a backbreaker for you if they take you on," said a voice from behind.

Nikias turned and saw a cheery man of middle age with a wavy brown beard, kindly eyes, and cheeks that stuck out like apples when he smiled. Over his stout body he wore a leather apron covered with pockets out of which poked the handles of his woodworking tools.

"You'll be assigned a bench on the lowest deck," continued the shipwright. "It's hot and it stinks down there. But you look like a strong lad. You'll work your way up fast."

Nikias realized that the carpenter assumed he had come from the country looking for work as an oarsman. He wondered, with frustration, why it was so obvious to every Athenian that he wasn't a local. "How many ships are in the fleet now?" he asked.

The shipwright scratched his beard, calculating. "Two hundred doubles, three hundred triples, and about a hundred of the smaller vessels fit for service. Most of the doubles and triples are guarding the shipping lanes now. The ones in the bay have just come in with cargo convoys from the north—timber and grain. Others are here to get supplies and men before heading back to the blockade of Potidaea. I heard say ten triples are going out to raid the coast of Megara."

"Good," said Nikias, thinking of the Dog Raiders of Megara. "It will be nice for them to get a taste of their own piss."

"The Megarians will regret their treaty with the Spartans," said the shipwright. "We'll cut off their grain supply and they'll starve."

"There's so many new ships being built," observed Nikias.

"Perikles loves ships," said the shipwright. "We'll keep building them until the treasury is bare of owls and the mines of Laurium are empty of ore. It's as good as anything to spend our silver on, at least in my opinion. I'm a boatbuilder, after all. They say the walls of Athens and the Piraeus protect Athens. But the wooden walls of the fleet are what keeps us safe from the Persians and Spartans."

Nikias had heard his grandfather say the same thing before when defending Athenian tax increases to pay for the fleet. "Do you know where the *Sea Nymph* is stationed now?" he asked, hoping to get information about his cousin's boat.

The shipwright laughed. "You'll never get a seat on the pretty *Nymph*, my son. That's Perikles's personal dispatch ship. He bought it with his own money and picked every man on it." He pointed at a magnificent two-hundred-foot-long ship beached on the shore. "Look at her. As pretty as any hetaera in the city."

"That's the *Sea Nymph*?" asked Nikias.

"She came in two days ago," said the shipwright, and went on his way with a nod.

Nikias headed down the road toward the port offices, thinking of his cousin as he walked. He hadn't seen Phoenix in almost four years—not since his older Athenian relative had come of age and shipped out as an oarsman. Nikias had met Phoenix only six or seven times over the years, and they'd never gotten on well. Phoenix, in Nikias's opinion, was a vain, loudmouthed braggart. The only thing they shared was the fact that their late mothers had been sisters. But he felt that he had to find him and tell him what had happened in Plataea. He wondered how he would locate the mariner in this port crawling with oarsmen on leave.

He passed a row of workshops filled with women working at looms. Out in front of their shops, hanging from hooks, were displayed expensive bolsters—cushions for oarsmen to put on the arse-numbing benches of the galleys. The Athenian navy, everyone knew, did not supply these necessary pads for their mariners. The slipcovers had the names of various ships woven onto them, or pictures of things from the sea—shells, dolphins, triremes, and fish. Some had images of men engaged in acrobatic sexual acts with other men, or women, or satyrs, or a combination of all three.

He saw a group of mariners bartering over the price of a cushion that bore the image of a grinning sea horse with a giant erection. The shoppers were obviously oarsmen because of their tremendously muscled shoulders and legs. He wondered if Phoenix had turned into one of these "sea-oxen," as Chusor disdainfully called them.

He kept going up the lane until he entered the busy square in front of the naval offices. A gang of workers had dug up the ground here to replace a clay water pipe. Several children were playing about in the mud caused by the broken conduit, but Nikias didn't see a one-eyed slave boy anywhere.

One of the slaves working on the pipe—a craggy-faced lout with a jutting jaw—stopped digging and glared at Nikias with a hostile expression. Nikias didn't like the look of him and was worried the man might be one of Kleon's spies, so he moved to the edge of the square where the slave couldn't see him.

"Stop right there, lad," said a commanding voice.

Nikias turned quickly and saw a handsome fifty-year-old man with silvery hair and a perfectly folded, expensive robe. He stood in a small wooden booth with a sign over the top that read: COLONISTS WANTED.

"Your destiny awaits!" said the recruiter, flashing a smile and pointing at the sign.

"No, thanks," Nikias replied. "I'm not looking to move to some rock farm on the arse-end of civilization."

Nikias heard a snort of laughter. He glanced over to a nearby food stall where a bearlike man was chewing on a chicken leg, watching them with a bemused expression.

The recruiter said with a scolding tone, "You are terribly misinformed, my lad. The colony of Thourion has some of the richest soil in the world." He smiled again, raising his eyebrows and leaned forward, dropping his voice to a whisper. "The local women of Italia—or the men or even boys if you prefer—are beautiful beyond compare. You can't imagine—"

"I can imagine quite well," interrupted Nikias. He'd heard about these Athenian colonies. Squalid places where the Athenians shipped off their poorer citizens to prevent overcrowding in the capital.

"You're right to be suspicious," said the man at the food stall. He wiped his mouth on a hunk of bread and ambled over to the recruiter's booth. "The only thing you'd have to look forward to in one of the colonies is catching some disease or getting murdered by the local barbarians."

"Not true!" exclaimed the recruiter. "The population of Thourion is fifteen thousand strong. They're building a new assembly hall and a gymnasium. Wheat production is rising—"

"Have you ever been there?" asked the other, picking a piece of chicken from a molar.

The recruiter's smile faded and he scowled. "No, I have not. But I have heard excellent reports."

The bearish man gave Nikias a conspiratorial grin. "That's what King Xerxes said before he invaded Greece, ha ha! And look what happened to him." And he slapped Nikias on the back.

Nikias laughed. He liked this kind of Athenian man. Straightforward and bluff—just like a Plataean.

"You've got a friend," said the bearish man.

Nikias felt a tug on his tunic and looked down to see a little black-haired slave boy—a one-eyed boy—staring up at him.

"Come with me," said the boy with a croaking voice. He gave the recruiter and the other man a suspicious look before darting off.

Nikias nodded at the two Athenian men and took off after the slave boy. He was fast and Nikias had to move quickly to keep up with him. He shot in and out of a maze of alleys, courtyards, and doorways until he came to a dark stair that led down to a foul-smelling tunnel. Nikias could see sunlight and the sea at one end and reckoned this was the main sewer conduit for the Piraeus District.

"I'm not going that way," he said to the boy when he saw the slave was moving away from the sea and into the darkness in the other direction.

The boy shrugged. "Timarkos said you might be afraid."

"I'm not afraid," said Nikias. "It stinks."

"You get used to it," said the boy.

"Isn't there another way?" he asked.

"Timarkos told me to bring you this way," said the boy. He smiled, showing a mouthful of broken teeth. "It's not far."

Nikias covered his nose with his hand and tried not to gag on the smell of the fetid wastewater. He had to crouch as they moved along a raised walkway, pressing his wounded shoulder to the clammy and slimy wall to keep from stepping off into the sewage. After a short distance they came to a small opening. He peered into it and saw the boy crawling down a dimly lit horizontal shaft.

"Zeus's balls," said Nikias, getting on his one good hand and knees. He inched his way down the shaft. After twenty feet he emerged into a small undercroft lit by torchlight. Somebody moved in the darkness and Nikias tensed. "Who's there?" he asked, clenching his left hand into a fist.

A man moved into the light and squinted at Nikias with weary eyes. "It's me, Timarkos," replied the wiry, goat-bearded Athenian spy. "Welcome to Athens, you sheep-brained fool."

NINETEEN

———◆———

Timarkos went to the opening of the shaft and shut a metal grate, then fastened it with a lock. "Climb," he ordered, pointing to a wooden ladder at the end of the chamber. The nimble slave boy was already ascending.

Nikias went slowly up the ladder—no easy task with one arm—and came up through the hole and onto a floor made of planks. He stood up and looked around. They were in a small room furnished with nothing more than a table and two chairs. There was a door at the end—locked with an iron bar—and two small square openings at the top of the opposite wall made to provide light.

"Sit," said Timarkos.

Nikias sat down on one of the chairs and glanced to the corner of the room where the slave boy was already curled up, staring at him like a little one-eyed bug. Timarkos took the chair across from Nikias, rubbed a hand across his face, and looked at him with an expression of contained exasperation. Finally he said, "You certainly have made things difficult for me."

Nikias smiled wryly. "Oh? The last time I saw you in Plataea you handed me an assassin's pig-sticker blade and sent me off to murder Nauklydes in the Assembly Hall. I would have been killed on the spot even if I *had* succeeded."

Timarkos raised his eyebrows. "You would have been remembered as a hero."

Nikias thought back to the terrifying moment. He had been about to run onto the floor of the Hall to stab Nauklydes in front of every citizen in Plataea. Fortunately his grandfather had arrived just in time. The Bull had exposed Nauklydes as a traitor without resorting to violence.

"My grandfather's way was better," said Nikias. "Nauklydes was executed by the people, not slaughtered by an individual."

Timarkos scratched the scraggly whiskers on his neck. "At the time I sent you to kill Nauklydes I did not know your grandfather was still alive. But everything worked out in the end, did it not? Nauklydes was given a stone tunic, as he well deserved."

"Do you know who drugged me last night?" Nikias asked.

"One of Kleon's whisperers," said Timarkos.

"Why did they dump me outside the city and order me to leave?"

"Athens is a snake pit of factions. But there are two main rivals vying for control of the empire. On one side there are men who will follow Perikles to Hades and back. And on the other are those who would gladly send his shade there forthwith, never to return."

"And which one are you?" asked Nikias. "Because that man who works for Kleon told me that *you* serve several masters."

"I do not serve any ruler or public official," said Timarkos proudly. "I am an agent of the Delian League and an enemy to all who would thwart its dominance. And I have eyes and ears in both camps—the supporters of Perikles as well as his enemies. You were stupid, yesterday, to create that ruckus in that theatre and have your things stolen. A bag of darics and a letter to Kleon's late concubine?" he added with an arch look. "I warned you not to trust Chusor."

"Who *is* Kleon?" asked Nikias. "What is his story?"

"He's a wealthy and powerful citizen," said Timarkos, "who hates Perikles and the other nobles and wants them all removed from power. Possibly even ostracized. He has started spreading rumors that Perikles has misused public funds—an offense that brings exile if proven!"

"How did *you* know about the gold?" said Nikias. "And the letter?"

"I told you already," replied Timarkos. "I have my sources in Kleon's inner circle."

"Is Kleon the one who tried to have Chusor murdered years ago?" asked Nikias. "Because Chusor was having an affair with the hetaera Sophia?"

Timarkos waved his hand in the air—a gesture of annoyance. "That is irrelevant. Your friend Chusor is a liar and a scoundrel. I warned you about him before."

Nikias glared at the spy. "Chusor risked his life to save Plataeans during the Theban sneak attack. We owe him a great debt."

"I wager Chusor had some other reason for being in Plataea," said Timarkos. "And I'll also bet he's long gone by now. Now, you must tell me something. Where did the Persian gold come from?"

Nikias quickly told him the story of finding the gold in the strongbox in Nauklydes's office.

"And what did you plan to do with the gold?" asked the spy.

"Hire mercenaries and bring them back to Plataea."

Timarkos smiled without mirth. "You've got balls, lad," he said. "Foolhardy idea, however. No mercenary in Athens would be stupid enough to walk into the middle of a Spartan siege, no matter how much gold you offered them. None of this has import, though. Kleon has the gold now and he'll be able to finance a pretty bit of espionage using those funds. Excellent work, young Oxlander."

"It was bad luck," said Nikias, burning with irritation at Timarkos's sarcasm. "Why is Kleon afraid of me?"

Timarkos burst out laughing. "*Afraid* of you? He's not *afraid* of you. He milked you for all of the information he wanted and cast you aside like a scooped-out pomegranate. You're nothing to him. An annoyance—a horsefly. But Kleon is the type of man who crushes those who displeasure him, like you or I would swat a bug."

Nikias sat back and sighed. He felt like an imbecile. He'd wasted an opportunity—squandered the Persian gold and accomplished nothing to help Plataea. "How goes it with the Plataean emissary?" he asked, hoping for some good news. Several days before he had left Plataea, his grandfather had sent two aged generals to Athens on a mission: to beg Perikles's permission to allow the Plataeans to sign a peace accord with the Spartans.

Timarkos's face looked truly sad when he said, "The two honorable generals have failed to sway Perikles, even with your city's promise of neutrality in the event Sparta and Athens go to war."

"But why?" asked Nikias. "What good can come if Plataea is besieged and destroyed by Sparta?"

"If Plataea is allowed to exit the Delian League," said Timarkos, "other city-states who are pressured by the Spartans will have no reason to resist. They will jump ship. If Plataea stands firm, however, then your city will be seen as a shining example of loyalty to the League. That is why Perikles cannot allow the peace treaty with Plataea and Sparta."

"And will Perikles give us no help at all?" asked Nikias. "No warriors or cavalry?"

"It goes against his policy," said Timarkos. "He believes that we Athenians can outlast the Spartans behind the walls of *our* citadel. That same strategy applies to you Plataeans."

"Perikles seems more like the enemy of Plataea than Kleon," said Nikias bitterly. "Maybe I should hope Kleon comes to power. Maybe then my city will get some warriors."

"It's not as simple as that, lad. The beating heart of the Athenian Empire is to the east of Athens: the islands and colonies under our control are where the real wealth comes from. The Spartans can't touch the islands because their navy is worthless. And all the treasure from those places can be shipped here to the Piraeus port and fed safely up the Long Walls to the citadel—grain to feed the people of Athens, and silver to fill our coffers. The Oxlands are merely an afterthought. It doesn't matter if Plataea falls, in the grand scheme of the empire. Even Kleon knows this to be true."

Nikias shook his head. He couldn't believe what he was hearing. "Plataea an *afterthought*? We stood by you at Marathon. And against Xerxes. We've fought in a dozen wars for Athens since the Persian invasions. My own father died at Koronea helping the Athenians fight Thebes and the other Oxland rebels. Yet we're merely an afterthought?"

"This coming war with the Spartans will be won or lost on the seas," said Timarkos. "We cannot defeat the Spartans on land. And so we must sacrifice that which we cannot afford to hold. That is Perikles's plan—to let the Spartans ravage the regions around Attika while we wait them out inside the citadel of Athens. The Long Walls will enable us to keep Athens fed from the sea."

Nikias thought of something his grandfather had told him a year ago: that if Sparta and Athens ever did go to war, Plataea would be caught between them like an olive crushed between two grinding stones. He felt like that olive now—flattened . . . utterly demoralized.

"Why were you even in Plataea spying on Nauklydes the traitor?" asked Nikias. "Why concern yourself with my city—why talk to me now—if what happens in the Oxlands is meaningless?"

Timarkos leaned forward and for the first time Nikias saw him drop his haughty mask. "I am not Perikles. Nor am I Kleon. And I think they are both wrong in regards to Plataea. I believe your city-state is crucial to this coming war. I am of the opinion that the Spartans will dash themselves to pieces on the rock of your high walls. If anything their siege will buy us more time to build up our fleet and make an attack into the heart of Spartan territory. The Spartans will gather their forces in Plataea and leave their back door wide open. There are no walled cities in Sparta, as I'm sure you know. An invasion force could wipe out their meager defenders and raise a second Helot revolt from which the Spartans would never recover."

"A new Helot revolt?" said Nikias, stirred by this notion. "So you see Plataea as a trap for the Spartans?"

"Yes," said Timarkos. "And I will do everything in my power to help prevent your city from falling. But things hang by a thread, Nikias. Athens is teeming with Persian spies. They are the ones financing the Spartan campaign in the Oxlands. You must take this message back to your grandfather—" He stopped mid-sentence, looking frantically around the room. "Where's the boy?" he asked.

Nikias looked to the corner of the room where the one-eyed boy had been sitting. But he was gone.

A moment later they heard the sound of metal crashing on metal from below—from the place where Nikias had followed the boy up to this chamber.

"The grate is open! The boy has betrayed me," said Timarkos. He turned toward the door that led to the street just as something heavy slammed against it from the outside.

"We're trapped!" said Nikias.

"Not quite," said Timarkos. "Let me get on your shoulders. Quickly!"

He scrambled onto Nikias's back and got into a standing position on his shoulders. Nikias craned his head and saw that there was a wooden trapdoor in the center of the ten-foot-high ceiling. Timarkos reached for a metal ring and yanked open the door. A knotted rope fell down into the room. Timarkos scrambled up the rope like a monkey. When he had climbed through the hole in the top he shouted down, "Come on!"

"I can only use one arm!" said Nikias. He glanced at the door in the wall—the top hinge broke away from the brick as the barred portal was pounded again.

"Grab on!" commanded Timarkos from the trapdoor. "I'll pull you up."

Nikias grabbed the rope with his one good arm and wrapped his feet around the end. Timarkos tried to pull Nikias up but he was too heavy. The spy let go of the rope and disappeared from the hole above.

"Timarkos!" Nikias shouted urgently.

The portal cracked and slammed to the floor. At the same time a man rushed up the ladder from the undercroft. Nikias kicked the man in the face, then spun around and smashed his fist into the nose of the first man bulling his way through the door.

But more men came.

Nikias crushed a man's nose. Dislocated another's jaw. Teeth and blood flew. But it was no use. There were too many of them. Five strong men pinned him down. They tied his wrists behind his back and he screamed from the pain in his wounded shoulder.

A hand grabbed him by the hair, yanked back his head, and forced him to stare into a familiar face. "Hello, lad," said the friendly bearlike man he'd met while talking to the recruiter in the shipyard marketplace.

"You?" gasped Nikias.

The man glanced up at the trapdoor in the ceiling, then he stared at Nikias with a wicked look—an expression that was entirely different from the cheerful fellow he'd been pretending to be a short while ago out in the marketplace.

"You were much easier to catch than they said you'd be," sneered the man, leaning in and breathing his rank breath into Nikias's face. "There's a ship waiting to take you on a little voyage to Sparta."

He crammed a wad of sailcloth into Nikias's mouth and tied a piece of rope around his jaw to hold the gag, muffling the young fighter's desperate screams.

PART II

The Athenian leader Perikles was a shrewd tactician, a charismatic politician, and an arbiter of taste. But when he gave the funeral speech on the Akropolis, declaring that "War is a necessity," the nature of his soul was made public; for wise men realized that he was a disciple of that most despised of all the Greek pantheon: Ares—the god of war.

—Papyrus fragment from the "Lost History" of the Peloponnesian War by the "Exiled Scribe"

ONE

———————◆———————

Kolax's stolen horse went three-legged lame a quarter of a mile from the walls of Athens. He immediately dismounted and inspected the animal. By the way it was holding its left foreleg he reckoned the animal had snapped a tendon. He wasn't surprised. He'd driven the ill-bred horse extremely hard over five miles of pitted and rocky territory.

He turned and looked up the long, straight road—the same road that he and Nikias had been traveling on when Nikias's horse had bolted yesterday. He could see the slave-hunters in the distance—the ones who'd been pursuing him all the way from the glade where he'd slaughtered the Mollossian hounds . . . five riders moving at a relentless pace.

Kolax faced the other direction—toward the walls of Athens. He could see the brick wall of the city snaking across the countryside, all the way down to the bay far to the south. He could even make out the figures of Skythian archers on the crenellated walkways. His father was so close now! But he knew the guards at the gates would stop him from entering—question him to see if he was a spy . . . an enemy of the Hellenes. That would give the slave-hunters enough time to catch up.

He started running, stripping himself of any unnecessary weight, casting aside his arrow case and cloak—even the beautiful short sword Chusor had made him. The only weapon that he had left was the small knife strapped to his ankle. Half-way to the gates he glanced over his shoulder and saw that the riders were much closer now, galloping in single file down the road.

Soon they would be on him.

Kolax pumped his arms, gasping for breath with each step. He felt a sharp pain in the lower part of his lungs, as though long tattoo needles were stabbing straight through his ribs.

The tall gray limestone towers of the Dipylon Gate loomed ahead. The oak portals spanning the gap between the towers were opened wide. The area in front of this entrance was crowded with people—all of them waiting to be scrutinized by the guards. A band of shepherds, however, had already been given leave to enter, and they were guiding their flock of a hundred or so sheep through the archway.

Kolax heard hooves pounding on the stones behind him. The slave-hunters were close now. Within bowshot. They were shouting to the guards at the gates. Trying to get their attention.

A Skythian curse burst from Kolax's lips. He could not let them catch him! But what could he do? Hide in the crowd? Scale the wall? Turn and fight? None of these seemed like good ideas. He was as good as dead.

He saw a little stray lamb gambol away from the flock and, without thinking, ran to the animal and scooped it up—he'd done the same thing a thousand times before tending his father's flock back home in Skythia. He kept running, straight into the herd, and lifted the lamb onto his shoulders, hunching down so the animal's legs dangled over his face on either side. He kept moving with the flock, past the armed guards, and into the dark space under the thick wall's arch.

He went into the inner courtyard, an area protected by another set of towers. Kolax recognized this place was designed as a trap—a way to trick invaders into thinking they'd breached the gates, only to be stuck between the archers who lined the high walkways. He glanced up at the battlements. All of the archers up there were Skythians! The sight of their distinctive peaked caps filled him with joy! He was about to call out to the men—shout that Kolax, son of Osyrus of the Bindi tribe needed help—when he noticed something that made him reel.

"By Athena's hairy gash," he uttered, his face turning pale.

The caps of the archers were woven with a pattern of black stripes. The Skythian archers up there were Nuris! The blood enemies of Kolax's tribe!

The sheep packed together in this small courtyard started bleating—a panicked noise that echoed between the narrow walls of the causeway and made the flesh on the back of Kolax's neck tingle. Then he heard shouts from outside the gates.

"—a Skythian boy! Murdered my slave! He must be here. Look for his red hair!"

"Yes, General Lukos!"

One of the shepherds turned and, seeing a strange boy holding one of his sheep, raised his eyebrows and asked, "What are you doing with my lamb?"

Kolax hefted the animal over his shoulders and tossed it at the surprised shepherd. Then he elbowed his way through the flock, sprinted through the second archway, and into the marketplace. There were thousands of people milling about and he swiftly lost himself in the multitudes, darting in and out of the merchants' stalls like a wary fox. Eventually he found an alleyway that was empty.

He stopped and crouched down against a low wall, trying to stop the frantic beating of his heart. He couldn't help but laugh—that stupid lamb had saved his life.

A familiar pungent odor hit him in the face. He stood up and looked over the low wall and saw animal skins stretched on wooden frames and a row of dyeing vats. The slaves who worked in the tannery—their arms stained dark brown up to their shoulders—sat huddled together eating a meal in the adjoining courtyard.

He jumped over the wall and strode to a vat of brown-colored liquid. He took out his ankle knife, cut the cord of his topknot, and let his long red hair fall to his shoulders. Then he dunked his head in the vat until his hair was thoroughly soaked. He stripped off his Skythian pants and jacket and used them to dry the excess dye from his head, then tossed the ruined clothes into a pile in the corner.

One of the slaves' tunics—a dirty gray rectangle of cloth—hung from a hook on the wall. Kolax grabbed this and put it on, fumbling with the thin cord that pulled the tunic tight at the waist. He finally got it tied and leapt back over the wall and into the alley before any of the tanner slaves noticed him. He walked slowly back to the marketplace and found an armor-maker, gazing at his reflection in the burnished bronze of a shield.

Kolax didn't recognize himself with his new hair color and absurd slave's outfit. The dye had stained the pale skin of his forehead and cheeks a dirty brown. It was a good thing his father had tattooed his back with the family gryphon, he thought, because his papa wouldn't recognize this boy standing here now.

But how was he going to find his father in this huge city? He'd never seen so many people in one place in his life. They were like bees in a hive. He looked in the direction of the rising sun and saw the limestone plateau of the Akropolis, and the colorfully painted Temple of Athena on top. The temple was so impossibly beautiful it looked as though it had been made by gods.

That was where he needed to go—the highest place in the citadel. He would be able to see the whole city from up there. Like climbing to the top of a towering fir tree back home.

He ran all the way to the base of the Akropolis and sprinted up the flight of seemingly endless stairs shaded by olive trees, climbing the five hundred feet to the top of the plateau. His young legs were strong, though, and soon he stood in front of the Temple of Athena, staring in wonder at the marble building with its lifelike statues of men, women, and even horsemen carved on the topmost part of the temple.

The Akropolis grounds swarmed with people, some going in and out of the temple while others walked around it with their necks craned, staring and pointing at the painted statues. Kolax spotted more Nuri archers and slunk away from the area of the temple. He knew that the city's treasure was inside the building, and the place was well guarded. But why did it have to be guarded by Nuri? He hadn't even known that the hateful Nuri were in the employ of the Athenians.

He walked quickly to the low southern wall and leaned on the stone, staring down at the teeming agora. A blast of warm wind swept up from below and hit his face. He squinted and peered to the northwest, in the direction of the Kithaeron Mountains, and saw the place several miles from Athens where he and Iphigenia had hidden in the little grove. He wondered how she was doing. He felt guilty that he had been forced to break his word. He'd told her that he would come back for her no matter what.

"How will I ever see her again?" he wondered sadly.

With his keen eyes he retraced his flight over the rolling hills to the Athenian Road, then through the Dipylon Gate and the marketplace. He could even see the tannery from up here. But where would his father be? He knew there were at least two thousand Skythian archers living in the citadel of Athens as well as the walled port five miles to the south. There was so much ground to cover.

He had to find his papa, he told himself. Everything would be good once he found his papa. . . .

He turned and squatted with his back to the wall, staring in the direction of the temple, searching desperately for a fellow tribesmen amongst the many guards. Bindi wore red stripes on the sleeves and leggings to signify the number of heads that a warrior had taken. But all of the guards that he could see up here were wearing Nuri hats woven with black-and-white stripes to mimic the markings of the deadly grass vipers of Skythia.

Curse the Nuri! Any one of these enemy archers would slit his throat if he knew that Kolax was a Bindi. Or push him off this high wall and send him plummeting to his death. At least that's what Kolax would do if he was given the chance of killing one of the enemy—the people who had been responsible for slaughtering his tribe and selling him into slavery.

Just then an archer strode by wearing the distinctive purple leggings of a Hippermolgi tribesman. The "mare-milkers" were allies of the Bindi!

Kolax jumped up and ran after him, holding up the palm of his arrow hand in the age-old Skythian greeting. But the archer—a ferocious-looking man with a high topknot and bright red beard—curled his lip in disgust, grabbed the handle of his whip, and spat in Greek, "Lower your eyes from mine, dirty thrall, or I'll blind you."

Kolax cringed and jumped out of the warrior's way. He'd forgotten he was dressed like the lowliest kind of slave—his hair, hands, and arms were stained with the dye. Back home defiant male slaves had their eyes put out and were made to milk sheep for the rest of their miserable lives. He turned his head away quickly, shielding his eyes from the archer—an expression of extreme deference to a warrior of his rank.

"Please, great warrior," Kolax said in Skythian. "I'm looking for my father. His name is—"

The archer took a step forward and slapped Kolax across the face with the handle of his whip. "Get out of my sight, you fucking whore's son," he said, and went on his way toward the Akropolis entrance.

Kolax stood rooted to the rocky ground, shaking with fury. Blood trickled down from his forehead and into his eye and he swiped it away with the back of his hand.

"Those archers are dangerous, lad," said a voice. "Better stay away from them. They've got terrible tempers."

Kolax turned and saw a dark-skinned man, naked except for a loincloth, carrying a long pole with a tortoiseshell harp hanging from the end. Kolax was about to walk away—he had no use for musicians or beggars—when a raven flew down from the pediment of the temple and landed on the bard's shoulder, rubbing its beak on the side of the man's head. The handsome bird's blue-black wings glistened in the sun.

The bard smiled and sang, "*Good people, a fistful of grain please give—or a small piece of bread so my raven may live.*" He took out a crust and let the raven take it from his fingers. "That's what I sing at every house I pass on my journeys. They usually give enough bread for me and Telemakos here."

Kolax ignored the talkative man and walked to the wall again, staring at the city morosely. He wondered what had happened to Nikias. Was he down there somewhere?

"You look like you're at a crossroads," said the bard, who'd sidled up beside him. "You've obviously never been here before. Come with me. I know this city as well as the head of my prick. You look hungry. I'll beg a little bread and we can eat together. Maybe even get some wine."

Kolax was about to turn and walk away when he realized the bard had just spoken in heavily accented but perfectly understandable Skythian. Kolax's jaw dropped and the bard flashed a smile showing a set of healthy white teeth.

"So you *are* Skythian," said the bard, tugging on his curly beard. "You're probably wondering how I could tell?"

"Yes," said Kolax. "Can you read minds?"

"There are many clues," said the bard. "I spent five years wandering through your country, so I'm able to read the signs. You've got the face of a Skythian, that's for certain. No amount of dirt or dye or whatever it is on your skin can mask the hideous upturned nose of your people—a curse from Zeus, methinks. But it's also in the way you walk. The bowlegged strut of a boy who's ridden a horse more than he's walked."

This bard was turning out to be a smart sort of foreigner, Kolax mused. Maybe he would help him find his father! He glanced over and saw the Skythian archer who'd threatened him had returned to pacing the grounds and was coming back toward him, eyeing him suspiciously.

Kolax smiled at the bard and pointed his chin in the direction of the agora. "Let's get something to eat," he said, pulling on the man's sleeve and leading him back toward the great stairs. He had gold. There was no reason he should starve to death in a city full of food. He could pretend that he was the bard's slave and blend into this strange city.

"Good idea," said the bard, keeping pace with him. "Let's earn some bread for Telemakos here. And I'll teach you how to tie that outfit you're wearing. You've got it on backward."

TWO

Nikias counted ten of the henchmen surrounding him. They were murderous-looking scoundrels with scars and missing teeth. They marched him down the main street of the Piraeus, his hands bound behind his back and a rope around his neck, pulling him along like a captured slave. The bearlike man, who the other men called "Commander," held the rope.

Nikias tried to walk as slowly as he could, buying himself some time before they arrived at the ship that would take him to Sparta. But every time he paused in his steps the commander yanked on the rope, tugging his head forward violently.

"Come on, pole-pleaser," said the man. "You'll wish you'd taken that recruiter up on his offer to go to the colonies after the Spartans get through with you."

The henchmen laughed. Several of them whispered things that they were going to do to Nikias once they got him alone in the hold of the ship. Things that made Nikias's skin crawl. He knew what men were capable of doing to other men. He'd witnessed the torture of a captured Theban general. The enemy had resisted beyond what Nikias thought was humanly possible before he'd given up vital information about the plans of his attacking forces. But not before he'd been ruined forever as a man.

Nikias's face tingled with a mixture of fury and terror. He felt humiliated to be paraded through the streets like a slave—people were leaning out the windows of their homes, gawking at him. But he didn't want this shameful walk to end. Once they got him on that ship, he knew that his life would be over.

His only chance was to make a break for it now, while he was still in a public place.

He remembered something his grandfather told him once: the most dangerous opponent is the one that you think is helpless.

If he could catch these men by surprise and take a few of them down, he might be able to make a break for the drydocks and then to the bay. He knew he could swim without the use of his arms. He'd done it before as a child countless times in the Korinthian Sea—a test of endurance with his friends. He could swim on his back out to a trireme and tell the sailors he was part of the Plataean emissary's entourage. They would take him on board. He would be safe.

He looked the commander's men up and down, searching to see if they carried weapons, but he didn't see any. And he was thankful that all swords, bows, and daggers were banned from inside the city walls of Athens and the Piraeus. "They'll wish they had metal in their hands in a second," thought Nikias, steeling himself for the fight. He wasn't going to let them defile his body. And he would die before falling into the hands of the Spartans.

Up ahead he saw a line of half a dozen mule carts coming toward them, each stacked fifteen feet high with bags of grain. Nikias realized the carts would take up most of the roadway, forcing the henchmen to stand on one side of the narrow lane. This was his chance. He slowed down, baiting his captor to jerk on the rope.

"Come on!" ordered the commander as he gave a vicious tug.

Nikias pretended to stumble forward and fell face-first on the ground, landing on his chest and lifting his face to protect his teeth from the stone pavers.

The commander leaned over him and wrenched the rope. "You hold us up one more time," he said, "and I'll kill you right here!"

Nikias looked up as the grain carts started to rattle past. The henchmen stepped aside, breaking up their tight ranks. Nikias struggled to a sitting position and refused to move as the wheels rolled by. One of the henchmen kicked him on his backside, but he glared at the commander with defiance.

The commander pulled back his fist to punch Nikias in the face and in doing so he let his hold on the neck rope go slack. Nikias moved as fast as a whip, sweeping out his legs and taking the commander's feet out from under him. The heavy man landed hard on his side. Nikias lifted his right leg and slammed his heel against the commander's throat, crushing the windpipe.

"Grab him!" shouted one of the henchmen.

Nikias did a somersault to gain some distance, then spun around on his buttocks to face the enemy, doing a move called "the crab"—the last defense of a wounded pankrator. He backed up along the ground on his haunches, kicking up with one leg and then the other, snaking between one of the slow-moving carts.

He glanced over at the commander—the man was writhing on the road, his face turning purple. Two of his men were trying to help him, but Nikias knew he would be dead in seconds.

Nikias sprang to his feet and hopped onto the back of one of the moving carts, squirming onto a grain sack. Now he was level with his attackers, and the first henchman to try and pull him off the cart got the flat of Nikias's foot to the face and his nose exploded in a spray of blood. The other henchmen backed off and shouted for the cart to stop. When the cart's driver ignored them they pulled the surprised man off his seat.

"Hey!" yelled the driver as he landed on the back of his mule.

The beast panicked and tried to flee, turning and running toward a nearby courtyard entrance. The cart came to a crashing halt as it got stuck in the doorway of the house. Nikias clambered up the precariously stacked bags of grain, climbing them like stairs until he was even with the flat rooftop of the house.

"Get the bastard!" shouted one of the henchmen. They clambered up the grain sacks after him.

Nikias whirled and caught one of the men in the chest. The man flailed backward and grabbed one of his companions as he fell. The two tumbled off the roof and landed headfirst onto the stone street below.

Nikias sprinted across the rooftop, flinging himself across the gap to another flat roof next door, then bounded down a flight of stairs that led to the street. At the bottom of the stairs was an empty sconce used to hold a pine torch. He hooked the rope that was tied around his neck onto one of the hooks of the sconce and jerked his head to the side. The rope came free, and Nikias spat the gag from his mouth. Through the doorway he could see the road that ran above the boat sheds. That's where he had to go!

Bolting from the entrance, he turned a corner and ran straight into a man blocking his path. The man landed on his buttocks, but the mariner—a living knot of coiled muscles—vaulted instantly to his feet as if shot from a bow and punched Nikias in the stomach with the force of a sledgehammer.

Nikias sank to his knees with the wind knocked out of him.

"Watch where you're going, blockhead!" roared the indignant oarsman, standing over Nikias in a threatening posture, his manly face set in a scowl.

Nikias stared up at his cousin Phoenix in amazement. He tried to say his cousin's name but the man's punch had been so powerful that Nikias could not take in enough air to make any noise other than a strangled groan.

"Leave him to us!"

The seven remaining henchmen converged on Nikias at the same time and tackled him. One of them wrapped his thick arm around Nikias's throat while the others clamped down on his arms and legs, hefting him up and hauling him away.

Nikias opened his jaws wide and locked onto the henchman's forearm that was strangling him, biting through the skin and straight into the muscle. The man shrieked and let go and Nikias screamed, "Phoenix! Phoenix!"

The henchman with the bleeding arm started pounding Nikias in the face. But Nikias kept calling his cousin's name, squirming like a mad thing to be free.

He lashed out with his knees. Flung his head. Tried to bite them. Anything to keep them from taking him away from his cousin.

He heard shouting and the henchmen dropped him to the ground. The next thing he saw was Phoenix's face—the face of a hero carved in marble—leaning over him.

"Who are you?" Phoenix asked. "Do I *know* you? How did you know my name?"

"Cousin," wheezed Nikias. "Nikias."

"Gods!" said Phoenix as recognition slowly came to him. "Nikias? What are you doing here?"

"I need your help," said Nikias.

"That's an understatement," said Phoenix.

"Leave the prisoner to us!" ordered one of the henchmen angrily.

Phoenix helped Nikias to a sitting position. Nikias squinted through swollen eyes and saw a wall of oarsmen—twenty or so mariners. They were restraining the seven henchmen—pinning their arms behind their backs. The ruffians looked like puny little children compared to the hugely muscled oarsmen.

"Prisoner?" asked Phoenix, baffled. He looked at the man who had spoken— a brute with a low brow. "You! What is going on here? You're no Skythian archer," he added with a sneer. "Where's your whip and topknot?"

The man refused to look Phoenix in the eye and no one responded. Phoenix turned to Nikias with a questioning lift of his eyebrows.

"They're Kleon's men," said Nikias, blood pouring from his mouth. "They're taking me to a ship. To send me to Sparta."

"The lad's crazy," said one of the henchmen. "We're taking him to the Piraeus jail. There's a bounty on his head. He raped a girl."

"He's lying!" spat Nikias through clenched teeth. "They're Kleon's men," he repeated.

Phoenix slowly wiped the blood from Nikias's lips with his own tunic. Then he stood up and faced the henchmen, eyes ablaze.

"Kleon's men, eh?" Phoenix said in a voice full of menace. He spat the name out again as if it were poison on his tongue. "*Kleon's* men?"

"Leave the country lad to us!" said the henchman. "Or you'll regret it, oar-puller."

Phoenix strode over to the man who'd just spoken and smashed him in the chin with his enormous fist. The man dropped to the ground, dead to the world. Phoenix glared at the other henchmen.

"Do you know who I am?" asked Phoenix with outrage. He raised his arms dramatically, like an actor on the stage, flexing his biceps. "I am Phoenix, captain of *Sea Nymph*! And if any of you dogs-of-Kleon—that pustule of a man who slandered our leader, Perikles—would care to say another word, I'll happily pull your tongue from your mouth with my bare hands and give you a taste of each other's arse-holes! Now, get out of my sight!"

He gestured for his men to let Kleon's thugs go. The oarsmen tossed the henchmen aside, kicking them as they skulked away.

Phoenix slipped a curved boat knife from a sheath on his hip and cut the ropes binding Nikias's hands. "Now," he said, helping him to his feet, "let's get you cleaned up, my young cousin. It appears you've got an interesting story to tell."

THREE

———————◆———————

"Telemakos always leads me to where I'm going," said the bard with a laugh, pointing at his raven flying above them on the tree-lined lane. "He has a way of finding us good luck."

Kolax, who was walking next to the bard and toting the man's staff and harp, nodded in understanding. His father had always told him that ravens were enchanted with a powerful magic. It was wise for this wandering musician to put his trust in such an intelligent animal. Because instead of being a smart sort of foreigner like Kolax had first thought, the bard had turned out to be one of the biggest donkey-brains he'd ever met.

In the short amount of time it had taken them to walk down from the Akropolis to this shady road, the bard had spouted a whole cartload of foolish sheep dung. Tales of lands far to the east where men could stand on red-hot coals without feeling pain, or make their spirits fly amongst the stars merely by concentrating on a third eye in their foreheads. Or the notion that the sun was a giant ball of fire rather than the Sun god's chariot flying across the sky. *That* one was really funny.

He glanced at the bare-chested bard and wondered how someone could get so muscular merely from walking from town to town and plucking catgut strings all day. The man had the biceps of a Skythian bowman and the rippled stomach of a wrestler. He would make a fine warrior if he tossed aside his tortoiseshell harp and grasped the handle of a sword. But the crazy Greek claimed he'd renounced violence! And refused to eat animal flesh! Absurd beyond belief.

Kolax knew a good thing when it came his way, though. The bard blended into Athens like all the other odd-looking characters in the capital, and as long as he stayed by this man's side, Kolax would fit in too. He'd offered to carry the musician's staff and harp for a reason: now he could pass for his servant. General

Lukos and his slave-hunters would have a difficult time spotting him in this improved disguise.

And it was a great relief to be around someone who could talk in Skythian after these long months away from home. Even if the bard did speak his tongue with an outlandish Greek accent.

"My name is Andros of Naxos," said the bard.

"Kolax of the Bindi," replied the boy.

"I don't suppose you can write out your name? Or anything for that matter?"

Kolax laughed. What a ridiculous question. "My father taught me the Three Skills—riding, shooting, and the counting of our gold," he replied.

"Illiterate like most of your barbarian kin," said Andros with a sigh. "I am writing a book and would have let you read some of it."

"What's it about?"

"The secret to eternal happiness."

Kolax grinned. "I know the secret to happiness already—riding better than any warrior alive, shooting three arrows in three heartbeats, and possessing a clay pot full of gold darics buried in the ground beneath the floor of a spacious round tent."

"The secret," said Andros, acting as though he hadn't heard anything that Kolax had just said, "is to let the world slip through your fingers like sand."

Kolax had absolutely no idea what Andros meant by that, but he made an admiring grunting sound in the back of his throat. Hopefully that would shut the man up.

"You must release everything," Andros went on. "Love, wealth, even happiness itself. Only then will you find peace of mind. For peace of mind is greater than any earthly glory, whether it be wealth or conquest."

This last idiocy made Kolax burst out laughing. He laughed so hard that he started to choke. His throat was still sore from where the slave-hunter had tried to strangle him with the whip.

"Gods!" exclaimed Andros. "Poor lad! Your face is turning as purple as a grape."

Andros led him to a nearby public fountain and encouraged him to drink. Kolax cupped his hands and held the cool water to his lips, gulping it down.

The raven flew over to them and landed on the edge of the fountain, and took a sip from the water pouring from the mouth of a stone satyr. The bird eyed Kolax, then let forth a low *carrrrock* sound. Andros reacted as though the raven had spoken an understandable word.

"Yes," said the bard. "You're right, Telemakos. Some leaf would be a good idea." He took the leather pouch from around his neck and emptied the contents onto the marble seat in front of the fountain—a clay pipe, a flint, and another, smaller pouch filled with dried hemp, the sight of which made Kolax's eyes grow wide with delight.

The bard filled the pipe and got the leaves smoldering. "Something I discovered in your country," he said and gave a rueful smile.

Kolax eagerly took the offered pipe from Andros's hand, sucking in the vapor. It was strong leaf and within a short time he felt his body start to change . . . as though he were made of arrow strings pulled taut and then loosened by the hand of a god.

Andros inhaled a long draft from the pipe and held the air in his lungs. "Good Skythian leaf," he said in the back of his throat.

Kolax grinned, then took several more puffs from the pipe. After a while he closed his eyes and imagined riding across a grassy plain with the sound of the horse's hooves thundering on the ground like war drums. He could smell the wet Skythian grass . . . and hear his mother's voice calling to him—"Come, child, come, my darling horseman. Your dinner is on the spit. Your skull cup is full." But no matter where he rode, he could not track her down.

A giant arrow—as tall as an ancient pine—slammed into the earth in front of him, blocking his path. The shaft was painted with black-and-white stripes to signify the arrowhead had been laced with poison.

Kolax's father had taught him how to make Skythian poison when he was a small boy. After trapping grass vipers in special baskets on the ends of poles, the snakes were subdued with hemp smoke, then the venom "milked" from their fangs. This whitish poison was mixed with human feces in a leather pouch and steeped underground for the cycle of one moon. A tiny scratch from a weapon tainted with this poison could send the mightiest warrior into paroxysms of agonizing pain followed soon after by death.

Kolax got on his knees and dug in the earth beneath the arrow and found a leather pouch. He carefully untied the drawstring's knots. When he pulled open the bag he could see nothing inside except an inky blackness. He put his face close to the opening. A viper leapt from the bag and bit him on the cheek.

He opened his eyes and looked around anxiously. He was lying down in front of the fountain. The bard and the raven were gone. He felt an ache in his guts and a powerful thirst. He glanced up at the position of the sun and reckoned he'd been there for over an hour. He'd never experienced that kind of vision while smoking hemp before, and wondered if the bard had mixed it with some other drug.

He drank some more water, then got to his feet and continued walking on the tree-lined road that led back to the agora. But no matter where he looked he couldn't find the bard. He felt lonely and chided himself for missing the foolish man. Andros had been kind to him, though. And he needed a friend in this huge city, especially one who spoke his language. He couldn't figure out why the bard had left him there by the fountain.

He sat down on a stone sidewalk in front of a crowded wineshop and rested his face in his hands. Hunger gnawed his guts. He still had the darics Nikias had given him for safekeeping, but he reckoned that using Persian gold in the market of Athens would draw suspicion. He pulled out the pouch that he wore around his neck. Then he opened it and started swallowing the gold pieces, one by one. That would keep his stomach from growling. And his guts were a much safer place to hide the gold.

He thought of the girl Iphigenia and wondered if she was still up in the tree where he'd left her. She had had enough food and water for only a few days. How would he ever get back to her and save her from her master? He wished the spear he'd thrown had found its mark in the Athenian warrior's chest, rather than slaying his pretty horse.

An old white-haired slave was sweeping off the sidewalk and he nudged Kolax with a tattered broom, saying, "Move on, my son," before giving him another gentle push.

Kolax got up and walked back into the packed agora, his heart as heavy as a lead ball for a sling. He thought of Andros's raven and looked to the sky, but all he saw were seagulls circling overhead and a few noisy crows in a treetop. He turned his gaze to the Akropolis. If the raven was flying anywhere in the city, he would be able to spot the bird from up there.

He sprinted all the way back and stood on the steps of the Temple of Athena, keeping an eye out for the Skythian archer who had struck him. He scanned the city below with his eagle's eyes. His father had always told him he could spot a flea on a fox's arse from five hundred paces.

But he saw only gulls—their white bodies and gray wings sailing the skies.

He walked over to the temple and stared up at the painted statues carved into the pediments. What impressed him most was a marble frieze showing a line of cavalry. The horses seemed about to leap right off the roof. Whoever had carved those animals knew his horses.

The wind shifted just then and he heard a sound that made the skin on the back of his neck tingle. It was the faint but unmistakable call of a raven. He ran around to the other side of the temple and gazed down.

Kolax smiled. He saw a raven, five bowshots away to the west. There was no mistaking the eagle-sized bird. Telemakos was flying in a wide circle over a cluster of brick buildings that were surrounded by a wall. It looked like an old fort of some kind—a stronghold built within the walls of Athens.

Kolax could see Skythian archers going in and out of the complex as well as

Athenian guardsmen standing on top of its flat roof. He watched as Telemakos dove into a courtyard of the fort and disappeared. He wondered what the raven was doing there. Was Andros in some kind of trouble? He had to find out.

He flew down the steps of the Akropolis as though his feet had sprouted wings.

FOUR

———————◆———————

Phoenix and Nikias sat together at a table in the back corner of the Golden Fleece. The wineshop was packed with customers, all of them mariners from the *Sea Nymph* and other ships loyal to Perikles, and the space throbbed with the din of boisterous talk and laughter.

Nikias wanted more than anything to eat, but his jaw ached from the punches he'd taken—and one molar felt loose—so he sipped his wine and told his cousin the tale of the Theban sneak attack on Plataea while Phoenix, unnerved by the story, picked at his food.

The mariner listened attentively for over an hour, stopping Nikias now and again to ask about particular details, or to exclaim with sorrow or wonder at the harrowing narrative. He was particularly shaken by the news that Nikias's mother had been murdered by the Theban invaders, and did not attempt to hide his tears for his dead aunt.

Nikias finished up with a short description of why he had come to Athens, and how he had run afoul of Kleon's whisperers. After he was done Phoenix poured his cousin another cup of wine and ordered him to drink up.

"How many Thebans do you think you killed in the invasion?" asked Phoenix.

Nikias shook his head wearily. "I don't know. Twenty, perhaps."

Phoenix blew out his cheeks. "Gods, Nikias! Those are respectable numbers!"

"It's the Theban who I *didn't* kill that matters most of all," said Nikias.

"The spy Eurymakus?"

"Yes. I'm afraid that grass viper will come back to bite Plataea again."

"Any man," said Phoenix, "who has the stomach to cut off his own arm to save his life is dangerous."

Nikias took a piece of bread and sopped up the oil on his plate, chewing gingerly with one side of his mouth, brooding. "I have to get an audience with Perikles," he said after a while. "I know it sounds foolish. But I must leave the Piraeus and get back to Athens."

"You've killed one of Kleon's hirelings," said Phoenix. "He'll not stop until you're on a spit." He slid a chunk of roasted meat off of a skewer and popped it in his mouth. "You're in bilgewater up to your chin, cousin, and that's no lie. And you can't just walk up to Perikles's house and knock on the door like some peddler."

"What do I do?" asked Nikias.

"The first thing we have to do is to get you back into the city."

"It's a six-mile walk from the Piraeus to the first gate of Athens," said Nikias. "Kleon's men will be able to catch me anywhere along the road."

"We'll simply walk along the Bulkheads," said Phoenix.

The Bulkheads, Nikias knew, was the name Athenian mariners used for the Long Walls—two parallel bulwarks with a narrow road in between, running all the way from the bastions of the Piraeus to the southeastern gates of Athens. Even in the event of a prolonged siege, the Athenians would be able to use the Long Walls to get supplies from the port of Piraeus. The construction of this fortification, with its thirty-foot-high walls, had infuriated the Spartans back when they were Athenian allies. It was the first sign to the Spartans that the Athenians were planning ahead for a potential war with them.

"I'll be recognized," said Nikias.

"That's easy enough to fix," said Phoenix. He grinned and looked around the room. He caught sight of the mariner he was looking for, put two fingers to his lips, and let forth a piercing whistle. "Ho, there! Bion. Come here."

A handsome young oarsman not much older than Nikias, but almost his exact same height and build, darted across the room and stood before his leader.

"Yes, Captain?" he asked.

"Take off your tunic," ordered Phoenix.

"Here?" asked Bion with a surprised voice.

"Don't get excited," said Phoenix. "We're not going to make love in a wineshop. Just take off your tunic."

"Switching clothes isn't going to fool anybody," said Nikias, annoyed.

"Just shut up," snapped Phoenix. "My cunning plan will be revealed shortly. Come on, man! Take it off!"

The young mariner pulled off his clothes and stood there naked, waiting for more instructions.

"Now, Nikias," said Phoenix. "Switch your tunic for Bion's."

The young oarsman stared with disgust at Nikias's blood- and dirt-stained clothes. Nikias stood up and gave Bion an apologetic look. He took off his tunic, then put on the clean one—an outfit cut in the distinctive style worn by mariners, with blue trim on the sleeves. He put his own belt back on and tightened it around his waist.

"I'll pay you back," Nikias said to Bion.

"You'll do no such thing," said Phoenix. He took a drachma from his purse and flipped it to Bion. "Get yourself a new rig." The young mariner smiled and tossed Nikias's tunic on the floor, then walked naked into the street to buy himself some new clothes.

"Don't worry about Bion," said Phoenix. "He's just a bottom decker. Great in bed—he could suck the rust right off a bronze doorknocker—but not much of a brain. Now wait here for a moment." He got up and whispered into the ear of one of his men—a short and swarthy heap of muscles who reminded Nikias of Diokles the Helot. The oarsman listened to Phoenix's instructions, took a proffered handful of silver coins, glanced at Nikias, then nodded and departed the wineshop.

Phoenix came back to the table and sat down, smiling smugly and signaling for a server. "We'll leave shortly," he said.

"I don't want you to get in trouble on my account," said Nikias.

"Don't worry," said Phoenix. "Kleon's men will never know."

"I don't see how wearing a mariner's tunic is going to fool anybody," said Nikias, picking at his sleeve and sighing.

Phoenix raised an eyebrow. "Just have patience," he said. "All will be revealed."

A server brought Phoenix a plate of chicken and the mariner dug into his meal with vigor. Nikias sipped his wine, wondering how his cousin was going to sneak him past Kleon's henchmen. When he started to ask him for an explanation Phoenix held up a hand for silence, humming in a self-satisfied way as he tore the meat from the bones with his teeth.

Nikias glanced at one of the wineshop walls. It was hung with battered Korinthian shields—trophies captured from the enemy in battles at sea. He'd heard descriptions of galley fights before. Two ships would come together side by side, grappling like wrestlers, and the mariners on board would toss aside their wooden oars for spears and shields. "It's just like a phalanx battle except that instead of good, solid earth beneath your feet, you're wobbling on the waves like some sort of drunken fool," was how his grandfather had described such an action.

Nikias studied his cousin's face. Phoenix had changed dramatically over the years. The last time Nikias had seen Phoenix he'd been a smooth-skinned, handsome rake with the elongated muscles of a swimmer. Now his chin was covered with a thick beard, his skin tanned the color of ancient oak, and his eyes creased with crow's-feet. His muscles were so massive they looked like the absurd pictures in the Athenian public gallery of Atlas holding up the world. The dashing, arrogant teenager had morphed into a stony-faced leader of men. He realized the man must possess tremendous skills as a seaman and a warrior to have become captain of the *Sea Nymph* at the age of twenty-seven. His grandfather had been a famous general, though, just like Nikias's grandfather. Fighting was in their blood.

"Tell me about your adventures," Nikias asked. "Or have you been guarding grain ships all these years?"

Phoenix smiled. "I've killed thrice as many men as you, dear cousin, since shipping out to sea."

Nikias knew by the serious look on Phoenix's face that he wasn't making an idle boast.

"The truth is we spend more time with spears in our hands than oars," continued Phoenix. "I was in the great battle off Sybota two years ago—the biggest sea battle since the Persian invasions. We sent twenty ships to aid the Korkyrans against the Korinthians. Nearly a hundred and fifty boats were in the water for each side, filled with enough hoplites to burst the planks. We came hull to hull with the enemy. Animal rage and brute force were swapped for seamanship. It was murder and chaos."

Phoenix took a long drink and stared at the table with a faraway expression.

"I heard that the enemy speared the survivors of ships that had sunk," said Nikias. It was a serious breach of the rules of war that had infuriated the Athenians—the killing of helpless fellow Greeks as they trod water in rough seas. And the rumor of it had come all the way to Plataea.

Phoenix nodded. "The Korinthians went mad with bloodlust after the battle. They even killed their own allies by mistake, such was their blind wrath. Both sides claimed victory in the end. But neither of us won." He paused then said, "The Skythian guards watch over Athens, keeping everyone in line. Well, we mariners do the same thing, only it's all of the islands in the Delian League that we have to worry about."

Nikias was stunned. "You mean you've been fighting Athenian allies too?"

"We call them mutinous city-states," said Phoenix. "Those who refuse to pay their taxes, or who make eyes at the Korinthians or Spartans or Persians . . . or any of our growing list of enemies. The League is in trouble, and that's one of the reasons this whole Plataean situation is so bad. Do you see now why Perikles can't let Plataea go? It will turn into another shit-pot."

"What's the shit-pot?" Nikias asked.

Phoenix looked at him incredulously. "Potidaea? *The* shit-pot? It's a city-state in the north that wanted to back out of the Delian League and go with Sparta. There are thirty Athenian triremes up there blockading their harbor—preventing help from Sparta or Korinth. We're building a counter-wall around the entire citadel while four thousand of our hoplites and a host of Skythian archers guard the place night and day. Perikles is not going to give up until he's starved the shit-pot into submission."

Nikias sat back and touched his aching left eye. It was swollen almost shut from a blow he'd taken from one of Kleon's henchmen. "And now the Spartans want to do to us what Athens is doing to this Potidaea."

Phoenix nodded in agreement. "It's a tangled rope, that's for sure. But at least you've got the Bull of Plataea. And we've got Perikles. Without them we'd both be in a sinking boat."

"Captain."

The mariner Phoenix had sent from the wineshop had returned with a canvas bag. He set it on the table.

"Excellent!" shouted Phoenix, opening the bag.

It was filled with theatrical masks—the cheap kind bought from a street vendor and worn at parties where the sole purpose was to get drunk and screw anonymously. Phoenix laughed as he pulled out a mask and put it on. He now resembled a pug-nosed satyr with a leering mouth and wrinkled brow. He reached in again and took out a giant phallus with low-hanging testicles, and wrapped this contraption around his waist.

"I don't have time to waste at a satyr party," said Nikias, annoyed.

Phoenix tossed Nikias a mask—the beauteous face of the god Dionysus, leader of the satyrs.

"We're not going to party *here,* arse-brains," said Phoenix, jumping on the table. He cupped his hands to the mouth of his mask and shouted, "I need twenty volunteers to go brothel-diving in Athens with me and my dear cousin!"

Mariners pushed and shoved each other out of the way to get to Phoenix first. He started tossing masks and phalluses to his men and soon they were ready for action. Phoenix led them out the door, followed by Nikias, disguised in his Dionysus mask and mariner's tunic, wine cup in his hand.

"Now you're just another drunken oarsman on shore leave," said Phoenix as they walked toward the entrance to the Long Walls with a gang of raucous mariners in their wake.

FIVE

By the time Kolax got to the fort where he'd seen the raven he was panting like a dog. He hid in the shadows of a building across the street from the entrance, trying to catch his breath. He thought about the strange vision of the giant arrow and the viper. He sensed danger now.

Two Athenian warriors stood on either side of the fort's double doors. And some watchmen paced the crenellated battlements above. Kolax wondered what this place was. A barracks? Some sort of armory?

He saw five Skythian archers saunter toward the entrance with three prisoners in tow—drunk men linked together with ropes around their necks and their hands manacled behind their backs.

"The place must be the city jail," he thought.

His eyes darted from one archer's face to another, looking for his beloved papa. But none of them even closely resembled his father. In fact this gang of Skythians was a butt-ugly lot with unkempt topknots and dirty orange beards.

The jail's front doors opened and three other Skythian archers exited the building. They stopped short when they saw the group with the prisoners. One of them laughed, pointing at the drunks, and said with a Bindi accent, "Nuri dogs! Did you find some new bedmates to fondle and braid your greasy beards?"

"Cistern-arsed Bindis," spat one of the Nuri archers. "Get yourselves some old Greek men and offer them your shaved hindquarters."

The Nuri archers laughed uproariously at this insult, but the Bindi warrior who'd called them dogs threw down his bow—a sign he was ready to fight to the death in a duel of long knives. The challenged Nuri smiled and tossed his bow onto the street, then started rolling up his sleeves.

Kolax crouched low and watched with anticipation. He hadn't seen a death duel in a long time. He wanted to see this Bindi pull the Nuri's intestines out and trample them in the dirt.

The Athenian guard on the battlements of the fort had been watching all of this, and now he called down to the inner courtyard. In no time at all a huge figure emerged from the fort. All of the archers in the street stopped what they were doing and shrank back, cowering before this giant Skythian.

He was taller by a head than any archer in the street, and his red-bearded face was set in a grimace of rage. The hair of his topknot was so pale it almost appeared white in the Athenian sun, and it stood high atop his handsome head like a horse's thick mane, making him seem even more colossal.

Kolax realized that tears were streaming down his cheeks. He'd recognized his father's wheat-white hair the instant he'd walked out the door. The raven—the canny raven!—had led him to his papa, Osyrus of the Bindi.

Osyrus pulled a whip from his belt and held it aloft, dangling it there as though it were a wicked snake. "The next one of you sheep ticks to start a fight," he said in a low voice charged with menace, "will taste my leather. These blood feuds end now. There are no tribes inside the walls of Athens. Now get back to your duties or I'll tie you all to the boards."

The Bindis went on their way down the street with spiteful backward glances while the Nuris entered the jail, shoving their prisoners.

Osyrus remained in the street, coiling his whip around his fist.

Kolax reacted without thinking. He ran across the lane and hurled himself at his father, wrapping his arms around his waist, crying with joy.

A powerful blow to the side of his head sent Kolax reeling. He stumbled backward and fell on his rump, looking up to see his father staring at him with an expression of horror.

"Dirty slave!" hissed Osyrus in Greek, and snapped his whip with an ear-popping crack.

Kolax touched his face and felt warm blood pouring from his cheek. He tried to speak but all that came out was a strangled sound. His eyes bulged in frustration. His mind reeled. He grabbed his long hair with both hands and pulled it back to reveal his face, grinning hopefully.

"Papa!" he yelled.

Osyrus recoiled, muttering the Skythian word for "insane," shielding his eyes with his arm so as not to be tainted by the sight of a lunatic. Warriors of the Grasslands feared little, but they had a profound terror of madness, as though it were infectious. Osyrus turned and disappeared into the fort.

Kolax leapt up and tried to run in after his father, but the guards at the door barred his way with their long clubs. One of them jabbed him in the stomach with the butt of his stick and yelled, "Get away, rabid mongrel, before we castrate you!"

Kolax walked backward on shaky knees. It felt as though the bones had been pulled from his legs. The delayed pain from the lash of the whip seared his cheek like fire. He staggered down the street, went around a corner, and collapsed against a wall, growling with exasperation.

Why had he acted so harebrained? There was no way his papa could have recognized him after these four long years, especially when he was dressed like a slave. He had to show his papa the tattoo. That would fix everything. The instant he saw the gryphon his papa would know who he was and embrace him. All he had to do now was figure out how to get into the jail.

He walked around the walls of the fort until he came to an empty alley on the opposite side. This uninhabited area—between the wall of the jail and the city bastions—was used as a garbage dump. The reek of rotting food and human feces made him gag, but the benefit of the stench was that there were no guards nearby.

He found a section of the jail's wall where the bricks were loose, leaving hand- and footholds. He climbed up the ten-foot-high barricade and dropped down the other side into a small alcove stacked with wood for cooking fires.

He heard a strange sound: men crying softly . . . like miserable shades trapped in the Underworld. And mingled with this mournful sound was the caw of a raven.

He crept around the corner and came face-to-face with a sight that snatched the air from his lungs—a courtyard filled with X-shaped wooden whipping stands on which a dozen men were tied spread-eagled, their backs flayed open like raw meat. Some had been dead for days and were in various states of decay. One was nothing but a skeleton, picked clean by the carrion birds. He realized that this was where the Athenians tortured their prisoners and left them to die. These were "the boards" his papa had threatened to tie the archers to if they had disobeyed him.

He couldn't see any guards in the courtyard—they'd left the prisoners who were still alive on these contraptions to roast in the heat of the afternoon sun.

Telemakos the raven was perched on the top of one of these torture racks, standing guard over a slumped body strapped to the wooden X. The bird stared at Kolax as he approached and bobbed his head as if to say, "Yes, yes, this one!"

Kolax recognized the bard's hair and felt a lurch in his guts. The skin of Andros's back looked like it had been slashed from side to side with a knife five or six times, but he knew the wounds had been made by a Skythian whip.

He crept to the other side of the wooden X so he could see Andros's face. The bard's lids were squeezed shut in agony and he whispered something to himself over and over again. Kolax touched him on the hand and Andros's eyes popped open to reveal whites that had turned red from burst blood vessels.

"Kolax?" he asked in a dazed whisper, speaking with great effort. "How did you find me?"

Kolax pointed at the raven. "I followed your bird and climbed over the wall."

Andros clenched his teeth as pain wracked his body. Then he said, "The Athenians are going to kill me."

Kolax raised his eyebrows and asked, "Why?"

"They have mistaken me for someone else," said Andros. He cocked his head to the side and said, "The ropes." And a moment later added, "Your knife."

Kolax moved without thinking. He unsheathed his knife and cut the cords holding Andros's hands and feet to the wooden X. The bard slumped to the ground and exhaled—a sound of mingled agony and pleasure. Kolax helped him stand and guided him with the raven hopping along behind.

"I knew Zeus had sent you to me at the temple," said Andros, his body shaking as though from chills.

Kolax led him back to the alcove with the woodpile and stacked some logs to create makeshift steps to the top of the wall. He gestured for Andros to escape over the top.

"Aren't you coming?" asked Andros, confused.

Kolax shook his head. The bard was too weak to argue and crawled on his hands and knees up to the edge of the wall. He glanced down at Kolax one last time.

"We'll meet again, one day," he said. "And I will pay you back for saving me."

Then he rolled over the side of the wall and was gone. The raven flapped to the top of the wall and looked the Skythian boy up and down before launching himself into the air and flying away.

Kolax hoped the raven would lead Andros to safety.

He stole back into the courtyard and found the door that led to the rest of the prison. He crept down a long hallway, knife held out in front. He smelled cooking and realized that he was near the kitchen. His heart pounded. He was so close to his father. After all these years. All he had to do was show him the tattoo—

He heard a sound and turned on his heels. A thin slave boy stood behind him holding a bucket. The child took one look at the knife-wielding, bloody-faced Kolax and screamed at the top of his lungs.

Kolax pushed past him and ran down the hall. An Athenian guard dashed around the corner and Kolax reacted instinctively—slamming his knife into the man's leg so hard that the blade embedded in the bone. The guard screamed and lashed out with a club, catching Kolax in the back of the head. The Skythian boy swooned and collapsed on the stone floor.

The next thing he knew, men had surrounded him. They pushed him facedown to the floor so he couldn't move and tied his arms behind his back so tightly that his shoulder blades were pressed together.

"Gag the rat so he can't bite," ordered a voice.

The men wrapped his ankles with cord so he couldn't use his legs. Then they dragged him into a cell and slammed the door shut. Kolax writhed on the floor, screaming and sobbing in frustration, trying to chew through the heavy rope gag.

It seemed like days passed before the door opened. He looked up to see the dumbfounded face of the blond-bearded Athenian who'd tried to spear him in the glade—General Lukos, Iphy's master.

Next to Lukos was Osyrus, peering at Kolax out of the corner of one eye as though the sight of him was poisonous.

"Is he the one who killed your slave-hunter?" asked Osyrus in Greek. "The one who killed your dogs?"

"Kronos's balls," said the general, awestruck. "That's the little brute, alright. He's dyed his hair. Clever barbarian. What was he doing here at the prison, I wonder?"

Kolax thrashed on the floor, flopping on his stomach. He croaked and screeched, trying with all his effort to speak through the gag.

"A mystery," replied Osyrus, replying to Lukos's question. "The gods love riddles."

Lukos said, "He's probably one of the numberless bastards your men have sired with the whores of Athens."

"I think not," said Osyrus flatly.

"I'll be back in a day to take him to the auction," said Lukos. "I'm going to sell him to the mines of Laurium to make up for my property he butchered. Along with that little bitch, if I ever find her."

"You can't have this one," said Osyrus. "He set free a Korinthian spy we'd caught today. But my whip will make him talk."

Lukos puffed out his cheeks. "The boy won't do me any good if he's ruined!" he complained.

"Not my problem," said Osyrus with a knife's edge to his voice.

Osyrus glanced at Kolax's face. Kolax pleaded to his papa with his eyes—prayed that his papa would recognize him. But Osyrus said to him in Skythian, "I know you can understand me, little dog. You came to murder me and failed, just like the last assassin. I turned his head into a drinking cup and yours will join his on my shelf. Soon we'll know who wants Osyrus the Bindi dead."

Osyrus slammed shut the oak door and Kolax heard the scraping of an iron bar on the other side. He pressed his face into the dirt floor to stifle his sobs.

SIX

———— ◆ ————

It was an hour after sunset and the mariners of the *Sea Nymph* were still hard at work, doing their best to exhaust the Athenian brothel's entire staff—both male and female—and getting as drunk as Skythians.

Nikias lay on a soft bed in the corner of the drinking room, resting his aching body after the day of physical punishment. He felt like he did after an all-day pankration event—as though a team of chariot horses had trampled on him. He went through a mental checklist of all of his injuries: ruined shoulder, useless right arm, sore jaw, loose molar, left eye nearly swollen shut, sharp pain in lower back.

At least Nikias's cousin had been right about the disguises—they had walked straight up the Long Walls road and into Athens without drawing the attention of Kleon's whisperers. The *Sea Nymph*'s oarsmen—the elite warriors of the seas—were untouchable, even if they were drunk and obnoxious and dressed as a gang of rowdy satyrs. Nikias, clothed like one of them and hidden behind the mask of Dionysus, had blended into their group.

They had made their way to the sex district and taken over a popular establishment, kicking out the stunned patrons with the enthusiasm they showed boarding an enemy galley. Nikias could imagine them slaughtering men with the same wild glee, and he was glad these warriors were on his side—they were the biggest, meanest, and loudest group of walking hard-ons he'd ever been around in his life. Quick to copulate and even faster to fight.

Phoenix had gone off into a private chamber with the mariner Bion and a pair of beautiful young men before emerging sometime later looking like a drained wineskin. He had told Nikias that he needed to dash off on some "errand of great importance," but not before ordering Nikias to "stay at your bench." And then his cousin had vanished.

That had been almost two hours ago and Nikias was growing restless. He closed his eyes and tried to make himself go to sleep above the grunts and groans of the orgy. After a few minutes he felt something tugging at his belt. He snapped open his eyes, grabbing at the wrist of a young slave boy—one of the wine servers—who stared back at him with a terrified look, squirming to be free.

"I've got nothing to steal, whelp," he said. "Now, get out of here."

The boy scampered out of the room like a frightened cat.

Nikias reached into his belt pouch to make sure the gold ring was still there. He found it and took it out, staring at the signet in the lamplight. It was a red gemstone carved with the image of a kneeling Persian warrior holding a bow. He tried to slip it onto the pinkie of his left hand, but the ring had been made for a man with much thinner fingers: Eurymakus the Theban.

He stared at his own signet ring, which he wore on his right hand. It had been his late father's ring and bore his family sigil carved in jasper: a boxing Minotaur. His signet finger had been broken in a fight last year with a warrior named Axe, and the knuckle had swollen so much that he would never again be able to slip the ring from his finger. Holding Eurymakus's ring next to his own, he compared the two.

Minotaur against archer . . . who would win?

He wondered if Eurymakus was still alive. He hoped so. For he wanted to kill the man with his bare hands. Clutching the spy's ring in his fist, he forced his aching body off the bench, picked his way through the orgy, found the back door of the brothel, and headed into the moonlit streets of Athens, ever watchful for Kleon's henchmen.

He thought of Kallisto as he walked. He wondered if she was recovering from her injuries. If she was gaining strength. He hoped his grandmother and sister had been looking in on her at Chusor's. His heart seemed to grow heavier in his chest. He'd betrayed Kallisto with the hetaera Helena. But he had not done so willingly.

Or had he?

"Love," Chusor had said on several occasions, "can lift you up like the wings of Daedalus, or bring you crashing back down to earth like a millstone around your neck."

He remembered that Chusor's friend—the hetaera Sophia—lived in this neighborhood near the pottery district, close to the edge of the agora. His friend would be angry if Nikias failed to deliver the message of introduction he'd written to her. And even though the letter had been stolen from him, Nikias had read it so many times he knew it by heart. He could recite it to her word for word:

My Sophia,

Not a single day has gone by since we parted that I have not thought of you. I have traveled the known world trying to forget you; and yet you still shine in my memory as brightly as the sun. . . .

Nikias saw a slave boy emptying a bucket of excreta into a gutter and asked him for directions to the hetaera Sophia's. He followed the slave's instructions and soon found himself on a lane of expensive homes. At the end of the block—where the courtesan's place should have been—was nothing but the charred remains of several houses that had burned to the ground some time ago. The crumbling shells of the lower walls were still standing. Blackened timbers were stacked neatly in piles, waiting to be taken away by a salvage crew. He thought of his own farm, destroyed by the Theban raiders, and felt sick to his stomach.

He went to the nearest house that had been unaffected by the fire and knocked on the door to the slave quarters. After a while an old Syrian answered, holding an oil lamp up to Nikias's face.

"What is it?" asked the slave.

"The hetaera Sophia?" asked Nikias. "Does she live on this street?"

The slave squinted and looked around the lane to see if Nikias was alone. "Who wants to know?" he asked.

"One of her friends," said Nikias. "I've traveled a long way to deliver a message."

"Then you'll have to go even farther," said the slave. "Though few have gone to Hades and returned. Those houses burned to the ground six months ago. And her place was one of them. We're lucky the whole block didn't go up in flames." And with that he slammed the door shut.

Nikias did not look forward to bringing this news to Chusor. His friend would be crushed. He wondered if Kleon had had anything to do with the fire. Nikias knew that Kleon had tried to have Chusor murdered for sleeping with the hetaera. Perhaps this Sophia had done something worse to provoke his anger.

He walked aimlessly down a narrow lane into a small square. He recognized the wineshop where he and Konon had eaten dinner the night before.

The sad-looking, skinny drunk with the prominent nose was at the same table, but there was no sign of his bitter wife and their two children. Nikias sat down on the stone curb and propped up his head with his one good hand, overcome with depression.

His adventure to Athens was a complete failure. He'd been robbed, drugged, and beaten. He'd lost his horse *and* the Skythian boy. And for what? Nothing. He felt like dashing his brains on the stones beneath his feet, but he was too weary to move.

"What's wrong with your shoulder?" asked the drunk in his strange accent.

Nikias glanced at the man and shrugged. "Fell from my horse."

"I noticed it last night when you were here," said the man, his voice thick with alcohol. "The way you held it. I could tell it was bad. You should wear it in a sling to take the pressure off the sinews."

"Thanks for the advice," said Nikias in a tone that said he wasn't thankful in the least. He opened his clutched hand and stared at Eurymakus's ring, then tossed it spinning into the air, catching it as it fell.

"My wife left me," said the man and let forth a tremendous sigh. He got up and stumbled over to Nikias, and sat next to him on the curb, offering him his wine cup. "She went back to her village. Took the children and what little money we had left. I deserved it, though. I am a terrible husband."

Nikias glared at the foreign-looking man—peered into his dark eyes with hostility. But all he saw there was abject despair, bitterness, and defeat. He felt a kinship with the drunk and his heart softened. On this night, at least, they were two of a kind. Hamstrung by the Fates. He took the proffered cup and drank.

"Thanks," said Nikias, wiping his mouth on the back of his hand. He spun the signet ring on the smooth curbstone, watching it until it came to a stop.

"I see you've taken a bad beating since I saw you last night," said the man. "That eyelid needs to be slit to let the blood drain, otherwise it will just keep closing. You'll be a one-eyed Cyclops soon."

"I've had worse."

"I'm sure of that! I can tell by your ugly ears that you're a pankrator. And your nose has been broken several times. Let me see the knuckles of your hands. Ah! Yes. The hands of a man who has spent his life punching other men in the face."

"You a fight trainer?" asked Nikias with a laugh, knowing the man was the furthest thing from serving in that profession.

"No," smiled the man. "I'm a physician. Though I'm sure you'd hardly believe me, looking at my sad appearance. I studied in Babylonia, where the skills of those illustrious doctors make your Greek physicians look like drooling barbarians. I came here several years ago to practice my trade. But I was never accepted here, being a tax-paying foreigner—or a *metic,* to use your ugly Greek word." He peered into Nikias's eyes for several seconds, then raised one brow. "You've had a blow on the head recently. I can see it in your pupils and the way you hold yourself. You need to be careful and get some rest. Have you been vomiting at all? Unable to keep your thoughts straight?"

Nikias smiled and laughed softly. "May I ask your name, Doctor?"

"Ezekiel," he replied, "son of Solomon the Babylonian. And I am a Jew—do you, by any chance, know what a Jew is?"

"Not in the slightest," said Nikias, grinning. He'd found Chusor's friend the doctor. The Fates had finally led him in the right direction.

"It is nothing funny to be a Jew," said Ezekiel, apparently taking Nikias's smile as an insult. "My people were enslaved by the Egyptians. We escaped because of a miracle. And then we were sent packing from Babylonia. We have no city-state to call our own."

"I'm not laughing at your predicament," said Nikias. "Forgive me, Ezekiel. My name is Nikias. And I would shake your hand but I can't lift my arm. I am a friend of Chusor. He gave me instructions on how to find you if I became injured. He said you were a great healer."

Ezekiel rubbed a hand across his face and stared suspiciously at Nikias. "Chusor told you to find me?"

"Yes," said Nikias. "He wrote directions to your home on a piece of papyrus."

"Let me see this papyrus," said Ezekiel, squinting.

Nikias could tell that Ezekiel had become mistrustful and on edge.

"I lost his note," explained Nikias. "It was taken from me."

Ezekiel flicked his eyes around warily, and then peered at Nikias with a guarded look.

"You don't believe me?" said Nikias.

"This Chusor," said Ezekiel. "What does he look like?"

"Tall," said Nikias. "Much taller than me, and broadly built. And dark-skinned. He is half Aethiope, though everyone in Plataea calls him the Egyptian—"

"Come, come," said Ezekiel with a sneering tone. "You can do better than that. Who sent you? Are you one of Kleon's men? If so, you can kill me now and get it over with like you did to my friend. I have nothing to live for."

Nikias shook his head. "Kleon? I'm not one of his spies. And Chusor isn't dead. He's very much alive."

"Pah!" spat Ezekiel.

Nikias stood up, his eyes blazing. "I don't like people to call me a liar. Go to Hades, you miserable sheep-stuffer. I don't need your help."

He turned and just as he did so he felt a rush of blood to his head and everything started to go black before his eyes. He steadied himself against the wine-shop wall with his left hand. In a few seconds his vision returned and he saw that Ezekiel now stood in front of him, staring at him with a concerned look.

"Come," said Ezekiel. "Come with me to my home. I will help you."

"I don't need help," said Nikias.

"I owe Chusor my life," said Ezekiel. "And now I must help you."

"So you believe me?" asked Nikias.

"Come," said Ezekiel. "And don't forget your ring. You left it on the curb."

Nikias glanced at the curb and saw the signet ring. He grabbed it, stuffing it into his pouch, then followed Ezekiel down the street. They walked a few doors away to the house with the sign hanging out front painted with a skull—the place that he and Konon had visited the day before. When they were inside, Ezekiel lit a lamp and led Nikias to a room full of shelves lined with hundreds of clay jars. He helped Nikias take off his tunic and carefully took hold of his right arm, turning it slightly this way and that, and stopping whenever Nikias winced in pain.

"You've got a torn shoulder ligament," said Ezekiel. "A very bad tear. You won't be able to use this arm for six months or more."

Nikias's heart sank. This was far worse than he had expected.

Ezekiel found some cloth and expertly tied a sling, placing Nikias's arm so that it was bent at the elbow and strapped firmly to his chest. With the weight of his arm off his aching shoulder joint, Nikias instantly felt less pain.

Next Ezekiel held a piece of thick glass to Nikias's left eye and peered through it. From Nikias's perspective the glass enlarged one of the doctor's own orbs in a comical way.

"What's that thing?" asked Nikias, laughing.

"Magnification glass," said Ezekiel. "A Persian invention."

"Chusor would like that."

"I need to drain the blood to take the pressure off your left eye," said Ezekiel.

"Do it," said Nikias.

Ezekiel took a small sharp knife from a little box and held it briefly over a flame, then he slit the skin at the corner of Nikias's swollen eye. The blood spurted out and Nikias sighed with relief.

"Where did you get the Persian ring you were playing with?" Ezekiel asked in an offhand manner as he cleaned his knife blade.

"I found it on a battlefield," Nikias replied. "The man who it belonged to had lost the ring . . . and his arm."

"May I see it?"

Nikias frowned. There was a strange glint in the physician's eye—a greedy kind of look. He reached into the pouch, took out the ring, and handed it to him. Ezekiel held it in his palm, staring at it through the magnification glass, pulling his lips back in concentration and revealing his big, wine-stained teeth.

"Was the man you killed a Persian nobleman?" asked Ezekiel.

"I didn't kill him," said Nikias. "And he's a Theban."

"I've only seen rings like this worn by retainers of Artaxerxes."

"Were you a physician to the king?"

"No!" said Ezekiel with a laugh. "But I lived in the capital of Persepolis, and treated many of the courtiers . . ." He trailed off in thought, holding the ring up very close to one eye.

Nikias considered this strange information. What would Eurymakus the Theban be doing with a Persian nobleman's ring? Where could he have gotten it?

He thought back to the battlefield in front of the gates of Plataea, when he and Eurymakus had been thrust together in the melee. Eurymakus had wielded a poison dagger that Nikias had managed to turn against him. Eurymakus had cut off his own arm to stop the poison, and then fled.

"There are words written on the inside of the band," said Ezekiel, interrupting his thoughts.

"I thought those were just scratches," said Nikias.

"It's Persian script," said Ezekiel. "A form of the old wedge writing. The ring itself is very old, you see. The gemstone, however, was added fairly recently. That's Artaxerxes, the present king, carved into the carnelian stone."

"What do the words on the band say?"

"*Magos*. It's the Persian word for a kind of priest," explained Ezekiel. "The man who wore this was a high priest and a follower of the one god Ahura Mazda."

Nikias remembered Chusor telling him how the Persians worshipped a single god. The smith had explained some of their strange beliefs. Something about good and evil and demons and protective spirits. But he couldn't remember the details. It had all sounded so fantastical and barbaric, it had gone over his head. He noticed, with a twinge of annoyance, that Ezekiel was prying at the top of the carnelian with a little metal tool.

"Hey, what are you doing to my ring?" he asked.

Ezekiel ignored him. He used his knife to bend back one of the tiny clasps holding the gemstone to the ring. "There we go," he said as he pulled off the gem to reveal the flat surface of the ring where the stone had been mounted to the band: the gold was inscribed here with a circle sprouting wings. "You see this? It's the symbol for a *fravashi*. A guardian angel."

"A guardian what?"

"It's a spirit that protects the wearer of the ring. Like your goddess Athena coming to help Odysseus in that story the bards all sing." Ezekiel turned over the carnelian stone and there, plainly visible, were deeply incised Persian letters. "Ahhhh, yes. Very interesting."

"What does *that* say?" asked Nikias.

"It's a name," explained Ezekiel. And he silently mouthed the word written there. He glanced at Nikias and passed a hand through his hair. "Like I said, the gold ring is very old. It's been passed down over the centuries from one *magos* to the next. When a new *magos* is initiated into this sect of priests, he is given a ring that's fitted with a new signet that is unique to him. The name of the wearer's *fravashi* is hidden on the opposite side of the gemstone because the name must be kept secret and only known by that particular *magos*."

"And that's what's written on the back of the gemstone?" asked Nikias with derision. "The name of Eurymakus's guardian angel?" He started laughing at the absurdity of what he was hearing.

"Yes," replied Ezekiel.

"How do you know all this? About the Persian gods?"

Ezekiel cocked his head and said, "One cannot grow up in Persia without learning about their beliefs. And I have made it a study to know everything I can about different gods. A man's body and mind are interconnected. You can't simply heal the body. You also have to heal the mind sometimes."

"You sound like Chusor," said Nikias.

Ezekiel shrugged.

"You still don't believe me," said Nikias.

"It is hard to swallow," replied Ezekiel. "I heard from a dependable source that Chusor was killed. And I have not seen the man for five years. And you show up claiming to be his friend, and all you can do is offer a vague description of the man."

"I could describe every scar on his body," said Nikias.

"So could anyone who had seen his corpse," replied Ezekiel.

"But you helped me anyway," said Nikias. "I appreciate that."

Ezekiel poured some water in a mug and put in various pinches of powders from different jars. "This will help your wounds heal faster."

"So you think this Eurymakus is a Persian priest?" asked Nikias, watching the physician concoct his potion. "He's a Theban."

"There were many Thebans in the court of Persepolis," said Ezekiel, stirring the mixture. "Thebes and Persia have always had close ties."

Something in Nikias's tired brain clicked into place, like a sword slipping into a scabbard.

Eurymakus. The Persian gold. The ring.

"The Persians financed the attack on Plataea," he said under his breath.

Ezekiel said, "The Persians will never forgive you Greeks for defeating them and starting your own empire." He handed Nikias the mug and ordered him to drink it.

"Why must the name of this *far*—" He paused, stumbling on the strange word.

"*Fravashi,*" prompted Ezekiel.

"Yes, why would it matter if somebody else knew the name of the *fravashi*?" He took a sip of the drink and screwed up his face. "This tastes like goat piss!"

"*Dried* goat piss," said Ezekiel. "It will help the swelling. Drink it all." He sat down opposite Nikias and scratched his beard. "If you know the name of this Eurymakus's angel," he continued, "you can call on that angel to protect you. And he cannot harm you if you do this in his presence."

"That's ridiculous," said Nikias, draining the contents of the mug in a few gulps.

"Men believe many ridiculous things," said Ezekiel. "Most of what you Greeks believe seems ridiculous to me."

"What is the name of Eurymakus's *fravashi*?" asked Nikias.

"Daena," replied Ezekiel. "A goddess. A daughter of Ahura Mazda."

"Daena," repeated Nikias. He thought of Eurymakus wearing his sacred ring and how it must torment the Theban to have had to cut off his own arm, knowing he was leaving something so precious behind.

"Why are you smiling?" asked Ezekiel.

"Pleasant thought," said Nikias.

They sat quietly for a while, and then Ezekiel asked, "Chusor had a friend. A constant companion who never left his side. Does *he* live as well?"

"The last time I saw him," said Nikias, "Diokles the Helot was still breathing air, though he was hiding in a storeroom, living on dried goat flesh, terrified the 'masters' had come for him."

As Nikias had been speaking he saw Ezekiel's eyes open wide in surprise, and a hopeful smile pulled at the corners of the doctor's mouth. "Diokles—" began Ezekiel, but he was interrupted by a faint knock on the door that made them both jump in surprise. Ezekiel got to his feet and sidled to the door, opened a sliding peephole, and peered out in the street. After a few seconds he looked at Nikias and whispered, "There's nobody there."

"Down here," came a girl's voice from the other side of the door.

Ezekiel frowned and unlatched the portal, opening it slowly. Standing on the threshold, far below the level of the peephole, was the hetaera Helena's slave girl.

"You!" said Nikias in surprise, jumping to his feet.

"My mistress wants to speak with you," said the girl.

"Why?" asked Nikias.

"I don't question my mistress," replied the slave girl. "But she told me that you can trust her. That she is a friend of Sophia."

"I'm not going to be tricked by her again," said Nikias. "I'm not coming back with you to that house where I was drugged."

"My mistress would not ask you to do that," said the girl. She leaned forward and looked into his eyes and put a trembling hand on his arm. "She knows it's not safe there. That is why she has come to you."

She turned her head and gestured with her thumb. Standing across the street, illuminated by the silvery moonlight, was the veiled figure of a woman. Nikias recognized Helena's eyes watching him, beseeching him to trust her.

"It's not safe here," said the girl, pulling on his wrist. There was something about her face and bearing that was so familiar to Nikias. She reminded him of someone but he could not put his finger on it. He allowed himself to be pulled out the door.

"Wait!" said Ezekiel. "Where are you going, lad?"

"Thank you," said Nikias over his shoulder.

"But the Persian signet ring!"

"Keep it as payment for your help," said Nikias. "I don't want it anymore."

SEVEN

———◆———

Nikias had the sensation of walking in a dream. It was the helpless feeling of being pulled along by an enigmatic force—a force that he had no way of stopping.

He could see the black shapes of Helena and the slave girl a few paces ahead, lit only by moonlight, guiding him through the deserted streets as though they were shades taking him to the Underworld.

He didn't know where they were headed. But for some reason it didn't seem to matter. Maybe Helena would betray him again. Maybe not. He felt too weak to fight anymore.

He imagined the Fates standing at their loom, weaving the destinies of men. His mother had always told him that even the gods were afraid of the "Old Sisters," as she called them. For the inhabitants of Olympus were also connected to the great hidden tapestry of the Fates.

He used to love being in the room where the women of his family worked the looms. He and his sister would crawl in and out of their mother's and grandmother's legs, clinging to them as they sang their weaving songs.

And the scent of that place . . . he could almost smell it now. The musky grease from the new-spun wool dripping down onto the hanging yarn weights and onto the floor; the mysterious natural perfume of the women's skin and hair.

When he'd turned six his grandfather had told him he could no longer play in the women's quarters. Nikias had tried to hide beneath his mother's gown, but the Old Bull had dragged him from the loom chamber and ordered him to stay outside and ride his pony, shoot arrows, and practice his whip—anything but "waste his time with females."

"Count yourself lucky," Menesarkus had told the sobbing boy. "Six-year-old Spartan lads are already living in miserable boy-herds, eating nothing but blood gruel and barley water and getting their arses buggered raw by bearded men. If you ever want to survive a fight with one of those man-reapers, you'll have to get tougher."

Nikias had wanted to kill his grandfather that day. He could picture his flinty eyes glaring at him now. As though he were standing in front of him in the practice arena. Snarling and pulling back a fist to punch him in the face—

Nikias jerked and realized he was so tired he was starting to hallucinate. There was a throbbing at the base of his skull that wouldn't go away and a faint nausea churning in his stomach. He stopped and swayed to one side, nearly falling over.

"Wait," he said softly.

Helena and the slave girl ran back to him and propped him up.

"He's exhausted, Helena," chided the girl. "I told you he was hurt. But you wouldn't listen. You never listen to me!"

"Melitta, hush."

"I will not hush, Helena. I will not hold my tongue any longer. I told you how Kleon's men beat him. I thought I would die watching them hurt him."

The slave girl stifled a sob and Nikias stroked her on the head. The child's concern touched his heart. "I've taken much worse than those feather-fists could serve out," he said, trying to make her feel better.

"It's not much farther," said Helena to Nikias in a soothing tone. "Come. You can rest soon enough."

He let himself be held by Helena and Melitta. Their slender arms did little to support him, but he liked feeling their warm bodies close. Earlier he had thought that they resembled shades . . . but now they felt very much alive.

The girl Melitta reminded him, in a way, of his hot-tempered sister, Phile. He wondered why Helena would let her slave talk to her in such an impertinent manner. And then it came to him in a flash, as if a secret thought had been spoken out loud.

"She's not your slave," said Nikias. "She's your sister!"

Helena gasped and glared at the girl. "You told him, Melitta?"

"No!" replied Melitta, amazed. "I said nothing."

"She didn't tell me," said Nikias. "I have a sister of my own. I know how siblings speak to one another."

They walked in silence for some time before Helena said, "I was going to tell you tonight. We are half sisters."

"It's no business of mine," said Nikias.

"It is, in a way," said Helena. "We're both the daughters of Sophia the hetaera. The one whom Chusor loved."

Nikias was speechless as they led him the rest of the way across a small square to an ancient temple made of timber frames and brick. It was enclosed like a house with a single porch and a front door.

"What is this temple?" asked Nikias.

"The old Temple of Aphrodite," replied Helena, opening the door. "One of the few buildings of the Old City to survive the burning of Athens by the Persians. We are members of this order, my sister and I."

They entered a sanctuary lit by a single oil lamp burning on the altar. A hunched woman—an aged priestess of the temple—nodded at Helena and went through a curtain, leaving them alone.

"We'll be safe here," said Melitta, shutting the door behind them and barring it with a board.

Helena took off her cloak and spread it out on the floor in a corner of the chamber. She gestured for Nikias to make himself at ease, and he lay with his back propped up against the wall. The place smelled of aged oak and burnt olive oil—a homey smell that reminded him of the great room at his grandfather's farm. His body relaxed for the first time all day and he let forth a great sigh.

Helena and Melitta left him for a while, disappearing behind the curtain at the back of the sanctuary. When they returned Helena carried a basin filled with water and some clean rags, and Melitta held a cup of wine that she put to his mouth so he could slake his thirst.

Helena moistened a cloth and started cleaning the blood and dirt from Nikias's face while Melitta sat nearby with her legs folded under her, watching him with her dark discerning eyes. Again he was struck by how familiar the little girl seemed.

He looked at Helena and realized she had taken off her veil and headscarf. She wore no makeup and her hair was pulled back in a single plait, accentuating the perfect oval of her face. Her beauty was beyond compare and when she looked into his eyes he felt a sudden pounding in his chest. It amazed him that this woman's mere glance could have such a bewitching power over him.

He asked, "Why did you want to see me?"

"So many reasons," said Helena with sadness in her silvery voice. "First I want to beg your forgiveness. Kleon is the master of my life, as though I were a shadow puppet moved by sticks and strings. And I feel such terrible shame for what happened to you at my house."

"Was the man in the room that night Kleon?" asked Nikias.

"No," she replied. "But he is Kleon's closest confidant."

"Does he threaten you?" asked Nikias.

"I am his toy. His plaything. But he threatens one whom I love very dearly." Helena glanced at Melitta and the two shared a doleful smile.

"Why would he threaten your sister?" asked Nikias. "What sort of man is Kleon to want to harm a little girl?"

"I'm not little," said Melitta angrily. "And I'm not afraid of Kleon."

"You should be, Sister," said Helena with an edge to her voice. "He is a man to be feared. He hounded our mother to her tomb. He told me that if I set one foot through any of the fifteen gates of Athens he will have me killed. And Melitta too. If we managed to make it out of the city . . . well . . . he would hunt us down to the Gates of Herakles."

"I saw your mother's house," said Nikias. "Did Kleon make that fire happen?"

"I don't know," said Helena. "But I suspect as much. She was trying to get Melitta and me out of Athens. She had bought passage for us on a ship. Kleon must have found out. When our mother died I had no other choice but to become a hetaera."

She put the dirty rags she'd been using to clean Nikias's face into the basin, stood up, and walked to the center of the small chamber. "Our mother never wanted this to be my fate. She abhorred the notion and saved enough for both my sister's and my dowries so that we could marry. But all of that was lost in the fire."

She paused and took a breath, touched a hand to her mouth as if she could not make herself speak.

"Please go on," said Nikias.

"When you were drugged," said Helena haltingly, "and spoke of the man Chusor, I thought the Fates had sent you to us. I knew him, you see, when I was a little girl. I was Melitta's age when he and my mother started their affair. He was very kind to me and I loved him. It broke our hearts when he was forced to escape Kleon and this snake pit of Athens. But Kleon's tentacles are long. And now he is drawn back into the mire."

"What does Chusor have to do with Kleon and his whisperers?" asked Nikias. "He fled Athens a dozen years ago."

"Tell Nikias how old you are, Melitta," said Helena.

"I'm several months past eleven," replied Melitta.

Nikias looked at her blankly.

"Plus the nine months I spent in my mother's womb," added Melitta with a wry smile.

Nikias closed his eyes and shook his head. He couldn't help but laugh. "I thought you were an Anatolian slave girl," he said. "But you're one-quarter Aethiope." He opened his eyes and looked at Melitta full in the face. "You're Chusor's daughter. Now that I look at you, Melitta, I see my friend's eyes staring back at me."

"You must help us," said Helena. "For your friend's sake if not for ours."

"What do you want me to do?" asked Nikias.

"Kleon is almost certain that Melitta is Chusor's child," said Helena. "And eventually he will kill her, such is his hatred for your friend." She crouched by Melitta, wrapping her arm around her sister's slender shoulders. "When you return to Plataea you must let Chusor know that his daughter—the legacy of his love for Sophia—exists in this dangerous place. Tell him that I am on my knees, asking for his help."

Nikias sat up and reached out his left hand. "Put your hands in mine," he said, encompassing both of the sisters' hands into his callused palm. "I promise to come back here with Chusor and take both of you away from this place. You understand? That is my oath."

"Are you leaving tonight?" asked Melitta with despair.

"No," said Nikias, laughing.

"Promise!"

Nikias reached into his pouch and took out a metallic disk, placing it in Melitta's palm and closing her fingers around it.

"Keep this safe for me," he said. "It's the marker for my sword—an heirloom of my house. I'll come to you to retrieve it before I leave Athens. To make certain that you are well."

Helena started crying and Melitta wrapped her arms around her body, holding her tight. Nikias leaned back against the wall and stared at the sisters with heavy lids. Soon exhaustion overcame him and he plunged into the realm of Morpheus.

Several hours later a hand touched his chest, rousing him from sleep. The lamp had gone out and the room was dark.

"Nikias," said Helena's voice close to his ear. "It is still several hours before dawn. You must leave before the priestesses open the temple."

He reached out and put his hand behind her head, guiding her mouth to his. Her warm lips kissed him back. He moved his hand down and felt the nakedness of her back. She pressed her breasts against his chest and reached between his legs, guiding him. They moaned at the same time, pushing their bodies together.

"Your sister," whispered Nikias.

"Asleep," came the breathless reply. Then she stopped moving and said, "Nikias, I wanted us to be together from the moment I saw you. In the street, outside the theatre."

He said, "The first time we made love I—"

But she cut him off saying, "The first time didn't happen. *This* is the first time."

Kallisto's face flashed in Nikias's mind . . . and he pushed the image away. The only face that he wanted to conjure up in the darkness was Helena's. Sweet Helena. The world and all its worries vanished and they were alone together, protected under the ancient temple roof, two disciples of Aphrodite.

EIGHT

Nikias made his way through the dark lanes of Athens in the direction of the Street of Thieves. It was that time of night, hours before dawn, when every living thing—except the owls and their prey—was asleep. Even the winds seemed to be at rest. It was a terrible time to be awake and alone.

He'd betrayed Kallisto—the woman he had asked to be his wife. But worse than that, he thought, was that he'd fallen in love with Helena, and with every step he took away from the temple of Aphrodite he felt a sort of wildness coming over him . . . a madness of unsatisfied desire. He wanted to sprint back to Helena and be with her again. To never leave her side.

He held his hand to his lips—the hand that had caressed her body with such pleasure. The intoxicating scent of her was still there on his fingertips. He couldn't stop thinking about her alluring voice, the tender way she had kissed him, the feel of her silky hair brushing against his face while they made love.

Men would kill and betray for a woman like her.

He heard the screech of an owl and looked up toward the Akropolis; he saw the dark shape of wings passing in front of the night-gray pillars of the Temple of Athena.

"Where have you been!" shouted a voice full of fury.

He turned and saw Phoenix walking toward him, bearing a torch. His cousin grabbed him by his left arm and started marching him in the opposite direction.

"Get off," growled Nikias, shaking off Phoenix's grip with a furious jerk of his arm and planting his legs like a stubborn mule.

"We need to put our oars in the water, mate!" said Phoenix. "We've got a meeting with the chief. And we're late."

"With Per—Perikles?" stuttered Nikias.

Phoenix raised his eyebrows and smiled wryly. "Who else?" He started walking quickly up the lane without glancing back to see if Nikias followed. Nikias had to run to catch up with him.

"But how?" asked Nikias.

"I went to see him," said Phoenix. "Told him my cousin the pankrator, Menesarkus's heir, was begging for an audience. The mad thing is that he'd actually heard of you! I've never said a word to him about you, mind. He wanted to see you straightaway. The chief only sleeps a couple of hours a night," he added. "It's already morning for him."

Nikias could hardly believe what Phoenix had just said. Was meeting the most powerful man in the Athenian Empire really this easy? After all of the insanity he'd been through in the last two days . . . it seemed absurd.

"It's who you know," said Phoenix, the smug tone in his voice implying that he was the main reason Nikias had been granted this meeting.

"Where are we meeting him?"

"Just follow, damn you," replied Phoenix with the air of a man who was used to giving orders, but not in the least bit used to being questioned.

They wended their way through the dark city streets lit by Phoenix's torch, moving closer and closer to the looming rock of the Akropolis. The bright moon shone in the cloudless sky, making the marble buildings glow. Eventually they arrived at the long flight of stairs leading up to the top of the Akropolis. But a guard of twenty or so armored warriors stood blocking the way. The men parted as Phoenix and Nikias approached, making a path between them. Before they got to the foot of the stairs, however, a warrior stepped forward and held up his hand for them to stop, and then he proceeded to search Phoenix's clothes for hidden weapons.

"Careful with my eggs, Akilles," said Phoenix sarcastically as the guard reached between his legs. "And my spear doesn't need waxing tonight."

Several of the warriors nearby laughed.

"Always a jest with you, oar-master," said Akilles.

"You're not my type anyway," said Phoenix.

Nikias sized Akilles up with his pankrator's eye. The guard was a sturdy warrior, with the crooked nose of a fighter. Nikias felt as if he'd met him before. The guard turned to Nikias and said icily, "Take your arm out of that sling."

Nikias did as he was told, slowly pulling his arm out of the bandage with his left hand, grimacing with pain. Akilles felt roughly under his armpit, and then, satisfied there was nothing dangerous concealed there, helped Nikias put his arm back in the sling with the efficient ease of someone familiar with the care of battlefield injuries.

"I know you," said Akilles, giving Nikias a steely look. "I fought you in the Oxlands. Two years ago. At the Festival of Demeter."

Nikias suddenly remembered. He'd only been sixteen at the time. He'd broken Akilles's thumb before getting him into a stranglehold and burying his face in the sand, whereupon the older athlete had raised his littlest finger in the sign of defeat. "Good match," said Nikias.

"Good for you," said Akilles. "You nearly broke my neck. I'd never been beaten before I fought you." He pointed at the marble stairs gleaming in the moonlight. "Proceed."

"We're meeting him up there?" Nikias asked Phoenix in surprise.

"The chief's office is up there," said Phoenix. "In the armory." He mounted the steps, taking them two at a time.

Nikias followed. He'd climbed much steeper and longer places in the mountains back home, but by the time he'd got halfway he was already winded. Fatigue. Not enough food or sleep. It wore him down. He glanced back and saw Akilles a few steps behind. The big man's eyes bored into him.

Phoenix waited for Nikias at the top by some wooden construction equipment—huge hoists with gears and pulleys, and a large crane.

Two Skythian archers stood nearby, eyeing them distrustfully, and Nikias could see several more of the barbarians patrolling the area higher up where the Temple of Athena stood.

"This entrance that's being built," said Phoenix proudly, "is the final building to grace the Akropolis." He swept his arm across the unfinished structure in front of them. "The Propylae Gates. We Athenians turn everything into something divine, cousin. At least that's what Perikles is always saying. He has a flair for the dramatic, our Perikles does."

"I haven't been here since I was a boy," said Nikias in wonder, turning his gaze from building to building. "And they had just begun the construction then. That was less than ten years ago."

"Wait until Perikles has his way with the rest of the city," declared Phoenix. He gazed out over the shimmering sea with a faint smile on his face. "The wealth we're bringing in from the other islands will turn Athens into a city that will last until the end of the world."

"Hmphh," muttered Akilles.

Phoenix nodded at Akilles and said to Nikias, "Akilles here is the chief's personal guard. We've been on a few voyages together, haven't we, Akilles?"

"I haven't counted," said Akilles in a monotone.

Before Phoenix could come up with a proper retort, a young clerk scurried from a nearby building and gestured for Nikias and Phoenix to follow. "Come," said the clerk impatiently. "You're late. Come, come." They followed him through an archway and past two lightly armored Greek guards, stopping at the threshold of a rectangular room. Nikias saw Akilles take up a position in the shadows, leaning against a wall, eyeing him with a blank face.

Inside the room was a long table—the longest Nikias had ever seen—almost entirely covered with papyrus rolls and scale models of machinery and buildings. The room was lit by several oil lanterns that hung by chains from the ceiling, casting the chamber in a flickering glow. Along one wall was a row of orange-and-black vases decorated with images of warriors engaged in combat.

A man stood at the end of the table wearing a plain robe wrapped over his shoulders against the chill of night. His palms rested on the tabletop, bare arms locked straight in an attitude of deep concentration as he stared down at a diagram on the table. He was in his sixties, but still had the muscular arms of an athlete in his prime. His pate, however, was completely bald, revealing an oddly shaped skull that reminded Nikias of the onion-like bulb on a bullwhip kelp.

Nikias reckoned this man must be an architect, studying his plans for the next day's work. But then Phoenix said, "Peace, General Perikles," and Nikias flinched, standing up a little straighter.

"So this is the man himself?" he thought.

Perikles. The leader of the Athenian Empire. The general who'd driven the last vestiges of barbarians from Greek territory and sacked any city that rebelled against the Delian League. The politician who'd brazenly moved the League's treasury from the island of Delos to Athens. The visionary who made no qualms about turning Athens into the seat of the empire and pouring tax money into its temples and public buildings. . . .

Perikles looked up from his work to reveal a long face with a thick beard streaked with gray. He had a full lower lip that jutted forward slightly, giving him a shrewd and contemplative look. His intelligent eyes flicked from Phoenix to Nikias.

"Peace, Phoenix," replied Perikles.

"My cousin," said Phoenix, gesturing for Nikias to step forward. "Nikias, son of Aristo of Plataea."

Perikles regarded Nikias for a long moment, then strode around the table with his right arm outstretched. Nikias stepped forward.

"I tore my shoulder ligament," he blurted. "An injury." He offered his left hand awkwardly. Perikles—a big, well-built man who towered over Nikias once they stood face-to-face—took his left hand and clasped it. The general took in the scars and scabs on Nikias's face with a raise of his eyebrows.

"I have heard the report of the battle," said Perikles. "The emissary from Plataea singled you out as one of the heroes in the defeat of the Thebans. But I had no idea you'd come with them from Plataea. I would have asked to meet you earlier.

I am an old acquaintance of your grandfather, whom I hold in great esteem, and I would have heard of the battle from your perspective—from the young man who led the cavalry charge against the Theban phalanx and routed it."

Nikias could not help the feeling of pride swelling his heart. To have a renowned man such as Perikles praise his deeds! He noticed that Perikles spoke with the refined accent of an Athenian nobleman, but there was a toughness in his voice and his face that Nikias immediately liked. None of the perfumed hair or stuck-up airs of the other Athenians he'd met in the city.

"I didn't come with the emissaries," Nikias said guiltily. "I came to Athens on my own."

"I'll wager you've got an interesting story to tell," said Perikles, clearly intrigued yet puzzled. He held a forearm across his chest, resting his other elbow on this shelf of an arm, and stroked his beard with his other hand—a calculating expression. "When I heard you were in the city I assumed your grandfather had sent you with a message for my ears alone. A message differing from the one I received from the official Plataean emissaries."

The way that he said this gave Nikias the distinct impression that Perikles had not been pleased at all with the message his grandfather had sent with the emissaries.

"And who could he trust more than his own heir?" continued Perikles with the slightest arching of his eyebrows.

Phoenix shot Nikias an angry glance as if to say, "Speak up, you idiot." Nikias clenched his teeth and glared at Phoenix. He wished his cousin would leave so he could talk to Perikles alone.

"I came to find men," said Nikias. "To raise an army of fighters to return with me to help defend Plataea." The instant he uttered the words they sounded so foolish to his own ears that he felt himself turning scarlet. But Perikles did not scoff. Rather he regarded Nikias with an even more serious expression.

"Did your grandfather give you leave to come here?" asked Perikles, staring at Nikias's long hair. "You're still underage."

"He did not," said Nikias, meeting his eyes again. "I came of my own accord. And I just turned eighteen. But I have yet to shear my hair and burn it. The ceremony was interrupted by the invasion." It was a bit of a lie, he knew. But he didn't want to tell Perikles he'd been in jail at the time of the ceremony of manhood, accused of murdering Kallisto's brother.

"You came alone? Through Megarian territory?" asked Perikles.

"Yes."

"A dangerous journey."

"A risk worth taking," replied Nikias.

Perikles turned to Phoenix and said, "Please wait outside. I need to speak with your cousin alone."

Phoenix nodded and bowed slightly. As he turned and passed Nikias he gave him a look that said, "You're on your own now. Good luck."

NINE

— ◆ —

Perikles stared into Nikias's face for the longest time, nodding his head slightly and smiling faintly. Nikias stared back, not knowing whether he should speak or not.

"You resemble your mother," said Perikles at last.

"So I am told," said Nikias. "You knew her?"

"*Knew?*" replied Perikles with a frown. "Then she is dead?"

"Killed by Theban raiders," said Nikias, his throat constricting as he spoke the hated words.

Perikles put a hand on Nikias's shoulder and dropped his head. "Yes, I knew her," he said with a note of deep sadness in his voice. "She was a famous beauty in Athens. My nephew wished to marry her, but she was carried away like Helen by a young Oxlander—a poet as I recall."

"My father *was* a poet," said Nikias. "He was killed at a battle near Koronea."

"That battle was a failure," said Perikles, removing his hand from Nikias's shoulder. "But your father's death was no less glorious than any warrior killed at Marathon."

Nikias felt his eyes welling up. He looked away from Perikles, ashamed that he couldn't control his feelings in front of this man, his gaze searching the room for something to focus on, to keep himself from bursting into tears. He felt like a child. He wanted to tell Perikles that his father hadn't died a glorious death. He'd been speared in the groin, and had perished in agony, amidst the carnage of a defeated army. What did his father's death mean?

Nothing but humiliation and horror.

His gaze passed along the row of painted vases showing scenes of warriors engaged in combat. The shifting light from the hanging lamps seemed to give movement to the painted figures: men from Homer's day, jabbing at each other with spears or riding war chariots pulled by galloping steeds. His eyes alighted on a vase showing a dead warrior carted from a battlefield by two smiling combatants. "They're grinning because they're still alive," thought Nikias. The corpse they carried hung limp and slack-jawed, his eye staring at the sky as dead as a fish's.

"Honorable," replied Nikias at last. "But not glorious."

Perikles's lower lip jutted forward. "The two go hand in hand."

"Do they?" asked Nikias.

Perikles peered into Nikias's eyes. "Why have you come here, lad?" he asked.

"I told you—"

"To raise an army? Ridiculous. Tell me the *real* reason. Why did you want to see me?"

Nikias took a deep breath. The words he wished to speak were bitter on his tongue. "If Athens will not help Plataea with warriors," he forced himself to say, "then we must be allowed to break our oath. Otherwise we will be destroyed."

Nikias had expected Perikles to react in disgust or rage. But Perikles merely nodded and said in a bemused tone, "That is impossible, you cannot break your oath," as though Nikias had suggested something absurd—that the citadel of Plataea should grow giant legs and march out of the Oxlands!

Nikias replied, "What good is Plataea to Athens if we're wiped off the earth?"

"No good at all."

"But—"

"Follow me," said Perikles. He turned and strode to the other side of the room, pausing to pick up a bronze oil lamp from the long table, and then he passed through a doorway at the end of the room into another chamber. Nikias followed. This anteroom was darker than the other. It took Nikias's eyes a while to adjust to the dim light. He saw at least twenty square tables. Each tabletop was covered with earth and rocks to simulate different kinds of terrain. And each table had a model of . . . what were they? It was hard to tell in this shadowy room.

Perikles set the lamp down upon the table in front of them and Nikias saw, illuminated in the lamplight, a model of a citadel. And then recognition came to him. It was as if he were standing on a familiar cliff top, gazing down into the Oxlands.

"Plataea," said Nikias with a tone of wonder, staring at the model of his city that had been meticulously constructed on this diorama. Everything was there. He could see the walls complete with each tower, and the Temple of Zeus, the Assembly Hall, the agora!

"As you can see," explained Perikles, "your home weighs heavily in my thoughts. I've stood on the heights of the Kithaeron Mountains several times in my life, gazing down on the plains of the Oxlands, and I've seen your citadel down below, at the foot of the mountain, rising up from the ground as though it had sprung from the earth itself. Strong! Like a hoplite in the best armor and shield—an Ajax ready to face down any foe."

"I fear the Spartans are too great an enemy," murmured Nikias. He glanced at Perikles, who frowned as if Nikias had said something distasteful. Or unmanly. And Nikias felt ashamed again.

"You think the Spartans can storm the mighty walls of Plataea?" asked Perikles. "They've never defeated a city-state in a siege. It is not in their nature. They haven't the mental faculties for such a campaign. They're bluffing. The walls of Plataea are twenty feet thick."

"They'll starve us out, like the Helots of Mount Ithome," said Nikias.

"A possibility," said Perikles. "Something my generals and I have contemplated. And that is why we have decided"—here he paused briefly, nodding his head sagely—"that you must bring all of the women and children to Athens immediately."

Nikias looked at Perikles in amazement. "Now?"

"Any loyal friend of Athens is a citizen of Athens," explained Perikles. "The people of Plataea can live in the citadel for one year with the stores you have accumulated. Your grandfather's own report told me as much. If your city were occupied by warriors alone, you could hold out for several years. The Spartans would never stay in the Oxlands for more than a season. They are stepping into bilge-water as it is. Soon they'll be up to their necks in it. We've had word that there have been more Helot uprisings in Sparta."

Nikias contemplated everything that Perikles said. It all sounded so reasonable. He imagined his grandmother, Kallisto, and his sister Phile protected by the high walls of Athens. Safe and well fed. He saw Plataea's warriors—inspired by the Athenian generosity—standing firm against an inept Spartan onslaught, the red-cloaked warriors attacking the high walls of Plataea like a gang of children attempting to break down a stone wall with nothing more than sticks and rocks.

Perikles said, "You can either submit to the Spartans and become their slaves, or stand up to them with the hope of survival. Which would you have?" he asked in a challenging tone.

"I would stand up to them," replied Nikias. And once he had said these words out loud—words uttered with passion—he knew that he could never question Plataea's path again. It was as if the Fates had, at his birth, woven a golden thread leading straight to the Spartan army camped outside of Plataea. And now that thread had been revealed to him. All that Nikias had to do was follow this thread to his destiny. Victory or defeat. There was no other choice. No middle path. "I fear slavery more than death," he said.

Perikles smiled. "And that's the kind of man with whom I would choose to be friends. Far better to die a glorious and honorable death than to skulk away like a whipped dog. The Spartans live wretched lives, Nikias, and so it is easy for them to face death. For those of us who have been blessed to be citizens of a democracy like Plataea or Athens—where the good things in life are revered and savored and enjoyed—dying in battle for us is . . . well . . . it's even *more* of a sacrifice. And that's why our deaths are held even higher in the eyes of the gods."

Nikias thought of all those he knew who had died in the Theban sneak attack. Did the gods really consider their deaths to be more honorable? It made perfect sense. The Thebans had broken the rules of war. The Plataeans, however, had died to save everything that they held dear—their family and friends and their beloved city-state. He wondered why his grandfather had never inspired him like Perikles. Never made him feel like he could take on an entire phalanx of the enemy all by himself. Perikles was a great man, just like everyone said. A kind and generous man. A thinking warrior. A builder of cities.

"What can I do?" asked Nikias, overcome with emotion. "How can I serve you, General Perikles?"

Perikles beamed at Nikias. "I would keep you here by my side and have you serve as my shield man if I could," said Perikles. "But I must send you back to your grandfather. You will return with the emissaries and deliver my message to Arkon Menesarkus with your own voice."

"And what is the message?" asked Nikias.

"Stand firm," said Perikles. "And give me your wives and children to look after. I will be their shepherd, their guardian, until the enemy is driven from the Oxlands."

His head swimming, Nikias followed Perikles out of the anteroom into the chamber containing the long table and the vases. As he passed the table he glanced at it and saw what Perikles had been looking at when he and Phoenix had first entered the room: it was a large map, spread out on the table. And on the map was a drawing of a narrow isthmus with the name POTIDAEA written above it. A small bronze warship had been positioned on the map next to Potidaea. Nikias remembered that this was the "shit-pot" that Phoenix had mentioned at the inn. The place the Athenians now had under siege. And to the northeast of Potidaea on this map was drawn another walled citadel. A model trireme advanced toward it menacingly. It was a city-state that Nikias had never heard of called Skione.

Perikles led him through the chamber and outside—into the cool night air and courtyard in front of the building. Here a gathering of men waited for Perikles: the armed guards, two clerks, and Phoenix, who had somehow procured a mug of wine and a chunk of bread. Nikias spotted the bodyguard Akilles as well, still standing in the shadows like a statue.

"Wait here," Perikles said to Nikias. "We're not done yet."

Perikles took one of his clerks aside and began a whispered conversation. Phoenix sauntered over to Nikias and offered him his cup. Nikias took it and drained the contents.

"What happened in there?" asked Phoenix.

"I don't rightly know," said Nikias.

"The chief has that effect on people."

Nikias noticed the clerk who Perikles was talking to shoot a curious glance his way, and then the man bowed slightly to the general before turning and dashing away into the armory, reaching for a ring of keys on his belt as he ran.

"Come," said Perikles, gesturing to Phoenix and Nikias. "To the Temple of Athena now. To beg the goddess's blessing for your journey home."

Nikias fell in behind Perikles. They walked through the half-built gates, and then up another flight of stairs to where the temple stood, and then up the steps of the temple itself. Now they were passing between the tall painted pillars that seemed so perfectly proportioned. Nikias remembered something Chusor had told him about the design of these pillars, but he couldn't remember exactly what his friend had said because his mind was in a whirl. He could see the gigantic statue of Athena up ahead, the gold shining in the torchlight, and he felt the skin on the back of his neck tingle with excitement. Perikles led them up to the base of the statue and stopped, holding up his hands.

"Bright-eyed goddess," intoned Perikles in a deep voice, "inventive, pure, savior of Athens, mother of arts, warlike, born from the wise head of Zeus himself wearing armor glinting of gold, the gods themselves were in awe when they gazed upon your beautiful form. . . ."

Nikias craned his neck, staring up at the ivory face of the goddess, the droning voice of Perikles lulling him into a trance. Nikias had no idea how much time had passed. He might have even dozed off, standing on his feet. For when he looked up he saw Perikles unsheathing a sword—the sheath held by the clerk who'd been sent off to the armory just before they'd come up to the temple.

"This sword has served me well in many battles," said Perikles. He walked directly to Nikias and handed him the weapon. "It is yours now, Nikias of Plataea. Yours to use in the defense of your citadel—our friend and ally until the end of time, blessed by warlike Pallas Athena, under her gaze, all-victorious, goddess of good fortune. "

Nikias took the sword with his trembling left hand. It was beautifully made. He held up the double-edged, leaf-shaped blade and looked upon his own face reflected in the polished surface. He saw tears streaming down his cheeks and was surprised. He wondered how long he'd been crying.

"Plow an oar in my arse," exclaimed Phoenix after he and Nikias were alone again, walking down the steep steps of the Akropolis. "I think the chief likes you."

Nikias smiled. He grasped the sword in its scabbard with a fierce pride. He glanced over his shoulder to where Akilles followed a few steps behind them. The bodyguard had the faintest smile pulling at the corner of his mouth yet a venomous gleam was in his eyes.

"Perfect conditions," said Phoenix.

"Huh?" asked Nikias.

"The water," said Phoenix, pointing down the length of the Long Walls toward the port of Piraeus four miles away. The bay was nearly flat. There was no breeze. "We leave after dawn."

"What are you talking about?" asked Nikias, confused.

"You and the Plataean emissaries," said Phoenix. "We're taking you back to Plataea via Delphinium, to the east of Thebes. I'm to captain the chief's own dispatch ship. After we drop you off you'll be given horses in Delphinium. You'll have to ride from there."

"But that will take us three times as long," said Nikias. "It's so much faster to just go back on the northern road to the fortress of the Three Heads at the pass."

"The Spartans have taken the Three Heads," cut in Phoenix. "Word came last night. One of our men who was at the stronghold escaped and fled to Athens on horseback with the news."

Nikias felt the world spin. The Three Heads was the fortress guarding the narrow pass through the Kithaeron Mountains to the Oxlands. It had never been taken by the enemy—not in the two hundred years since it had been built.

"How was it captured?" he asked incredulously.

"How am I to know?" replied Phoenix. "But the Spartans control the pass, and there's no other way back over the Kithaeron Mountains now. It's the water road for you, cousin."

TEN

———◆———

Osyrus the Skythian strode toward a great *kargon* burial mound built on the top of a treeless hill. The wind howled in his ears and a vast black cloud hung in the sky overhead. He saw flashes of lightning, but strangely heard no thunder. The world was grim and dark.

As he slowly climbed the hill and got closer to the *kargon* he was struck with awe: the mound was the biggest he'd ever seen—fit for a king of Skythia. It rose like a firm breast from the crown of the hill, and surrounding it was a ring of dead horses. These animals had been gutted and stuffed with chaff, then affixed to poles that were stuck into the ground. An offering to the dead man buried beneath this heap of sod.

Osyrus perceived that on each of the horses was mounted a human corpse that had been prepared in the same way as the steeds. And they were positioned in the customary way so that they appeared to be riding at full gallop, both hands on the reins, heads bent down and leaning over the horses' manes, racing into the afterlife with their dead eyes wide open.

This was an exceptional offering, considered Osyrus, and he felt a thrill of wonder. What an honor! If only he might be so lucky one day to receive such a *kargon*. But then the lightning flashed directly overhead, and he clearly saw the nearest faces and he cried out, for he had recognized the corpses of his mother and father mounted on two of the horses.

Osyrus ran from horse to horse, peering at each dead rider, seeing his aunts and uncles and cousins and childhood friends . . . even a priest of Papaeus. All of his kin had been killed and positioned on the dead steeds. He looked down and saw, with horror, that his own torso had been ripped open and stuffed with chaff.

And then he noticed there was one riderless horse waiting for him.

The dead began to hiss a whispered chorus. The riders were calling to him.

Osyrus forced himself to look away from the *kargon*. In the distance he saw a red-haired boy riding across the grasslands, chased by a band of enemy Nuri.

"Kolax!" he tried to scream, but his voice made no sound. His lungs had been stolen from his breast. The bloody organs lay at his feet, glistening on the dark grass.

Osyrus awoke in the dark with a gasping breath, clutching his aching stomach. He lay very still for a while, lost in a haze of nightmarish images that were slowly fading back to the world of dreams from which they'd come to torment him, as they did on most nights.

For a while he had absolutely no idea where he was. The hemp did that to him sometimes. He'd been smoking more and more of it to ease the terrible pain that had been growing inside his belly for the last year. It burned in the pit of his stomach like a hot coal.

He stood up, swaying precariously, then reached out probing hands for the shutters that he knew were there, somewhere on the wall. He found the wooden panels and opened them, leaning on the sill and breathing in the cool air. The light from the stars still shined brightly. He could see the constellation of the Archer and the three bright stars in a row that made up the god's belt; but a dim glow to the east told him the great god Papaeus would soon show his bright face to the world, riding his fiery chariot across the sky and covering the stars with his multicolored cloak.

The nightmare came rushing back into his memory. The same nightmare he had had for months.

A message from the horse goddess!

Last week a grain ship had come to the port of Piraeus from Skythia with a disturbing tale: old King Astyanax had died and his bastard son had usurped the throne, supported by the Nuri, who had taken this opportunity to massacre their enemies, ending the decades-long truce between the tribes.

The Bindis, Osyrus's tribe, would be the first to suffer at the hands of this new regime.

A cock crowed in one of the courtyards near the jail. The smell of woodsmoke wafted across his face and made him feel queasy. He cursed himself for this weakness. Smells had never made him sick before. Something evil was working on him in this city of the Athenians. Six years he'd lived here, seeking gold to bring back to Skythia. Six long years he'd paced the tops of the citadel's stone walls—a dull job without a single enemy skull to show for it. He couldn't even remember the last time he'd ridden a horse.

He clutched at his stomach as a stabbing sensation nearly caused him to double over in agony. He knew he was dying. He'd seen this before—the wasting disease that turned a strong man into a living corpse. He didn't have much time. If the tales of Astyanax's death and the Skythian massacres were found to be true, there was only one thing he could do. He must take a ship back to Skythia and try to find his son. He would be nine seasons now. The Horse Goddess had let him know that Kolax was still alive by showing him the red-haired boy in his dream—the one chased by the Nuri.

He gathered his long, loose hair and tied it into a knot on the top of his head. Then he reached for his dagger, taking it down from the wall where it hung by a metal hook. He strapped it to his waist, then removed his captain's whip from its hook and clutched it in his right hand. He'd had to use the scourge to stop three blood duels in the last week between various tribesmen who made up the five-hundred-man Skythian police force.

It was the Nuri who were causing all the problems.

They'd become cocky, emboldened by the rumors of their tribe's ascendancy back home. The archer called Skandar had been sneering at Osyrus all week—pissing on him with his eyes. Skandar coveted Osyrus's position as a captain of the police. Skandar most likely knew that Osyrus was ill. He was like a dog waiting to attack the wounded leader of a hunting pack.

Osyrus wondered if he could beat the younger man in a knife duel. No. Not in the weakened state he was in now. The only way he could get the upper hand with Skandar would be by surprise.

Osyrus took a few deep breaths to steady himself—to will away the pain in his gut. He strode to the door and opened it. The guards he'd posted there were alert. They were good men. Bindis like himself. But there were only twenty-five of his tribesmen still in Athens. One hundred and fifty Bindis had been sent up north, to help lay siege to Potidaea, because, of course, Bindis were the very best of all the Skythian archers. Those men had been gone a year and Osyrus had no idea when they would return. Until then, he and his brethren were far outnumbered by the other tribes in Athenian employ. And if the bastard king had taken over the throne and massacred their kinsmen back in Skythia, Osyrus and his tribesmen were now in grave danger, even here in Athens. The Athenians had no notion of Skythian laws, and let them govern themselves.

"Bring the boy to the yard," commanded Osyrus. "And strap him to the whipping posts."

Osyrus went down to the courtyard and waited. Torches burned in the sconces on the walls, but the sun rose and the sky glowed red. More cocks crowed in the houses nearby the jail, and the hens chattered excitedly. A billow of woodsmoke from the jail's kitchen wafted over his face and before Osyrus knew what was happening he was bent over, retching onto the stones.

"What's this, Osyrus?" asked a voice dripping with mockery. "Can't hold your drink? I guess it's true what they say—'Bindis are all mare-milkers.'"

Osyrus looked up to see Skandar chewing on a piece of bread. Standing next to him was one of his constant companions—another Nuri. Each had the image of a coiled snake tattooed on their left cheeks and they wore their hair in braided topknots festooned with gold loops. They were the only two Nuri assigned to the jail right now. The rest were on duty guarding the long walls.

Osyrus was astonished at Skandar's insolence. He felt an overpowering urge to stick his dagger into Skandar's brain, but all his strength had left him. He was relieved when the door leading to the underground cells burst open and his men appeared, dragging the frantically squirming boy. They brought him to the X-shaped post and tied him spread-eagle by his wrists and ankles.

"That's the one the Athenian general wanted," said Skandar. "What are you doing with him?"

"Do not question my actions," said Osyrus.

Skandar shrugged and remained to the side with his companion, chewing on his bread.

Osyrus walked across the courtyard to the whipping blocks. The gagged boy flailed against his straps, screaming deep in his throat. Osyrus peered deep into the child's blue eyes and said, "Why have you come, little beast? Why did you release the Korinthian? What game do you play?"

The boy's tear-filled eyes opened wide and he shook his head from side to side. Osyrus pulled his dagger from the sheath and held the point close to the boy's right eye and the boy became still.

"I think I'll snatch one of your evil eyes to start," said Osyrus. "I'll stuff it in your mouth and you can chew on it while I peel the skin off your back."

The boy shook his head and made a tortured grunting sound. Osyrus grinned. This child was a coward. He was already willing to talk. Osyrus slipped the dagger under the gag and slit it with a quick flick of his wrist, yanking the cloth from the boy's mouth.

Osyrus felt several eyes on his back and glanced around him. There were ten or so Skythians in the courtyard now, chewing on their morning bread, watching the show with interest. They loved a good whipping.

"Speak," Osyrus commanded.

The boy took in a rattling breath and cleared his throat. "Papa," he said with a voice full of sorrow. "It's me. Your son. Kolax."

The Skythians within earshot laughed.

"A fine son too," said Skandar snidely. "He favors you, Osyrus."

Osyrus glared at the Skandar. "Did you put this vermin up to this?" he asked.

"Not I," said Skandar, holding his belly and laughing. "I wish I had, though. It's the best joke ever."

"Papa," said the boy faintly, tears streaming from his eyes. "Believe me——"

Osyrus slashed his cheek below the eye. "Don't call me Papa!" he snarled.

The blood dripped down the boy's face and into the corner of his mouth. He licked at the blood and a crazed gleam appeared in his eyes.

And then he spat a huge gob of blood and mucus into Osyrus's face.

Osyrus staggered backward, swiping at his face with his sleeve. He glowered at the boy, but the wicked little goat actually smiled at him, flicking his eyes to the scourge in Osyrus's hand as if to goad him into whipping him. Osyrus lashed out, striking the boy across the face with the handle of the whip—a cruel blow that left a red welt across his cheeks and broke his nose. Blood gushed from his nostrils.

"I'll have every inch of his flesh!" screamed Osyrus. He moved around to the other side and whipped at the boy's bare legs. Once. Twice. Blows that ripped flesh from skin. The boy gasped in agony and Osyrus relished the sound. He paused and looked at the eager faces of the men in the courtyard. He would show them that Osyrus of the Bindi could still wield a captain's lash. That he could be merciless and fierce.

Osyrus heard a strange sound that made his blood run cold. The boy had stopped screaming, and now he was laughing. Laughing!

"Strip him!" bellowed Osyrus. He turned and walked away twenty paces, boiling with rage. The boy wouldn't laugh when he felt the full force of a *running* whip blow that would strip the skin of his spine and rib cage down to the bone.

One of Osyrus's men grabbed the boy's tunic, ripping it from his back with a swift downward movement, and then backed out of the way.

Osyrus focused on the boy's back in the dim light of dawn. He saw a dark pattern there. A tattoo! So the boy *was* a Skythian! A spy sent by the enemy. Perhaps the Nuri were now in league with the Korinthians!

Curiously, he realized that the boy had stopped moving. He was now as still as a statue. Excellent. He would cut the boy so deep his kidneys would spill from his wounds. Osyrus started running with the whip held out in front, snapping it back just before he reached the boy's still torso.

"Ayyeeeee!" screamed Osyrus, flinging the whip from his hand at the last instant and coming to a stop.

Osyrus couldn't breathe. The world seemed to tilt. He placed his hand on the boy's tattoo, ran his trembling fingers over the pattern. A memory came rushing back: the ceremonial tent and the smell of burning hemp, the priests chanting while Osyrus had sat next to the opium-drugged body of his only son, pounding the inked needles into his heir's skin to mark him in this world and the afterlife . . . so that they would never be separated.

The gryphon of the Bindi!

It was emblazoned on the boy's back in blue ink, just as it had looked when it had first been imprinted into his flesh. It was unmistakable. Tears burst from

Osyrus's eyes. He raised his hands skyward and called out, "Goddess of Mares! What is happening?"

Shaking violently and ignoring the mutterings of the men watching him, Osyrus staggered around to face the boy, whose head now drooped down like a poppy heavy with rain. Osyrus placed both hands gently on each side of the boy's head and lifted his face to his own, choking out his name, "Ko—Kolax?"

Kolax smiled wanly and nodded.

"How did you come here?" asked Osyrus.

Kolax's eyelids fluttered, struggling to keep them open. Osyrus put his mouth to Kolax's ear and whispered, "Is Astyanax dead?" then looked at Kolax full in the face to see his reply. Kolax nodded almost imperceptibly.

"Did the Nuri massacre our kin?" breathed Osyrus.

Another nod, and then Kolax let forth a great sigh. "The Snow Dog seized the Grass Throne," he managed to say. "I was captured and sold to a slaver . . . and sent to the Oxlands." His eyes turned inward and he stopped speaking. Osyrus couldn't help himself as sobs ripped from his breast.

"Osyrus has gone mad," muttered Skandar, stooping to pick up the whip that Osyrus had dropped. He strode forward and prodded the captain in the back with the handle, causing Osyrus's body to tense up. "Step aside. If you're not going to kill the boy, I'll deliver him to General Lukos and—"

There was a blur of movement and then Skandar staggered away from Osyrus, clutching at the side of his neck, scowling in surprise, staring at the bloody dagger now clutched in Osyrus's hand. He sank to his knees, then toppled over, pouring his lifeblood onto the dirty stones from the gash in his neck. Before the other Nuri tribesman in the courtyard could react, Osyrus leapt on him next, stabbing him through the heart. The man dropped dead at his feet.

The other eight Skythians exchanged surprised looks. They'd seen their own kind die before, but this slaughter had occurred without any seeming cause.

"Captain?" asked one Osyrus's men in astonishment.

"Why did you kill the Nuri?" asked another.

Osyrus moved swiftly, cutting Kolax free from his bonds. "Find all the Bindis who would still follow my hoofprints," said Osyrus as he lifted Kolax's drooping body in his arms. "The rumors are true—Astyanax is dead. Krouspako has taken the throne. This boy here is my son. The goddess has brought him to me. I'm leaving Athens with him now."

He kissed Kolax on the forehead and his son smiled faintly. Osyrus strode toward the archway that led to the stables. Word would spread quickly about the two Nuri he'd slain, and their brethren would come hunting for his head.

ELEVEN

———◆———

Menesarkus hated that he had to rely on a walking staff now at all times. His wife told him that it made him look venerable—like a wise seer in a play. But Menesarkus felt more like a doddering old man in an absurd comedy. He had no choice but to use the prop, however, with his knee getting worse daily. He could barely put weight on it now, and he could feel bone grinding against bone every time he walked.

He strode across the busy agora toward the closed gates, the metal-capped end of his staff banging on the stones with every step. The crowds of refugees got out of his way, nodding at him with respect, wary not to approach him because of the fierce look in his eye.

He wasn't angry, however. He was in pain. Every step hurt.

The injury to his knee had happened almost fifty years ago, during the Persian Wars. The Persians had burned Athens and its temples to ashes, and then King Xerxes had come north, into the valley of the Oxlands, halting two miles from the small but proud independent city-state of Plataea. There his army of half a million men had constructed the massive earthen redoubt that became known as the Persian Fort. It was four times the area of Plataea and big enough to contain the Persian king's vast retinue of warriors, women, and slaves. The Greek allies had come from all over Greece and assembled around Plataea for a final stand against the invaders.

On the tenth day after their arrival in the Oxlands, Persian heralds—each wearing enough gold to finance the building of a temple—had ridden on their fine black steeds to the Greek allies, demanding that they present a challenger to fight the Persian champion as a prelude to a battle. The Plataean generals had picked a mere lad of sixteen—selected more as a sacrifice to the god of death than as a serious opponent. The "Baby Bull," as his friends at the gymnasium called Menesarkus back then, had been chosen to fight the biggest and tallest man that Menesarkus had ever seen—Arshaka the Eye-Snatcher, bane of the Greeks, a famous, undefeated Persian pankrator.

This fight of heroes had only one rule: neither opponent could raise his little finger and yield, for it was a fight to the death.

"Hera's jugs," cursed Menesarkus, wincing in pain.

He came to a halt near the entrance to the citadel—the memory of that long-ago pankration match taking flight from his thoughts. He looked about him and saw that a thousand men were hard at work on a new inner defensive wall that was being built across from the two wooden gates. This "stone barricade" had been Chusor's plan. He'd gotten the idea from the wooden barricade that the Theban invaders had built in front of the gates to trap the Plataeans in their own city on the night of the sneak attack.

"Whoever controls the gates to Plataea controls the city," Chusor had said to Menesarkus in one of their meetings. And so Menesarkus had agreed to the building of this new wall. Several older structures in the citadel were being pulled down for the stones, their pieces reassembled into this new bastion—a second line of defense in case the Gates of Pausanius were rammed and breached.

Menesarkus entered the tower on the right side of the gate and climbed the steps leading to the top. Climbing stairs hurt even more than walking. He glanced up at the topmost landing and saw the tall figure of Chusor staring down at him with an impassive look. Menesarkus gritted his teeth and willed his body the rest of the way, sweat pouring off his brow despite the cool of dawn.

"I can make you a stanchion brace," said Chusor as Menesarkus reached the final step.

"What's that?" asked Menesarkus, pausing to wipe his forehead and catch his breath.

"A device of my own design using rods to support the knee on either side," replied Chusor. "I made one for the Naxos of Syrakuse."

Menesarkus grunted. "Don't concern yourself with me. The defense of the city is all that matters now." They walked to the tower battlements and Menesarkus gazed out over the fields to the Persian Fort two miles away. Gray woodsmoke from many fires rose high into the sky. The Spartans had at least ten thousand men inside the fort—five hundred full-blooded Spartans, three thousand free-man warriors, and the remainder in Helot slaves. Scouts had ridden close to the fort and reported that nearly all of the oak trees in the surrounding area had been cut down—far more than were needed for cooking fires. The Spartans were most likely building siege machines.

The sounds of hammers and axes carried on the wind from the fort—an endless din that lasted from sunrise until sunset.

"How many days do we have?" asked Chusor.

"A week, perhaps," replied Menesarkus. "As soon as the emissaries have returned from Athens the Spartans will press us to give them a decision. When we refuse to join the Spartan League they will start their attack." He had received a carrier pigeon message from Athens when the emissaries had arrived two days ago. They would not risk sending another message, however. It was too risky.

Chusor nodded grimly and tugged on the braided goatee. "I believe they will assault the gates with a battering ram," he said. "And that is why we're building the inner wall. But I think the Spartans have probably learned from the Syrakusans to attack everywhere at once with hundreds of lightweight scaling ladders."

"Everyone in the citadel must be ready to man the walls," said Menesarkus. "Old men and women included. How goes the excavations under the citadel?"

The night that Nikias escaped from Plataea during the Theban sneak attack, he had done so through an ancient tunnel that led from under the Temple of Zeus to the graveyard outside the city walls. But this passageway had collapsed, nearly burying Nikias alive. Chusor had suggested clearing it as well as making new tunnels to provide other ways out of the citadel—underground sally ports in case they had to launch a counterattack against the Spartans outside the walls.

"It goes well," said Chusor. "I have a team of a hundred men working day and night. The old tunnel that leads to the graves is almost clear and has been supported with beams. It won't cave in again. New passages are being made as well. These can be used to thwart Spartan miners who might dig under the walls to make them collapse."

"Good," grunted Menesarkus. He knew all about sappers and the undermining of walls. He had been at the second siege of Sardis—a brutal siege that had lasted for months. The Athenians who had been leading the attack on the citadel had dug deep down under a section of wall, causing the entire bastion to collapse like a child's sandcastle. Menesarkus had been in awe of the terrible sight—a sturdy wall turned to a pile of rubble . . . a gaping hole in the city's defenses like a huge hole in a bronze breastplate. He looked at Chusor and thought, "Thank the gods this capable man was sent to us in our time of need."

He saw something out of the corner of his eye—a flash of white in the foothills of the mountains. Snapping his head around, he saw a horse picking its way down the slope toward the citadel. He felt the blood drain from his face.

"That's Photine!" said Chusor. He shielded his eyes from the sun, staring at the horse with a grimace. "Nikias's mare!"

"But where is the rider?" said Menesarkus. "Where is my grandson?"

"Men on the road!" called out one of the lookouts standing nearby.

Menesarkus and Chusor stared east in the direction that the lookout pointed; they saw a line of carts pulled by Helots. The Spartan slaves, with their squat bodies and dark, bowl-shaped haircuts, were yoked to the carts like animals. Menesarkus counted ten carts.

"What are they bringing?" asked Chusor.

"I can't see what—"

Menesarkus stopped short as he caught sight of a line of twenty naked men, roped at the neck and ankles, shuffling along behind the carts. And marching behind these prisoners was an army of the enemy—at least five hundred men strong.

"Spartans!" cried several voices from along the walls and watchtowers.

The Helots pulling the carts stopped just out of bowshot range of the citadel. The roped men came to a halt behind them, and they stood with downcast heads, full of shame, Menesarkus thought, looking like children who been caught doing something bad and were now getting punished. The enemy hoplites fanned out in a phalanx formation and stood still.

A lone Spartan stepped from the mass of carts, prisoners, and warriors and made his way up the road toward the gates, striding alone and without a hint of fear. Even from this distance Menesarkus recognized the familiar gait of his old comrade from the Persian Wars. The man whom Menesarkus had fought in a pankration match in Sparta: a match without rules, fought in the Spartan way—a match in which he'd bitten off the Spartan warrior's nose to force him to release his death grip on Menesarkus's balls.

Drako the Skull.

The Spartan general sauntered right up to the gates and pounded on the oak planks as if he were knocking on the door to Menesarkus's farmhouse.

"What do you want?" Menesarkus called down unceremoniously.

Drako craned his neck toward the voice. "Ah, Menesarkus," he said. "The fortress of the Three Heads is taken. We bring your dead so you can bury them."

"Gods, no!" uttered the lookout. "Those are Plataean corpses in the carts!"

"Shut up!" hissed Menesarkus. He scratched his beard and peered into the distance, in the direction of the Three Heads—the fortress guarding the narrow pass through the Kithaerons. This was a disaster! The Spartans had succeeded in taking a fort the Plataeans had always thought was impenetrable. With this crucial stronghold in Spartan hands, Menesarkus realized with a sinking heart, the Plataean emissaries would not be able to return from their mission to Athens by the shortest path. And neither would Nikias, for that matter. They would have to take an alternate route by sea that could take many days or even weeks.

"I'm coming down, Drako," Menesarkus said in a booming voice, then turned and clambered down the stairs to the ground level, followed by Chusor. His knee ached with every step.

When he got to the bottom of the tower he went out the door and paused in the area in front of the gates. The throng of men had stopped work on the interior bastion wall and were milling about near the sally port door that was locked and guarded by armed warriors.

"Open the door!" commanded Menesarkus. "Let me through."

"But Arkon!" protested the guard. "There's a Spartan—"

"Open the damned sally port," barked Menesarkus. "There's only one Spartan out there."

"But you're unarmed!"

Menesarkus whacked the guardsman on the side of the head with his staff. "Weapon in hand," he said.

The guards unbarred the door and Menesarkus stepped outside the walls and went straight up to Drako, stopping a few feet away. They stared into each other's eyes for a long time.

"There are forty-three bodies," said Drako. "They all died fighting. None were put to death, as you will clearly see from their wounds. We took another twenty-one Plataeans prisoner." He gestured with his thumb at the roped and naked men standing listlessly in front of the Spartan phalanx.

Menesarkus was speechless. The dead Plataean warriors were a hard loss, but to see twenty-one prisoners in the clutches of the Spartans was worse. "And what are you going to do with our brothers?" he asked at last.

"I will trade them," said Drako.

"Trade them for what?" asked Menesarkus.

"Prince Arkilokus."

"Are you still missing your precious royal?" asked Menesarkus in a mocking voice. "Perhaps he went whoring in Thebes."

"Come, Menesarkus, old friend," said Drako. "Do not lie anymore. There is no place else he could be. He foolishly went riding alone that day. Your men must have captured him."

Menesarkus smiled wryly. "And if I had your prince, why would I trade him for a mere twenty-one men? That's not a fair trade at all for a man who must be worth his weight in gold."

"If you wish to see your men again," said Drako, "you will give up Arkilokus. Otherwise those warriors will be sent to Sparta as slaves and you will never see them again."

"I'll make you a bargain," raged Menesarkus, spit flying from his mouth in fury. "I'll trade you Arkilokus's ten fingers and toes and his cock for those twenty-one men. One piece of the prince per man."

"You would not do such a thing to your own grandson," said Drako.

"He may be my flesh and blood," said Menesarkus. "But he's a Spartan. And I'll skin him alive with my own knife if I must."

The two men locked eyes. Drako cocked his head and raised one eyebrow. "I do believe you *would* skin Arkilokus alive," he said with admiration. He turned his head and whistled. The Helots started pulling the carts toward the walls.

"Stop the Helots!" said Menesarkus. "Tell your slaves to leave our dead where they are. We will carry them into the city in honor. And if you do not leave me the prisoners, I will go get you Arkilokus's signet ring right now with the finger attached to show you that I am serious, and then you'll have your proof that I've got him."

Drako smiled and, turning to his men, held up one hand, giving a quick signal in Spartan battle code. Twenty Spartan warriors drew their long daggers and moved menacingly toward the prisoners, and Menesarkus suppressed the urge to cry out. Each of the Spartans grabbed a prisoner's bound hands with one hand, raised his blade . . . and cut through the bonds, setting the Plataean free.

Menesarkus swallowed the lump in his throat and forced himself to breathe again.

"I intended to give them back all along," said Drako with a mirthless smile. "And now I know that Arkilokus lives and is your prisoner. Take care of him, Menesarkus. When we storm the citadel we will expect to find him alive and unharmed. Or else every single man, woman, and child in Plataea will pay for his one death. For *that* is how much a Spartan prince is worth to us." He turned around and marched back toward his waiting hoplites.

Menesarkus cursed himself for an old fool. Drako had played him like a harp. He'd used the threat of sending the prisoners to Sparta merely as a ruse to trick him into revealing that he did indeed have Arkilokus.

"Open the gates!" he ordered.

The gates slowly opened and Menesarkus turned to look into the citadel. Thousands of men and women were now standing there, staring at him with anticipation.

He looked back toward the Spartans. The enemy and their Helots were already marching away, back toward the Persian Fort.

The survivors of the Three Heads started pulling the corpses of their brothers from the carts, carrying them across the field and laying them in front of the gates. Many of the freed warriors were weeping, and almost all had bloody wounds, but they did not rest until they had brought all of the dead to the walls of Plataea.

"Hold up your heads," Menesarkus said to the naked warriors, his voice strained with emotion. "Any honor you lost at the Three Heads you will regain in the coming siege. Thank the gods you've been blessed to live to fight the enemy another day."

As he stood watching the men he heard the sound of a horse's hooves on the rocky ground behind him. He turned and saw Photine walking toward him, breathing hard through her nostrils, tail swishing in agitation, a wild look in her eyes. But she seemed to recognize Menesarkus and bowed her head slightly as if in greeting. She still wore her bridle but the reins had been torn loose. And her haunch was streaked with blood from a wound that looked like claw marks. It had been three days since Nikias had left Plataea on his foolhardy quest to Athens, and now his horse had returned riderless, apparently having come over the Kithaerons from Megarian territory. What had happened to the lad? Had he been killed by a mountain lion? Attacked by Dog Raiders?

"Come . . . come here, girl," Menesarkus said in a voice breaking with emotion. He reached out a trembling hand to seize her noseband, but she whinnied and tossed her head, then bolted in the direction of their ruined farm. He glanced over at Chusor, who stood next to him, watching Photine disappear down the road. Then the smith hung his head low and went back into the citadel.

TWELVE

———————◆———————

Nikias stood on the shore of the Piraeus harbor amidst an armada of beached black warships: a dozen triple-decked galleys as big as temples, and twice as many sleek dispatch ships with single masts sat on the rocky shore. The triremes were built with copper-covered rams projecting from their prows like strange beaks, and all had ornate eyes painted on their prows: the sight of these beached ships brought to mind a throng of forlorn sea monsters that had been stranded at high tide.

"They bring them on to the beach at night to keep the hulls from becoming waterlogged," said General Agape at Nikias's side. "The fir planks soak up water and make them slow. A triple-decker can lose two and a half knots speed if it's left in the water overnight. Now the Persians make their hulls out of the wood of . . ."

Nikias rolled his eyes and tried to ignore the older man's voice, listening instead to a multitude of noises: the cries of birds, the shouts of men, the sounds of hammers and adzes from the nearby shipyard, and the splash of waves. There were thousands of men at work unloading sacks from a massive grain ship that had just arrived from Sicily.

General Agape had been talking nonstop since Nikias had met up with the Plataean emissaries at the port half an hour ago. Back in Plataea the young people referred to the man as "General Windbag" because he never seemed to stop talking or offering advice.

Nikias was relieved that Krates, the other emissary whom his grandfather had sent to Athens, had virtually ignored him since they had come face-to-face on the beach. Agape had been flabbergasted but pleasantly surprised to find Nikias in Athens, but Krates had been furious and scornful, promising him that Nikias's grandfather, the Arkon, would flay his hide for running away from Plataea and interfering with the mission. Nikias and the weather-beaten stonemason had never gotten along. Even when Nikias was a little boy Krates had treated him with disdain, calling Nikias arrogant and a bad influence on his friends.

"Ah, the triple-decker's crew is all assembled now," said Agape. "Observe this maneuver now, lad. It's a thing of beauty."

Nikias watched as a crew of three hundred oarsmen moved into position on either side of one of the ships, gripping the hull along the waterline and pushing it the two hundred feet into the bay with a magnificent ease and efficiency. The noise of the wood scraping on stones cut through the air, and then the ship was in the water with a great splash. The crew climbed on board, swarming over the sides like insects, moving to their seats along the three decks and taking hold of the oars. Within thirty seconds of the warship moving onto the water the oars stroked backward in unison and the ship moved away from the shore.

Nikias turned his gaze farther up the beach to where a smaller crew carried a fifty-man dispatch vessel to the water. Nikias could see Phoenix standing on the ship, barking out orders.

"That one is a scrupulous captain," said Agape, pointing at Phoenix. "You'll notice his men are carrying the boat so the hull does not get a single scrape."

"That's my cousin Phoenix," said Nikias.

"And he is the one who introduced you to General Perikles?" asked Krates with disdain.

"Yes," said Nikias. "He's the captain of Perikles's own ship—the *Sea Nymph*."

"Hmmph," said Krates under his breath. Nikias reckoned Krates must be fuming that their mission to Perikles had failed. The Athenian general had refused to give the Plataeans permission to parlay with the Spartans, and then he'd sent them packing.

"Your meeting was illuminating, then?" asked the old man.

"Perikles is a great leader," Nikias said.

"He told you nothing of import? Anything you would like to share with us?"

"No."

"And yet we are to be delivered to Delphinium with such urgency," said Krates in a scoffing tone. "In Perikles's own personal dispatch vessel? This is such a high honor for a pair of old emissaries who were given no more than ten minutes of the general's precious time and sent away like naughty schoolboys."

Nikias shrugged. He wasn't about to reveal to Krates the message that Perikles had given him to deliver to his grandfather. He felt proud that he had been selected by the Athenian general to bring this information—a message that Perikles had entrusted to him and not to the emissaries.

"We were told this dispatch vessel can make seventy sea miles per day," said Agape. "It's one of the fastest in the fleet."

"It's two and a half days of hard rowing to Delphinium if we're lucky," said Krates. "If this weather holds. And then we'll have two days of hard riding to Plataea near enemy territory."

"Nikias is a good rider," said Agape. "He won't slow us down, I'm sure. Even with one arm in a sling."

"That's not the point I was getting at," fumed Krates.

Nikias glanced behind him where the six Plataean cavalrymen who had escorted Agape and Krates to Athens stood. They were dressed in tunics, holding their light armor and weapons in leather sacks. He was glad these warriors were with them. He'd known all of them his entire life and they were battle-hardened hoplites and good riders. Nikias would not have relished the notion of riding near Theban territory with just Agape and Krates. They had both been capable warriors in their primes, though Agape was a little stout to be a fast rider, and Krates was in his late eighties and becoming feeble.

"We can go now," said Agape, pointing at the dock that stretched into the bay. The dispatch vessel had rowed over to the dock and waited for the Plataeans to board.

Krates walked quickly on his bandy old legs toward the dock, followed by General Agape. Nikias fell in line with the cavalrymen. One of them, a man in his early thirties named Teuker, flashed a smile at Nikias behind his black beard.

"So what happened to your arm, Nik?" he asked.

"Photine," said Nikias, shamefaced. The other riders laughed.

"That white mare of yours will get you killed one day," replied Teuker.

"But she's the fastest thing in the Oxlands," said another one of the cavalrymen. "I couldn't keep up with you when you charged the Thebans!"

A big warrior named Alexandros slapped Nikias on the back. "I'm glad you're with us," he said. "Nikias brought us luck against the Thebans," he announced to the others, "and he'll bring us luck on *this* journey back home."

Nikias was pleased. Krates might be scornful of his presence in Athens, but these warriors were glad to have him.

"Why did you come to Athens, anyway?" asked Teuker under his breath. "Did your grandfather send you on a special mission?"

"Long story," said Nikias. "I'm just glad to be going home."

"Have you ever been on a lengthy sea voyage?" asked Teuker.

"No," said Nikias. "Just on a little sailboat in the Bay of Korinth. Like that one," he added, pointing to a small, dilapidated sailboat an old fisherman was pushing from the shore into the water.

"You might not be so glad an hour from now," replied Teuker.

As Nikias walked across the gangplank with the others Phoenix grabbed him by the arm and hissed in his ear, "Stay out of the way, cousin. And don't fall overboard."

Nikias made his way down the aisle between the two sides of the *Sea Nymph*'s oarsmen. He recognized most of the men—Phoenix's crew from the inn. They stared straight ahead, sitting stone-faced, as if steeling themselves for a long fight. He noticed that every mariner had his cushion under his arse and this made him smile.

Shields were stowed next to each bench and held fast to the wall of the ship with leather straps. Nikias knew that shields used to be attached to the bulwarks of ships in the olden days—to protect the rowers from enemy arrows. But the Athenians had come up with the clever idea of raising the bulwarks high enough to shield the oarsmen, protecting them within the walls of the ship itself. Weapons such as bows and quivers and boarding axes were stowed under the benches.

The ship felt like a safe place. A phalanx that moved upon the sea.

Nikias joined Krates, Agape, and the Plataean cavalrymen at the stern, where his cousin stood by the man at the tiller. Phoenix cried out, "Oars down!" The oarsmen reacted as one, dropping their oars into the water and flexing their muscled backs. "Pull easy, now!" commanded Phoenix. The poles squeaked as they pivoted against the rope oarlocks.

The ship eased forward, moving away from the dock, gaining speed with every unified sweep of the oars. Nikias turned and stared at the Parthenon, shining in the morning sun atop the Akropolis. He thought of the impromptu ceremony in the temple led by Perikles. The Athenian general's prayer echoed in his mind. He leaned back and closed his eyes, trying to picture the ivory face of the statue of Athena, but instead he saw Helena. He felt a surge of longing, like a fist digging into the pit of his stomach. Would he ever see her again? Hold her in his arms? Feel her body? Take her? But then he thought of Kallisto—pictured her lying on a bed, so frail and frightened after she had awoken from her unconscious state—and he felt a rush of guilt.

The ship hit some choppy waves and started to rock back and forth. Nikias opened his eyes and frowned. He saw Teuker staring at him.

"I think Nikias needs to be near the side," announced Teuker. "In case he has to feed the fish."

Nikias swallowed slowly and realized that something wasn't right in his gut. He moved to the edge of the boat and gripped the side with a white hand, feeling his breakfast churn in his stomach. The strong scent of pine pitch and brine mingled in the stultifying air with the smell of greasy sheep tallow used to coat the oarlocks; the reek clawed at his nostrils.

Krates stared at Nikias and smiled cruelly. "It's going to be a long journey," he said. "Oh, yes. A *long* journey for young Nikias."

Nikias glanced behind the ship and saw, in its wake, the tiny sailboat the old man had pushed off from the beach. It had unfurled its sail and was tacking into the wind. Watching the sailboat made him feel even queasier, so he looked up above and saw a black bird hovering near the top of the dispatch vessel's mast.

The bird was too big to be a crow, Nikias mused. It must be a raven. It seemed strange that such a creature would be flying over the sea—the realm of gulls and other seabirds. He took it as a good sign: the gods were telling him that an Oxlander like himself, unused to ships and waves, would be safe upon the water.

He realized his heart was beating quickly and that he had broken out in a clammy sweat all over his face and armpits. He was overcome by a strange panic the likes of which he'd never felt before. It was as though he were intoxicated—a sensation of spinning—but without the pleasurable feeling that came from being drunk.

"The fried squid was good this morning," said Krates in an affected offhand manner. "You can say one thing about the Athenians: they know how to cook. I can still taste that fermented fish sauce on my tongue."

Nikias tried to drown out Krates's voice and think of anything but the smell of fried squid and fish sauce, and the sound of that hateful old man's smacking tongue. But it didn't work. He felt the boat veer in another direction, and his stomach lurched. He let forth a groan, then jerked forward, leaning over the side of the boat to be sick into the sea as laughter erupted from behind him.

The ship passed through the narrow gap in the stone sea walls that guarded the entrance to the harbors of the Piraeus, and a shrill horn sounded from one of the towers, signaling to the god of the sea that an Athenian ship was leaving the safety of the port and heading into his realm.

"Poseidon . . . have mercy on me," moaned Nikias.

As the Athenian dispatch vessel headed south—its oars sweeping powerfully and rhythmically, propelling it onward into the Saronik gulf—the little sailboat that had been following in its wake wore sails, catching the increasing wind, and turned fast, sweeping around and heading westward toward the island of Salamis.

To all eyes it appeared to be a shabby fishing boat laden with nets, guided at the tiller by a weather-beaten old fisherman. But in reality it was a speedy craft of Phoenician design, disguised to hide its sleek hull and sophisticated rigging. And the old man was no fisherman, although his face was as dark brown and wrinkled as anyone who'd spent his entire life on the sea.

The raven that had been hovering over the dispatch vessel veered back toward the sailboat, as though responding to a call. It flew over to the small craft, hovering there on the wind, staring down with its intelligent eyes. Then the black bird tucked its wings and dove, landing on the pile of nets in the prow, cawing and stabbing at the netting.

The netting stirred, and slowly a man extricated himself from where he hid under the meshwork. Andros could barely move from the torture he'd suffered at the jail, and his face was swollen nearly beyond recognition. But he was so happy to be alive that he didn't care if he were crippled for life. The odd little Skythian boy had saved him from excruciating torture and a certain death.

The Fates wove strange threads and cast curious nets.

After escaping from the jail, Andros had made his way to the port without being spotted. There, in a building owned by a Lydian silk merchant in the employ of the Persians, he'd been reunited with his fellow conspirators, who had just received new information from their highly placed man in Perikles's inner circle. Andros had been briefed on the situation, and then he'd written coded messages, sending them via homing pigeons to the city of Korinth to the west and, most importantly, north to the island of Euboea, where the Athenian vessel was headed. The speedy pigeons could fly fifty miles in an hour. In a few hours they would be at their destinations. . . .

The raven hopped onto Andros's shoulder and rubbed its beak against his ear. Andros found a fish head on the bottom of the boat and handed it to the bird, who took it gently from his fingers. "Good Telemakos," said Andros, smiling. "Smart bird."

"Who was on that Athenian galley?" asked the old man.

"The Plataean emissaries," said Andros. "And orders for the generals at the siege of Potidaea, including the most recent code key."

The wind picked up and filled the sail, making it taut. This wind would be in the faces of the Athenian ship, Andros mused. The old sailor pulled on a rope and sent up a second, smaller sail. The ship jumped and moved forward even faster.

Andros realized he would never be able to return to Athens after what had happened. It was too dangerous for him there now. But that didn't matter anymore. He had accomplished much in his two years pretending to be a bard in the enemy citadel. And there were many other men in place to carry on his work. Now he could shift his efforts to the forthcoming siege of Plataea.

He pictured the two fifty-oared attack ships that were beached in a deserted cove on the west side of the island of Euboea. The sleek, long-keeled boats were manned by the strongest Korinthian oarsmen and outfitted with a complement of archers and hoplites. The spy in Perikles's employ had given the silk merchant the latest shield signals, and Andros had sent these along with the message borne by the carrier pigeon. The Korinthian ships would be able to intercept the Athenian galley in the Straits of Euboea by luring the sailors with the signals, then attack miles before it reached the safety of the harbor of Delphinium.

Once the Athenian dispatch ship had been captured, all of its surviving oarsmen would be taken to Syrakuse and sold—they would spend the rest of their lives cutting marble in the dreaded Prison Pits or chained to an oar bench in a slave ship. And the boat itself would be added to the growing Korinthian fleet.

Perikles would never know what had happened to his galley. It would become yet another Delian League vessel that had vanished without a trace. . . .

"We'll have a quick journey home to Korinth," said the old man. "The wind is in our favor."

Andros smiled, ignoring the pain on his back where the Skythian whip had ripped his flesh. Closing his tired eyes, he let the sun warm his swollen face.

"The *gods* are in our favor," he said.

PART III

The Persian gods were strange to us. But that did not make them any less formidable.

—Papyrus fragment from the "Lost History" of the Peloponnesian War by the "Exiled Scribe"

ONE

On the day before his impending execution by suicide, Eurymakus the Theban sat alone in his library, composing a letter in coded glyphs, starting the missive over several times because his writing was shaky and illegible. But it wasn't fear of his coming death that caused such an unsteady hand. The problem was that his writing hand was no longer attached to his arm—he had amputated it at the elbow on the field of battle in front of Plataea, and now he was forced to use his left hand to hold the stylus. He felt like a child learning to write all over again.

The coded words in Persian script resembled the tracks of bird feet made in sand. It was based on the ancient wedge writing he had seen on old clay tablets on his first trip to Persia when he was a young man. He had found one of these tablets for sale in the market of Persepolis. The tablet fit into its own baked clay envelope. And even though he hadn't been able to read the writing at the time, he had bought the old thing and kept it as a souvenir of Persia. It sat on his desk now—a weight to hold down sheets of papyrus.

Later, after he learned to read the ancient Persian script, he discovered that the clay tablet and its envelope were nothing more than a mundane record of grain shipments, written by some lowly clerk. The letter he wrote now was of a far different kind. He read over what he had inscribed:

> *"Greetings, my most beloved and honored King Artaxerxes, son of Xerxes, lord of Persia and blessed of the true god Ahura Mazda. I, Eurymakus, magistrate of Thebes and your loyal vassal, offer news that will sadden your heart. By the time you receive this letter I will be dead. The sneak attack on the city-state of Plataea—that city of demons, your father's bane, where he suffered his greatest defeat against the depraved Athenians and Spartans and their allies—has utterly failed. And this loyal servant has been blamed for the disaster.*

There was a gentle knock on the door and a slave, his eyes red from weeping, poked in his head. "There is a doctor, sent by the council, to see you, master."

Eurymakus put down his stylus and touched his upper lip where the Skythian boy had bit it off during the fight at Menesarkus's farmhouse. The missing flesh had left Eurymakus with a perpetual sneer on his otherwise handsome face.

"Send him in," he said to the slave. He tried not to move his mouth when he spoke, for the pain was severe.

"Dr. Pisenor," said the slave, and then disappeared.

The doctor, as thin as a reed, white-haired, and decrepit, shuffled into the library and stood before Eurymakus's desk. "Every slave in your house is in tears," said Pisenor with an impressed tone, stroking his beard with a hand shaking from palsy. "They must love their master."

"They don't cry for me," said Eurymakus. "They are all to be sent to the quarries after I'm dead. My wives and children too. Or hadn't you heard?"

"I—I was away for the trial," said Pisenor, embarrassed. "I just returned from the coast. I was taking the sea air. I have a small house near Anthedon. It was my mother's uncle's house and he died childless, leaving it to me and . . ." He trailed off, having caught the withering look on Eurymakus's face. "My apologies, Eurymakus," he continued. "I blather on. Your punishment is harsh. *Too* harsh, in my opinion."

Eurymakus put down his stylus and placed a hand on the stump of his right arm. It ached fiercely. But none of it mattered anymore. None of the physical pain or mutilation of his body meant anything. Soon he would be dead, and his spirit would be reunited with his perfect and unchangeable form in the Other Realm.

Now he just wanted it all to be over. He had failed to kill Menesarkus and his scion, the citadel of Plataea was still standing, and Eurymakus was an outcast from the city in which he was born. After he had escaped the massacre at the gates of the citadel, he had fled back to the Spartan camp at the Persian Fort. He had hoped to rest there until he could take passage to Persia—the place he had gone to study in his youth and where he'd been recruited by the Persian king's high whisperer: a man who had trained him and sent him back to Greece as a spy to help bring about Artaxerxes's reconquest of Greece.

But the Spartan general Drako, who hated Eurymakus, had handed him over to the Thebans, knowing full well that they would turn the spy into a scapegoat for the disastrous outcome of the attack on Plataea. Somebody had to be punished. Who better than the man who had planned the whole thing?

"What do you want?" asked Eurymakus.

"Tomorrow at dawn," said Pisenor, "I will mix the hemlock and watch over you while the poison takes effect. I am here to instruct you on the procedure."

Eurymakus lowered his head and rubbed his eyes. He knew all about poisons and their effects. He didn't need to be told by some senile old man what would happen. First his toes would become numb and cold, and then the numbness would pass up his legs, to the testicles, then the torso, and finally to his heart. And then his heart would stop beating and his soul would abandon this wretched husk for another . . . a perfect celestial body.

He brought his right hand to his mouth to kiss his signet ring—the ring with the name of his guardian angel inscribed on the stone. But when he looked down he saw only the stump. The hand and ring had been gone for ten days now. Many times over the last several days his mind had tricked him this way, as though his brain were mocking his soul.

The doctor cleared his throat and said, "I assure you it is painless, Eurymakus. Shall I explain exactly what happens—"

"Pain?" shouted Eurymakus, his face contorted in wrath. "You think I am afraid of pain? You idiot! Pain is meaningless to me. Humiliation, however, is worse than any pain this world could inflict upon me."

"I didn't—"

"Shut up, old fool!" sneered Eurymakus. "Why do you think they sent you to me? A palsied old shit-for-brains who has just returned from a vacation at the sea! It's ludicrous. At least they could have given me the honor of having my head severed from my body by the public executioner. No! A jury convicts me of treason against my own city, when the truth is that my plan was ruined by the incompetence of the generals leading the expedition and the cowardliness of the men under their command. But they punish *me* by sending my entire household into slavery, and they make me live with the wretches for days, listening to their howls and sobs, in an attempt to degrade my spirit even more. And now they send you, Pisenor—a doddering herb-grinder—to be my executioner. It's galling. It's mortifying." He stopped and wiped the spittle from his mouth, twitching with fury, glaring at the old man.

Pisenor had watched in silence as Eurymakus vented his spleen. "So you don't want the hemlock tutorial, then?" he said at last.

Eurymakus reached for the clay tablet on his desk, intending to throw it at the doctor's head, and realized with dismay that he was trying to clutch the object with his missing hand. He gasped and turned away from Pisenor, hiding his face. "Get out," he hissed. "Get out."

Pisenor left him alone, and Eurymakus picked up the clay tablet with his left hand and hurled it against the wall, where it shattered.

He stumbled back to his chair and sat, staring at the clay lamp on the desk with its unlit charred wick floating in the dark oil. He thought of his imminent death and funeral pyre with misery.

The slave poked his head in the door again. "Master," he whispered. "Nihani begs to see you."

Eurymakus sighed and shook his head. Nihani, his Persian wife, was his favorite of all his consorts. She had been a gift from King Artaxerxes: a temple prostitute skilled in the arts of love-play. She had known how to please him from the moment of their first night together.

He hadn't been able to face her since coming back from the disaster at Plataea. He didn't want her to see his mutilated mouth, his missing right arm. He had been filled with a shame so profound after the loss to the Plataeans that he felt as though his spirit had already left his body. There was nothing left but a hollowed-out gourd.

"Master?" pressed the slave.

"No," said Eurymakus. "I don't want her to . . . I don't want to see her."

"She said she would kill herself if you didn't let her come to you."

Eurymakus considered this for a moment. Nihani was perfectly capable of committing self-violence. She was a bold, strong-willed woman, unlike his other docile and lazy wives, who were good for nothing but breeding pudgy little brats. Nihani had yet to give him a child. He didn't care, though. He loved her more than any of them put together. But after his execution she would be sent away to the quarries with the rest. It was such a waste. Like casting aside the most splendid jewel into a heap of dung.

"Bring her," he said, half-miserable, half-relieved.

He rested his face on his remaining hand with his eyes half-closed. His heart started beating wildly as he waited for Nihani to enter. What would she say to him? Would she chastise him for his failures? Berate him for the dismal future that now lay before her? He feared her reprimands more than the poisoned cup. By the time the door opened he was shaking from nerves and felt like he would be sick. He kept his eyes hidden by his hand as she approached the table. He couldn't look at her. She stopped on the other side of the table, standing in silence.

"My husband," she said at last in a stern voice, speaking in Persian. "Why do you cry like a little girl?"

"I can't look upon you," he replied with a quaking voice in the same language. "I have lost you. And I have lost my honor. I am ugly."

"You haven't lost me, or your honor," said Nihani. "And you are still as beautiful as an angel."

She placed something on the desk. He spread his fingers apart so he could peer at the thing: a knife handle sticking from an onyx box; the weapon and box were fitted so precisely together that it appeared the blade had been driven into the stone.

"My assassin's dagger!" thought Eurymakus.

The sheath was filled with the deadliest poison known to Persian whisperers: "Dragon Blood" it was called. The slightest scratch from the tainted blade caused an excruciating and nearly instant death. He had learned to make the concoction in Persia, mixing the powerful venom of saw-scaled vipers along with the juices of wolfsbane, oleander, and hemlock, and then brewing this noxious potion for several months in a sheep's bladder. He had brought the vipers with him to Thebes from Persia, and he'd bred the snakes for years in the undercroft beneath his slaves' quarters. He grew all of the poisonous plants in the courtyard of his house—his garden of death.

The dagger and its slightly rounded stone sheath were rotating slowly on the tabletop where Nihani had set it spinning like the iron pointer on a lodestone.

Why had she brought this tool of death to him?

"You wish that I should kill us both now?" he asked.

The sound of Nihani's harsh laugh caused him to jerk his hand away from his face and stare at her for the first time since she had entered the room. He was taken aback by what he saw now, for Nihani resembled a young man: she wore one of his tunics and his leather riding boots, standing with her hands on her narrow hips, shaking her head with a scornful expression on her handsome face. She had cut off all of her long curls so that her hair was as short as a man's, which made her more ravishing than ever in Eurymakus's eyes.

"Die together?" she sneered. "That's the last thing I would want."

"Then why have you come?" he asked. "Why did you cut your hair?"

"I have come to plan our escape," she said. "And I cut my hair and burned it, in the manner of these Thebans when they come of age and offer their hair to their war god. I am ready to join you in your battle against the demons."

Eurymakus looked at her in disbelief. "Where will we go?" he asked. "I am nothing. I am ruined. My own people have sentenced me to death. The Spartans spurn me."

Nihani tilted back her head and looked down her nose at him with her black eyes. "Where is my husband?" she asked, her thick dark eyebrows arching. "Where is he hiding?"

Eurymakus recoiled. "Your husband is here," he said, pointing to his heart. "This ruined body is not me."

"I wasn't talking about your body," she spat. "You look the same to me as when you set out from Thebes to kill the Plataeans who murdered your brother. What care I if you are missing an arm? What care I if your face were *covered* with scars? You have the wounds of a hero." She put her palms on the table, leaning close to his face. "I want my husband to come back. The *spirit* of my husband. What I see in your eyes is a cunt staring back at me!" And she repeated the word in Greek, spitting on the table.

Eurymakus stood up, mouth agape. "What do you say to me? How dare you!"

Nihani strode to the other side of the table and lifted up the front of his robe, peering at his loins with disdain. "I expected to see the petals of a woman's lips down there. But your manhood remains, however shriveled it may be." She grabbed his balls in one hand, squeezing them hard. Then she lifted up her tunic to reveal the carved phallus that she always wore during their lovemaking. "Bend over," she commanded.

When Eurymakus hesitated, Nihani grabbed his long hair at the nape of his neck and shoved him toward the desk.

"Bend over, I say!"

He let himself be pushed down until his stomach was flat on the tabletop, and then he stretched out his arm and stump. Nihani lifted up his robes, baring his naked buttocks and legs. She picked up the oil lamp that sat on the table and poured its contents onto his backside. He felt the cool oil dripping down his inner thighs and legs as her fingers worked the lubrication into his crease. He waited with anticipation, and gasped with pleasure when she slowly entered him.

"Ah," she said, reaching around and stroking his growing erection. "There's still blood running through those veins."

"Tell me what to do," said Eurymakus, grabbing the edge of the table with his remaining hand as she slammed against him. "T-tell me."

She pushed all the way inside him and leaned over his back, whispering in his ear. "The men who guard the front door to this house take their pleasure with me every night. All three of them at the same time. When they are all inside me, heedless and witless, you will slay them with the poisoned dagger." She started pumping again, slapping his buttocks with one hand. "Do you understand?"

"Unnnhh," he gasped. "But the guards—"

"The guards are beasts," she replied. "I have brought them under my control like dogs."

He stared at the dagger on the table. It would be easy to kill three unarmed men. He could already see their corpses writhing in agony on the floor. "But where will we go?" he asked. "The city confiscated all of my wealth."

"I have darics," she said. "They were hidden in a secret compartment in my dowry chest that I brought from Persia. Enough to get us back to Persepolis. I have already purchased horses. They're at a stable near the gates. We will ride down the eastern road through the night. You told me once you have allies in other city-states. Once we get away from Thebes, we can plan how to get to the coast and hire a ship."

Eurymakus nodded his head. It was a good plan. She had learned much from him. His life in Thebes was over. But that did not mean he should give up his duties to the one true god. Why should he throw his life away because an assembly of incompetent men had cast their votes against him? Eurymakus had not been born to serve as a scapegoat!

"You are a good wife," he said.

"I am your secret *husband* now," said Nihani. "Nihani *was* your wife." She thrust her hips, stroking him with her hand at the same time. "Tell me I am your husband."

"Yes—my husband!" cried out Eurymakus. He imagined Menesarkus's heir. He saw the young pankrator in his mind's eye, on his knees, groveling and submissive, bleeding from many wounds, raped and defiled.

In no time at all Eurymakus bucked and shuddered violently, crying out in ecstasy, "My husband!"

TWO

———————◆———————

Chusor led a sleepy, and therefore sulky, Barka through the Sarkophagi—the cemetery that stood outside the western wall of the citadel of Plataea. The eunuch, as Chusor was well aware, liked to sleep in very late. But he'd roused Barka from bed a few hours before sunrise and had asked him, with all of the politeness he could muster, to follow him to the graves.

"I always knew you were going to be the death of me," Barka joked as he stared at the cemetery.

Like the streets of Plataea the Sarkophagi was laid out on an orderly grid. Family tombs were constructed of black marble and made to resemble miniature versions of houses. The little pathways of the cemetery were lined with tall cypress trees and low-growing juniper. A few crocuses had started to poke through the ground, and the vines of the everlasting flowers—snaking around the monuments— were beginning to sprout their tiny gray leaves.

Chusor thought back to yesterday in front of the walls: the terrible omen of Nikias's riderless and bloodied horse returning to Plataea alone. Was the lad dead? He clung to the hope that his friend still lived. But his stomach felt heavy and sick, as though it were filled with ore slag.

"A pretty little city for shades," commented Barka, the irritation in his voice contradicting his words. He wore a woman's dress, veil, and straw sun hat—all of which he'd purchased in the marketplace of Plataea—and now resembled a female Oxlander. "These Plataeans know how to make domiciles for their dead," continued the eunuch.

Chusor paused to look back at the high wall of the citadel. Every ten feet along the battlements stood a watchman with a spear. He saw a figure waving at them and frowned.

"Who is that?" he wondered aloud.

Barka sighed. "It's the man from the gates. The one who was tasting me with his eyes that first day we entered the citadel. Damon."

Damon gave a lingering look at Barka before continuing on his inspection of the battlements.

"At least he's not too hairy," said Barka. "I can't abide the hairy ones. Like smelly monkeys. And he gives me pretty things like this bracelet." He held up his wrist to show a cheap bauble.

"You don't have to pleasure the man," said Chusor.

"My dear Chusor," said the eunuch, "you know as well as I that having a man like Damon, captain of the Guards, wrapped around my pinkie is a boon to our endeavors."

Chusor rubbed a hand over his scalp. Barka was right. The more their group was integrated into Plataean society, the less suspicion would arise toward their activities. He gestured for Barka to keep following and they walked in silence until they came to the outlying section of the Sarkophagi. Here there were tombs in the ancient style—elongated rectangles with lids, carved from limestone and granite. These cracked and crumbling memorials had been worn away over the years by wind and rain and were a stark contrast to the well-kept marble grave markers of recent centuries.

"How old are these?" asked Barka, running his fingers over the rough edge of a gravestone.

"Five hundred years, perhaps," said Chusor. "Maybe longer. They were built by the race of men who lived in this valley long before the Greek-speaking Plataeans arrived. The citadel here was built on top of the ruins of their city. They spoke a language akin to Phoenician, but their writing is mostly indecipherable, at least to me. The legends say that these people—whom the locals call the "Ox Turners"—had a vast treasure in gold which they buried under their city. But they were wiped out by the invasions of the Sea People. A Greek tyrant discovered the buried hoard, but then he was slain by a democratic hero named Androkles. And the secret of its location died with him."

"Ah!" exclaimed Barka. "The statue in the agora of that delicious youth."

"That is the hero Androkles," said Chusor. "Slayer of the Last Tyrant."

"And how did you come to know all of this?" asked Barka.

"The architect Hippodamos of Miletus told my former master Phidias," said Chusor. "I overheard them speaking one night while they drank. Hippodamos was the man the Plataeans brought to improve their city after the victory against the Persians. They paid for this construction program with the gold they'd gleaned from the bodies of the dead princes in King Xerxes's army. The Persian nobles went to war covered in gold, the fools, and their corpses made the Plataeans wealthy beyond compare."

"And where is this Persian gold kept?" asked Barka. "Perhaps we should just steal *it*."

Chusor waved a hand at the citadel. "They spent every granule of gold on the city itself. No expense was spared. Hippodamos—the greatest architect in Greece—was kept busy for ten years expanding these walls, building temples and public spaces. During his work he discovered a network of tunnels under the citadel."

"And?"

"They led nowhere. They were all dead ends. And so he gave up looking for the hoard of the Ox Turners. When I moved here with Diokles I began my quest. But after two years of searching I hadn't even found a single tunnel entrance. Until the night of the Theban sneak attack, that is."

He recounted that fateful night when he and a handful of warriors tried to figure out a way for Nikias to escape from Plataea and warn the men outside the walls that the Thebans had taken the citadel. The invaders had controlled the gates that night—the only exit in and out of the city—as well as the battlements. Breaking out had seemed impossible until the oldest man in Plataea, the priest of the Temple of Zeus, had shown them the entrance to the secret tunnel hidden under the temple altar. Nikias had crawled through this shaft, making his way under the city walls and emerging outside.

"The shaft led to a tomb," said Chusor.

"Where?" asked Barka.

Chusor pointed to a granite box—about the size of a table—that was missing its top. The smith jumped inside and squatted in front of the opening to a narrow shaft that ran back in the direction of the western wall, less than twenty paces from the tomb.

"This is the tunnel Nikias used to escape," said Chusor. He peered into the gloom of the shaft and breathed in the dank odor of the underground passage. A shudder passed through him. He hated any cramped space and had a terror of being trapped underground.

"And what makes you believe this tunnel has anything to do with the treasure of the Ox Turners?" asked Barka.

Chusor clambered out of the tomb and stood over a broken stone slab where it lay on the ground next to the tomb. The face of the slab was covered with inscribed letters. "When Nikias came out of the tomb he had to push off this lid to get out, flipping it over so the side facing down was revealed. It's cracked in several pieces, as you can see, but I put them back together." He passed his hand over some letters etched into the stone. "Unlike the outside of the tomb, this underside of the lid was never exposed to the elements, and it looks like the day it was carved."

"Those are ancient Phoenician words," said Barka.

"Of course," said Chusor. "I knew that when I first saw them because there are no vowels. But I can only pick out a few of the words. There"—pointing to the center of the slab—"are the words 'trove gold' and the numbers are recognizable, but as a whole they're meaningless."

Chusor watched as the eunuch knelt down and ran his hands over the letters and numbers, this way and that, up and down, even in circles.

"I don't need your seer-sight now," snapped Chusor, thinking Barka was going into one of his trances. "I need your knowledge of Phoenician. You were educated in the library of Karthago. You must have seen any number of ancient Phoenician texts and—"

"Shut up!" said Barka. "I'm trying to think."

If any other man had told Chusor to "shut up" he would have twisted his neck and popped off his head. But Barka was different. He was so much like a woman in both aspect and demeanor that Chusor was always thrown off guard whenever they interacted. Especially when he snapped at him like an angry female.

Barka stared at the sky, tracing a finger up and down his neck. He shuddered, then walked quickly away.

"Wait," said Chusor, running after him. "Tell me what you discovered about the words on the slab."

"Take me to the highest place in the citadel," said Barka. "I need to see something."

The Eagle's Turret was the tallest point in the citadel—a tower on the southeastern section of wall, directly behind the smithy building. The guards on the walkway below the tower were used to seeing Chusor up there and let him and his pretty veiled companion gain access to the stairs leading to the top.

"The view of the citadel is on the other side," said Chusor as Barka went and stood at the low wall on the top of the turret facing the Plataean valley.

"I don't want to look at the city," said Barka. "I want to look at the countryside."

"What do you see?" asked the smith.

"There," said Barka, pointing in the distance.

"What?" asked Chusor.

"A plowman and an ox," said Barka.

Chusor cursed under his breath. "This is not the time for games, Barka." He glanced at the farmer and wondered what sort of optimistic fool would be plowing a field in front of a city that was about to be besieged.

"You didn't understand most of the words on the slab," explained Barka, "because they're written in an old dialect of Phoenician, which I can read. And the order of the letters is confounding, unless you know the secret of the way they were transcribed."

Chusor gave Barka his full attention. "And what is the secret?"

Barka said, "You told me the ancient inhabitants of this place were called the 'Ox Turners.' But the name has nothing to do with their occupation, though I'm sure they worked these fields just like the Plataeans. What the name refers to is the way a plowman, once he has reached the end of his furrow, turns his ox and plow, and walks back across the field, only to turn around and go back the other way."

Chusor stared into the distance and watched as the plowman got to the end of his rectangle of earth and made a tight turn.

"You see?" asked Barka, smiling. "The language is read from left to right. But the line below is scanned from right to left, then left to right, then right to left, and so on. That is called the turning of the ox."

"Ah," said Chusor. "I did not know that."

"And thus you were scanning the words in the wrong direction," said Barka smugly. "You need to start from the bottom and work your way to the top."

The smith tugged on his goatee with excitement. It was so simple! "So could you read it?" he asked.

"Oh yes," said Barka. "And you were right. They're instructions on how to find the 'treasure trove.' You must start with the 'navel of the city,' as they called it. Everything is paced out from there to an arm's length with the use of a special rock for directions—magnetite I think it is called in the Greek."

"A compass," said Chusor. Then he started laughing. "Zeus's Thumb," he said. "The 'navel of the city' is Zeus's Thumb."

"Whatever are you babbling about?" asked Barka.

He pointed down into the city. "In the oldest part of the citadel is an ancient stone. Some kind of marker worn by centuries of rain. The people call it Zeus's Thumb because it looks like a great finger jutting from the ground. That is where we start."

"I'm happy to have helped," said Barka. "Now I need to go back to bed."

Chusor grabbed Barka's arm and said in a low voice, "No one must learn about our secret."

Barka glanced at him. "Who would I tell?"

Chusor seized Barka under the arms and raised the eunuch up in the air as though he were a child—lifted him up near the tower's battlements. The eunuch let out a terrified scream, but Chusor brought him back down to his feet and hugged him to his chest.

"I thought you were going to throw me to my death," said Barka, wide-eyed.

"Only a madman would throw away his treasure," said Chusor, laughing.

THREE

———◆———

"Lad! Lad!" said General Agape with a cheerful and excited tone, probing him with his foot where Nikias lay in the hold of the ship, covered in sick. "We can see the Parnes Mountains!"

Nikias groaned and curled up into a tighter ball. He would have enjoyed seeing the famous sight, but he could barely open his eyes, let alone utter a reply. He'd been felled by Poseidon's wrath for the last two days, shivering and vomiting until there wasn't even bile left in his guts, dry heaving like a dying dog. If Agape were to announce that he had come to slit Nikias's throat, the young pankrator would have smiled and welcomed a quick death, such was the profound agony of his seasickness.

Every so often during the voyage General Agape had come to visit Nikias in the dark hold—where the Plataean cavalrymen had carried his incapacitated body—and fill him in on the journey's progress, droning on like a persistent and irritating Olympian tour guide. But Nikias had missed it all, alone in the hold, listening to the ceaseless creak of the oars and the slap of the waves on the hull, cursing the day he'd been born, cursing the day he'd decided to set out from Plataea, and even cursing the man who'd built the first boat.

"Here," said Agape, kneeling down and holding a skin filled with water to Nikias's parched mouth. "Take a sip."

Nikias shook his head. He tried to say the word "no" but it came out as a feeble moan. Even the thought of water repulsed him. But Agape poured some in his mouth anyway, saying, "Just a sip. You must not get dried out. Your blood will become thin."

"Thanks, General," Nikias forced himself to say after he'd swallowed.

"It will be dusk in an hour or so," said Agape. "The wind is picking up. We're going to put into the next cove and beach the boat for the night. You might be able to eat something and get some sleep. Tomorrow we'll be on the last leg of the journey. Captain Phoenix says we'll arrive at Delphinium before zenith."

"Praise Zeus," said Nikias with a shuddering sigh.

"Ships!" called out the voice of a lookout on deck.

"What's that?" said Agape, cocking his head to one side. "What did he say?"

Nikias listened. He heard Phoenix's voice asking, "Who are they?"

"They're Athenian," replied a voice from the other side of the deck. "Fifty-oared attack ships by the look of them. I count two. They're flying the proper flags."

"They're flashing a shield signal," said a second voice. "It says: 'Put up oars.'"

After a pause Nikias heard Phoenix say, "Poseidon's prick! Why do they want us to put up oars?"

"They say: 'Urgent news,'" called out the second voice again, relaying the signal.

There followed some muttering between Phoenix and a few of his men at the tiller—a disagreement that Nikias couldn't quite hear. After a few minutes Phoenix said, "Stop pulling. We'll wait for them to get within shouting distance."

"I wonder what news the other ships bring?" said Agape. "I reckon it's about the siege of Potidaea."

Nikias drifted into a dreary and fitful state, half between waking and sleep. Several minutes must have passed in this way, for when he opened his eyes with a start, Agape was no longer by his side, and men were shouting on the deck above—frantic and surprised shouts and the rapid thump, thump, thump of dozens of objects peppering the hull.

Arrows!

And then a massive bronze spear point—like one of Poseidon's trident prongs—ripped through the side of the boat a few feet above Nikias's head. He lurched to his feet. Water was rushing through the breach in the ship, swirling around his ankles.

A scream cut through the din: "Board the other ship!"

It was Phoenix's voice. A desperate call to arms followed by the sound of many feet treading on the platforms above.

Nikias stumbled over to the stairs at the aft of the boat. He clambered onto the deck. An arrow whizzed past his head. He ducked, crouching low, surveying the chaotic scene. Dead men on the decks. Athenian oarsmen leaping onto the bow of the enemy ship: a fifty-oared warship—the one that had rammed them—stuck in the hull like a colossal swordfish with its painted eyes glowering.

Phoenix's men had grabbed shields and axes and were chopping their way onto the enemy ship, some falling into the water, others spurting blood as their limbs were hacked from their bodies. Nikias saw Phoenix barreling his way through a mass of enemy fighters with old Agape by his side. He saw Teuker the Plataean cavalryman beheaded—

"Boy!"

Nikias looked down. Krates was slumped with his back against the wall of the ship, an arrow protruding from his left shoulder. He stared at Nikias with a wild, terrified look in his eyes.

"Krates—"

As Nikias bent down to inspect Krates's wound, something shook the ship and pitched him forward, slamming him against the wall. He looked to the other side of the deck and saw that another fifty-oared ship had rammed the dispatch vessel from the opposite side. Enemy warriors were already leaping onto the top deck, running toward Nikias and Krates.

There was no time to grab a shield. No time to board the enemy ship and join the others. Nikias reacted without thinking. He grabbed Krates around the collar with his good hand, pulled him to a standing position, and flung himself backward over the side of the ship, taking Krates with him.

Nikias hit the shockingly cold water and all sounds were muted for a few seconds, and then he floated back up, his head breaking the surface. He swam to Krates, who was flailing and gasping. The waves pulled them toward the prow of the enemy ship—to the spot where its ram was stuck into the *Sea Nymph*. Here they were hidden from the view of the enemy mariners above—warriors who were peering over the side, searching for them with spears in hand.

An Athenian fell off the enemy ship he'd just boarded and the enemy leaned over, skewering him in the water with a long spear. The man died and sank under the water.

"Can you swim?" Nikias asked Krates in a harsh whisper.

"A little," said Krates.

"Get on your back," Nikias ordered. "And start to kick." Krates obeyed and Nikias wrapped his left arm around the man's neck and kicked hard, swimming along the hull of the dispatch vessel. When he got to the prow he kicked off it and moved them away from the cluster of ships. Nikias was a strong swimmer and soon, helped by the rising tide that moved toward the shore, they were racing away from the sea battle. From this vantage point Nikias could see the two enemy ships stuck into either side of the dispatch vessel and the fight raging on the decks. He looked behind him. They weren't far from shore. He could see the waves crashing on a rocky beach in the setting sun.

He glanced back toward the pandemonium of the battle. The Athenians were still fighting. They had seized shields and weapons from the enemy ship and had made a shield wall at the prow of the ship they'd just boarded, stopping the mariners from the second vessel from coming across the captured *Sea Nymph*.

He saw the distinct figures of Phoenix and Agape. His cousin had grabbed an oar and swung it back and forth, screaming insanely, knocking the enemy over the side. And Agape brandished an axe like a hero. It was a desperate battle and the Athenians were fighting bravely. But the enemy had overwhelming numbers.

Nikias saw oars start to pull on the ship that Phoenix and his men had boarded. The Athenians were attempting to disengage the enemy boat from the *Sea Nymph*. They were trying to escape in the captured ship!

"Lead them, Phoenix!" Nikias shouted.

Just then a big rolling wave slammed into his face and he took in a mouthful of water. When he finished coughing he looked back toward the cluster of boats—but they had spun around so that now he couldn't see the ship that Phoenix and the others had boarded. The screams of men were carried away on the increasing wind.

Lightning flashed in the distance: a storm front coming in from the east.

Nikias kicked hard, putting more and more distance between themselves and the battle. The tide pushed them quickly toward the shore, and the sun was about to set. Night would soon hide them.

"Who were they?" asked Nikias with outrage.

"Korinthians," replied Krates. Then he said simply, "I'm dying."

"I can swim us both to land."

"Thanatos," said Krates, uttering the name of the god of death.

"Hold on," Nikias said in his ear. "Just kick with your legs."

"You must get back to Plataea," said Krates. "Bring your message from Perikles."

"We both will, old man. Now just—"

"Nikias. Your father . . . he had the most beautiful voice I had ever heard . . ." Krates's words trailed off and he stopped kicking. His body became very still, rising up and down on the waves like a piece of driftwood.

"Krates?" asked Nikias urgently.

Nikias refused to let go of the old man's body, and he swam with it all the way to the beach, where they were tossed to and fro on the rocky shore. He finally managed to pull Krates's corpse from the shore break and drag him to a dry place.

The beach was empty. It was dark now. Nikias peered out onto the water, but he could barely see the ships half a mile away, still locked together. The storm clouds were directly over the ships now. The wind shifted, and Nikias heard a lusty victory shout—the sound of many men celebrating as one—carried on a gale.

He was filled with despair.

He sat on his haunches for a while over the dead body. Krates looked so small and frail and childlike. There was a faint smile on his craggy face.

The Athenian ship was taken. Phoenix, Agape, the Athenian oarsmen, and the Plataean cavalrymen were either dead or captured. Krates was a shade. He was alone on a beach, many miles from home, with only one good arm. And he had lost the sword that Perikles had given to him.

He went to work, quickly stripping Krates of his belt upon which was fastened sheaths holding a sword and dagger. He readjusted the leather straps, fitting them around his own waist. Krates had a small leather purse around his neck filled with coins. Nikias took this off and slipped it over his own head.

He started to walk away, then stopped. He opened the leather pouch around his neck, searching in the dim light for a Plataean coin amongst the Athenian owls. When he found one he went back to Krates and knelt, placing the coin on Krates's palm, then closed the dead man's fingers around the silver disk—payment for the Ferryman.

"Here comes a warrior of Plataea," said Nikias, uttering the ancient Plataean farewell.

Then he stood and walked up the beach on wobbly legs toward a path that wended its way up a cliff face, climbing toward dark mountains beyond.

FOUR

"Pretty skull cup, my best drinking cup—
Don't put down the cup, raise it up, up, up!"

Kolax sang happily, nestled in his father's lap where Osyrus sat cross-legged in front of a roaring fire. The Skythian boy had never felt happier in his life. His father's strong arms were wrapped around him, and he was thousands of horse strides from that hateful city of Athens. The god Papaeus was smiling on him. He didn't even mind the searing pain from the whip marks on his legs that still burned two days after his father's lashing.

Nothing in the world mattered anymore, for he had found his father.

They had made camp for the night on a flat outcropping high in the mountains, with their backs to a wall of stone. Beyond the fire was a dark forest of pine trees swaying in the wind. Their horse was tied to a tree nearby, staring at them with one black eye shining in the light of the fire. Kolax felt safe and content. He stared up at the stars twinkling in the sky and sighed.

"Are you comfortable, my son?" asked Osyrus in a gentle voice. He adjusted his cloak so that it covered Kolax's legs.

"Of course, Papa!" rasped Kolax. "Please tell me all about the stars. What are they made of?"

Osyrus laughed and held Kolax tighter. "The stars are needle holes made in the tent-skin of the sky."

"Papaeus made those holes in the sky-skin with a giant tattoo needle," said Kolax. "You told me that when I was little."

"Yes," said his father. "You have a good memory. It was a needle made from the tooth of the biggest dragon that Papaeus slew with his lightning arrow."

"I would like to shoot *that* bow!" said Kolax.

Osyrus kissed Kolax on the head. "On the other side of the dark skin is Heaven," he continued in a voice full of reverence. "But the light of Heaven is so bright that it would blind us were we to see it all at once. So the Great God poked little holes for us to catch a glimpse of that light. And the holes are in the patterns of the gods and monsters so that we won't ever forget the stories of our heroes and their enemies."

Kolax loved hearing his father talk. He was so wise and seemed to have an answer for every question. Why was the sky blue in daytime? Why did horses have hooves and not feet? Why were the Greeks such terrible archers?

It had taken them two days to ride from the gates of Athens to this spot in the eastern Kithaeron Mountains. Kolax had ridden the entire way sitting in front of his father, for he had been too weak to ride a horse on his own. At first he had been filled with shame and had wept hot tears, but his father had said, "You have been whipped in the legs by Osyrus of Skythia, my son! Of course you cannot ride on your own. I am amazed that you are still living." These words had filled Kolax with such pride that he had cast aside his shame and let himself be borne like a stripling.

"Papa," said Kolax. "Are we going to Plataea?"

"I have not yet decided, my son."

"Oh please!" whined Kolax. "The killing is good there. And they will pay us in gold." A sudden stabbing sensation in his intestines made him shift and grimace. He needed to relieve himself, but his father had told him he must stay in his lap, for he had sensed danger lurking in those dark woods.

"I am still waiting for a sign," said Osyrus, staring into the night sky. "We could go to Potidaea and join the hundred and fifty of our Bindi brothers sent to the siege of that city. But Potidaea is far to the north. It's many days' ride from here, and we would have to take a ship for part of the journey."

"Will the Hellenes be angry that you left Athens?"

"The Athenians can suck my balls," replied Osyrus.

"Ha ha!" cried Kolax. "Good one, Papa! That one Athenian general can suck my balls too."

Kolax thought about the little girl Iphy with a pang of sadness. He had forgotten about her until they had ridden many miles from Athens. He wondered if she was still up in that tree. He vowed to go back there someday and get her down.

"Osyrus of the Bindi is tired of that foul and grassless city full of oar-pullers," said Osyrus.

"Plataea is just over these mountains," said Kolax, pointing to the west. "We could be there in a day! They have grass everywhere. So much grass!"

"I am unsure," said Osyrus. "I do not know if we would be welcomed by the Oxlanders. From what you say they are in the midst of a war with the Spartans."

"They would welcome us, Papa!" said Kolax. "They are my friends! I am a hero to them. You'll see. Oh, Papa! Please let's go to Plataea. Let's help kill the Red Cloaks."

"Hush," said Osyrus. "I hear something."

Kolax squinted across the flames and into the dark trees at the edge of the clearing. He thought he saw shapes moving there. The fire crackled and spit as the pitch-filled branches burned.

"I'm not afraid of the Dog Raiders," said Kolax in a harsh whisper. "I killed fifteen of them on my own."

"Fifteen, eh?"

Kolax could tell by the tone of his father's voice that he was smiling. "I am not making it up!"

"That is a great number, my son, for someone so young."

"Papa," said Kolax, "you don't believe me? But I swear by Papaeus I killed fifteen of them on my way to Athens alone. I didn't have time to collect their skullcaps. But I do have several of the Theban skulls back in Plataea. My little friend Mula, a slave, is keeping them for me in a leather steeping bag. You will see when we get to the citadel. I'll bet they stink good and proper by now. I'll make my poison from the decayed flesh and—"

"Quiet now," said Osyrus. "We must be quiet. Someone is coming."

He wrapped Kolax in his cloak to hide him, but the boy pushed aside the cloth so that he could peek out. He saw a black shape moving across the clearing. The man stopped on the other side of the fire, peering at Osyrus from the dark slits of his dog hair–covered helm. He wore plate armor, greaves, and big iron bands on his wrists. He was a tall man with trunks for legs and broad shoulders.

"Greetings," said Osyrus in a friendly voice, speaking in Greek. "Come and join us by the fire."

The dark figure cocked his helmeted head to one side. "I thank you," he replied in a tone of mock politeness, but remained where he was. The man looked past Osyrus, scanning the rocks behind and above him, peering into the blackness.

"He's a Dog Raider," whispered Kolax from the tent of his father's cloak.

"Quiet," hissed Osyrus.

The Dog Raider looked directly at Osyrus and asked, "Who are you?"

"I am Osyrus of the Bindi. You don't need to bother with me. I am just passing through with my injured son."

"Just passing through?" said the Dog Raider with a scornful laugh. "With your injured son. And where are you headed, Skythian?"

"Who is to say," said Osyrus. "The god chooses my destiny. Come and sit. We have wine we'll share with you."

"Do you think I'm an idiot?" said the Dog Raider. "I won't drink your poisoned wine, Skythian horse-raper." He made a quick gesture with his left hand, drawing his sword with his right. More shapes moved from the woods and came up behind him, fanning out in a semicircle, their weapons glinting in the light of the fire. All of them wore helms and had round shields slung on their backs. Kolax quickly counted fourteen men. He reached around and clutched the handle of his father's dagger where it was attached to his belt, inching the blade from the sheath.

"We're travelers," said Osyrus. "In my country travelers are afforded certain rights of safe passage."

The Dog Raider laughed and glanced from side to side at his men. "Did you hear the Skythian?" he asked in an amazed tone. "I think he left his sheep-shit brains in his Grasslands."

Kolax could not believe this Dog Raider spoke to his father in such an insolent manner. He started to say something insulting, but Osyrus clapped his hand over his mouth.

"Which way would you like your heads to be facing when we lay out your corpses?" Osyrus asked the Dog Raiders calmly.

"Come again?"

"East or west?" asked Osyrus. "Answer me, quick, you maggot from a buzzard's arse, because you're all about to die."

The Dog Raider chief turned to his men. "Skin the boy first, then roast him on the fire."

Osyrus let forth a Skythian war cry.

The instant the sound had passed his lips a barrage of black arrows flew down from the rocks above, striking the Dog Raiders where they stood. The dumbfounded warriors jerked and gasped as they were struck, for the tips of the arrows were coated with a poison that acted nearly instantaneously, filling the men's veins with a terrible fire. They fell to the ground, screaming and writhing.

All but one.

The Dog Raider chief had somehow avoided being struck. An arrow had clanged off the forehead of his helm. Another had glanced off one of the iron bands on his wrist. He reacted without hesitation, leaping straight through the roaring fire—charging at Osyrus, who still sat on the ground.

Kolax, in a blur of motion, sprang from his father's lap, his dagger clutched in his hand. He ducked the Dog Raider's furious sword stroke and plunged the dagger into the man's groin, pulling the blade upward and spilling out the enemy's guts.

"Stop your arrows!" shouted Osyrus, jumping to his feet.

The Dog Raider chief howled in agony, dropping his sword and falling to his knees, clutching his intestines as they oozed from his abdomen. Kolax kicked him in the face with the flat of his foot, then sliced across the man's eyes, blinding him. The warrior clapped his hands to his face and Kolax drove the dagger into his chest—three quick stabs that pierced his heart.

The Dog Raider chief crumpled to the dirt. Before his head hit the ground Kolax was already bounding over to the nearest enemy warrior who lay on the ground, slitting the man's throat to make certain he was dead, then moving on to the next one.

"Kolax!" shouted Osyrus.

"Yes, Papa," said Kolax without glancing up, driving his dagger into the brain of a twitching Dog Raider.

Osyrus stood with his mouth agape. "Good kill," was all that he could manage to say.

Kolax smiled at his father and nodded. But then another powerful gut cramp wracked his bowels and he squatted on his haunches, groaning in pain. He peered up at the rocks behind his father, watching as the black silhouettes of Skythian archers moved down the steep face. There were twenty-four of them. They were all men of the Bindi tribe who had left Athens with Osyrus and Kolax.

The archers fanned out on the killing ground, carefully removing their individual arrows from the bodies, for each man marked his own arrows with a particular pattern on the shaft. They put the arrows back into their lidded quivers, careful not to touch the razor-sharp and tainted arrowheads.

"Strip them of the armor and clothes," said Osyrus in a commanding voice. "Cut off their heads and put their faces in their arses so that they can smell their own bungholes for eternity."

"Ha ha!" laughed Kolax, before doubling over in agony. He watched as the archers quickly completed their task, making a pile of clothes on one side and armor and weapons on the other. The fourteen naked corpses were lined up in a row, their skin shining white in the light of the rising moon. Kolax thought they looked like strange fish. He giggled as their heads were hacked off and arranged in the humiliating position. But the painful spasms in his bowels cut his laughter short.

"Where do we go now?" asked one of the archers.

Kolax turned to see Jaro—an archer nearly the same age as his father—standing face-to-face with him. Jaro was a tall and muscular man with the reddest hair Kolax had ever seen. Osyrus wasn't looking at him, though. He had his arms crossed on his chest and gazed at the sky.

"I don't know," said Osyrus. "I'm waiting for a sign."

"Well, we can't wait here forever," said Jaro. "Killing these Dog Raiders is a waste of time. They don't wear gold like Persians. Where are we, anyway?"

"The Kithaeron Mountains," said Osyrus. "Didn't you ever look at a map when you were in Athens? On the other side of this range is the Oxlands and the city-states of Thebes and Plataea."

"I say we set out for that other place," said another archer. Kolax glanced over at Skunxa—the fattest and smelliest Skythian he'd ever met. The man stood near the fire, trying on one of the Dog Raider helms. "We should join our fellow Bindis at the Athenian siege of Potidaea or whatever it's called and make some coin."

A few of the Skythians made sounds showing their agreement with Skunxa. But others complained. It was a difficult decision to make: Plataea or Potidaea.

"Potidaea is too far," said a slender young man with a neatly trimmed beard and a splendid topknot. He chewed on a piece of dried meat and smiled in a self-satisfied way. His name was Griffix and he was one of Kolax's cousins. "I heard it takes weeks to get to Potidaea on a trireme," he continued. "And I don't see any ships up here in the mountains. Plataea, however, is just a day's ride over this mountain."

"We should go to Plataea," agreed Kolax.

"My son," said Osyrus, holding up a hand. "Please. You are too young to have an opinion on such a matter."

"Let the boy talk," said Jaro, throwing up his arms. "He's the one who got us into this shit-pit in the first place."

Osyrus waved a hand for Kolax to speak.

"Plataea is a wonderful place," said Kolax. "The people aren't like Athenians at all. They are tough and don't ride in boats. There's heaps of gold too. You could each make enough in a year to buy fifty of the best horses back home."

"Come on," said Griffix. "The boy is talking shit. Are you *certain* he's your son, Osyrus?"

Kolax flew at Griffix, but before he could get close enough to throw a punch, Osyrus grabbed his son around the waist and lifted him above his head. The archers all laughed as Kolax kicked the air, screaming in his hoarse voice.

"Calm yourself," said Osyrus, "or I'll have Skunxa sit on you."

Kolax stopped struggling and glanced at the potbellied Skunxa. All of a sudden it felt like a knife was digging into Kolax's guts. He let forth a howling scream, clutching his midriff. Osyrus quickly set him down.

"What happened?" he asked. "What is wrong?"

"It's my stomach," said Kolax. "I've got to make shit."

He squatted down right in front of the men and started straining, his eyes bugging.

"I don't need to see this," said Griffix, rolling his eyes.

"Watch!" barked Kolax. "I'm going to prove it to you."

"Prove what?" said Griffix, a disgusted expression on his face. "That you're as crazy as a hemp-smoking hare?"

A great fart erupted from Kolax's hind end, followed by a noisy bowel movement that splattered on the ground.

"He looks like a sheep with the drips," said one of the men, peering at Kolax.

"Hey, what's that coming out of his arse!" cried out another, pointing.

"He's shitting darics!"

"You're kidding."

"Look!"

"Thank Papaeus!" said Kolax after he was done. He fell on his side and lay very still.

Many hands grabbed at the pile of feces, cleaning off the gold coins and holding them up to the firelight. Griffix, after thoroughly rubbing one of the darics on his tunic, bit into it, exclaiming, "It's real!"

"There must be thirty of them!" said Jaro in amazement.

"I had to swallow them," said Kolax. "To keep them safe. They're the coins my friend Nikias gave me."

He looked at his father, who stared back at him with a dumbfounded expression that slowly changed to a smile. Osyrus nodded, as if finally coming to a decision. He turned to the men and said, "Everyone take one gold coin. Consider it a first payment. And we'll keep the Dog Raider heads as well."

Kolax grinned. They were going to the Oxlands. They were going to Plataea!

FIVE

"Is anyone there? Help!"

The plaintive voice had called out three times before Kallisto finally forced herself to get out of bed, drawn by the urgent tone. It was late morning, and Phile and Eudoxia had gone to the market, leaving Kallisto alone in Menesarkus's house in Plataea.

Well, not quite alone. There was the Spartan, Arkilokus, in the room at the end of the hall. Phile had whispered to her, practically right after they had passed the threshold of the house, that there was a Spartan under the roof and that he was Menesarkus's illegitimate grandson. Kallisto had been fascinated by this remarkable news and had been curious to see what the man looked like.

But Kallisto had been ordered by Eudoxia to stay away from the Spartan's room. Phile had told her that the prisoner was utterly defenseless—paralyzed in both his arms and legs. And now the man was crying out in fear, but not loud enough for the guardsmen standing watch downstairs at the front entrance of the house to hear him.

Even in her weakened state Kallisto reckoned she could fight a man who could only turn his head from side to side. And so she started gingerly down the long hallway, holding one arm over her sore ribs—the place where she had been struck by a Theban arrow. She wondered where Menesarkus was. She had yet to see the Arkon since she had been brought to his house. She'd been told that he spent most nights at the city offices. She dreaded the moment when they finally would meet. They hadn't seen each other since the night she had helped defend Menesarkus's farmhouse from the invaders. But now Menesarkus knew the truth about her father's part in the sneak attack on Plataea, and he must hate her for being her father's daughter.

"Help!" cried the Spartan again. His voice sounded terrified now.

Kallisto said, "I'm coming!" What she saw when she pushed open the door made her burst out laughing, for the Spartan was flat on his back, naked except for a sheet over his lower half, with a huge black crow sitting on his chest, staring at him with its beady black eyes. It was the same crow that had flown into the bedchamber at Chusor's house the other day—the one with the distinctive white tail feather.

"Why are you laughing, you idiot girl!" raged Arkilokus. "Get it off me!" His fingers and toes wriggled frantically.

"I thought you were being mauled by a vicious dog," said Kallisto.

"These things will pluck out the eyes of the dead," said Arkilokus. "Now get it off me."

Kallisto crossed her arms on her chest. "Say 'please.'"

Arkilokus turned his head and stared at her openmouthed, evidently astonished at her impudence. He thrust out his jaw and appeared to be on the verge of saying something vicious when the crow hopped closer to his face and let forth a menacing sound—a low gurgling deep in its throat.

"P-please!" sputtered Arkilokus. "Yes! Please! Just get the thing off of me!"

Kallisto grabbed a pillow from a chair and strode toward the crow. It cocked its head at her as she pulled back and whacked it. The bird went flying toward the open window with a raucous cry, and Kallisto fell onto the bed with a howl of pain. She lay across Arkilokus's body for a while, then sat up, hugging her rib cage.

"You're injured," said Arkilokus.

The concern in his voice surprised Kallisto.

"I'm all right," she said, glancing over to the window. The crow perched on the sill, eyeing her with fury. She flung the pillow across the room—a perfectly aimed throw. Both the pillow and the bird disappeared out the window.

"Thank you," said Arkilokus, sighing.

"You're welcome," said Kallisto.

"Now, could you scratch me?"

"What?"

"With your fingernails."

Kallisto rolled her eyes. "Are you mad?"

"It itches *so* much along my spine," said Arkilokus. "It's agony. It started as a tingling early this morning. Now it feels like ants crawling over my back. Come, now, girl! Don't be squeamish. My arms are useless. Your mistress would tell you to do it if she were here."

Kallisto stared at Arkilokus as if for the first time. It struck her, in that instant, how much he resembled Nikias . . . an older, fiercer version of Nikias. As if her beloved had gone away for ten years and returned a hardened but still recognizable man. This Spartan had nearly the same color hair and eyes as Nikias. Even his physique resembled Nikias's, with his broad chest, long legs, and huge hands. But the older man had a full beard, and his brow was thicker. And there was nothing of Nikias-the-poet in this haughty prince's eyes.

She thought of the terrible rumor that Phile had told her yesterday . . . that Nikias's horse, Photine, had returned to the city, riderless and covered with blood. She could not believe it. Would not believe it. But she had been praying desperately to Artemis all morning that it was untrue. That her beloved was safe. . . .

"Please?" asked Arkilokus, as if taking her silence for a rebuke of his manners. She shook herself from her reverie. "Where should I start?"

"Anywhere," he said. "My chest. Start there."

She started scratching his skin with her right hand, moving it over his pectorals. He let forth an almost orgasmic sigh—the same deep-throated sound Nikias made when they made love.

"Gods," he said. "So good."

"She's not my mistress," said Kallisto.

"Who isn't?" asked Arkilokus, his eyes squeezed shut in rapture.

"Eudoxia. Menesarkus's wife. I'm not their servant. I'm a guest in this house."

"I don't care who you are," said Arkilokus. "With fingernails like those I'll build a shrine to you."

She moved down his legs, her fingernails making little red marks across his skin, but he smiled and made no complaints.

"Your name?" he asked.

Kallisto bristled. She didn't like being asked her name like a slave. "My name is for my family and friends," she replied.

Arkilokus opened one eye.

"I have been rude," he said. "I should have introduced myself first. My name is Arkilokus, even though I'm sure you have already been told my name."

Kallisto shrugged.

"You don't seem to be squeamish around men," observed Arkilokus. "Athenian women are always so high-strung. So different from Spartan females."

"I'm not Athenian," said Kallisto. "I'm Plataean. And I grew up with a house full of older brothers."

"Did you?" asked Arkilokus with a raise of his eyebrows. "A fortunate father."

"My father is dead," said Kallisto, and stopped scratching. "He was in league with the traitor Nauklydes, but the Thebans cut off his head once he'd helped them inside the citadel. And most of my brothers were slaughtered." She gave him a black look, as if he were the cause of all her woes.

Arkilokus nodded his head. "Helladios," he said solemnly. "You are the daughter of Helladios."

Kallisto said, "I am no longer the daughter of Helladios. His name is poison to me. My name is simply Kallisto. I'm nobody's daughter anymore."

"I am not a lover of the Thebans," said Arkilokus, as if to apologize for her misfortunes. "I argued against the sneak attack on Plataea. I called for our elders to use diplomacy to sway your men to reason. You cannot understand such things, though"—this last part spoken to himself, as if she were no longer sitting right there in front of him—"because it is beyond your ken."

Kallisto threw back her head and laughed scornfully, her eyes flashing. "Ha! You are in a precarious position to insult my intelligence, Spartan." She glared at him and felt her pale cheeks turn red. "I could claw out your eyes faster than that crow could have pecked them. Or I could cut off your precious balls and send them flying out the window after that pillow!"

Arkilokus made a meek face. "My apologies again, Kallisto. I'm impressed. You speak with the lashing tongue of a Spartan maid. My own sister has scolded me in the same manner. And I beg your forgiveness, just like I do with her."

Kallisto's look softened. She couldn't believe she had just threatened to cut off the balls of a Spartan prince. "Are Spartan girls really allowed to wrestle naked in the gymnasium?" she asked.

Arkilokus grinned. "They ask the same question in Persia," he said. "And the answer is: yes, they do. Our women are trained to be warriors, and to breed warriors. Women don't wear veils in my country. And they can own property as well."

Kallisto considered this information for a moment, then asked, "Do women in Sparta really have their heads shaved and their breasts bound on their wedding nights?"

He nodded. "I was brought up in my father's palace," he replied. "But most Spartan warriors are sent away as little boys and raised with the men. By the time they are of breeding age they are wholly unused to women. The shearing and binding lessens the . . . the shock of their new circumstances."

"So King Menelaus had Helen's breasts bound?" asked Kallisto, astonished. "Beautiful Helen's head shaved?" She started scratching Arkilokus's other leg in an absentminded way, trying to imagine Helen of Troy treated in such a strange manner.

"Menelaus was a king," he replied. "He was sophisticated enough to appreciate a woman's beauty. Like me."

Kallisto stared into Arkilokus's eyes. She was surprised to see a hunger and yearning there. He glanced down the length of his body and smiled. She followed his gaze to his loins, where the sheet was now propped up like a tent.

"I think you're getting better," said Kallisto hurriedly, springing to her feet and departing the room as fast as she could. She slammed the door behind her and stood with her back to it, listening. Arkilokus's laughter emanated from the chamber.

Later that day Phile came into Kallisto's room to inform her, with a kind of subdued excitement, that the Spartan had started to move his limbs.

"The phoenix is coming back to life," said Phile.

The next morning Kallisto heard the noise of several men in the hall. She got quickly out of bed and opened the door a crack, peering out. She saw Menesarkus and a doctor, as well as the two guardsmen, walking toward the Spartan's chamber. "This itching he complains about," the doctor was saying, "is a very good sign. I've seen this many times before. It means the spine was merely bruised and . . ." His voice trailed off as the Arkon and the doctors entered the room.

Arkilokus improved rapidly—as if Asklepius, the god of healing, had blessed him. The next day Phile dashed into Kallisto's chamber and informed her, breathlessly, that the Spartan had actually risen to his feet. "He's several inches taller than Nikias," said Phile, her voice mingled with admiration and fear. "He stood there naked, stretched out to his full height. And he's hung like a bull," she added with a sour look. "It's disgusting."

The next morning—just three days after Kallisto had gone into the Spartan's room to chase away the crow—Kallisto stood at her window staring down into the courtyard, watching Arkilokus as he took his first awkward steps. He was supported on either side by the guards, moving hesitantly, but he made his way on his own two feet, albeit stiffly, like a corpse that had come to life. The Spartan prince's face was rigid with determination as he concentrated on each small step.

He glanced up and saw Kallisto in the window above. He smiled at her and made a ludicrous cawing sound like a crow. Kallisto saw the guards exchange puzzled looks. She stepped back from the window and closed the shutters, smiling despite herself.

SIX

———————◆———————

The sun was westering when Nikias, dog-tired and limping, emerged from a wooded path and onto a dusty road, supporting himself with a staff made from a branch. Directly ahead, a mile up this cart-rutted road, he saw a familiar citadel made of gray stone, built atop a hill of white chalk that rose above the northern bank of the Asopus River. He said a silent prayer to Zeus, for he had arrived at the city-state of Tanagra and was now only twenty miles from home.

He wiped the sweat from his face and lurched down the road toward a stone bridge spanning the river. His right ankle was swollen to three times its normal size. He'd never had an ankle injury like this before. He'd never realized it could be so debilitating. All he wanted was to find a bed at an inn and get some sleep. He didn't dare risk going the rest of the way home on foot tonight. The Spartans would most likely be patrolling the road from Tanagra to Plataea, hunting for any messengers attempting to get in and out of the Oxlands.

And Nikias felt about as agile as a bull with a broken leg.

He would have to take an alternate route—through the mountains. And to do that he would need a decent horse. In the morning he would buy a mount with the money he'd taken from poor old Krates's corpse. He would have to chance running into Dog Raiders again, but he would rather fight those warriors than attempt running a blockade of Spartans.

At least for now he was safe. Tanagra lay just on the other side of the river, and he knew the place well. He had been to the citadel many times over the years to fight in pankration matches with Tanagraean boys. The city was about half the size and population of Plataea's twenty thousand, and had been under the control of Athens for many years. But it had always been a fiercely independent place. "The men of Tanagra might just rebel against the Athenians someday," his grandfather had told him. "Though the people of that city hate the Thebans just as much as we do."

Nikias arrived at the bridge and paused halfway across it to rest his ankle, leaning on the ancient stones. Two dirty boys were wrestling on the riverbank below, grappling halfheartedly, laughing in a good-natured way. A group of veiled women were nearby, dipping amphoras into the river and balancing the water jugs on their heads. Woodsmoke from cooking fires drifted from little stone houses lining the top of the riverbank. He heard a baby crying, and a woman singing to soothe it. All was normal. Everything was at peace.

It had taken four days to get to this haven. Four punishing days of hiking across the Parnes Mountains, a rugged and mostly uninhabited range covered with a thick forest of pine and fir trees. He should have made the trip in half that time. But he'd gotten lost at the start of the journey, and had been forced to double back time and again after getting stuck in dead-end ravines. Then he'd nearly broken his neck slipping down a crumbling slope. He'd been lucky to come away with only a sprained ankle. But this injury had slowed him considerably.

On the evening of his second day in the mountains he had chanced upon a well-used footpath. He had known, immediately, that it was one of the old pathways the Athenians had made connecting their city to their northern allies. He'd seen the route before, marked on one of his grandfather's maps. This trail was interspersed every few miles with guard towers, each manned by a small band of Athenian warriors, and Nikias had been overjoyed when the path had led him to one of these forts, for by that time he'd become delirious with hunger and thirst.

He'd called out to the guardsmen in the square tower, telling them that he was a Plataean. The men had been surprised at the sudden appearance of a lone and bedraggled traveler and had let him in. Nikias had immediately told the commander of the tower about the loss of Perikles's dispatch vessel, and the veteran warrior had sent a runner back to Athens with this urgent news and a note written by Nikias. They had given Nikias food and water and let him rest for the day and all through that night inside the safety of the stone tower. The next day, he'd walked the rest of the way to Tanagra along the footpath.

And now he was so close to home he could practically smell Plataea on the wind. Steeling himself against the pain in his ankle, he continued across the stone bridge, wincing with every step, and then started up the switchback road that led to the city gates. He passed a theatre built into the side of the hill below the town, and looked down upon the curving rows of empty marble benches and the bare stage.

The face of Perikles flashed before his eyes. He reckoned the Athenian general had heard the news about the dispatch ship by now. He wondered if the great man would be distraught that Phoenix and his crew had been killed or captured. At least he would know that it was the Korinthians who had attacked, thanks to Nikias's message. He thought of the beautiful sword that Perikles had given him. It must now on the bottom of the sea, lost forever—a gift to Poseidon.

Nikias knew he was lucky not to have been killed or captured during the sea battle. But all he felt right now was numb and exhausted. And his ankle burned like it was on fire. He paused for a moment to rest, leaning on the makeshift staff, scanning the road up ahead. The only other traveler he saw was an old man walking slowly and leading a tired-looking donkey. Nikias gritted his teeth and walked as fast as he could, keeping his head down as he passed. The old man smiled at Nikias.

"Peace, young man."

Nikias had learned not to trust smiling strangers anymore. The old man could easily be a Theban or Korinthian spy. He scowled, refusing to look at him, and quickened his pace despite the pain in his ankle. When he got to the city gates he found eight guardsmen milling about. Glancing up, he saw many archers along the battlements. The Tanagraeans were on alert. They had obviously heard about the sneak attack on Plataea, and were not going to get caught with their balls in their hands.

One of the guards stepped forward, blocking his way. He was a short, wiry man with a pointed beard and sly eyes. "What's your business, lad?" he asked.

"The Three Thieves," Nikias said. It was the name of the inn that he and his grandfather always stayed at when they came to Tanagra.

"Where are you from?"

"Plataea."

"Plataea?" the guard asked incredulously. He looked Nikias up and down, and then his eyes opened wide with recognition. "You're Menesarkus's grandson, aren't you? That young pankrator."

Nikias nodded but made no reply. All of the guards were now gawking at him and starting to crowd around. Nikias glanced over his shoulder. The old man with the donkey was still out of earshot.

"You fought my younger brother," said the guard with sly eyes. "Two years ago. You broke the stupid sheep-stuffer's arm."

Nikias remembered the fight. The man's brother was an arrogant boy who'd spit in Nikias's face during the bout, sending him into a blind rage. He'd broken the boy's arm on purpose, to teach him a lesson. "Sorry," he said.

Sly Eyes gave a merry laugh that was out of sorts with his crafty-looking face. He slapped Nikias on the back, saying, "Don't apologize. I wish you'd broken both of his arms. I hate the little bastard."

"What's the news from Plataea?" asked another guard—a young man of about Nikias's age with a missing front tooth and a hunted look on his gaunt face. "We haven't heard anything for a week. Our general sent some scouts to Plataea three days ago, but they saw Spartans five miles east of the Persian Fort, and so they came straight back. Are the Spartans really camped right outside the gates of Plataea?"

"Not within pissing distance," said Nikias, "but close enough to make everyone nervous." He glanced over and saw that the old man with the donkey had stopped ten paces away and was eyeing Nikias surreptitiously. He was now close enough to hear their conversation.

"Did you fight in the battle at the gates of Plataea?" asked the younger guard.

Nikias nodded. "I did."

"No modesty, now," said the biggest guard standing there. He was an older man with a blond beard and huge scar across his cheek. "We want to hear what happened firsthand. All we've heard until now are rumors."

Nikias knew he would have to tell them something or they would think he was lying about fighting in the battle. But he didn't want the suspicious old man to know anything about him. "Perhaps you could let this old fellow in first," said Nikias. "I'm holding him up."

The guards barely glanced at the aged traveler and waved him through the gates. The old man smiled warmly at Nikias and led his donkey through the arch. Once he had disappeared into the city, Nikias began his tale. He told them about being trapped in the citadel during the Theban sneak attack. About escaping through the secret tunnel and riding to the northern garrisons. He described the wild charge against the mass of Theban hoplites and the great battle that had ensued just outside the city walls.

The guards listened with rapt attention, staring at him with admiration. Nikias felt himself getting carried away, but he kept on talking despite the nagging voice in the back of his head that told him to shut his mouth. He even told the guardsmen about his fight with Eurymakus. How the Theban whisperer had killed Nikias's horse out from under him—killed it instantly with a poisoned dagger—and how the horse had collapsed, pinning Nikias underneath it with the Theban standing over him, bearing the poisoned blade and gloating.

"How did you survive?" asked the young guard, awestruck.

"I had my Sargatian whip," said Nikias with a smile. "I got one hand free from under the horse, grabbed the whip, and snapped it around the Theban's left arm, yanking as hard as I could against the hand that held the dagger. The spy's fingertip brushed against his own tainted blade, drawing blood."

"You killed the man with his own poisoned blade?" said Sly Eyes, laughing.

"No," said Nikias. "Eurymakus grabbed a sword from off the ground, and cut off his own arm before the poison could travel up his arm. He did it faster than you could fart."

"This Eurymakus sounds fierce," said the young guard, a hint of awe in his voice. "Cut off his own arm! Gods!"

"He sounds like a Theban goat-stuffer," sneered the guard with the scar. "Only cowards use poison, Priam." He smacked the young guard on the back of the head.

Priam bowed his head. Nikias felt sorry for him. He was obviously the whipping boy of the group. "May I pass?" Nikias asked, and then added with a forced laugh, "Because I'm starving."

"Leave your weapons," said Sly Eyes.

"But I'm Plataean!" said Nikias indignantly.

"New law," said the big guard gruffly. "You can keep your walking stick."

Reluctantly, Nikias took off his sword and dagger. He felt more naked than if they had stripped him bare.

Priam reached for his weapons and handed him two markers in return. "I'll lock these up in the tower," he said, smiling in a fawning manner. "You can get them when you leave the citadel." He slipped away from the others and disappeared through the gates.

The guards stepped aside to let Nikias enter.

"Don't break any arms," said Sly Eyes.

Nikias forced himself to smile and nodded at the guards as he passed. He walked as quickly as he could, limping on his swollen ankle through the archway and into the public square. There were many people milling about and enjoying the warm evening: families with children and old men and women. A group had gathered to watch some performers on stilts, and just then a piper struck up a happy tune. Nikias felt foolish for having been so reluctant to give up his weapons. This place was just like Plataea. He might as well have already been home.

There was a little fountain house in the center of the square designed to look like a miniature temple. Nikias stepped inside and went up to the bronze cistern filled with water from a marble spout shaped like the head of a water nymph. There was a cup attached to the basin by a chain. He dipped the cup in the basin and drank the cool, clean water. He thought of the Well of Gargaphia back home and how he'd sat in the little building the night before he departed Plataea, staring at the signet ring of Eurymakus. He tried to remember the Persian name that Ezekiel had found inscribed on the stone, but the guardian angel's name had slipped from his mind.

He felt eyes on his back.

He turned quickly and thought that he saw, out of the corner of his eye, a hulking figure of a man ducking into a building across the square. Nikias's heart jumped, but he didn't panic. He pretended that he hadn't seen anyone. He calmly took another drink of water, then put the cup in its holder on the basin.

He slipped out of the fountain house and walked casually to the opposite side of the square, where he stood in the doorway of a busy wineshop, lingering there for several minutes, but he didn't see the hulking figure again.

"I must have imagined it," he told himself and laughed. He'd thought he'd seen Axe—a Plataean warrior who had been one of the traitor Nauklydes's followers. Axe, a violent and ruthless giant of a man, had vanished from the citadel after the trial of Nauklydes. He'd last been seen walking down the road that led to the fortress of the Three Heads. There was no way Axe would be here in Tanagra, he told himself, so close to Plataea, where he was a wanted man.

"Idiot," he chastised himself under his breath. "You're seeing things."

As he was about to leave the wineshop he saw a slight young man exit the dark doorway that he had been watching. The youth had black hair and brown skin and very smooth cheeks. Nikias reckoned he must be a Persian slave. The young man walked directly up to the fountain house and peered inside, then looked around the square as if searching for Nikias.

He exited the wineshop, walking slowly across the square to the other side, making certain that the Persian spotted him. Then he turned and headed down a lane lined with pottery shops that had all been shuttered for the night. At the end of the lane he saw the familiar sign for the Three Thieves inn—a board painted with a comical picture of three housebreakers on tiptoe bearing various stolen objects, their heads looking furtively behind them. He heard footsteps behind him and whirled.

The Persian slave was there, smiling in a friendly way.

"What do you want?" asked Nikias.

"Don't hurt me!" said the youth, holding up his hands. He spoke with a thick Persian accent. "My master see you at the gates and send me."

"Sent you for what reason?"

The Persian raised his arched eyebrows coyly. "Only one silver coin. Two for whole night. *And* I have room with bed."

Nikias let forth a relieved laugh. The young man was nothing more than a prostitute—a gate-lurker looking for lonely travelers. "No, thanks," he said. The Persian looked crestfallen. "But tell your master I'm flattered," added Nikias. "I've no doubt he sent his prettiest boy to tempt me."

He turned his back on the Persian and ducked through the doorway of the inn.

SEVEN

Nikias had only been standing in the entrance of the Three Thieves for a few seconds when the innkeeper, a tall balding man with a brown beard and a kindly face, appeared from an inner doorway. Hypatos took one look at Nikias and said, "Why, it's Aristo's son, Nikias! Are you here with your grandfather, Menesarkus?" he added.

"No, just me," said Nikias. "But I need a room all the same. I have silver." He reached under his shirt and held up the bag, jiggling it.

"You've come to the right place to spend it, young Nikias!" said Hypatos, clapping his hands. "You must have a story to tell. I'm sorry that I don't have time to hear it, though. I'm off to the kitchen to make sure that things are not amiss. The evening meal will be served quite soon, and I have hungry travelers waiting. Please, go into the dining hall and wait."

Before Hypatos could walk away Nikias said, "I need a horse."

Hypatos screwed up his forehead. "Horses are hard to come by, as of late. I've got an old nag down at the stables, but I only use her to pull the cart when I drive to Delphinium for the great market."

"I need a *fast* horse," said Nikias in a confidential tone.

Hypatos frowned harder and said, "I'll see what I can think of. Have patience. The gods always provide." And cupping his hand to his mouth he called out, in a voice that was far louder than was necessary for the small room, "Karpos! Show young Nikias to the dining hall."

A downcast slave of indeterminate age appeared from where he'd been lurking around the corner. He eyed Nikias sullenly and gestured for him to follow, leading him down a narrow hallway to an arched entrance. Karpos looked the same as when Nikias had first seen him ten years ago, when he and his grandfather had stayed at the inn for the first time. Karpos stopped at the entrance and gestured grandly for Nikias to enter the dining hall, a windowless room with a low ceiling. He counted six men at the tables drinking wine and talking amongst themselves, waiting for their meals.

"Find a seat," said Karpos with a bored expression, "and I'll bring you wine."

Nikias found a spot in the corner where he could sit with his back to the wall and keep an eye on the doorway. It felt good to sit down, and even though he was still on his guard, he let himself relax a little. But he kept one hand on his walking stick, just in case. He looked at each of the men in the room in turn, sizing them up. They all wore dusty traveler's clothes. And the only accents that he detected were either Athenian or of Oropos and Delphinium.

Karpos brought him a drinking cup and two jugs—one with wine and the other with water—then slunk out of the chamber. Nikias poured himself some uncut wine and quaffed it in a few gulps. In a few minutes the wine's magic started to take hold.

Slaves brought in plates from the kitchen, and Nikias was grateful when his meal was finally set before him: bread and cheese, olives, a steaming bowl of bean soup, and skewered lamb braised with garlic and mint. He ate greedily and in no time at all there was nothing left but an empty plate. He used the bread to sop up the olive oil and grease and, catching the attention of one of the serving slaves, called for another meal, even though he was already filled with a sense of peace and well-being.

Hypatos appeared at the entrance and cleared his throat for attention. "Listen, good travelers. I have a surprise for all of you. The great bard Linos has arrived in the citadel tonight after ten years of travel away from the Oxlands, and he has agreed to sing for you all tonight. I am greatly honored to have him under my roof."

Nikias sat up and stared at the doorway eagerly. He had seen Linos perform when he was a boy. The man had passed by their farm and had performed the "Song of Troy" for his supper. He remembered the man as being very handsome—as regal as a king, with a black beard and a handsome face. But the person who slowly doddered into the room was bent with age and white of hair. Nikias realized, with embarrassment, that this was the same old man leading the donkey that he'd passed on the switchback road—the one who had said "Peace" to him but whom Nikias had so rudely ignored. He felt like a fool for suspecting this poor old wandering bard of being a spy.

Linos shuffled to the other end of the room and sat down. A slave brought him a leather bag and Linos opened it carefully, taking out a tortoiseshell harp. He tuned it softly, holding it to his ear and plucking each string. The men in the room quieted down and stared at him expectantly. All except one—a fat-faced oaf sitting next to Nikias who slurped his soup noisily and hummed under his breath. Nikias gave the man's chair a swift kick.

"Shut up," he hissed. "Linos is about to sing."

The soup-slurping man shot Nikias an angry look, but when he saw the murderous expression in the younger man's eyes he smiled meekly and pushed his bowl away, wiping his mouth on the hem of his tunic and sitting up very straight on the bench.

Linos closed his eyes and held his pick to one of the strings, pulling it taut like an archer with an arrow in the nock. He snapped the pick and the string thrummed violently, a single note that filled the room with an ominous noise while at the same time his voice exhaled a throaty growl. And then his hand flashed on the strings, once, twice, thrice, and his nearly toothless mouth let forth a honeyed voice:

"Sing to me! Sing to me, Muse, of the man whose journey home
Is filled with twists and turns, blown time again off his course
After he had plundered the high walls of Troy.
Countless cities he saw, and learned the minds of many men
Many agonies he suffered, homesick, heartsick on the wine-dark sea
Fighting to save his life and bring his comrades home."

Before long Nikias realized he was watching Linos through a mist of tears. He listened raptly to the "Song of Odysseus," the tale of that unhappy wanderer struggling for so many years to make his way back home to Greece from the shores of Troy. He was carried away to far-off lands, brought to life by the bard's words and music: to Kalypso's cavern, and the land of the Aethiopes; to high Olympus, where the gods argued about the fates of men, and Odysseus's home, where his worthy son cursed the horde of suitors who had come to win his mother's hand, longing for the return of his magnificent father.

Linos played for two hours straight before pausing briefly to take a drink. But no sooner had he sipped from his cup than the men in the room were already calling out for more. Nikias glanced around and saw that Hypatos stood in the back of the room, smiling. And surrounding the innkeeper were all of the servants and slaves under his roof: they had all been allowed to listen to the bard. Even the sullen old slave Karpos was there, a dreamy look on his face. Linos the bard had cast a spell.

"My father had the same power to enchant," Nikias mused sadly. Aristo would have been another Linos, if he had not fallen in battle.

Linos played for another two hours or so before his voice became thin and weak and he begged to stop for the night. The men in the room pleaded with him to continue, but the bard's voice was spent. The room erupted into applause. Nikias waited until the other guests had gone off to bed and then went up to

Linos and shyly made his introductions. The old man smiled at him enigmatically and said that he remembered visiting his grandfather's farm.

"Where are you going next?" Nikias asked.

"To Plataea," said Linos. "I have some business to attend to there before I die."

Nikias laughed, and then realized that the old man was not joking. The smile faded from his face. "What do you mean?"

"I'm sick," said Linos. "My heart tells me it isn't long now."

"But you can't go to Plataea," said Nikias. "The Spartans guard the road. I am going to go by way of the mountains. It's a hard path, but you'll be safer with me."

Linos laughed softly. "Kindly offered, young Nikias. But I have no fear of Spartans. It is true that they have no use for poetry in their bleak country, but they would not harm an old wandering storyteller like me. I am too feeble to go traipsing through the mountains at my age. And my poor old girl would balk at such an effort."

"Your poor old girl?"

"My donkey," said Linos. "She's on her last legs too."

Karpos led Nikias down a dark corridor, holding a burning lamp to light their way. When they got to the door at the end of the hall the slave took out a ring of keys and unlocked it. He entered, setting the burning oil lamp he'd been holding on the table. Then the slave jerked his thumb at the pot in the corner and said, "For your convenience," before leaving the room and shutting the door behind him.

Nikias slid the bolt on the door, locking it. He picked up the lamp and inspected the room. There was one window, high up on the wall, but it was shuttered and locked. The only furniture was the bed and the table. He relieved himself in the pot, then set the lamp on the floor by the bed and lay down on the mattress. Leaning over, he blew out the flame and the room was cast into utter darkness. It had never felt so good to lie down on a bed. He felt as though his body weighed as much as the giant statue of the hero Androkles back home. He felt himself floating. . . .

He dreamt he was in the Cave of Nymphs with Kallisto, making love. And then he looked over to see Helena watching them from the corner. She was naked and unadorned. Nikias invited Helena to join them, and together the three became entwined, rolling on the floor of the cave, seeking out each other's mouths and nipples, writhing like eels. And then Nikias looked up and saw his best friend Demetrios standing over them, holding the golden fleece. But the sheepskin dripped with blood.

"I'm coming home," said Demetrios, his handsome face breaking into a smile. "I bring healing treasure."

Demetrios laid the fleece on the fire and smoke poured forth into the cave, filling it with black vapor. Nikias started choking. He heard someone outside the cave screaming—

"Fire! Fire!"

Nikias awoke in the dark chamber. He was on the floor and his eyes burned from smoke. He got up and fumbled for the door ring, panicking because he couldn't breathe.

"Get out!" yelled Karpos's voice from somewhere outside the door, followed by frantic screams.

At last he found the door ring, but it burned hot to the touch. He slid the bolt, unlocking the door, and wrapped his tunic around the door ring, pulling hard. But the door would not open. It had been blocked from the outside! Nikias pounded on the door, calling out for help, but nobody replied. The smoke was getting thicker. He felt dizzy.

All at once the shutters on the high window flew open. "This way!" called a young man's voice. Someone was outside the window, holding up a torch so he could see.

Nikias grabbed the table and pushed it up against the wall, then jumped on top of it and clambered out the window, landing on the stone pavers on the other side. He was in the alleyway at the back of the inn. Two men stood over him. One was an enormous man covering his face with a cloth to filter out the smoke. Nikias recognized the face of the other in the torchlight—Priam, the young guardsman who had taken his weapons at the gates of Tanagra.

Nikias choked and gasped for air. "Thank—thank you."

The bigger man shifted, quickly raising something above his head. "You're welcome," he said with a familiar voice—a deep, callous voice that sent a shock wave of terror through Nikias's brain.

Axe!

Before Nikias could react, the warrior Axe swung a club downward, smashing Nikias on the side of the head with a devastating, skull-rattling blow, and the world went black.

EIGHT

———◆———

Eurymakus could not take his eyes away from the gift that the one god had delivered to him—a gift that lay in chains on the floor of a windowless undercroft beneath the streets of Tanagra, unconscious and mumbling deliriously.

It had been less than two weeks since Eurymakus and Nikias had fought at the gates of Plataea. Eurymakus had felt such heartache in the aftermath of that defeat. A soul-crushing desolation like he had never felt before. It had been worse than the blinding sorrow he had felt after Menesarkus had murdered his brother Damos in the pankration championship. But how quickly life could change when the hand of Ahura Mazda was at the tiller of one's Ship of Destiny. For lying helpless at Eurymakus's feet was the wily Nikias himself—heir to General Menesarkus, scourge of Eurymakus and Thebes!

Eurymakus wished that Axe had not struck Nikias so hard in the head. He was concerned that Nikias might have suffered brain damage, or that he might never awake from his insensate condition. For the Theban whisperer wanted Nikias to be fully aware when the torture began. Eurymakus was an expert in inflicting pain—he'd trained with the king's own torturer in the prisons of Persepolis, where the art of agony had been perfected by centuries of practice. Eurymakus had skinned men up to their necks and thrown them in holes filled with hungry rats. He'd snapped bones and yanked teeth, burned out eyes and sliced off noses and genitals.

But those efforts had been meant to merely punish and maim a man's body. The most valuable thing he had learned how to do was to destroy a man's soul. He had taken the stoutest and most defiant warriors and turned them into gibbering apes who would eat Eurymakus's shit when commanded to do so. To do something like that meant taking one's time. And that was what he planned on doing with Nikias.

He squatted by the pankrator, setting down an oil lamp by his head, then pulled the young man's long hair back from his face so he could study his strong features in the flickering light.

"Of course, your body will be ruined by the time I'm done with you," Eurymakus said softly. "No fingers with which to touch your beloved, no teeth with which to chew delicious food. Lipless and earless. A hideous mockery of what you once were." He saw Nikias's eyes moving rapidly behind his lids, as though he heard what was said but was unable to speak.

"I will, however, leave one of your eyes intact," continued Eurymakus in a cheerful voice. "So you can see the expressions of utter horror on the faces of your fellow Plataeans and kin. But by that time there will be nothing much left of your mind but a shrieking, sickening agony that never fades, for you will be mad. And then I will send you back to Plataea so that your grandfather can look upon you, and his heart will wither in his breast."

Eurymakus felt a twinge in his guts—a sensation of excitement mingled with expectation.

Just then Nikias shifted and mumbled something in his sleep. Eurymakus leaned forward, listening.

"The name," said Nikias, barely audible.

Eurymakus frowned. Nikias had been muttering in his sleep ever since Axe and the young Tanagraean guardsman had carried him to this building for safekeeping a day ago. But Nikias had spoken only nonsense. He kept rambling on about a talking white horse that could turn into a shaft of light and fly away; and a magical singing sword—given to him by Perikles, of all people!—that lay at the bottom of the sea. Several times during his fevered nightmares Nikias had opened his eyes, staring into the distance, hallucinating that gold darics were spilling from his stomach, or that he was trapped in a collapsing tunnel made of bones, or stuck in the hold of a sinking ship that was filled with the corpses of his kin.

Eurymakus had to admit they were interesting nightmares. He wondered what kind of elaborate fantasies Nikias would retreat to when the suffering began.

"I can't remember her name," said Nikias in a strangely coherent voice, though his eyes were still closed tightly. "Why?"

"Whose name?" asked Eurymakus in a soft voice, his lips so close to Nikias's ear that he could smell the oily scent of his hair.

"*Her* name . . . the stone . . . the doctor told me . . ." muttered Nikias, his voice incoherent again. He shifted in his sleep and shivered. Then he laughed. "The Babylonian doctor knows . . . but he's drunk. Demetrios would know how to figure it out. But he's found the golden fleece. . . ."

Eurymakus reached for a blanket and covered Nikias with it. Then he held a skin filled with water to Nikias's lips, squirting some into his mouth and making certain that he swallowed. Then Eurymakus prayed to his *fravashi*—his guardian angel—to bring Nikias out of this delirium. To make him sound of mind. Torturing a deranged man was a fruitless and dissatisfying effort.

He chewed on one of his fingernails, a nervous habit from his youth that he had corrected long ago but which had come back all of a sudden—ever since he had laid eyes on the unconscious form of Nikias.

Ten years of waiting!

Several times over the previous decade since his brother's death, Eurymakus had risked venturing into Plataean territory and spying on Nikias, hiding in the olive grove above Menesarkus's farm, watching the family of Plataeans like the most patient of spiders. He had seen Nikias grow up, changing from a wild boy to a savage young man. And all that time he had planned how he would one day capture him and take him apart, piece by piece, in front of his grandfather's horrified eyes. That plan had failed on the night of the sneak attack, though he had come so tantalizingly close to having both Menesarkus and Nikias in his grasp.

Nikias the cunning. No! Nikias the fortunate. A young man seemingly protected by the entire pantheon of Greek gods.

But now he was here. A prisoner, chained in an undercroft far beneath the streets of Tanagra. Helpless and alone. No god could touch him here. It was like a beautiful dream. But this was real. He had been led to Tanagra by his guardian angel, and given this gift as a reward for all of his efforts. There were no coincidences in life. This was destiny.

He heard Nihani stirring in the corner of the room where she had fallen asleep on the floor. He thought back to the night they had escaped from Thebes. Eurymakus had crept down to the main room of his house, where he'd found the guards ravaging her body. He had sprung on them like a wild cat—three swipes from his poisoned claw and they lay writhing on the floor, blood pouring from their eyes and nostrils as the venom did its work.

Eurymakus and Nihani had found the horses she had purchased in the Theban stable. Then they had gone to a sally port on the eastern gate where a guard who was still loyal to Eurymakus had let them out of the citadel. They had ridden hard through the night, arriving in Tanagra just as the gates to the city-state were opened in the morning. They had been admitted without incident and had gone to the home of a wealthy Tanagraean merchant named Polykarpos—a staunch anti-Plataean who had been secretly plotting with Eurymakus for over ten years to overthrow the Athenian rule of Tanagra.

Thirty years ago this Polykarpos had married off one of his daughters to a Plataean citizen, and she had borne him a son named Kiton who had spent much of his youth in Tanagra, where the boy had been coddled by his grandfather.

Kiton had grown up to be a fearsome Plataean warrior, and had been given a nickname based on his favorite weapon.

"Axe" was what the Plataeans called him.

Axe hated the Athenians and was loyal to his Tanagraean grandfather. And he had been one of Eurymakus's spies inside the Plataean citadel on the night of the sneak attack. Eurymakus had been surprised to find Axe still alive and taking refuge in Polykarpos's house, for he had thought the Plataean had perished during the battle. Eurymakus had been even more astonished when, a few days later, Axe's cousin, a young man who guarded the gates, had burst into Polykarpos's house, breathless and excited with news: Nikias of Plataea had arrived in Tanagra!

Axe had slipped out of Polykarpos's house before Eurymakus could stop him, and the great oaf had nearly been spotted by the young Plataean in Tanagra's public square. But Axe had ducked back into Polykarpos's house before Nikias had seen him. Eurymakus had quickly sent Nihani to follow Nikias through the citadel. The clever woman, still in the guise of a man, had trailed him to the Three Thieves, pretending to be a male prostitute when confronted by Nikias.

The plan to burn down the inn and force Nikias out of his room had been Eurymakus's scheme. And Axe and his cousin had carried it out perfectly, smoking Nikias out like a mountain badger from his hole.

Eurymakus heard a sound outside the chamber door and stood up. The door opened and Polykarpos lumbered into the room, followed by Axe bearing a pine-pitch torch that crackled loudly.

The merchant was a big man in his sixties. He resembled a much older, gone-to-seed version of his nephew, for he was corpulent and wore perfume in his hair like an Athenian. The small chamber was quickly filled with its overpowering scent. Polykarpos's eyes, like Axe's, were too small for his head, and his bushy beard hid his face.

"Is he awake?" asked Polykarpos, casting a dark glance at Nikias.

"No," said Eurymakus. "Axe does not know his strength. He hit him too hard."

"I tried to kill him," said Axe with a slanted smile. "I don't care if that sheep-stuffer lives or dies."

"Oh, he will die," said Eurymakus. "But he will die *slowly*."

"Is this torture necessary?" asked Polykarpos, twisting one of his many rings on his fat fingers. "Why don't you just extract the information you need and slit his throat?"

"I don't need any information," said Eurymakus. "There is nothing about Plataea that Nikias could tell me that I don't already know."

"Then why—"

"He must pay for what he and his family have done," said Eurymakus, trying to keep his voice calm. He despised having to explain himself to this merchant.

Eurymakus watched as Axe walked over and squatted by Nikias, holding the flame close to the young man's face.

"Be careful," said Eurymakus. "You'll set his hair on fire."

Axe put the torch a little closer with a mischievous grin, singeing Nikias's hair until it curled and smoked.

"Stop!" ordered Eurymakus. "There will be time for that later."

"Just checking to see if he's really unconscious," said Axe with a shrug.

"Disgusting smell," said Polykarpos, waving away the smoke.

Axe cleared his throat and spit on Nikias's face. "There," he said. "That will put out the fire for good. Or should I piss on him? I say we start in on him now," he added. "We're wasting time. My uncle has a big Median slave who's hung like a donkey. Let's have him rape Nikias to start. That will give us all a good laugh."

"We have all the time in the world," said Eurymakus. "I will not begin until Nikias is fully aware of what is going on."

Axe stood up and kicked Nikias in the stomach. "Awake or not, I would enjoy it either way. I've hated this piece of shit since he was a boy. Just like I hated his worthless father, Aristo."

Polykarpos scratched his bushy beard with a nervous gesture. "Listen, Eurymakus," he said, speaking in a lower voice, "we need to talk about what comes next."

"I told you already," said Eurymakus. "We wait until the Spartans destroy Plataea. In the meantime we start bringing together all of the Tanagraeans who are ready to kill the Athenian loyalists in the citadel. When the time is right we take over the city and then send emissaries to the Spartans."

"*We* ally ourselves with the Spartans?" mimicked Axe. "*You* are not a Tanagraean, Eurymakus. You're not even a Theban anymore from what I can gather."

"You are not a citizen of Tanagra either," replied Eurymakus icily. "But I still have the ear of the Persian king as well as the Spartans, and I will be the bridge that connects Tanagra to them both. I can bring Persian gold to Tanagra. Enough to buy armor for a thousand men. Can you say as much, Axe? The Persians would indeed be willing to finance Tanagra, just as they had given gold to Thebes."

Eurymakus turned to Polykarpos and said, "You cannot hope to remain independent from the Spartans unless you have the backing of Artaxerxes and the Persian Empire. Otherwise the Spartans will make you their vassals."

By the looks on their faces his words had worked, for Axe shrugged and turned away as if accepting defeat, and Polykarpos nodded contritely.

"What about Thebes?" asked Polykarpos. "Won't the Spartans give Thebes the power to rule in the Oxlands once Plataea is destroyed?"

"Thebes is like a one-legged man," said Eurymakus. "We lost too many warriors in the battle against Plataea. We . . ." Here he paused and rubbed his hand on the stump of his arm. ". . . *they* are now powerless. Thebes will fall under the Spartan yoke. Tanagra has the opportunity to become the most powerful city-state in the Oxlands. But only with my help."

Eurymakus turned and saw that Nihani now stood beside him, staring at Polykarpos and Axe with her haughty gaze. Eurymakus noticed Axe ogling her. Nihani saw this, too, and stepped closer to Eurymakus's side.

The room was silent except for Nikias's mumbling.

Polykarpos put a hand on his chin and stared at Nikias, thinking for some time. "I don't want this Plataean to be alive much longer," he said at last. "There are men in Tanagra who are still loyal allies of the Plataeans. They would have me sharded for torturing the heir of the Plataean Arkon. I say we kill him and bury his corpse in the forest."

"I agree with my grandfather," said Axe. "The sooner, the better."

"I need a week," said Eurymakus. "That is all that I ask."

"You shall have three days," said Polykarpos. "You can do whatever needs to be done with this poor lad in three days. 'Death is a terrible discharge that we all must eventually pay,'" he recited with a sigh. He cast another glance at Nikias, then exited the chamber.

Axe followed after his grandfather, saying over his shoulder, "Don't start the fun without me," then slammed the door shut behind him.

After the two men were gone Eurymakus stood for a long time staring at Nikias.

"I don't like either one of them," said Nihani.

"I would gouge out Axe's eyes for undressing you with his eyes that way," said Eurymakus. "But we need him. And we need Polykarpos, even though he is as spineless as a snail. We will use them for as long as we can."

"We should go to Persia now," said Nihani. "Kill Nikias and be done with him. Your revenge is in your grasp."

"No," replied Eurymakus. "Death is not enough. He must suffer. Only then will my brother's spirit find peace." He chewed on a nail, pulling it off, causing his finger to bleed. "The game has shifted, my love," he said. "We have been shown the path by Ahura Mazda. If I can bring Tanagra to the Spartans, I will be back in their good favor. I can't run away to Persia like a dog with its tail between its legs. Not when Plataea is so close to being destroyed."

"God be praised," she replied in a wooden voice. "Come now."

She led him to the corner of the chamber with the makeshift bed.

"Take off your tunic," she commanded him. "Get on your hands and knees."

As they made love Eurymakus kept his eyes locked on Nikias the entire time, and exploded in the most violent of orgasms. He lay next to Nihani, breathing hard, and then fell into a deep slumber. When he awoke she was kneeling next to him, staring into his face, smiling impishly.

"My love," she whispered. "The Plataean is awake."

Eurymakus got up very slowly and turned to face Nikias. The young pankrator stared back at him, hair and face wet with sweat, struggling against the chains, an expression of horror on his pale but lucid face.

"Zeus, no," hissed Nikias.

NINE

When Diokles the Helot was a child he had found a puppy cowering in a ditch—a stray that was near death. He had cared for the animal in secret, feeding it milk from a goat, and the dog had grown strong.

But then the tall, lean, noseless Spartan master who owned the village and all of its inhabitants came for an inspection and discovered what Diokles had done. Helots weren't allowed to have dogs. Dogs could be used to hunt and Helots were forbidden to hunt. Or a dog could act as a sentinel—to alert Helots engaged in secret meetings that their Spartan masters were in the village. So the master killed the dog by smashing its head against a wall, and then he ordered his men to hang Diokles upside down by his ankles and whip him until his skin was in shreds.

Diokles had lived. But just barely. And he had never stopped hating the masters. Especially the one with the face like a skull: Master Drako.

Diokles had asked his father if the Helots had ever been free of the Spartans. His father hadn't known. But he had said that the Spartans were good masters. His father had told him a story. "Long ago, when the beasts could talk, a sheep said to her master: 'We sheep do so much for you. We give you wool, lambs, and cheese. But we get nothing except what comes from the land. Yet you share your house and home with your dog who gives you none of the things we give you.' The dog heard this and replied: 'Stupid sheep! The master and I protect you from thieves and wolves. Without us you would not even be able to graze for fear of being killed.'"

As he had grown into manhood Diokles had come to realize that, not only were his people exactly like the sheep in the story, but the Spartans were the *wolves*. The word "Helot" in the Spartan tongue meant "the captured ones." Each year at the summer harvest, Master Drako would come to the village with his small army of soldiers and read from a scroll: "As we have done every year since conquering this land, we the Spartan people declare our everlasting war upon the captured ones." This "war" was enforced with the *krypteria*—the Spartan initiation into manhood. Every so often a Helot man would be taken from the village and marched high into the mountains, where he was released . . . and then hunted down by a Spartan boy. Diokles's father had been one of these butchered men. Diokles was ten years old at the time.

Over the years he had heard rumors of some Helot slaves who had run away during a great earthquake that had shaken Sparta. It was said they had started their own city on the top of a volcano, and had beaten back an army of Spartans who had come to take them back. He vowed to find that city one day.

Perhaps his Spartan masters had known how to read his mind. For when he had entered the breeding age, they had picked him out as a troublemaker and sold him off to a slaver. And that's how he'd ended up in a Spartan mine, where twenty thousand men pounded the earth to bring up the ore to make iron. Somehow he'd survived the agonizing labor, the cave-ins, the beatings, the poor diet. The guards at the mines had given him the name "the beetle" because he was so short and squat, dark-skinned and sturdy. His body was suited to crawling into tight crevices to search for ore. It was as if the weight of the earth he toiled under had compressed him, packed him together.

He had worked in shafts so deep, the only light came from sooty lamps, the only smells the ore dust and the smoke of burning wicks. He had pounded holes in the solid rock for hours on end. He had fantasized about killing himself many times. All he would have had to do was anchor the digging spike into the rock and impale his neck on it. But he hadn't been able to stand the thought of dying underground, in the darkness. . . .

"And how did you finally escape?" asked Ajax and Teleos at the same time.

Diokles stopped hammering for a moment and glanced at the faces of the brothers staring back at him, illuminated by the lamplight of the dark tunnel. He had been telling them his story as they dug under the streets of Plataea in the tunnel entrance beneath the ancient marker called Zeus's Thumb—the place where Barka had told them that the treasure was sure to be found. The eunuch had come to the tunnel an hour ago to inspect their work, and then he had disappeared. But where had his pretty Lylit gone?

"Diokles?" urged Teleos.

"Eh?"

Diokles had become so lost in his own tale that he'd forgotten he had been speaking his thoughts aloud to the brothers.

"What happened next?" asked Ajax.

"Earthquake come," said Diokles. "Biggest earthquake ever. Wall around slave quarters split open. And we run. All of us. I don't know how many make it to the sea. Maybe I the only one. I find a ship on a beach in a little cove. A pretty ship full of pirates. They getting water from a spring. I beg them to take me on board. I cry at them. Big tears."

"And that was Chusor's ship?" asked Ajax.

"*Zana's* ship," replied Diokles and started hammering a spike in between two rocks. The first blow made a strange hollow sound and he cocked his head to the side. He struck the spike again and frowned. This was a wall. A wall of stacked stones.

"But Chusor was there," said Teleos. "Right? He brought you on board."

"Chusor was one of the sailors," said Diokles. "Barka who kept them from killing me. My Lylit ask Zana to take me on ship."

"Why?" asked Ajax.

Diokles pounded the spike several more times, driving it into the rocks. The blockage crumbled suddenly and filled the tunnel with debris. For an instant Diokles thought the roof of the tunnel might collapse, but the wooden supports they had installed held. Once the dust cleared he held up the lamp and thrust it into the darkness. He wiped the sweat and dirt from his face and said under his breath, "Barka tell me I going to save her life one day."

"And did you?" asked Teleos.

Diokles ignored the question. "Clear this," he ordered.

The boys went to work, hauling the mound of debris up the tunnel and out of the way.

Gripping a large stone that jutted from the floor of the tunnel, Diokles pulled on it with all his might and it came from the earth like a rotten tooth. Now there was enough room for him to squeeze into the dark space on the other side. He held the lamp out in front of him and crawled on one hand and his knees into some sort of man-made chamber.

"What do you see in there?" said Teleos from the tunnel.

"Stay out," said Diokles.

On the other side of the chamber, leaning against the wall, was a decayed wooden shield and a rusted bronze corselet.

"Diokles?" said Ajax. "Can we come in too?"

"Stay out," said Diokles. "Not enough room for you monkeys."

"Did you find the treasure?"

He ignored the boys as he crawled around the chamber. He found the skeleton of a dog, curled up as though in eternal sleep. And stone boxes. Diokles pulled off the top of one of these and held up the lamp to peer inside. He couldn't tell what was contained in it. A black substance. He reached inside and took out a clump of something and sniffed it.

Grain. To sow in the afterlife.

At the other end of the chamber he found a narrow alcove with a body stretched out on the floor, and skeletal hands clutching a sword in a rotting wooden scabbard. On the dead man's head was a helm fashioned from the curved tusks of boars. A shelf had been carved into the alcove, and on it were arrayed dusty objects that reflected the lamp flame with a pale yellow gleam.

He put the lamp next to the corpse's head and saw a metallic face smiling back.

"Forgive me for disturbing your sleep, warrior," said Diokles, and reached for the golden mask with a trembling hand.

TEN

———————•———————

Nikias laughed, even though doing so caused him immense pain—like knives stabbing into his lungs. He laughed because he couldn't figure out why his blood floated *upward*, toward the low ceiling a few inches above his head. He felt the blood pooling in his mouth and let another gob of it out, and watched curiously as the red stream flowed up rather than down, joining the pool of fluid and vomit and piss.

And there was a voice in the back of his mind—a nagging voice that wouldn't stop. It kept saying over and over again, "Remember the name." He could picture the fellow. Dark eyes, curly beard, plump—strange accent.

Remember the name, Nikias. . . .

"What name?" Nikias said aloud. "I told you, I can't remember." He laughed again and winced. He realized that his ribs were broken. That's why it hurt so much to laugh. He tried to move his arms but they were pinioned behind his back. Everything seemed so strange. Where was he? Why couldn't he move his arms? Why couldn't he walk?

The ring. The stone. The angel. She will save you. . . .

"What's he doing?" asked an annoyed voice—a cruel voice that was so different from the kindly one in his head.

"He's hallucinating," came a silky reply. This second voice had a Theban accent.

"I need to rest my hand. My knuckles ache from punching him."

"Axe, you surprise me. I reckoned you could punch a *defenseless* man all day."

"I've been beating on him for three hours. I think I've broken all his ribs. I say we start cutting into him."

Nikias saw the upside-down face of a man with almond-shaped eyes come into view. The man was missing part of his upper lip. With a sickening twist in his guts, he remembered where he was. Tanagra. Hanging by his ankles from a beam in an undercroft. And the man looking at him was his enemy—the Theban Eurymakus.

"Hello, Nikias," said Eurymakus, pulling back his ruined lip in a ruthless smile. "You left us for a few minutes."

Nikias squirmed and tried to lash out, but he was helpless. When they had first strung him up by the rope, hours ago, he had felt like his eyeballs were going to pop out of his skull from the pressure of his blood rushing to his head. But then Axe had started beating on him as though he were a stuffed leather punching bag at the gymnasium, and now every organ in his body felt as though it were going to burst. He had blacked out several times during the ordeal, drifting into fevered dreams that brought a few moments of escape.

But every time he woke up again to this horror.

Now his heart started pounding as the panic returned. There was no escape. He was utterly helpless, far from home and friends. No help would come if he were to scream. All he wanted now was for them to kill him and put him out of this misery. A wave of sadness bathed his soul. Eurymakus had told him that he would torture and mutilate him and send him back to Plataea in a cart. He thought of his grandfather and Kallisto seeing his destroyed body and he fought back tears. He didn't want Eurymakus or Axe to see him cry.

"I'm sorry, Grandfather," Nikias whispered. "I'm so sorry I didn't listen to you."

"He's sobbing, the little bitch," said Axe. "What's he saying?"

"He's terrified," said Eurymakus in a gentle tone. "Lower him down, Axe. Let's give our friend a little rest."

"Stuff giving him a rest!" said Axe. "I want to make him eat his balls. You promised."

"Lower him," said the spy, a hint of anger creeping into his voice.

Eurymakus supported Nikias's head as Axe lowered the rope, and Nikias let forth a body-wracking sigh as he slumped to the floor. He lay with his head in Eurymakus's lap, feeling his enemy's hand stroking his head. He tried to stifle his sobs, but he couldn't help himself. He wept like a child.

"There, there," cooed Eurymakus. "You may weep, Nikias. You must rest now. We will be here for many more hours. Many more days. There is so much I need to teach you. So much that you need to learn about pain and humility. Just like your beloved friend Demetrios will have learnt in the Prison Pits of Syrakuse. He'll be dead by now, of course. He was no use to the Spartans after his father, Nauklydes, had been turned to our cause. And the Syrakusans do whatever the Spartans tell them. They are good little dogs. They have learnt to heel. Just like you will, my frightened pup," he added, and patted Nikias's head.

"Please let me go," said Nikias. He couldn't help himself. He didn't want to speak but the words came pouring out of him. "Please. I'll do anything. Just tell me what to do."

"Ha!" barked Axe. "I love this! Listen to him! Pathetic."

"I was supposed to die . . . as a warrior," gasped Nikias.

"You want to die like your father did?" said Axe with a scoffing laugh. "You want to die in *battle*?"

"Yes," said Nikias. "This is . . . dishonorable."

"Ah," said Eurymakus. "Now you're learning something. Now you know what my brother Damos must have felt when your grandfather murdered him in the pankration arena, in front of forty thousand men. When he pushed his face into the sand, smothering him. Humiliation," he hissed.

"I want to tell you something," said Axe, kneeling down and putting his leering face close to Nikias's. "Your father wasn't struck down by the enemy at the Battle of Koronea. *I* killed him." He started laughing giddily.

Nikias stared back at Axe, eyes bulging.

"I always hated Aristo," continued Axe. "Such an arrogant piece of shit, just like you. In the chaos of the battle, after our shield wall broke and we were running away, I speared your father in the guts. You should have seen the look on his face. I've never seen anyone look so surprised. I was on my back, helpless, when Aristo cut down a warrior who was just about to kill me. He saved me! Can you believe that? Aristo saved *me*. He was such a right-minded prick. And then the sheep-stuffer reached out a hand to pull me up and"—here he made a horrible squelching sound, screwing up his face in a look of mock surprise—"Aristo sang no more."

Nikias remembered seeing his father's bloodless blue-skinned corpse in the back of the cart. He remembered cradling his father's cold funeral jar in his arms. He remembered his mother's anguished cries and the blood pouring from the cuts she had rent in her own face with her fingernails. And all this time . . . all these years . . . the man responsible for his murder had walked free in Plataea, mocking him behind his back. Never in Nikias's life had he wanted to kill somebody more than now. To squeeze the life from Axe's body.

"You should see the look on *your* face now!" said Axe with vicious delight. "You look just like your father!"

Nikias lunged at Axe, clamping onto the man's cheek with the only weapons he had left—his teeth. He ripped back his head and tore out a chunk of flesh, then spit it back into Axe's face.

Axe fell on his haunches, clapping a hand to his bloody cheek. Then he dove at Nikias, raining blows upon his face.

"Stop!" barked Eurymakus. "Not yet!"

"I'll kill him!" shouted Axe, whipping out his short knife.

Eurymakus stood up and pulled forth his poisoned dagger from its stone box. The blade shone with dark poison. "Not yet!" he screamed.

Axe was about to stab Nikias, but the sight of the tainted blade inches from his face stopped him short. He backed up and glared at the Theban.

"Now go clean yourself up," ordered Eurymakus. "And tell Nihani to come back down here."

Axe sheathed his knife and clapped a hand over his cheek. He got up slowly and backed to the door, then exited the chamber, slamming the door behind him with such force that the hinges rattled.

Eurymakus got a wineskin filled with water and held it to Nikias's swollen and bleeding lips. "Drink," he said.

"Why are you doing this to me?" asked Nikias plaintively. He had started shaking uncontrollably, his teeth chattering. "Why, Eurymakus? It debases you. It makes you less of a man."

Eurymakus said in a chiding tone, "You do not understand, Nikias of Plataea. It is my duty. My *fravashi* has brought you to me. To teach you things. You will understand soon enough."

Fravashi!

Nikias's thoughts spun. The stone on the signet ring. And the name that the doctor Ezekiel had found inscribed there. What had he called her? An angel. A *guardian* angel. But what was her name? He couldn't think straight.

The door to the cell burst open. Axe strode into the room with one of his big arms wrapped around the neck of Nihani, his other hand holding a dagger to her throat.

"What is this?" said Eurymakus in a shocked tone.

"I'm going to show you how to get this job done," said Axe, blood pouring down his face.

From the doorway the Tanagraean magistrate Polykarpos entered, followed by Axe's cousin Priam and two armed guards. The guards shut the door and barred it behind them.

"We can't let the Plataean live any longer," Polykarpos said to Eurymakus. He shook his head and glared. "He is too dangerous. Look what he has done to my poor grandson even though he is bound at the wrists and ankles!"

"But—but he is my prisoner!" sputtered Eurymakus.

"He is *my* prisoner," said Polykarpos. "Under *my* roof. You're going to kill him anyway, Eurymakus. What difference does two days make?"

Axe shoved Nihani to the floor so that she was on her hands and knees. He turned to Priam and said, "If she moves a muscle, cut off her head."

Priam drew his sword and stood over Nihani, arms raised for the deathblow. Nihani looked at Eurymakus, who held a trembling hand for her to be still.

"Now," said Axe. "I'm going to make Nikias chew on his own balls. And then I'm going to cut off his head and throw it down the hole of the public shithouse."

Axe walked over and shoved the stunned Eurymakus out of the way. "Come here," he said to the two guards. The men sauntered over and grabbed Nikias, lifting him off the floor and positioning him on his knees with his face pressed into the floor, holding him tightly between them. Nikias squirmed desperately.

Nikias felt Axe's hand groping underneath him, reaching for his testicles. Then he grasped hold of them, yanking them down like a farmer getting ready to castrate a young bull. Nikias sucked in his breath and bucked his hips frantically. This couldn't be happening!

"Hold him still!" Axe growled at the guards. "I can't get a firm grip."

And then, for an instant, Nikias felt himself leave his body, as though he were in a flying dream. Everything went quiet save for a rushing sound in his ears. The evil chamber vanished, and he saw Ezekiel in his mind's eye, peering at the stone he'd pried from the signet ring, uttering a woman's name. . . .

Nikias felt the touch of cold iron against his thigh. He locked eyes with Eurymakus, who stared back at him.

"Daena!" screamed Nikias. "Daena! Protect me!"

Eurymakus's eyes opened wide in disbelief. He held up his arm, screaming, "Axe, wait!"

Axe turned to look at Eurymakus with a curious expression, such was the powerful force of Eurymakus's cry, but he kept the dagger poised against Nikias's testicles. "What?" he asked angrily.

Eurymakus rushed to Nikias, knelt in front of him, and peered into his eyes with a desperate look. "What did you say?" he asked with anguish in his voice.

"Daena!" whispered Nikias frantically, tears pouring from his eyes. "Your *fravashi*! I found your ring. And the name inscribed on the stone. Daena. I will call to her after I die and she will come to me and not to you."

Eurymakus's eyes flicked around the chamber. He stood up and passed a shaking hand across his brow.

"Take me to the Spartans," pleaded Nikias. "They can trade me for Prince Arkilokus, who is a prisoner in Plataea."

"What's he talking about?" asked Axe.

"Gibberish," said Eurymakus faintly.

"Get ready to taste your own seed," said Axe, pulling on Nikias's testicles again and tensing his arm for the cut.

Nikias squeezed his eyes shut, screaming deep in his throat. He started thrashing again.

"No!" he screamed. "No, no, no!"

All of a sudden Axe released his grip and so did the guards. Nikias heard choking sounds and opened his bleary eyes. Axe and the guards were on the floor, writhing in agony. Blood oozed from their eyeballs. Axe clutched his hand.

There was a wound there—a thin scrape, no bigger than a cat's scratch. Eurymakus stood over the dying men, his poisoned blade grasped in one hand. It glistened with gore.

"What is this?" croaked Polykarpos from across the chamber. "What have you done?"

Priam stared in amazement at the men flailing on the floor. It had all happened so fast. In the blink of an eye. He brought the sword down to cut off Nihani's head, but his sword clattered on the stones and he staggered forward, for Nihani was no longer on her knees at his feet—she had slipped behind him and, pulling the young man's dagger from his belt, plunged it into his back, both hands grasping the hilt. Priam, groaning, fell to the stones, and Nihani yanked the dagger from his back, then drove it in again and again until he became still.

Polykarpos ran to the door and tried to unbar it, but Eurymakus flung his dagger across the room. The short blade stuck in the magistrate's head and he clutched his skull, shrieking. Falling to his knees, blood started gushing from his nostrils and eyes. His lips curled back to reveal his red-stained teeth—blood seeped from his gums. He looked back and forth from Eurymakus to Nihani, gasping for air, and then fell on his back, convulsing violently, biting off his tongue with a spray of blood.

Nihani stared wild-eyed around the chamber. She made to speak, but Eurymakus held a finger to his lips for silence. He darted to the portal and put his ear to the keyhole, listening . . . waiting to see if anyone in the house above had heard the slaughter down in the undercroft. When he was certain no one was coming, he pulled the dagger from the magistrate's head and slipped it back into the stone sheath on his belt.

Nikias lay on the floor, breathless and unable to move. He craned his head and saw Axe slumped against a wall, twitching in his final death throes from the dreadful and potent poison.

Axe was grinding his teeth—gnashing them together so hard that they were breaking apart in his mouth. He spit some teeth from his mouth along with a gob of blood. "N-no!" he sputtered, his bleeding eyes locked onto Nikias's. "H-h-how?" he asked, his voice now coming out as a desperate squeak from his constricting throat.

"You," said Nikias, mustering every effort to speak, "should see the look . . . on *your* face."

ELEVEN

———— ◆ ————

Barka crawled along a passageway under the streets of Plataea, a small lamp clutched in his slender fingers. Even though he had been reassured by Diokles that the tunnel had been shored up with stout timbers, he was still unnerved by being alone in such a quiet and solitary place. He felt like he was on a path leading straight to the Underworld.

He hummed to himself. It was a jaunty tune he'd learned in Syrakuse from a young man with whom he'd fallen in love.

> *The lion sprang, and Herakles leapt*
> *His cudgel flew, the lion wept*

The lyrics of the drinking song were idiotic, like all songs men sang when they were tipsy with wine. But they had a soothing effect on Barka. The image of a weeping lion made him smile. He thought of his lover—how he resembled a painted statue of Apollo come to life. How his eyes glowed like jewels. His smile like the sun. From the moment Barka had laid eyes on him two years ago in Syrakuse, he had known that he would die for this man.

Or kill for him.

Barka had been the guest-friend at the palace of the richest and most influential citizen in the city-state of Syrakuse: General Pantares. Barka's soothaying skills were famous in the lands of Greater Greece and "the Tyrant" had always welcomed the eunuch whenever he came to port, marveling at his skills as an oracle, asking him advice about his enemies—advice that nearly always came true. Pantares had even asked Barka if Syrakuse should join with Sparta, which Barka had declared was inevitable, telling him that, years hence, the alliance would lead to a colossal victory for the general's city against the Athenians.

But Barka had not predicted his *own* fate in the house of Pantares: falling madly in love with the general's new ward . . . a beautiful young man who had arrived from the backwater of the Oxlands to further his studies in that cultivated city.

Barka stopped short as he came to a fork in the corridor. Diokles had taken him on a thorough tour of the tunnel system the day before, proudly showing him all of the twists and turns of the underground labyrinth that the work crew had been excavating, and so he knew exactly where he was. This particular corridor had only just been cleared, and it led to the city's cistern. He could smell the scent of dank stones coming from the right, and so he turned and continued in that direction.

He never would have taken the risk of sneaking out of Plataea if not for the unsettling dream that he'd had the night before: a vision of his beloved in chains, an executioner standing over him with an axe. Barka felt that he had to see the Spartan face-to-face. The only important thing was to know for certain if his beloved was still alive. All that he had to do was to peer into the Spartan's eyes and he would know if he told the truth or not.

He glanced down at the ring on his right hand. The ring bore a stone that opened with a hinge. Under the stone was a short needle containing a deadly poison. If Barka discovered tonight that his lover was dead, he would kill the Spartan, and then himself.

He could hear the sound of dripping water up ahead. And then he saw moonlight shining through a metal grate and a pool of water. He had come to the cistern. He set down his lamp and put a piece of flint next to it so that he could relight it if he were to return from the Spartan camp. Then he blew out the flame and let his eyes adjust to the moonlit chamber. He eased himself into the pool, treading water, then took a deep breath and dove down, feeling for the metal grate overhead. For a terrifying moment his dress got caught on the bottom of the grate, and he panicked, shooting to the surface and ripping his clothes.

He took a breath and sighed with relief. He was on the other side of the city walls. He climbed out of the cistern and wrung out his dress, then crept toward a road lined with plane trees, looking over his shoulder at the city walls to see if he'd been spotted by the guards manning the towers. But fortunately nobody saw him. He took the road for a mile, keeping in the shadows of the trees, and then headed off across the countryside, bearing east. In a short while he could see the earthen walls of the Persian Fort looming up ahead.

A moment later he felt many eyes watching him.

He stopped and stood still and said in a firm voice, "I am Barka. I have come to see Drako."

Men slipped from the shadows of the trees like ghosts and surrounded him. One of them stepped forward and quickly bound his hands behind his back, then searched his body for weapons. Satisfied that he was not a threat, two of the warriors silently led him toward the entrance to the fort, while the others went back to their hiding positions for their night watch.

The warriors led Barka down a row between Helots—thousands of them sleeping on the ground without blankets, many of them snoring peacefully. Up ahead he could see a cluster of tents lit by a roaring fire. These tents were surrounded by guards bearing spears and wearing armor.

They led Barka inside where Drako sat on a wooden camp chair in front of a desk that was covered with papyrus scrolls. The Spartan general was naked except for a cloth wrapped around his loins. He was in his late sixties, but he had the lean and muscular body of an Olympic athlete half his age. Barka stared at his skull-like visage—the noseless face with its high cheekbones and deep-set eyes. Even if he still possessed a nose, Barka mused, he would not be a handsome man.

The general looked up at Barka and fixed him with his killer's stare. "Why have you come?" he said in his raspy voice.

Barka turned the poison ring on his finger nervously. "It's too risky sending messages by pigeon anymore."

"And *this* is not taking a risk?"

"I had to see you," said Barka. "I had a dream about Demetrios."

"Your Plataean lover?" said Drako. "What care I for dreams about the traitor Nauklydes's son? He is the prisoner of General Pantares. And the Tyrant of Syrakuse is a valued friend of Sparta. Unless you do our bidding, your Demetrios will die a painful death."

"Then Demetrios is still alive?" asked Barka, trying not to betray the hopefulness in his voice. He stepped forward and peered into the Spartan's eyes. Drako stared back—the predatory look of a hawk regarding a mouse that has crawled into his nest. "You promised me that he would be treated well by the Tyrant if I did what you asked. If I infiltrated Plataea."

"I told you," said Drako. "He lives. And so you must go back to Plataea and glean whatever information you can. You have not been very useful to me thus far."

Barka couldn't help himself. He let forth a cry of relief and the tears burst from his eyes. Drako had not been lying. He could see the truth in the man's cold eyes. His nightmare vision of Demetrios, chained and awaiting execution, had merely been a bad dream.

Drako got up, walked over to Barka, and led him through a curtained-off area containing a simple cot.

"Your clothes are wet," he said. "Did you swim the river to get here? Take them off."

"My hands are bound," said Barka, biting his lip coyly.

Drako found a knife and cut through the ropes and watched silently as Barka removed his wet gown. Then the Spartan ran his rough hands over the eunuch's naked body.

"Female and male intertwined," said Drako, sinking to his knees and staring up at Barka with a hungry look. "You are androgyny in perfection."

Barka forced himself to think of Demetrios—so gentle yet manful. He smiled inwardly, remembering the day he had first seen the young Plataean arrive at the house of General Pantares, wearing his unfashionable Oxlander clothes, but looking more refined than any bejeweled nobleman in the Tyrant's house.

Then—footsteps in the tent and the sound of a man clearing his throat.

Drako cursed and swiftly stood.

"General. Eurymakus the Theban is in the camp. He has a Plataean prisoner. He begs to see you."

"Stay here," Drako ordered Barka, then pushed aside the curtain and stepped into the other part of the tent, wrapping his loincloth around him. "Bring the Theban here," Drako said to his subordinate. "He wears a poisoned dagger in a stone sheath. Take it from him. And bind his arm behind his back."

Barka put his wet dress back on. It felt clammy and clung to his skin. He sat on the cot and fixed his hair, thinking longingly of Demetrios. Then someone entered the tent and he cocked his head, listening with half an ear.

"You should be dead by now," rasped Drako's voice. "You were to be given hemlock."

"As you can see," came a smug reply, "I am still alive."

"You are a fool to come to me," said Drako. "I'll happily do the job your own people have apparently failed to do."

"I bring you an important prisoner," said the other.

"Really?" said Drako. "I hardly believe that is possible."

"Nikias of Plataea—the heir of Menesarkus."

Barka tensed. He knew that name. Nikias was Demetrios's best friend. He never stopped talking about him. They were like brothers. He pulled back a corner of the curtain and peered into the room. There stood Drako now wearing a red cloak, hands on his hips, facing a one-armed man with flowing hair and a long beard. The guard had said that this Eurymakus was a Theban. But he looked like a Persian, even though he did not speak with a Persian accent.

"How did Nikias come to be your prisoner?" asked Drako.

"God brought him to me," said Eurymakus.

"Let me see the prisoner."

Two guards dragged in a naked body bound at the feet and wrists. The young man's blood-splattered face was so swollen that Barka could not tell if his eyes were open or closed. And his torso was covered with livid bruises. He lay there, unmoving.

"And what am I supposed to do with this?" asked Drako. "It looks like you've ruined him."

"He lives," said Eurymakus. "The damage is not permanent."

"Where did you come from?" said Drako.

"Tanagra," replied Eurymakus. Drako bent down and put his hand on Nikias's neck, feeling for his pulse.

"Menesarkus will not sign a peace treaty in exchange for his heir," he said. "Even if this is Nikias."

Eurymakus smiled coldly. "But he *will* give you back Prince Arkilokus," he said in a self-satisfied manner. "Think of the praise that will be heaped upon you if you are responsible for gaining the release of a Spartan prince."

"And what do you want in return?" Drako sneered.

"Safe passage to Korinth for myself and my servant," replied Eurymakus. "From there I will travel to Persia and beg Artaxerxes to redouble his efforts to help Sparta in its war against the Athenians."

"That is all?" asked Drako.

"You and I are not enemies," Eurymakus said. "I am the best friend Sparta has at the moment."

"How can I be certain this is Nikias?" said Drako. "His face is beyond recognition."

"He wears the signet ring of his house," said Eurymakus. "Look, there. On his right hand. The boxing Minotaur."

Drako took a torch from one of his men and knelt by the body, grasping Nikias's hands, which were tied behind his back. He found the ring and tried to pull it off, but it would not budge.

"Knuckle . . . broken," muttered Nikias weakly through his swollen lips.

"Give me your knife," Drako ordered one of his men. The guard handed him a dagger.

"What are you doing?" asked Eurymakus.

"Shut up," spat Drako. He put the knife to Nikias's littlest finger and gave a quick flick of his wrist.

Nikias sucked in his breath, then screamed.

Barka gasped, covering his mouth with his hands.

Eurymakus watched apprehensively as Drako studied the ring on the bloody finger, holding it close to the torchlight. "Do you see?" asked the Theban spy. "That is Nikias's ring."

"You have redeemed yourself, Eurymakus," said Drako. "You will leave at dawn for Korinth."

Eurymakus let forth a relieved sigh. "You will not regret this, Drako."

Drako made a guttural sound. "All of my actions with you end in regrets," he said. "Now leave me."

Barka watched wide-eyed as Eurymakus bent over and looked at Nikias with a curious expression: hatred mingled with yearning. Nikias wept, muttering something under his breath. Eurymakus seemed about to speak, and then he turned and exited the tent, followed by the guards.

Drako went back to his desk and sat with his back to Barka. He started writing a message on papyrus. Barka, his heart beating wildly in his breast, opened the curtain and crept over to Nikias, putting his mouth close to Nikias's ear.

"Take heart," he said. "Demetrios is alive."

Nikias turned in the direction of the voice. "Who are you?" he murmured.

"A friend."

"Demetrios is dead," said Nikias. "Eurymakus told me. They no longer needed Demetrios alive after his father was killed."

Barka's pulse raced. His heart told him what Nikias had just said was true. Had Drako deceived him about Demetrios? Or did the Spartan not know the truth himself? Was Demetrios really dead? How could he know for certain?

Drako turned around and glared at Barka. "What are you doing?" he asked.

"The lad seemed to be choking," Barka lied.

"Get away from him," Drako ordered.

Barka dropped his head and obeyed, stepping back into the corner of the tent and standing very still, twisting the ring with the poisoned needle with the fingers of his opposite hand. A wild thought flashed through his brain: he could slay Drako and put Nikias out of his misery and kill himself before the guards outside had time to react.

But what if Nikias was wrong? What if the Theban Eurymakus had been lying?

He watched as Drako put Nikias's bloody finger and its ring, along with a small of papyrus, into a leather bag. Then he whistled and his subordinate entered the tent. Drako handed him the bag, saying, "Remove the prisoner from my tent and guard him well. And take this bag to Plataea at sunrise and nail it to the gates."

TWELVE

———————◆———————

Chusor stood outside the eastern walls to the citadel the next morning, inspecting a crew of stonemasons who were reinforcing a section of wall that had sagged during an earthquake years before, when he heard one of the lookouts on the battlement cry out, "Spartan on the road! Shut the gates!"

Snapping his head around, Chusor peered down the road, where he saw a single red-cloaked warrior striding toward the citadel. The Spartan walked slowly with both hands held up to show he had come in peace, but even so, the gates were slammed shut, and Chusor heard the big beams sliding into place on the inside, locking him and his work crew outside the walls.

The ten stonemasons picked up their shovels, picks, and chisels and walked hesitantly toward the gates.

"Should we attack him?" asked a young man.

"He's just a messenger," said Chusor, for he could clearly see a dispatch bag around the man's neck. He looked like a typical Spartan—lean to the point of looking starved, with whipcord muscles, a gaunt face, and hair as long as a woman's.

"It might be a trick," said one of the other masons and brandished a pickax.

"Don't do anything stupid," said Chusor, grabbing the man's pickax and flinging it on the ground. "We're not at war with Sparta."

"No *yet*," said another Plataean.

Chusor and the others stopped at the edge of the dirt road and watched as the Spartan walked up to the gates. The invader was not very tall—the top of his head barely reached Chusor's shoulder—but he had a menacing air about him. He turned and regarded the work crew with his cold eyes, looking at each man in turn. Then he went straight up to the gates, removed the dispatch bag, and pulled a dagger from his sheath.

"What do you want?" called one of the men on the battlement above the gate.

The Spartan ignored him, holding the dispatch bag to the wooden planks of the gate with his left hand, and drove the dagger through it with the other, pinning the bag there. Then he turned without another word and strode away.

The stonemasons exchanged mystified looks.

"What was that all about?" the lookout called down.

"It's a message," said Chusor. He strode over to the gate and yanked the dagger from the wood. Then he opened the bag and peered inside it. When he saw the finger his eyes got big and he uttered an oath under his breath.

"What is it?" asked one of the stonemasons.

Chusor reached into the bag and took out the finger and turned it over. "Some unfortunate man's—" He stopped short. The flesh on his back and neck tingled.

Nikias's signet ring!

"Open the gate!" he said in a quavering voice as he put the ring back into the bag. "Open the gate!" he shouted, pounding on the door with all his might.

The portal opened and Chusor bolted through the gap, nearly knocking over the men inside. He sprinted across the agora toward the public buildings. He could see Menesarkus coming down the steps from his offices, throwing his robe over his shoulder and clutching his staff. Chusor ran up to him, holding out the bag.

"What is it?" asked Menesarkus, taking the bag. "Where is the Spartan?"

"Go back inside," said Chusor. "Into your office. Now!"

Menesarkus's eyes narrowed. "Did you just *order* me—"

"Forgive me, Arkon," said Chusor, bowing. "Please, take this dispatch bag into your office." He stared hard into Menesarkus's eyes.

Menesarkus frowned and shooed away his clerks who were trying to take the bag from him. He turned and walked back inside, saying over his shoulder, "Follow me, Chusor."

When they were inside his private office Menesarkus shut the door, went behind his desk, and put the dispatch bag down. "You've seen what's inside?" he asked.

"Yes," said Chusor.

Menesarkus opened the bag and dumped the contents onto his desk. The finger fell out along with a small papyrus scroll. The Arkon stared at the finger for a long time before picking it up with a shaking hand and examining it. "It's a trick," he said at last, but his voice came out as barely more than a whisper.

"What does the scroll say?" asked Chusor.

Menesarkus set down the finger and picked up the scroll, breaking the wax seal and pulling it open. His eyes darted back and forth across the words written on the papyrus, then he tossed the scroll aside and put both palms on the desktop as though to keep himself from falling over. He'd gone pale, and his eyes were staring blankly into the middle distance, but when he spoke his voice was clear and resigned:

"They have Nikias," said Menesarkus. "He was captured in Tanagra, on his way back to Plataea. They are going to send another finger tomorrow. And then another. Piece by piece until they get what they want."

Chusor felt as though he might be sick. He stumbled over to a chair and sat down, staring in horror at the bloody finger. "What do they demand?" he asked. "A treaty?"

"No," replied Menesarkus. "Drako wants something else. And I cannot give it to him. And so Nikias is dead."

"What is their demand?" asked Chusor, aghast. "Surely you cannot think of letting Nikias be cut apart like a—"

"I have a Spartan prisoner!" shouted Menesarkus. "Prince Arkilokus."

"A Spartan *prince*?" Chusor asked in wonder. "Send him to the Persian Fort now and save Nikias's life."

"I cannot give up our prisoner," said Menesarkus with exasperation, as though speaking to an idiot child. "He is the only piece I have left to play in this game. He is the only security I have in case we have to get the women and children out of Plataea to the safety of another city-state. One Spartan prince—an heir to a throne—is worth thousands of Plataean lives."

"This isn't a game of pebbles," said Chusor, standing up and pointing at Nikias's finger. "They're going to cut apart your grandson. Torture him. Until there's nothing left but a sick and twisted mockery of a man."

"Leave me," said Menesarkus. "I must compose a letter to General Drako."

"No!" shouted Chusor.

"Get out!" bellowed Menesarkus.

Chusor could not control his anger. It surged inside his heart like a fire stoked by a bellows. He picked up his chair and smashed it against the wall, screaming, "I won't let you throw away Nikias's life!"

"He threw his life away the moment he defied me and went on his idiot's quest to Athens!" raged Menesarkus.

Chusor felt an overpowering urge to attack Menesarkus. He wanted to strike him down, put his head through a wall, anything to make him come to his senses. He could see the Bull was thinking the same thing, for his fists were clenched and he took a step toward Chusor, his mouth twisted in fury. "Take your best shot," he said.

Men pounded on the door. "Arkon! What's going on?" they shouted.

"Nothing!" spat Menesarkus. "Leave us!" He stared into Chusor's eyes with a truculent expression—the detached gaze of a pankrator sizing up an enemy before a match began.

"You think I'm afraid to fight you?" said Chusor, his voice soft yet dangerous. "I'm not. I could beat you to a bloody pulp. Even when you were in your prime. But what good would it do? There's no way to pound any sense into that thick skull of yours. Let your beloved grandson die. It's on your head."

Chusor went to the door and pulled back the bar lock, flinging open the portal so that it smashed against the wall, then pushed past the surprised clerks and guards and strode out of the building.

THIRTEEN

Menesarkus slammed shut the door to his office and slid the locking bolt. He was suddenly aware of his own heartbeat pounding in his ears. It was as though his heart had become a war drum inside his chest, vibrating through his body, pulsing in his head. And it beat twice as fast as normal.

All at once his heart stopped for two full seconds, and when it started again it seemed to roll in his chest like an animal squirming inside a box. He had never had this happen before and it terrified him. His heart beat rapidly again, but a few seconds later the squirming sensation repeated.

Then again. And again.

He felt a tightness in his chest and gasped for air. He stared at his hands. His own fingertips had gone white. As white as Nikias's severed finger. His heart fluttered and stopped again, then felt as though it were expanding, churning, roiling.

A seizure of the heart!

His heart beat faster still and his face broke out in a clammy sweat. He was dimly aware of the men outside the door who were hammering on the portal with their fists.

He staggered over to his armor on its stand and punched it. The helm and corselet flew across the room and clattered on the floor.

His heart had gone mad inside his breast. He fell to his knees, trying to breathe slowly, but he felt a palpitation so strong that it took his breath away and he was seized by a severe coughing fit.

"Arkon!" shouted his clerk from the other side of the door. "Are you unwell?"

Menesarkus swayed over to the desk and grabbed Nikias's finger, clutching it in his hand. He lunged to the door and unbolted it, avoiding the anxious eyes of his clerk and the guards.

"Your face is drained of blood!" said the clerk anxiously.

"Water," rasped Menesarkus.

The clerk ran to the other side of the room to fetch something to drink.

"Should we arrest the Egyptian?" asked one of the guards.

"For what?" snarled Menesarkus.

"We heard you shouting at each other," began one of the other guards hesitantly.

"Leave Chusor alone," said Menesarkus. "He is doing his duty." He took the proffered cup from his clerk. But his hand shook so hard he couldn't put the cup to his lips.

Ba-boom. Boom. Boom. Boom.

The sound of his own heartbeat in his ears was maddening. He flung the cup against the wall and bulled his way past the guards, stepping into the sunlit court-yard outside his offices. His clerk tried to follow him, but Menesarkus struck out at him.

"Leave me be!"

He made himself walk though his legs felt as though they'd been carved from marble. He was panicking. That was all. A fit of panic. He'd seen it happen to men in battle. They lost their wits. Said their hearts were going to leap out of their chests. Cowards.

"But I am no coward," he thought bitterly.

He headed into the agora . . . making his way blindly through the crowds of refugees. The woodsmoke from cooking fires choked him. Made him queasy. He saw women and children. Old men. The helpless citizens of Plataea whom it was his duty to protect. He stopped when he got to the statue of the hero Androkles and leaned against the plinth, looking up at the carven figure. The hero's sword was raised in triumph. He read the words etched onto the slab:

NO SHAMEFUL FLIGHT OR FEAR!
MAKE YOUR SPIRIT VALIANT!

They were the last words that the hero spoke before slaying the despotic madman—the Last Tyrant of Plataea. And then Androkles had been cut down by the Tyrant's guardsmen.

He thought of Nikias. His beautiful grandson. So fearless. So foolish. He imagined him tied up in the Spartan camp, bleeding from his hand, awaiting the next cut, and his heart churned so forcefully behind his ribs that the sensation took his breath away.

His heart pounded even faster. Faster than it had ever beaten in his life. He'd held a frightened rabbit once when he was a boy. His heart beat faster than that creature's organ. How much longer before his heart split itself open? Tore itself apart?

He felt many eyes upon him. He looked around. A crowd of people had gathered and were gawking at him with curiosity. The sun beat down on him. But he felt cold. He was shaking. A woman stepped forward and took him by the hand. She was in her forties. Black hair. Kind eyes.

"Arkon?" she said. "What is wrong?"

He tried to smile. But he could not make his mouth work. He shook his head. Unclasped her hand. He started walking again. Lumbering and limping away like a wounded man. The people parted for him. He saw the Temple of Zeus up ahead. Every step was an effort. He passed between the pillars and stepped inside the sanctuary. He flung himself on his knees at the altar. He placed Nikias's finger on the cold stone. He gasped for air.

I'm dying. This is the end. A pitiful way to die.

He thought back to the day, fifty years ago, when he'd fought against the Persian invaders in the Battle of Plataea. His heart had been steady throughout that entire frantic day. That glorious day that he had killed the Persian cavalry general Mardonius and turned the tide of the battle in favor of the Greek allies—

He beat his breast with his fist. Over and over again, as if to tame his heart. To pummel it into submission. But it would not obey. It continued to race as though he were running the hoplitodoros—the footrace run around the citadel in full armor. He gasped and put his hand to his mouth, biting it until his teeth drew blood.

Drako would carve up Nikias. Each finger. Then each toe. Then his ears and nose. His lips. His teeth. One by one. Until there was nothing left.

But he could not trade Arkilokus for Nikias. The Spartan prince was worth every woman and child in Plataea. It would be too great a sacrifice. The city was far more important than one man . . . than one mere lad—

His heart stopped for several seconds. Then it swelled in his breast and pounded furiously.

He reached for Nikias's finger and kissed the cold dead flesh. He stared at the statue of Zeus looking down at him with its merciless eyes.

He thought of Nikias's horse, Photine, returning riderless that day, covered with blood and marked with a mountain lion's claw. It would have been better if Nikias had died in the forest—killed by a beast—than be in the clutches of the Spartan monsters.

"Forgive me," he said to the idol. "Forgive me," he whispered. "Forgive me," he said over and over again. He had made a decision that he knew would haunt him even into the afterlife. But the decision had been made.

And yet the pounding did not cease.

FOURTEEN

———— ◆ ————

"It's a death mask," said Chusor miserably as he stared at the object Diokles had brought back from the tunnel. He sat at one end of the long table in his work-shop with Ji standing behind him, peering over his shoulder. The discovery of the treasure that he had so long searched for had done nothing to diminish his dejected state of mind. He could not stop thinking about Nikias and the sight of that bloody finger. . . .

"Perhaps this tomb is cursed," said Ji. "We should put this mask back on the body."

"Don't be a fool," replied Zana from where she sat sprawled in a chair on the other side of the chamber, sipping wine from a golden cup, her face shining with exultation. "We've robbed graves before and nothing happened to us." At her feet sat a wooden chest. The lid lay open to reveal all of the treasures from the tomb: vessels bearing the likenesses of bulls and horsemen that had been made by hammering the images from the insides of the cups; intricately crafted neck-laces and bracelets and rings; the head of an ox the size of a man's fist . . . all made from solid gold. Her eyes blazed with delight. "Oh, Chusor. You have outdone yourself this time. You have made up for all of your treachery. There is enough wealth here to buy the finest ship in the port of Piraeus and outfit it for a year!"

Chusor held the mask out in front of him. It had been hammered as thin as papyrus and resembled the face of a bearded man in the prime of life. The face appeared to shift from a maniacal grin to a sinister frown as he tilted it this way and that. He felt as though the death mask were mocking him—as if it knew the turmoil in his heart, his abject despair concerning the fate of Nikias.

"Such treasures," breathed Zana in a tone of awe mingled with lust.

Chusor turned the mask around and held it to his own face, peering through the eyeholes to the other end of the table where Diokles sat eating voraciously after his day of backbreaking labor. The Helot was covered in soot and streaked with sweat, so that he resembled a mound of living rock splotched with rain. On the table in front of him sat the strange helm fashioned from the tusks of boars.

"Don't forget the sword too!" said Ajax. "I found it!"

"See!" put in Teleos, holding up the ancient blade that he had been stabbing into a wooden beam.

"Give me that!" barked Chusor. "That sword is a relic!" Teleos brought him the sword blade and Chusor set it on the table next to the golden mask. "Now go into the street and play," he ordered. "And don't tell anyone about what we have found or I'll flay your arses." The boys slunk to the door like scolded puppies. As they got to the portal it opened and Barka entered.

"Look what we found, Barka," declared Ajax, pointing to the box at Zana's feet.

"Treasure!" said Teleos, jumping up and down.

Barka did not seem to hear their words but stared at the floor, chewing on a fingernail.

"Out," Chusor said, striding to the door, for Teleos and Ajax were lingering on the threshold, staring with curiosity at the eunuch. When they saw Chusor coming at them the boys scurried into the street and the smith shut the door behind them, sliding the bolt to lock it.

"My little Lylit," asked Diokles. "Where have you been? See what I found." He placed the boar tusk helm on his head and smiled foolishly.

Barka glanced at him with a haunted look.

"Where have you been?" asked Chusor, staring hard at the eunuch. Barka's hair was lank and wet and his clothes were soaked, dripping onto the floor. "The sun shone all day and yet you are drenched."

Barka stared at everyone in turn with a wretched expression. His face was pale, and his lower jaw trembled. No one spoke. They had seen Barka this way before—one of his dark moods that always came after experiencing a mystical vision.

Chusor noticed that Barka nervously turned a ring over and over again on his finger.

"We must leave this cursed place," said Barka. "Immediately. We must go back to Syrakuse."

Shouts erupted in the street and everyone in the room looked toward the shuttered window.

"What's that?" asked Ji. "What is going on?"

"Is something wrong?" asked Zana, springing to her feet. "What have you seen?" she asked Barka with a mounting tone of hysteria in her voice. "The Spartans? Attacking?"

"*That* is inevitable," replied Barka without emotion. His eyes alighted on the box of treasure with a disinterested look. "I must go back to Syrakuse," he said in a whisper.

"But have we found all the gold?" Zana asked Chusor, shutting the lid on the box and standing over it like a dog guarding a haunch of meat.

"Damn your insatiable greed, Zana!" said Chusor. "We have enough. Staying alive is all that matters now."

He went to the window and opened one of the shutters, staring into the street. He saw people running in the direction of the agora, but they were smiling and laughing.

"Nothing dire," said Chusor. "But something *is* indeed happening."

"We must leave this place," said Barka. "This city will be our tomb."

Zana's eyes grew big and she brought a hand to her mouth.

"The poppy," said Barka, squinting at Chusor and holding out one hand like a petulant child demanding a toy. "I need poppy."

Chusor knew better than to argue with Barka when he was in this mood. He went to a cupboard and took out a small bowl filled with resin and gave it to the eunuch, who clutched it to his chest. Ji reached into the folds of his robe and brought out a long pipe, which he handed to Barka.

"Do not interrupt me during my meditation," said Barka. "*Any* of you. And I suggest we depart before dawn. Death hangs over this city like a funeral cloth. The guard Damon—the one I've been lying with. He will let us through the gates without searching us." He headed up the stairs and disappeared from view without uttering another word.

The room was silent. Chusor stood chewing on his cheek with his arms crossed, wondering what had brought about such a sudden transformation in Barka's mood. Where had the eunuch been all night? Why was he wet? It was odd. But then, Barka had always been a mystery.

He glanced at the others. Ji had sat at the table and was looking at the mask with an inquisitive expression. Diokles chomped on his food with a frown on his face, the strange tusked helm still perched on his head. Zana bored her eyes into the ceiling with a worried look, as if she were trying see through it into Barka's chamber.

Chusor's gaze turned to the floor where Barka had tracked mud across the stones. He bent down and touched the mud, smelling it. It gave off the distinctive odor of musty earth and slime.

"We must go," said Zana. "Barka has never been wrong."

"Remember Tyre?" asked Ji.

"And Karthago," said Zana.

"And many more," said Ji. "We can leave the city tonight and sleep in the cave on the mountain. But then which way do we go?"

Zana, Ji, and Diokles all looked at Chusor. He avoided their probing eyes, pulling on his goatee and staring into space. There was no way that Menesarkus would give up the prisoner Arkilokus for Nikias, he thought bitterly. His friend was as good as dead. But he would be damned if he would linger in Plataea to see Nikias returned home piece by piece.

He thought of the strange sign that he had seen on the path in the mountains the day he had gone to the Cave of Nymphs to meet Zana: the tortoise entangled in a dead goat's fleece. After he had set the animal free, it had headed west. . . .

"I will not become entrapped like that creature," he thought.

"Chusor?" asked Zana. "What are you thinking?"

He picked up a sharp knife, held it to his own chin, and quickly sliced off his long goatee, tossing it on the floor.

"We follow the mountain toward the setting sun," he said. "It's only an eight-mile walk to the port of Kreusis. We'll find a boat there to take us south across the Gulf of Korinth to the Diolkos." The Diolkos was the stone-laid trackway that the Korinthians had built to transport goods and ships from the Ionian Sea to the Aegean across the narrow Isthmus of Korinth. It was a marvel of machinery. There were many skilled shipwrights in that area separating Attika from the Peloponnese. "From there we can walk overland to the town of Isthmia and purchase a suitable galley. The sea will be our road thereafter."

"To the sea," exhaled Zana. "Gods, how I long to be on the sea again!"

"I will start packing," said Ji and went to work gathering up their belongings.

Chusor looked keenly at Diokles, who smiled back and cocked his head. "If Lylit says I must go from Plataea, then I must go." He picked up Chusor's goatee and stared at it with a quizzical expression.

Chusor nodded and gave a heavy sigh. "So be it." He had a mind to go to Kallisto—to ask her to come with them. But he knew that she would refuse. He dreaded the thought of what Nikias's slow death at the hands of the Spartans would do to the girl. It would kill her soul.

Someone banged on the portal. Chusor went to it and peered through the peephole, then he slid back the bolt and opened the door. Leo stood there wearing the uniform of a city guardsman.

"Come look!" he said breathlessly. "A sight to behold!"

Chusor, Diokles, Ji, and the brothers followed him into the street. Leo started running through the marketplace in the direction of the gates and they fell in behind him. When they got to the agora they saw a huge crowd had gathered there. The two gates had been opened wide and riders were coming through, holding the reins of many riderless mounts. The agora was already filled with hundreds of horses and more were coming in.

"Zoticus has returned," said Chusor, spotting the Plataean cavalry general astride his charger. Zoticus, one of the heroes of the Battle of Plataea, had gone on an expedition north to Thessalia in search of horses to supplement the Plataean cavalry. He had made fast work of his task.

Chusor spotted Menesarkus on the other side of the agora, leaning on his staff, nodding appreciatively at the sight. There was a festive atmosphere amongst the city's inhabitants—people were laughing and stroking the horses. Parents held their small children up to stroke the noses and necks of the beasts.

"Where are we going to keep them all?" asked Leo, a grin on his face.

"They can't stay outside of the citadel," said Chusor. "The Spartans will kill or capture them for food."

"Horses good to have," said Diokles. "The masters did not bring any horses with them. We saw Nikias and the others charge the Theban army. Smash into their shield wall. Bam! I like to see them do that to the Masters."

"You mean the mounts will all stay in here?" Ji asked Chusor. "Inside the citadel?" A horse nearby lifted its tail and dumped a huge load of manure onto the stones and another followed suit.

"Indeed," said Chusor. "We might end up eating them all before the siege is done. Whatever the case, Plataea will soon become like the Augean Stables."

"Augean Stables?" asked Ji. "What's that?"

"A very messy place," said Chusor.

FIFTEEN

A glimmering fleece hung from the limb of an ancient oak. The sun shone on the metallic curls of the sheep's wool, coruscating in the sun, and Nikias realized that the fleece was made of gold. He was filled with wonder at the sight of the magical object—for he knew it was the thing that the hero Jason had journeyed to fabled Kolkis to find.

"It has the power to heal," said a familiar voice. "The power to bring health and prosperity to the city that possesses this treasure."

Nikias turned and saw Demetrios standing by his side. A rush of happiness flooded through him. It had been so many years since they had been together. How Nikias had missed him! He tried to speak but no words came out of his mouth. Demetrios slapped him on the cheek and grinned, showing his straight teeth.

"Just reach up and take the fleece," said Demetrios. "Take it home to Plataea."

Nikias tried to do as he was told, but he looked down and saw that he no longer had any arms.

"Let me help you," said Demetrios. He grasped Nikias with his muscular arms and lifted him toward the fleece—lifted him with a godlike strength as if Nikias weighed no more than a feather. He was eye level with the fleece now, and he was overcome by desire to possess this thing. But the tree suddenly came to life, its limbs lashing out at him as if to protect the fleece. One of them brushed him across the face—

Nikias woke up with a start and squinted through the slits of his swollen eyes. The dream faded instantly from his mind, to be replaced by the reality of his situation: he was in the Spartan camp, bound and gagged, and Drako stood in front of him, slapping him to wake him up. Nikias felt as if his head were on fire, but his torso was shaking from cold.

Drako pulled the gag from Nikias's mouth and stared at him with his stony eyes. Nikias tried to speak, but his tongue felt as though it were glued to the roof of his mouth. Drako held a skin full of water to his lips and squirted some in. Nikias couldn't swallow at first and gagged. But soon he was gulping greedily, trying to slake an unbearable thirst.

"Bring him," said Drako, and started walking. Nikias saw that the Spartan general held a shining axe.

One of the guards cut the ropes binding Nikias's feet and looped a noose around his neck, leading him through camp in the direction Drako had gone. Nikias stumbled along and fell several times but was quickly lifted to his feet by the Spartans who followed close behind. They passed through the southern entrance of the Persian Fort. A hundred paces away, near a stand of trees, Nikias could see a group of Helots digging a pit. They were guarded by a handful of Spartan warriors. Drako was already there, staring down into the pit with a contemplative look.

The warrior holding Nikias's rope led him to the edge of the pit and pushed him to his knees. Nikias stared at the ten Helots as they worked methodically with their picks and wooden shovels in the red and rocky soil. They must have been at it for hours because they had dug the pit up to their shoulders.

Nikias could not stop himself from shuddering.

"They're digging the pit for me," he thought with horror. "They are going to cut off my head and throw me in this pit." He glanced at Drako, who stood still, holding the axe. He heard an eerie sound from the sky above and craned his neck. A flock of red-winged geese flew overhead, honking their sad cries. . . .

"Nikias of Plataea," said Drako without deigning to look at him. "We Spartans will not stand for noncompliance. Bravery is one thing, but stubbornness is unacceptable. Your grandfather has put your city on the brink of ruin. One word from him and we would be your loyal friends. But Menesarkus is like a mule that balks at a fork in the road. Or one of these wretches here." He gestured at the Helots in the pit.

Nikias started weeping and the shame of crying in front of Drako and the other Spartans was unbearable. He retched, but all that came up was the water he had drunk a few minutes before.

"I won't beg for my life," he said defiantly, but his voice cracked when he spoke. His body hurt everywhere. The stump of his missing finger throbbed. With every breath he took he felt stabbing pains where Axe had cracked his ribs. His nose was broken—he could barely breathe through one nostril. Half the teeth on the left side of his jaw ached. It felt like a knife was digging into his brain. "Death would be a relief," he mused. But he knew he was lying to himself. He wanted to live more than anything. He didn't want to die in this pit. But he wasn't going to beg to stay alive. He glanced up at the sky and saw white clouds. "A pillow fit for Zeus," as his father used to say when Nikias was a little boy. The geese were already far in the distance, their honking now barely audible . . .

"Deep enough," said Drako. He gestured for the Helots to come out of the pit. They lined up in a row and the Spartan warriors dragged Nikias over so that he was on his knees in front of them. Drako handed the axe to the Helot at the head of the line. The slave took the axe and turned to face Nikias.

"Prepare yourself," said Drako.

Nikias's teeth chattered.

Fevered images flashed across his mind's eye. He saw his dead mother as she'd looked when he was a child, standing in front of her tall loom, brushing aside her beautiful hair, glancing down at him where he lay curled at her feet. Then he saw Kallisto's face grinning at him as she rode her horse at breakneck speed toward the Cave of Nymphs, her eyes flashing. Then Helena, in the Temple of Aphrodite in Athens, her beguiling face lit by the lamplight as she leaned over him.

"Begin," said Drako.

The Helot with the axe moved aside and the second slave in line stepped forward and squatted in front of Nikias with his head bowed. The Helot with the axe did not hesitate. He raised the axe high, then brought it down on the neck of the kneeling Helot. The slave's head flew off and Nikias was splattered with the blood that sprayed from the stump of the dead man's neck. Nikias gasped in surprise, then watched in shock as the Spartan warriors dragged the corpse into the pit and tossed the head in after.

The Helot who had just performed the beheading handed the bloody weapon to the next slave in line, and then he got on his knees in front of Nikias, bowing his head just as the last victim had done. The new Helot executioner dealt the slave a swift blow. The body and severed head were thrown into the pit with the other. And then this grim act was performed again and again: the next Helot in line taking the axe and beheading his fellow slave until, finally, there was only one Helot left and nine headless corpses in the pit.

The evil noise of buzzing flies filled the air. Many of them landed on Nikias, sipping the Helot blood that covered his face and neck. Fury boiled inside him. He licked his cracked lips. He could taste Helot blood.

The last Helot left standing stared down at Nikias with a wild terror in his dark eyes.

Nikias glanced at Drako, who stood close enough for the Helot to kill him with the axe. The noseless Spartan just stood there with his arms crossed on his chest, head cocked to one side, staring back at Nikias with his dead eyes.

The imperious piece of shit!

"K-kill Drako," Nikias stuttered, his body shaking uncontrollably. "Kill him!"

The Helot stared back at him, tears welling up in his eyes. The Spartan slave clutched the axe and bowed his head. Then the man dug the edge of the axe blade across his own stomach. His innards spilled onto the bloody grass, steaming in the cool morning air.

"No!" screamed Nikias.

The Helot staggered to the edge of the pit and, with his final act, threw himself on top of the others.

"They tried to escape last night," explained Drako. "They were caught."

"Why—why did they d-do that to each o-other," Nikias faltered, his jaw twitching violently.

"Because they know that if they disobeyed the death sentence their entire families would be skinned alive back home in Sparta."

"If you g-gave m-me that axe," said Nikias with an effort to stop the spasms in his jaw, "I—I—I would k-kill you."

"That is because you are a human," said Drako. "Helots are merely automatons."

"Y-you have made them w-what they are," replied Nikias, seething.

"Now it's your turn," said Drako. He kicked out with his foot, striking Nikias in the stomach. Nikias fell forward with his face in the blood-soaked dirt.

"Go to Hades," spat Nikias.

Drako raised the axe.

Nikias closed his eyes.

Thump!

The axe drove into the ground in front of Nikias's head. Nikias remained silent for a few seconds. And then rage surged through his veins. Drako was toying with him, like a cat that had caught a bird and broken its wings.

He clenched his jaw.

Then without warning he rolled over, locking his legs around Drako's ankles, twisted over again, and pulled the surprised Spartan into the pit. They landed in a tangled heap on the headless corpses. Drako sprang up like a cat, spitting curses, and clambered out of the hole. But Nikias lay helplessly on his stomach, struggling to free his hands from his bindings, writhing on the Helot corpses. After several minutes he had exhausted himself and lay still, gasping for breath.

"Get him out of there," said Drako. "It's time to move."

SIXTEEN

———— ◆ ————

Spartans jumped into the pit and dragged Nikias out. Then two warriors, one on either side, half carried, half dragged him through the woods away from the Persian Fort. Ahead Nikias saw a company of Spartans waiting in a clearing—perhaps twenty armored men with spears and shields.

Drako gestured with his hand—a battle sign—and his men started quick marching.

Nikias stared at the ground, moving his legs feebly, wondering where they were taking him now. Were they going to attack Plataea with this small band of warriors? It seemed preposterous. Maybe they were taking him to Thebes. Nikias tried to dig in his heels but Drako was on him in an instant, smashing him in the stomach. Nikias sucked in his breath as a dark mist appeared at the corner of his vision, and he knew that he was blacking out. When he opened his eyes again he was facedown on a hard surface. He had no idea how much time had passed. When he lifted his head he saw a road lined with plane trees stretching out ahead.

"Keep your eyes open," Drako said to his men.

"What's going on?" asked Nikias in a daze.

"Shut up," said Drako and lifted Nikias off the ground, putting him in a kneeling position.

Nikias looked around and realized, with surprise, that they were on the Kadmean Way—the road that led from Thebes to Plataea. He squinted into the distance in the direction of his citadel. He saw a cloud of dust on the road. Men were coming toward them. He could see a phalanx of armed warriors bearing Plataean shields a quarter of a mile away. He watched with anticipation as they approached. They stopped just outside of arrow range of the Spartans and stood silently with their shields raised.

"I don't see the prince," said Drako under his breath, and drawing his sword he held the flat of the blade against Nikias's neck.

"Where is Prince Arkilokus?" shouted Drako.

The Plataean warriors in the front of the phalanx parted and a big man in gleaming armor stepped forward, his face hidden behind a helm with a horsetail crest. He took a few paces forward, walking with a pronounced limp.

"Where is Arkilokus?" shouted Drako again.

The Plataean ignored Drako and stared at Nikias through the slits of his helm. "Nikias?" he asked with undisguised shock in his voice. "What have they done to you?"

Nikias nodded and squeezed his eyes shut, dropping his head with shame, hot tears leaking from the corners of his eyes. He had recognized his grandfather's armor the instant he had stepped from the phalanx.

"Grandfather," said Nikias through his sobs. "I'm sorry for what I did. Don't trade me for Arkilokus. Kill him now!"

He felt Drako's blade tense against his throat, the edge cutting through the skin.

"Shut your mouth," hissed the Spartan.

Menesarkus held up a hand, then took off his helm and put it under one arm, revealing his leonine head of black hair streaked with gray. Even from this distance Nikias could see the stricken look on his face.

"What have you done to Nikias?" Menesarkus asked, his face twisted in wrath.

"I didn't do this to him," said Drako. "It was Eurymakus the Theban."

Menesarkus tore his gaze away from Nikias's swollen and blood-spattered face and glared at Drako. "But it was you who mutilated his sword hand," he said.

"You're lucky I didn't send you the whole hand," Drako replied in a bored voice.

Menesarkus smiled without mirth, then turned and gestured with one arm at the Plataean phalanx. Nikias watched as a tall, blond, naked man with his arms tied behind his back stepped forth from the mass of warriors. Arkilokus started walking toward Menesarkus with a strange halting gait, as though he had just learned to walk. When he got near to Menesarkus, the Bull grabbed him by the biceps, pulled a dagger from a scabbard at his belt, and held the point to the Spartan prince's abdomen.

"So what do we do now?" asked Menesarkus. "Do we slaughter them in front of each other out of spite?"

"Send Prince Arkilokus over to us," demanded Drako.

"Let him kill me!" shouted Nikias.

"Silence, Nikias!" commanded Menesarkus. "Do not speak again!"

Nikias clamped his teeth together and sat trembling.

"Come, Menesarkus," said Drako in a cajoling tone. "This is a foolish game. Send over Prince Arkilokus and then I will set Nikias free."

Menesarkus threw back his head and burst out with a belly laugh. "Drako, I'm not one of your idiot Helots to kick about. I agreed to your terms. I have met you on the road with my twenty hoplites. I have brought your precious prince. Now let my grandson go and I will release Arkilokus."

"I cannot trust you, Menesarkus," said Drako. "You have already proved yourself to be a liar. You told me that Arkilokus was never your prisoner, and yet I see him standing next to you now."

"He was never my *prisoner*," said Menesarkus. "He was my *guest*. He'd been injured—a fall from his horse. And he is my own flesh and blood, after all. My own grandson."

Nikias squinted in confusion at his grandfather. What had he just said? *Flesh and blood? Grandson?* Had the Bull gone mad? He stared at Arkilokus, who gazed back at him with an enigmatic expression.

"And I will take no lessons in trustworthiness," continued Menesarkus, pointing at Drako, "from a man who allied himself with that Theban goat-raper Eurymakus and plotted to bring down Plataea by means of treachery!" His voice had risen at the end of this speech to a thunderous climax on the word "treachery"—a hateful word that seemed to linger in the air like the stink of death. After a prolonged silence he said, "We helped you defeat the Persians at the Battle of Plataea. We renamed the very gates of our citadel after your General Pausanius—the Spartan who led us to that glorious allied victory. And you and your kindred swore in front of those gates never to invade the Oxlands. You are oath breakers!"

Nikias took a deep and painful breath and shouted, "Grandfather! Krates and Agape are dead! Attacked by Korinthians on the sea—" He stopped as he felt the flat of Drako's sword press against his neck.

Drako said, "Say another word and I'll slit your throat!"

"Take Arkilokus back to Plataea!" continued Nikias, heedless of Drako's warning. "When the time comes, trade him for safe passage for our women and children! Perikles told me they are welcome in Athens! That was the message he ordered me to bring back to Plataea—"

Drako brought the pommel of his sword down on the top of Nikias's head and he pitched forward onto the road, his ears ringing.

"You've just sealed your own fate," muttered Drako, raising his sword for the kill. But before he could bring it down a man screamed in agony, and a commanding voice in the Spartan tongue cried out:

"Stop!"

Drako hesitated.

"Stop!" repeated Menesarkus in Dorik.

Nikias lifted his head from the dirt and stared down the road. Menesarkus held something in his hand and he threw it in the direction of the Spartans—a bloody finger bearing a signet ring.

Arkilokus's face was constricted in pain, his jaw jutting forward. "My finger!" he howled. Menesarkus held a bloody dagger to the Spartan prince's throat.

Drako stood with his sword still raised, staring back and forth from Arkilokus to Menesarkus with a feral look in his beady eyes.

"Piece by piece!" Menesarkus called out to Drako. "A finger for a finger! And if you kill Nikias now I will slit Arkilokus's throat before my grandson breathes his life into the dust, whether he's my kin or not."

"You're bluffing," said Drako.

"Drako, you fool!" Arkilokus shouted with wrath. "He's going to kill me! My father will have your family skinned alive like Helots if you let me die on this road!"

There was a long and tense silence, broken only by the sound of crows crying harshly in the treetops. And above this rose the sound of a voice—a clear voice, singing from somewhere behind the Spartan phalanx, along with the plodding clop of a donkey.

"What is that?" Drako asked with surprise.

Nikias started laughing softly, for he knew the sound of that distinct voice. He was transported back to the Three Thieves in Tanagra . . . listening to the bard Linos. The singing got louder and soon the old bard came into sight, his face hidden by a hood, leading his ancient donkey by a frayed rope. Nikias was glad to see that Linos had survived the terrible fire at the inn.

Linos, for his part, seemed oblivious to the two groups of armed warriors facing each other across that stretch of empty road. As Linos passed by the Spartans he stopped singing and glanced at Nikias seemingly without recognition, but raised his eyebrows—an expression of baffled curiosity.

"Peace," he said to Drako by way of greeting.

Drako grunted.

Linos continued on his way in the direction of Plataea. As he went by Menesarkus he waved at him cheerfully as well. "Peace," he said again.

"Peace," replied Menesarkus gruffly.

Linos disappeared from Nikias's view behind the Plataean warriors and started up his song again.

After a long silence Drako said, "We send our prisoners at the same time."

"So be it," said Menesarkus.

Drako yanked Nikias to his feet. Nikias swayed, hunched with pain. Menesarkus cut Arkilokus's bindings, then he gave the prince a little shove in the back. A moment later Drako sliced through Nikias's ropes.

"Go," said Drako.

Nikias shuffled down the road. Every step was agony, every breath caused him pain. He saw Arkilokus stop by his severed finger and stoop with difficulty, picking up his digit with his unmutilated hand. Then he straightened and started walking again.

The two men locked eyes as they approached each other at the midpoint in the road between the two packs of warriors. When they were a few feet away they came to a stop, looking each other up and down.

Nikias gaped at the Spartan's face—a face that was so strangely familiar. He could see his grandfather's eyes staring back at him from the same wide brow. He looked so much like a Plataean with his sandy-colored hair, broad shoulders, and high cheekbones. But there was a hardness in the Spartan's eyes that was different from his grandfather's wise gaze. Arkilokus's countenance displayed the haughty and merciless spirit of a Spartan royal.

Nikias drew himself up painfully to his full height.

"Now we both have nine fingers," he said.

"You don't look good, *cousin*," said Arkilokus in a taunting voice. "I don't know if the lovely Kallisto will recognize you."

"What did you say?" asked Nikias, amazed to hear Kallisto's name pass his enemy's lips.

"Once your city is defeated," said Arkilokus, smiling contemptuously, "I'll take Kallisto back with me to Sparta."

Nikias reacted without thinking. He threw himself on the Spartan, grappling him with his one good arm, kicking the bigger man's feeble legs out from under him. Arkilokus fought back, and they rolled on the road together, biting and thrashing.

"Enough!" bellowed Menesarkus, grabbing Nikias by the arms and dragging him away. At the same time Drako seized hold of Arkilokus and pulled his writhing body toward the Spartan warriors.

"You have one more day," Drako shouted at Menesarkus. "And then we attack."

"We'll kill you all!" screamed Nikias in an insane voice. Then he went limp in his grandfather's arms. The world swam before his eyes.

"I'm sorry, Grandfather," he mumbled. "I'm . . . so sorry."

"Do not speak, my son," said Menesarkus in a voice choked with emotion.

Nikias couldn't focus on his grandfather's face. He felt as if he were floating. As if he were rising up toward the tops of the trees. A brilliant light engulfed his vision, and then he became still with his eyes wide open.

"Nikias?" asked Menesarkus. "Can you hear me?"

Suddenly Nikias started twitching and Menesarkus quickly set him down on the road. Nikias's body was wracked by spasms—the muscles of his arms and legs became rigid. Plataean warriors rushed forward and surrounded him. One of them pulled off his helm to reveal a pug nose set in an anxious face.

"Is he dying?" Leo asked frantically.

"He's having a seizure," said Menesarkus. He whipped off his leather belt and jammed it in Nikias's mouth to prevent him from biting off his tongue.

"What did they do to his face?" asked one of the younger warriors with horror.

"You were brave, Nikias," said another, touching him on the head. "You were brave."

"Nikias?" asked Menesarkus. "Can you hear me?"

But he made no reply.

Four strong Plataeans lifted Nikias's limp body onto their shoulders and bore him back toward the city in the manner of a corpse carried in honor from the battlefield.

SEVENTEEN

———— ◆ ————

Menesarkus followed his men in utter despair down the long road to Plataea. His thoughts were only for his grandson. They had been walking for two miles and still Nikias had not stirred. The lad's arms hung limply at his sides. His chest barely rose as he breathed.

When he had first laid eyes on Nikias today he had not recognized him, so altered was his grandson's face. Menesarkus had seen many pankrators beaten to a pulp. But Nikias had always come through his bouts relatively unscathed, such was his prowess in the arena. He had never seen him look this bad.

But Eurymakus had tortured him. Broken his body. There were black bruises all over Nikias's torso. He had livid bruises on his forehead. Menesarkus knew that serious head wounds could cause seizures. Had his brain been affected?

What would Eudoxia say when she saw her poor grandson?

When he was in the Temple of Zeus yesterday he had begged the Storm-bringer to forgive him for making the decision to save Nikias, for he had realized what his wildly palpitating heart had been trying to tell him. He wondered if Zeus would take away his protection from the citadel and its people because Menesarkus had made such a selfish act.

They passed the old man leading the donkey: he walked with fast strides that were at odds with his withered legs. He had thrown back his hood to reveal his features and he was still singing softly to himself, a smile fixed on his weather-beaten face. All of a sudden Menesarkus recognized him: the old man was Linos, a famous bard with whom his son Aristo had studied in his youth. Linos was a Plataean who had departed the citadel soon after the Persian Wars had ended, and had returned every now and then over the last fifty years. Menesarkus had not seen him in the Oxlands since Nikias was a little boy.

Linos glanced at Menesarkus and smiled genially without recognition. "Peace," he said again. Menesarkus nodded back. He suspected Linos had become senile.

They were a quarter mile from the closed gates of the citadel of Plataea when Menesarkus heard the sudden thunder of horses in the distance, followed by warning cries from the lookouts on the tops of the walls.

"Dog Raiders!"

Menesarkus ordered his men to stop and peered south. He could clearly see the horsemen—a troop of over twenty raiders in black cloaks—charging down the foothills of the Kithaeron Mountains, heading straight toward the citadel. The enemy would cut off Menesarkus's armored men before they could run to the gates. And they were out of range of the protection of archers from the walls.

Better to stand and fight than be ridden down by riders, he mused.

"Make a wheel," Menesarkus said in a loud but calm voice. "Lay my grandson by my side," he said to the men bearing Nikias. He glanced over at Linos, who was a hundred paces behind them. The old man looked about him with a bewildered expression. "Leave your donkey, Linos!" Menesarkus ordered. "Come here now!"

Linos seemed torn. His head moved back and forth from the approaching Dog Raiders to his animal. Finally, and very reluctantly, he dropped the animal's lead and dashed over to the warriors, who had formed an orderly circle of shields around Menesarkus and Nikias. He squeezed through the ranks and gave Menesarkus a mystified look.

"I don't have a spear," said Linos with a sheepish smile.

"Here." Menesarkus drew his sword and handed it to Linos.

Linos took the leaf-bladed sword and gripped it in his gnarled hand, screwing up his lined face.

The Plataean warriors raised their left arms bearing their shields and planted the butt spikes of their long spears in the ground.

Menesarkus clenched his teeth. The military part of his mind raced. Dog Raiders had never been so bold as to come this close to the citadel in daylight, preferring to lurk in the mountains or attack farms at night. Perhaps these horsemen were a decoy—an advance force of a much larger army attacking the other side of the citadel. Had Drako used the prisoner exchange as a way of distracting Menesarkus from his duty? An army of Spartan warriors might already be sneaking around to the western walls with scaling ladders.

He cupped his hand to his mouth and shouted up to the walls, "Keep the gates shut! Do you hear me? This might be a trick! Do not open the gates, even if we are overwhelmed!"

"Yes!" the guards on the wall shouted back. "We understand, Arkon!"

Menesarkus realized that his heart beat regularly now. It had been churning inside his breast during the confrontation with Drako, but now it felt surprisingly normal and this filled him with a sense of calm. He was actually looking forward to this fight. He stared down at Nikias, who lay dead to the world with half-closed lids and mouth slightly agape, but his mutilated hand twitched slightly. Was he dreaming now?

A fearsome battle cry from the horsemen shook Menesarkus from his thoughts. The Dog Raiders turned away from the city walls and charged straight at them—a mass of riders that split apart and rode in a circle around the Plataeans. Menesarkus perceived that each carried some sort of strange weapon in his hand—a black rope attached to a roundish shape.

Menesarkus gripped his shield and raised his spear, his body tensed for battle.

Suddenly the lead horseman threw one of the objects at his shield. It hit with a dull thud and fell at his feet. He glanced down and saw a black-bearded decapitated head with its tongue sticking out. A barrage of heads hit the shields, one after the other, until each of the riders was empty-handed.

"What are they doing?" called out Leo. "Are they trying to kill us with severed heads?"

The Dog Raiders stopped all at once and tore off their helms to reveal red hair tied in topknots. They cast off their black cloaks and threw them on the ground, baring their muscular arms painted with tattoos.

"They're Skythians," said Linos with a dumbfounded laugh.

Menesarkus glanced at the old bard who grinned back.

"Greetings!" said Linos in the Skythian tongue, smiling and handing Menesarkus's sword back to him. "May your ewes never come out arse first."

The lead rider bowed to Linos and addressed him, speaking in halting Greek, "Elder one, I am Osyrus of the Bindi. I have come to offer my services to the city of Plataea."

Menesarkus and the Plataeans stared back at the Skythians in astonishment. Osyrus and the other Bindis exchanged tense glances.

"We bring these Dog Raider heads as a sign of our skills," said Osyrus. "We—"

"We've come to kill the Red Cloaks!" interrupted a croaking voice. Menesarkus recognized the boy Kolax as he drove a white horse forward past the other riders until he was next to the leader. Osyrus tried to clap a hand over Kolax's mouth, but the young barbarian ducked and looked directly at Menesarkus, "Peace, Arkon! Forgive me. But I lost Nikias in Athens. I found his mare, though."

"Photine!" exclaimed Leo with sudden recognition.

Menesarkus gazed at the tempestuous animal. He hadn't seen her since the day she had appeared outside the citadel, streaked with blood. "Where did you find her?" he asked, bewildered by the arrival of Kolax and his kin.

"I found her wandering in the olive groves above your farm," Kolax said. "I reckoned Nikias had come back to Plataea and had fallen off her again! Where is he? He'll be happy to see I caught her."

Menesarkus dropped his chin to his chest.

Leo took off his helm and held it under one arm. He caught Kolax's eye and gestured toward the center of the ring of men. "He is there," said Leo in a funereal tone.

Kolax frowned and slid off Photine, elbowing his way through the armored Plataean warriors, leading Photine to the center of the wheel formation. When he saw Nikias he let forth a cry and knelt by his body.

"Ah, Sky-Father Papaeus! What happened to him?" he said in Skythian, tears pouring from his eyes. "Who did this to him?"

Menesarkus put a hand on Kolax's shoulder and turned to Osyrus.

"I am Menesarkus, Arkon of Plataea. You are welcome here," he said. "The boy Kolax is known to us. He is accounted a hero in my city."

Osyrus nodded and translated Menesarkus's words for those of his men who did not speak Greek. The Skythians who had doubted Kolax before now stared at him in wonder.

Menesarkus heard the sound of a dagger being unsheathed and turned. He saw Kolax slicing a deep cut across his own palm, then the boy held the wound to Nikias's lips.

"My blood is a healing potion," Kolax intoned. "I bear the blood of the gryphon of Skythia in my veins. I will save him from death."

Photine dropped her head and sniffed Nikias's head, then ever so gently she nudged him with her nose. But he did not move. The horse pawed the ground as if in anger, then threw back her head and let forth a bloodcurdling neigh.

"She's calling the Horse God for help," said Kolax with a sigh. "All will be well."

EIGHTEEN

Menesarkus stood in the doorway to a bedchamber at his house in Plataea watching his wife, granddaughter, and Kallisto caring for Nikias. They had cocooned him in blankets and were chanting a hymn to Demeter as they rocked him back and forth—an old method for curing a fever.

The room smelled of dried rosemary and mint mingled with the musky scent of poppy resin. They had clipped all of Nikias's long golden hair to tend to his several head wounds.

Kallisto knelt by Nikias's side holding a bowl of water and a sponge. Every now and then she put the sponge to Nikias's lips and squeezed in a little bit of water. She gazed at him with eyes full of concern, but she did not look faint of heart. None of the women had reacted in the way that Menesarkus had thought they would when he brought the unconscious Nikias back to the house. They had been grief-stricken, of course, but they had conducted themselves swiftly and efficiently, setting up the room for the wounded lad—covering the window to block out the light and administering opium and other medicines while cleaning his wounds and applying poultices.

Kallisto glanced over at him and smiled. "He is in our care now," she said.

Menesarkus chided himself for being so hard on her—for telling Nikias he would never let him marry this brave and strong girl.

Eudoxia whispered something to Phile, then got up from the bedside and walked over to the doorway.

"You should go eat something, husband," said Eudoxia. "There's no use for you to stand there for hours on end. This is going to take time."

"Will he live?" whispered Menesarkus.

Eudoxia put a hand on Menesarkus's chest. "He clings to life. Have you sent for Chusor? He saved Kallisto—"

"Nobody can find him or his companion, Diokles," broke in Menesarkus. "His smithy is empty and the forge fire is dead. One of the city guards, Damon, said he saw them heading up into the mountains—toward the Cave of Nymphs. I sent riders up there but they found nothing except the remains of an extinguished campfire. I offered the man citizenship if he stayed in Plataea," he said, grinding a fist into his palm. "I thought I knew how to work on a creature like him. I was wrong."

"Strange," said Eudoxia, rubbing her eyes with fatigue. "Chusor loved Nikias like a brother."

"Did you save Nikias's hair?" asked Menesarkus.

"Yes, of course," said Eudoxia.

"He can burn it on the altar of Zeus when he is able," said Menesarkus.

He went downstairs to the kitchen and found his Persian slave Saeed cooking the evening meal with his ten-year-old boy, Mula. The two had taken over the domestic duties so that the women of the household could tend to Nikias. All of Menesarkus's other slaves had been butchered by Eurymakus when he and his Theban killers attacked Menesarkus's farm on the night of the sneak attack. But Saeed was more of a member of the family than a mere slave. He had been with Menesarkus since he was Mula's age. Menesarkus had captured Saeed in the Persian Fort nearly fifty years ago, killing the groom's ruthless master and thus gaining Saeed's loyalty for life. Saeed had gone to battle with Menesarkus countless times and had helped raise the wild Nikias after his father had been killed.

"How is Young Master?" asked Mula in a quavering voice. The frail boy was recovering from an arrow wound suffered during the Theban attack, and he stared at Menesarkus with a woeful look on his ashen face.

"His life is in the balance," said Menesarkus, putting his hand on the boy's head of curly dark hair. He knew that Mula worshipped Nikias.

"He will live," said Saeed with a confident tone. "I'm making him a new Sargatian whip for the one that he lost in Athens. The silly lad. Always losing things. Losing weapons. Losing his horse." He pretended to wipe his face of sweat, but Menesarkus knew that he was wiping away his tears.

Menesarkus tore off a piece of bread from a round loaf sitting on the table, then went to the courtyard and sat on a bench, stretching out his aching knee. He tried to chew a mouthful of the bread but it stuck in his throat. He tossed the bread aside and it was immediately set upon by some house sparrows, fighting beak and talon to possess it. He watched them numbly. He had never felt so useless in his life. He did not know what to do. He should be in his offices right now, preparing for the Spartan siege, but it was as if his spirit had been plucked from his chest and cast down the deepest well.

He heard the sound of Saeed clearing his throat.

"What is it?" Menesarkus asked.

"A visitor to see you, Arkon," said Saeed.

Menesarkus stood slowly, grunting with pain as his bad knee locked up. Linos, the bard, entered the courtyard. The old man walked over and stood in front of him, smiling. He held his sandals in one hand.

"Linos," said Menesarkus.

"My sandals," said Linos with a laugh, holding up his dirty footwear. "I stepped in horseshit. There are horses everywhere in the citadel!"

"Have you recovered from your fright outside the walls?" Menesarkus asked.

"An adventurous return to Plataea," said Linos with a grin. "I am invigorated by it."

There was an awkward silence and then Menesarkus asked, "Have you a place to stay?"

"With my cousin Kallinikos," said Linos, naming the ancient priest from the Temple of Zeus. He glanced toward the doorway where Saeed stood watching them. The bard cleared his throat as if to say, "May I speak with you alone?"

"You can leave us, Saeed," Menesarkus said. The Persian slave bowed and disappeared. He looked at Linos and raised his eyebrows. "Speak freely."

The agreeable smile faded from Linos's face and his eyes hardened. His entire aspect became stern and shrewd. The change was so sudden and dramatic that Menesarkus flinched. It was suddenly apparent that Linos had only been masquerading as a doddering old fool. But he was something far different.

"I have returned just in time, it seems," said Linos in an icy voice. "This ship is filled halfway up the hold with bilgewater. My appearance in Plataea is no accident. I was sent here to offer you counsel."

Menesarkus scratched his beard and stared at Linos as if for the first time. "You're a spy, aren't you?"

"Not a spy," said Linos. "Not like that scheming Athenian Timarkos, who has been in and out of Plataea like a mad jackrabbit. I am, rather, a member of a confederacy of like-minded men who oppose tyranny wherever we can. I have spent most of my life scuttling the schemes of the Spartans and Persians, ever since the end of the Persian Wars, wandering throughout Greece and the barbarian lands in the guise of a bard. I was on my way back to Plataea when I met your grandson in Tanagra."

"You met Nikias in Tanagra?" said Menesarkus, amazed.

"Before he was captured by the Theban Eurymakus," said Linos. "The lad asked me to travel with him back to Plataea. But I declined. Meeting him there seemed to be too much of a coincidence. I thought perhaps my enemies were trying to set a very clever trap for me. Now I know the gods were attempting to bring us together for his safety. I hope that he lives," he added, glancing toward the upper floors.

Menesarkus shifted his jaw back and forth warily. "And why should I trust you? Perhaps you are a trap set for *me*."

"You and I stood next to each other in the shield wall against the Persians," said Linos. "Do you forget? I saved your life once, Menesarkus."

"How could I forget?" said Menesarkus. "But men change. Look at what became of Nauklydes."

"Nauklydes was corrupted by money and power," cut in Linos. "I am not Nauklydes. I crave neither of these ephemeral things. I seek only to thwart the tyranny of the dual kings of Sparta."

"So you know about Nauklydes and his treachery," said Menesarkus under his breath, more as a statement than a question. "This league of yours must have eyes and ears everywhere."

"We do," replied Linos. "My cousin Kallinikos is part of our order. He is much shrewder and more sharp-witted than he lets on."

Menesarkus sat down on the bench and sighed. "The water clock is running out for Plataea. The Spartans will attack soon," he said. "We will either hold them at bay or not. Everything now depends on the courage of our warriors."

"Those are the words of a defeated man," said Linos.

Menesarkus scowled at him.

"I am not afraid of your black looks, Menesarkus," said Linos, crossing his slender arms on his chest and smiling. "I knew you when you were a fat beardless lump of a boy, dreaming of glory. You don't have to trust me," he added. "You merely need to heed my advice."

"And what is your advice?" asked Menesarkus with disdain.

"Attack the Persian Fort immediately!" shot back Linos. "Tonight! The Spartans are expecting you to lock yourselves behind these walls like frightened rabbits. Listen to me, Menesarkus. There are no more Spartans coming to the Oxlands. It was a ruse to force you into a treaty. The enemy has already sent their reserve forces to aid Potidaea. There are only five hundred or so full-blooded Spartiates in the Persian Fort right now. The other three thousand warriors are Spartan vassals. The rest are mere Helot *slaves*. Seize this moment! Storm the Persian Fort with every man that you have. Slay the Spartans. Free the Helots. Send the enemy running back to their homeland with their tails between their legs, and you will deliver a message to anyone in the Oxlands—be they Theban or Tanagraean—that attempting to destroy Plataea is a dangerous business."

Menesarkus kept silent for a long time. Linos's words were well-spoken, but they did nothing to bolster his morbid spirits. He shook his head. "That would be suicide, Linos the bard. We wouldn't get an army halfway to the fort before the Spartans came out to meet us on the fields. We cannot beat them in a phalanx battle. You, a veteran, should know that."

"I'm not suggesting that you attack them in broad daylight with an army of hoplites!" said Linos scornfully. "I'm not telling you to send a herald inviting them to battle on foot, you great ox-headed lump! You need to start thinking like a barbarian now. Not a general of Plataea."

"Like a barbarian?" asked Menesarkus, bristling at Linos's insult.

Linos smiled. "Like a *Skythian,*" he said with a glint in his eye.

NINETEEN

—◆—

General Drako gazed at a monster in the fading light of dusk.

Instead of feet this strange beast had giant wooden wheels, and its stout body was covered with bronze shields like the scales of a lizard. An iron wedge as big as a tree trunk jutted from its maw like a fang. It sat silently inside the walls of the Persian Fort on the eve of the assault on Plataea like a hunched and sleeping Titan.

"What a shock Menesarkus will get when he sees my Helots pulling this battering ram up the road to the gates of his citadel," thought Drako. He stood admiring the thing with his arms crossed. He reached up and touched the head of the ram—felt the cool, smooth metal. It weighed over four thousand pounds and would easily smash through the oak and iron-banded portals of the citadel. It would have been impossible to bring something this massive all the way from Sparta, so every piece of this machine had been constructed here inside the Persian Fort. Spartan engineers had built a smithy and forge. The iron for the ram head had been brought from Sparta, carried a few ingots per man by the thousands of Helots.

"'Many Helot hands make easy work,' as the old saying goes," Drako mused.

He walked over to a gang of the squat, black-haired slaves fitting together the scaling ladders. There were over two thousand twenty-foot-tall ladders ready for tomorrow's attack. Watching the thralls at work always gave Drako a feeling of satisfaction. They were like an army of efficient and tireless ants. All they needed was food and discipline—a hardy people that Drako's ancestors had been wise to enslave.

The siege would begin at dawn with an assault on the main gates using the battering ram. That would draw the attention of the Plataean defenders to the eastern wall. Then the Helots would charge the western wall with the ladders. Many of the slaves would die, of course, in the attempt to take the walls. But once the battlements were in Spartan control the Plataeans would be trapped in their own citadel. And after the gates were smashed, the Spartan hoplites, along with a contingent of Theban warriors, would storm the citadel and slay everyone.

The plan for this attack had originally been conceived by Arkilokus. The prince had studied with a siege master in Persepolis—with the Persian known as "the City-Killer"—and had learned many useful stratagems from that wily race. But now, thankfully, the pompous royal was gone, and Drako would not miss him an iota. He was glad to be rid of the man who had been a burr in his balls for so many years. He had sent Arkilokus to Korinth with a contingent of guards immediately after he had been handed over by Menesarkus. In Korinth, Arkilokus would board a ship for Sparta, where the prince could recuperate in the palace of his father. And thus he, Drako, would reap the benefit of having both secured Arkilokus's release as well as defeating Plataea . . . alone.

It was growing dark. Hesperos, the evening star, was already shining. Scores of bonfires burned brightly in the camp. Drako heard the distinct hooting of an owl from somewhere on the other side of the earthen wall, and it was answered by the screech of another in the distance. Night was coming.

"The Helots can rest now," said Drako to his second in command. The warrior nodded and barked out an order that was taken up throughout the Persian Fort. The Helots put down their tools like automatons and started trudging off to the fenced area in the center of the stronghold where they ate and slept, guarded by an outer ring of ever-watchful Spartan warriors.

Drako took a long look at the guarded and gateless entrance on the southern wall of the fort, then scanned the tops of the high earthen walls, picking out the silhouettes of the warriors stationed there. Satisfied at what he saw, he walked in the direction of his tent. Just then a swallow flew so close to his face that he could feel the rush of wind created by its wing.

He smiled faintly. Good things were coming. The swift birds, returning from their winter homes for the summer season, were a happy omen.

He entered his tent and took off his cloak. Then he lay down on his cot and started to touch himself, thinking of the coming siege. There would be no prisoners or slaves taken. Plataea was to serve as an example for the rest of Greece. If Menesarkus survived he would make him watch as everyone in his beloved city was executed, and then he, Drako, would cut off the Arkon's head.

For some reason he couldn't make himself hard.

He tried to think of the pretty eunuch, but the only face that came to mind was Eurymakus's, snarling at him with his mutilated lip. He took his hand away from his loins in disgust and crossed his arms on his chest, frowning as he fell into a deep slumber. . . .

He was awakened an hour later by the sound of screams and the pounding of horses' hooves. He leapt out of bed, the sword he kept by his bedside in hand. He saw the shapes of his guards writhing in the torchlight outside the tent. And then the shadows of horses galloped past.

One of his guards stumbled inside the tent and fell at his feet, clutching an arrow sticking from his neck. The warrior—a powerful man who had served Drako on many campaigns—thrashed as blood gushed from his eyes and nostrils.

What in the name of Zeus is happening?

Then Drako heard a sound that made him break out in a cold sweat and panic for the first time in his long life of battle and bloodshed: the eerie and un-earthly shrieking of Skythians—archers whose poisoned arrows brought instant and excruciating death from the slightest scratch.

He saw the shadow of a rider outside the tent. An arrow ripped through the cloth, passing by Drako's ear—closer than the swallow's wing had done.

Drako turned and slashed a hole in the back of the tent and dashed headlong through the rent and into the fray.

"Death!" crowed Kolax as he rode through the Persian Fort, shooting surprised Red Cloaks with his tainted arrows.

It had been so easy to breach this stronghold! The Skythians had simply split into four groups and charged up each of the four sloping earthen walls, shoot-ing the Spartans manning the tops of the battlements, and then riding straight down and into the heart of the encampment. The Spartans were completely unprepared for this kind of crazed attack—it had never even crossed their minds.

Kolax's head moved like a hawk's with rapid jerks from side to side. He scanned the battlefield lit by the Spartan campfires, seeking out the enemy. He let forth a piercing war cry and wheeled his horse around and charged toward a campfire where a group of Spartans, naked as pigs, had been combing their long hair. His bow twanged, arrows sang, and five Spartans lay writhing.

"Glory to the Arkon!" he shouted in his raspy voice.

Nikias's grandfather was a great man to conceive of such a smart plan!

He saw Skunxa try to ride through a mass of Helots, but the Spartan thralls merely sat unmoving on the ground where they'd been sleeping, blinking like perplexed children woken from dreams. Skunxa's horse balked at running over so many men, and threw its rider to the ground. Two Spartan warriors who stood nearby ran at Skunxa with their swords raised, but Kolax shot one through the hand and the other in the ankle. They screamed and fell with their faces in the dirt, twitching as they vomited their life into the dust.

Kolax rode up to Skunxa and said, "Hurry up! We must get to the entrance!"

The fat man was taking far too long to remount his horse, at least in Kolax's opinion.

He heard his father's voice calling out in the distance in Skythian, "To the southern entrance! Ride!"

Kolax kicked his horse and headed back toward the sound of his papa's voice. The plan had been simple: the Skythians were to breach the Persian Fort and scatter the Spartan warriors manning the heavily guarded entrance. But Kolax couldn't resist killing a few of the enemy on the way there.

"Die!" he shouted as a Spartan tried to hold up a shield to block his arrows, but Kolax merely shot him in the foot and he fell dying just the same as if he'd been struck through the guts. "If only this night could go on forever!" he thought.

Suddenly a spear flew out of the dark and struck him in his armor-plated chest. He fell off the horse and landed on his rump. He grunted in pain and watched in outrage as a naked and noseless Spartan ran out of the shadows, grabbed his horse's reins, leapt onto its back, and charged away.

"No!" screamed Kolax, jumping to his feet and taking off after his mount. He sprinted toward one of the blazing campfires and stopped short when three Spartans, each of them wearing armor, started running toward him with spears raised. There were no other Skythians in sight. Swiftly Kolax reached back and grabbed an arrow. But his eyes nearly shot out of his head when he realized the string of his bow had snapped in his fall. The bow was useless!

Kolax smiled wolfishly and tossed aside his bow. He grabbed another arrow from his quiver, holding one in each hand. The Spartans surrounded him, jabbing at him with their spears, closing in on him, their eyes fierce with hatred.

Kolax let one of the arrows slide down his palm so that he clutched it by the fletching feathers. Then he reached back and flung it like a dart. The arrow grazed the wrist of one of the Spartans, and the man screamed and fell on his back. The other two warriors stared at him in horror as blood started to gush from the man's nose. Kolax ran straight at the dying Spartan and jumped over his body, flinging his other arrow. It struck one of the two remaining Spartans in the unprotected thigh and he fell, clutching his leg in agony.

But the third Spartan swung out with his spear, whacking Kolax across the shins and tripping him. He landed hard, his face slamming into the ground. He rolled over but the Spartan who had just knocked him down landed on his chest, pinning him with his knees. The warrior quickly drew his sword, pulling it back to stab Kolax through the face.

"Poison!" shouted Kolax in Greek, pinching the Spartan on his naked buttock with his sharp fingernails. The Spartan bellowed and jumped off him, twisting around and staring with wild eyes at his arse. Kolax pulled his dagger from his belt and flung it. The Spartan sank to his knees, grasping the blade now sticking from his throat, glaring with outrage at the Skythian boy who had just tricked him.

Kolax sauntered over to the choking Spartan, laughing maniacally as he pulled one of his poisoned arrows from his quiver. "As fast as a nighthawk," he said, and flicked the arrow across the man's cheek, drawing blood, bringing death.

Menesarkus charged down the road to the Persian Fort astride Nikias's horse Photine. The moon had just risen and cast the world in a gray and lustrous glow, as though the entire landscape had been painted in silver.

He wore no armor except for an old-fashioned Oxland helmet—a bronze head covering without a face guard that allowed for the best visibility when on horseback. On his back was strapped a scabbard with a curved Persian blade he had taken as a war prize almost fifty years ago, and he held a javelin under one arm.

And he had never ridden so fast in his life.

His heart beat strong and steady. He felt like a young man again. The skin at the nape of his neck tingled with excitement. Down the road, a quarter of a mile away, he could see Spartans flooding out of the dark entrance to the fortification. The Skythians had done their work. They'd kicked the ant's nest and created chaos.

The Plataean cavalry was nearly to the fort. But first they had to cross the bridge that spanned the Asopus River. Spartans bearing shields were running toward the bridge—a desperate attempt to hold off the onslaught.

He glanced to his left. There rode Zoticus the horse master—going to battle with nothing but an Oxland helm for protection, his exposed face set in a grimace of anticipation. He looked to his right—there was Saeed wearing a shirt of Persian plate armor, and next to him rode Linos the bard, his silver hair flowing in the wind like a horse's mane. Menesarkus's ears were filled with the thunderous noise of six hundred Plataean cavalrymen riding at their backs.

"Look, master!" shouted Saeed.

Twenty or so Spartan hoplites had made it to the opposite side of the bridge, making a shield wall to stop the riders. But the Plataeans were not about to be thwarted by a handful of men. They charged onward like a monstrous and unstoppable force of nature. Menesarkus was the first to cross the bridge, and his javelin slammed through the eye slit of a Spartan's helm, nearly ripping off the man's head. He let go of the javelin as he passed, then quickly drew the sword from the scabbard that was strapped to his back, slashing at the faces of the Spartans. He passed through the small body of hoplites and headed toward the entrance—an open gap that the Spartans, in their hubris, had not even bothered barricading.

Hundreds of the enemy hoplites were now flooding through that open gap, fleeing the fort and the terrible poison of the Skythian arrows. Menesarkus had never seen Spartans panicking before. It was a glorious sight.

"To the entrance!" cried Zoticus, racing past Menesarkus. "Push them back inside!"

"Thanatos!" bellowed Linos, singing out the name of the god of death. The cry was taken up by all the riders in the pack—a breathtaking sound that swelled Menesarkus's heart with joy.

"Thanatos!" roared Menesarkus above the din.

"For Nikias!" yelled Leo's voice from behind.

And then, like a crash of thunder, the lead riders slammed into the Spartan warriors, skewering them with javelins, slicing off arms and heads, trampling them into the dirt, pushing them back on themselves, pinning them against the earthen walls of the Persian Fort. The survivors were driven back inside the fortress.

But a lone Spartan rider charged headlong through the mass of horses and men, escaping from the killing ground. He rode right by Menesarkus, ducking the Bull's sword stroke, and knocked Saeed off his mount with a blow to the chest—a sword stroke that would have cut Saeed in half if he hadn't been wearing armor plating. The slave fell to the ground and lay there, unmoving.

Menesarkus turned Photine and charged after the rider, shouting angrily, "Come back, Drako!"

Drako galloped along the length of the southern wall, away from the chaos of the battle. Menesarkus knew where he was going—a footbridge spanning the river. If Drako made it there he could head into open country and ride straight for the mountains and the protection of the fortress of the Three Heads.

But Menesarkus was not going to let Drako get away. He kicked his heels into Photine's sides and leaned forward. The white mare tore up the earth with her hooves. When Drako reached the southeast corner of the fortress, he turned abruptly and headed toward the river, and so did Menesarkus.

Photine was gaining on the other horse. Her ears were laid back, her neck outstretched. But Drako had almost made it to the bridge. Menesarkus cursed and reached back, pulling his sword from its scabbard and flung it forward. It soared from his hand like a spear and grazed the rump of Drako's mount. The animal neighed in fear and came to a sudden stop. Drako sailed over its head and hit the rocky ground, where he lay still.

Menesarkus reined in Photine and got off her back. He approached Drako warily. But the sound of heavy footsteps coming from behind made him turn.

He saw a band of Spartans—hoplites who had managed to escape the fray—running toward the river.

When Menesarkus turned back toward Drako, the Spartan's fist slammed into his nose, followed by another that caught him in the gut, and he reeled.

"Over here!" shouted Drako, waving frantically to his men heading for the river. "This way!" Then he lunged at Menesarkus again.

But Drako's punches had sent a rush of energy coursing through the Bull's veins. It was the ikor of the gods—the blood of the Olympians infusing Menesarkus's body with strength. The old pankrator was ready for the Spartan this time. He dodged Drako's fist and kicked out with the flat of his foot, breaking Drako's kneecap. The Spartan cried out in pain and lurched. Menesarkus threw himself onto the enemy, hitting him on either side of the head with two powerful haymakers. Drako's knees went wobbly. Menesarkus slipped behind him and wrapped his arm around his neck, putting Drako in the dreaded Morpheus hold. The Spartan squirmed and clawed at Menesarkus's face as his larynx was slowly crushed, but he could not stop the champion pankrator.

"Release him!" shouted a voice.

The Spartan warriors Drako had summoned had arrived and now surrounded Menesarkus, coming to a halt a spear's length away and forming a semicircle around him. There were four of them. Two had swords. Two were unarmed. They were completely naked and their long hair was untied and hung about their faces like women's tresses—a strange contrast to their lean and muscular male bodies. Their chests heaved with every breath, and their teeth were bared like feral animals, eyes shining in the moonlight.

"Come any closer and I snap his spine," threatened Menesarkus, tensing the muscles of his arms.

Drako raised his hand, moving his fingers quickly—speaking in battle sign: "Kill him."

With a final effort Drako jerked and trembled and went limp.

Menesarkus let go of Drako's body and the Spartan slid to the dirt—a lifeless heap. Clenching his fists and gritting his teeth, the Bull of the Oxlands braced himself for the final fight of his life.

The Spartans charged. Their swords flashed in the silver light.

"Zeus!" bellowed Menesarkus, raising his right fist to throw a final punch before the enemy swords claimed his flesh.

And then, in the blink of an eye, all four of the Spartan warriors dropped to the ground . . . dying at Menesarkus's feet. Three of them were writhing and gagging on their own blood as it gushed from their eyes and nostrils, while the fourth clutched a spear point that had been plunged through his stomach, a look of agonized surprise on his face.

"And that was my last poisoned arrow!" called out a voice in Skythian. "Or else I would have killed all four!"

Menesarkus had neither seen nor heard the horse bearing its two riders as it charged down from the Persian Fort to rescue him from certain death. But there they stood: Leo and Kolax astride a single mount. Menesarkus wanted to kiss both of their unlovely faces.

The barbarian pushed himself off the animal's rump, landed spryly on his feet, and dashed over to the Spartan with the spear in his guts. He bent down and swiftly slit the man's throat.

"I claim all four as my kills," Kolax said to Leo, pointing his bloody dagger at him. "Your poorly aimed spear hadn't killed him yet."

Leo ignored him and said to Menesarkus, "Are you hurt, Arkon? You're bleeding."

Menesarkus shook his head. "Just my nose," he said.

Leo, however, had lost his Oxland helm and had suffered a deep gash that stretched from his left ear to his chin. He seemed oblivious to his wound, however, for he replied with a smile, "Me neither."

At that moment a wild roar of "Plataea!" erupted near the entrance to the Persian Fort, and Menesarkus knew that the army of fully armored Plataean hoplites who had quick-marched behind the cavalry—two thousand men strong!—had made it to the fortress. The real slaughter of the enemy would now begin in earnest.

Menesarkus wiped the blood from his upper lip and let forth a sigh of relief. Then he knelt cautiously by Drako and put his fingers to his wrist, feeling for a pulse.

"This is the one who stole my horse," Kolax said, gesturing at Drako. "Ah! There she is!" he declared with relief, pointing to the riverbank where his animal stood eating grass.

"Does Drako still draw breath?" asked Leo.

Menesarkus nodded. "He is harder to kill than the Hydra."

"May I slay *him* too?" said Kolax hopefully.

"No," said Menesarkus. "We keep *this* Spartan alive."

EPILOGUE

---◆---

Never waste new tears over old sorrows.
—EURIPIDES OF ATHENS.

"And then what happened?" asked Nikias. He was propped up in bed, squinting through puffy eyes at Kolax and Leo, who sat on either side. Mula was at the foot of the bed.

Leo was about to continue when Kolax raised his hand in a self-important manner and exclaimed, "Let me tell! Leo got the last part all wrong. I felled *six* Spartans who were going to kill Grandfather Arkon, not *four*! And besides, Leo didn't even see what happened next."

Nikias glanced at Leo, who rolled his eyes and smiled in a good-natured manner. "It's true," he said. "The Arkon took my horse and left me to tie up Drako and guard him."

"Menesarkus and I galloped back to the Persian Fort," said Kolax with enthusiasm, pretending he was astride his mount. "Inside it was a slaughter ground. I wanted to join my people and chase down the enemy who were still fighting, but Grandfather Arkon ordered me to stay by his side. He started shouting that he had captured Drako, calling on the surviving Red Cloaks to throw down their arms. And do you know what those mare-milkers did? They gave up! Curse them to the Barren Lands Below!"

The Skythian looked so comical in his wrath that Nikias laughed, even though doing so caused him immense pain. He touched the wrappings wound around his rib cage and winced.

"Over two thousand of them were killed," said Leo. "And we only lost thirty men."

"Only three Skythians were killed," observed Kolax. "My cousin Jaro was one of them. But he died a glorious death. We buried him with fifteen Spartan heads."

"A great victory," said Nikias. "If only I could have ridden with you," he added faintly.

"And me too," said Mula morosely. "I'll never get to be in a battle."

"Don't whine about it," Kolax said to Mula. "Some are born to be warriors like me and others are born to cook, like you."

Mula scowled and punched Kolax in the shoulder.

"Ouch!" said Kolax. "I didn't insult your cooking."

Nikias thought it was amusing that Kolax, the most brutal killer he had ever known, would allow himself to be punched in the arm by a puny slave boy, but the two had escaped from the citadel together on the night of the sneak attack and had formed a brotherly bond that, apparently, would never be broken.

"We should leave you now," said Chusor from the other side of the chamber where he'd been sitting silently during the entire visit. "Nikias was in Morpheus's arms for three days and has only been awake for two more. We must let him rest and heal."

"But let me finish!" said Kolax, and speaking very quickly he told how the Helots—those docile sheep-people—had merely sat in their pens during the entire attack. And how the five hundred Spartan survivors were chained together and led back to the citadel. He also described the battering ram that the Spartans had built and how it had taken twenty oxen to pull it back to Plataea. "And I sat on top of it the entire way," he exclaimed, "laughing at Skunxa the whole time and mocking him for his feeble number of kills. I bested him by ten. And—"

Leo, realizing that Kolax would never stop chattering, started pulling the boy away from the bed.

"—now I'm going to make a drinking cup from one of my enemy's skulls for the Skythian celebration my father is . . ."

Leo and Mula dragged him out the door and Nikias could hear him babbling all the way down the hall.

Chusor walked over to the bed, bringing his chair with him, and sat by Nikias's side. He took his pulse, then examined the wounds on Nikias's skull with a pensive look.

"What do you think?" Nikias asked.

"You are proving most difficult to kill," replied Chusor.

"How do I *look*, though?" Nikias said, touching his swollen face.

Chusor stared into his eyes. "It will take you a long time to heal from these facial wounds. And your right shoulder is bad. But you do not seem to have suffered any hurt to your brain, which is a relief. Your face might never look the same, although I set your broken nose while you were comatose. You should be able to breathe through it again once it has healed."

"Am I that hideous?" Nikias asked.

"I never thought you were particularly good-looking to begin with," said Chusor with a wry smile.

"Thank you for doctoring me," said Nikias. "If someone had to poke holes in my skull, I'm glad it was you."

"A simple procedure," said Chusor, getting up to take a closer look at the back of Nikias's skull where he had drilled three small holes. "I had to do it to relieve the pressure on your brain from the swelling." He lifted the wrapping. It had been two days since he had performed the operation, and there was no sign of infection—no necrotic stink. The skin looked healthy too. He put Nikias's wrapping back on. "You are young. You will heal," he said, almost to himself.

"You saved my life," said Nikias.

"The women of your household were the ones who kept you alive," replied Chusor. "Your grandmother, sister, and Kallisto refused to let you die. But it was fortunate that I came back when I did."

"Where *did* you go, Chusor?" asked Nikias with a searching look.

Chusor ignored his question. He went to the table in the corner of the room and picked up an object covered in a leather wrapping—a thing that he had brought into the chamber earlier—and put it on the bed within Nikias's reach.

"What's this?" asked Nikias, unfolding the leather cover to reveal a sword in a plain scabbard.

"Diokles found the blade under the city. When we were excavating tunnels to serve in case of a siege," explained Chusor. "He discovered an old tomb. This was the only treasure that we found. I set it in a new handle."

Nikias gripped the handle and slid the double-edged leaf-shaped sword from the scabbard. It shone like polished silver. He saw a stranger reflected in the mirrorlike surface: a young man with a head shorn of all its hair, and a face that was swollen beyond recognition and covered with scabs and bruises. "It's a beautiful blade," he said softly. "I've never seen the like."

"Nor I," said Chusor. "It's made of a curious amalgam of metals. It's lighter than iron but stronger. And the edges were incredibly sharp, even after being underground for centuries. It's almost like it's been charmed by a god."

"It must have been made by the people who lived here before the Sea Raiders came," said Nikias. "What are the words etched here?" He squinted at the strange script running up the center of the sword's blade. "This is in the language called the Ox-Turning, isn't it? The same script written on our ancient stones."

"Yes," said Chusor. "As best I can tell it's a blessing: 'Light-god-help-me-slay.'"

"The Sword of Apollo," said Nikias.

"Indeed," said Chusor with a smile, nodding his head. "Apollo: god of light."

"I lost two swords on my journey," said Nikias. "My grandfather's old blade and one given to me by Perikles."

"The Sword of Apollo is yours now," said Chusor. "You'll need a good weapon in the coming days. The Spartans won't give up, you know. They suffered a great loss at the Persian Fort, that is true. Over two thousand warriors in their service were killed. Five thousand Helots have been freed. Hundreds of full-blooded Spartiates breathed their lives into the dust, and hundreds more are captive here in the city. But the two kings of Sparta and the elders of their high council will not let this disaster go by unpunished. They will send an even bigger force next time. They will avenge their dead, free their prisoners, and recapture every single Helot in the Oxlands. And they will besiege this city for a lifetime if that is what it takes to destroy Plataea."

Nikias smiled grimly and slid the sword back into the scabbard. "I know that the Spartans won't give up," he said. "And thank you for the sword."

Chusor stared into space, stroking his smooth chin.

"You cut off your hair and goatee!" said Nikias. "Strange that I only just now noticed."

Chusor glanced at him and smiled slightly, then looked away. "I am like the sheep from the old tale that sheds its wool to disguise itself from the wolves, forgetting that they can still smell its scent."

"Where is Diokles?" Nikias asked. "I haven't seen him yet."

"He has gone away with some old shipmates," said Chusor. "They departed several days ago. I went with them to Kreusis, but I returned to Plataea because . . . well, I came back because I had a feeling that I must. And I was right to return, for I found you near death. But now that you are on the mend I have to join my companions."

"Then it's true?" asked Nikias. "Leo said you're going away for good. Where?"

"The sea," said Chusor. "To roam the sea on a galley."

Nikias nodded and stared at the sword.

"I'll leave you to rest, friend," said Chusor. He cleared his throat. "Good-bye, Nikias. I don't know if we will see one another again."

He made to leave but Nikias reached out and gripped his wrist. "There's something I have to tell you. About Athens."

Chusor looked at him curiously. "What is it?"

"Your lover Sophia," said Nikias. "I don't know how to say this." He paused and lowered his eyes. "She's dead. She died in a fire several months ago."

The smith dropped his chin and passed one of his large hands back and forth over his smooth head, then covered both eyes with his palms. "Barka prophesied truth again," he hissed under his breath. Awe and anguish were intermingled in his voice. "Years ago he told me that Sophia would die in a fire lit by our love. And so I never went back to Athens for fear of condemning her to death. But such is the nature of prophecies: you are damned by either path that you take at the intersection of the roads." He took his hands from his eyes and they were wet with tears.

"I asked to see you the moment that I awoke from my stupor last night," said Nikias. "So that I could tell you. I'm sorry to bring you such sad news."

"I knew it in my heart," said Chusor. "A sadness has touched my soul for some time."

"I met Sophia's daughter," said Nikias. "She told me how kind you were to her when she was little."

"You met Helena?" Chusor asked. "Is she well? The last I saw her she was a boyish, skinny little thing," he said with a fond smile. "Sophia would never tell me who her father was," he added under his breath.

"She is beyond compare," said Nikias. "And intelligent. And so many other things. We became . . . friends."

"Indeed?"

"There's more. Listen. Sophia had *another* daughter."

Chusor's eyes narrowed. "Another daughter? That cannot be. Sophia was barren after Helena was born."

"The gods sometimes bless women with fertility again later in life. At least, that's what I've heard my grandmother say."

Chusor scowled and said, "Then she's Kleon's daughter."

"No," said Nikias. "She's *your* daughter."

Chusor smiled out of the corner of his mouth. A slanted and humorless smile. "Impossible," he said.

"She was born seven months after you left Athens," Nikias said. "She has your eyes and dark skin. I thought she was part Aethiope when I first saw her. And she's very tall for her age." He met Chusor's intense and fixed gaze. "And she's in great danger because of you."

Later in the day, after Nikias had been alone for some time at his rest, Kallisto entered the room with a plate of food. She set it on the table by his bed and then lay down next to him, gently pressing her body against his side. He stared out the window, gazing at a crow standing on the rooftop of the adjacent house.

"The one with the white tail feather," he said. "He knows you've brought me food. He'll land on the windowsill soon and beg for bread."

"I'll shoo him away with a pillow," she said. "Dirty old thing. He haunts this house like a ghost."

"No," said Nikias. "Apollo sends him. And I like the bird. He brings me good luck."

After a long silence Kallisto said, "Why won't you look at me, my love?"

Nikias glanced at her and said with a mournful voice, "Can you still love me after all that's happened?"

She kissed him very gently on the cheek. "I didn't fall in love with you for your face," she said.

"No?" he asked with a faint smile. He wanted to tell her everything . . . about his shame for all that had occurred. About how Eurymakus and Axe had broken him in the chamber in Tanagra—how he had begged for his life like a coward and revealed the secret of Arkilokus being a prisoner in Plataea. About the horror of watching the Helot slaves behead each other, one by one, until the terror had nearly made him lose his mind. About making love with Helena . . . and the fact that he longed for her still. But the words stuck in his throat and he was silent.

"It was your words," said Kallisto with a playful laugh.

"My what?"

"I fell in love with you for your poems. Even the *bad* ones."

Nikias could not hold back his tears. He wept like a child while she covered his swollen face with soft kisses. "Don't be sad," she said in a soothing voice, full of love, full of compassion. "There is so much to be joyful about. Your grandfather is going to let us marry. And there is this."

She took his hand and placed it over her womb, smiling mysteriously. Nikias stared deep into her shining eyes . . . and in that moment he understood.